THE FINAL GAMBIT

∞ AN INHERITANCE GAMES NOVEL ∞

#1 *New York Times* bestselling author

JENNIFER LYNN BARNES

Little, Brown and Company
New York Boston

Little, Brown and Company
Hachette Book Group
1290 Avenue of the Americas, New York, NY 10104
Visit us at LBYR.com

Originally published in hardcover and ebook by Little, Brown and Company in August 2022
First Trade Paperback Edition: July 2023

Little, Brown and Company is a division of Hachette Book Group, Inc.
The Little, Brown name and logo are trademarks of Hachette Book Group, Inc.

The publisher is not responsible for websites (or their content) that are not owned by the publisher.

Little, Brown and Company books may be purchased in bulk for business, educational, or promotional use. For information, please contact your local bookseller or the Hachette Book Group Special Markets Department at special.markets@hbgusa.com.

The Library of Congress has cataloged the hardcover edition as follows:
Names: Barnes, Jennifer (Jennifer Lynn), author.
Title: The final gambit / Jennifer Lynn Barnes.
Description: New York ; Boston : Little, Brown and Company, 2022. |
Series: An inheritance games novel | Audience: Ages 12+. |
Summary: "Eighteen-year-old Avery Grambs is weeks away from inheriting the multibillion-dollar Hawthorne fortune, but first she'll have to survive a dangerous game against an old enemy looking for vengeance."—Provided by publisher.
Identifiers: LCCN 2022017764 | ISBN 9780316370950 (hardcover) |
ISBN 9780316371124 (ebook) | ISBN 9780316466301 (int'l) | ISBN 9780316485050 (Walmart exclusive edition) | ISBN 9780316451338 (B&N exclusive edition)
Subjects: CYAC: Inheritance and succession—Fiction. | Wealth—Fiction. |
Puzzles—Fiction. | Secrets—Fiction. | Families—Fiction. | LCGFT: Novels.
Classification: LCC PZ7.B26225 Fin 2022 | DDC [Fic]— dc23
LC record available at https://lccn.loc.gov/2022017764

ISBNs: 978-0-316-37102-5 (pbk.), 978-0-316-37112-4 (ebook)

Printed in Indiana, USA

LSC-C

Printing 9, 2026

PRAISE FOR

THE INHERITANCE GAMES

A *New York Times*, *USA Today*, and IndieBound Bestseller
A Goodreads Choice Awards Finalist
An Edgar Award Nominee for Best Young Adult Mystery
A *Kirkus Reviews* Best Young Adult Book of the Year
A *Publishers Weekly* Best Book of the Year
A New York Public Library Best Book for Teens
A YALSA Teens' Top Ten Winner
A YALSA Best Fiction for Young Adults Book

"Barnes is a master of puzzles and plot twists. *The Inheritance Games* was the most fun I've had all year." —E. Lockhart, #1 *New York Times* bestselling author of *We Were Liars* and *Again Again*

"A thrilling blend of family secrets, illicit romance, and a high-stakes treasure hunt, set in the mysterious world of Texas billionaires. The nonstop twists kept me guessing until the very last page!" —Katharine McGee, *New York Times* bestselling author of *American Royals*

"Impossible to put down." —Buzzfeed

★ "Part *The Westing Game*, part *We Were Liars*, completely entertaining." —*Kirkus Reviews*, starred review

★ "This strong, *Knives Out*–esque series opener…provides ample enjoyment." —*Publishers Weekly*, starred review

"Perfect for any reader seeking suspense, romance, and glamour.… Fun and fast-paced, fans of Karen M. McManus's *One of Us Is Lying* and Maureen Johnson's *Truly Devious* will find a new home at Hawthorne House." —*SLJ*

"[A] well-characterized mystery that's packed to the brim with twists and tricks." —*Booklist*

Also by Jennifer Lynn Barnes

The Inheritance Games

The Inheritance Games

The Hawthorne Legacy

The Final Gambit

The Brothers Hawthorne

Coming next: *The Grandest Game*

The Naturals

The Naturals

Killer Instinct

All In

Bad Blood

Twelve: A Novella

The Debutantes

Little White Lies

Deadly Little Scandals

The Lovely and the Lost

For William

CHAPTER 1

"We need to talk about your eighteenth birthday." Alisa's words echoed through the largest of Hawthorne House's five libraries. Floor-to-ceiling shelves stretched up two stories, encircling us with hardcover and leather-bound tomes, many of them priceless, every single one a reminder of the man who had built this room.

This house.

This dynasty.

I could almost imagine the ghost of Tobias Hawthorne watching me as I knelt and ran my hand over the mahogany floorboards, my fingers searching for irregularities in the seams.

Finding none, I stood and replied to Alisa's statement. "Do we?" I said. "Do we *really*?"

"Legally?" The formidable Alisa Ortega arched an eyebrow at me. "Yes. You may already be emancipated, but when it comes to the terms of your inheritance—"

"Nothing changes when I turn eighteen," I said, scanning the room for my next move. "I won't inherit until I've lived in Hawthorne House for a year."

I knew my lawyer well enough to know *that* was what she really wanted to talk about. My birthday was October eighteenth. I would hit the year mark the first week in November and instantly become the richest teenager on the planet. Until then, I had other things to focus on.

A bet to win. A Hawthorne to best.

"Be that as it may..." Alisa was about as easily deterred as a high-speed train. "As your birthday approaches, there are some things we should discuss."

I snorted. "Forty-six billion of them?"

As Alisa gave me an exasperated look, I concentrated on my mission. Hawthorne House was filled with secret passages. Jameson had bet me that I couldn't find them all. Eyeing the massive tree trunk that served as a desk, I reached for the sheath fixed to the inside of my boot and pulled out my knife to test a natural crack in the desk's surface.

I'd learned the hard way I couldn't afford to go anywhere unarmed.

"Moping check!" Xander "I'm a Living, Breathing Rube Goldberg Machine" Hawthorne poked his head into the library. "Avery, on a scale of one to ten, how much do you need a distraction right now, and how attached are you to your eyebrows?"

Jameson was on the other side of the world. Grayson hadn't called once since he'd left for Harvard. Xander, my self-appointed BHFF—*Best Hawthorne Friend Forever*—considered it his sacred duty to keep my spirits high in his brothers' absence.

"One," I answered. "And ten."

Xander gave a little bow. "Then I bid you adieu." In a flash, he was gone.

Something was definitely exploding in the next ten minutes. Turning back toward Alisa, I drank in the rest of the room: the seemingly endless shelves, the wrought-iron staircases spiraling upward. "Just say what you came here to say, Alisa."

"Yes, Lee-Lee," a deep, honeyed voice drawled from the hall. "Enlighten us." Nash Hawthorne took up position in the doorway, his trademark cowboy hat tipped down.

"Nash." Alisa wore her power suit like armor. "This doesn't concern you."

Nash leaned against the doorframe and lazily crossed his right foot over his left ankle. "Kid tells me to leave, I'll leave." Nash didn't trust Alisa with me. He hadn't for months.

"I'm fine, Nash," I said. "You can go."

"I reckon I can." Nash made no move to push off the doorframe. He was the oldest of the four Hawthorne brothers and used to riding herd on the other three. Over the past year, he'd extended that to me. He and my sister had been "not dating" for months.

"Isn't it not-date night?" I asked. "And doesn't that mean you have somewhere to be?"

Nash removed his cowboy hat and let his steady eyes settle on mine. "Dollars to doughnuts," he said, turning to amble out of the room, "she wants to talk to you about establishing a trust."

I waited until Nash was out of earshot before I turned back to Alisa. "A trust?"

"I merely want you to be aware of your options." Alisa avoided specifics with lawyerly ease. "I'll put together a dossier for you to look over. Now, regarding your birthday, there's also the matter of a party."

"No party," I said immediately. The last thing I wanted was to turn my birthday into a headline-grabbing, hashtag-exploding event.

"Do you have a favorite band? Or singer? We'll need entertainment."

I could feel my eyes narrowing. "No party, Alisa."

"Is there anyone you'd like to see on the guest list?" When Alisa said *anyone*, she wasn't talking about people I knew. She was talking about celebrities, billionaires, socialites, royals....

"No guest list," I said, "because I'm not having a party."

"You really should consider the optics—" Alisa began, and I tuned out. I knew what she was going to say. She'd been saying it for nearly eleven months. *Everyone loves a Cinderella story.*

Well, *this* Cinderella had a bet to win. I studied the wrought-iron staircases. Three spiraled counterclockwise. But the fourth... I walked toward it, then scaled the steps. On the second-story landing, I ran my fingers along the underside of the shelf opposite the stairs. *A release.* I triggered it, and the entire curved shelf arced backward.

Number twelve. I smiled wickedly. *Take that, Jameson Winchester Hawthorne.*

"No party," I called down to Alisa again. And then I disappeared into the wall.

CHAPTER 2

That night, I slid into bed, Egyptian cotton sheets cool and smooth against my skin. As I waited for Jameson's call, my hand drifted toward the nightstand, to a small bronze pin in the shape of a key.

"Pick a hand." Jameson holds out two fists. I tap his right hand, and he uncurls his fingers, presenting me with an empty palm. I try the left—the same. Then he curls my fingers into a fist. I open them, and there, in my palm, sits the pin.

"You solved the keys faster than any of us," Xander reminds me. "It's past time for this!"

"Sorry, kid," Nash drawls. "It's been six months. You're one of us now."

Grayson says nothing, but when I fumble to put the pin on and it drops from my fingers, he catches it before it hits the ground.

That memory wanted to loop into another—*Grayson, me, the wine cellar*—but I wouldn't let it. In the past few months, I'd developed my own methods of distraction. Grabbing my phone, I navigated to a crowd-funding site and did a search for *medical bills* and *rent.* The Hawthorne fortune wasn't mine for another six weeks, but the partners at McNamara, Ortega, and Jones had already seen to it that I had a credit card with virtually no limit.

Keep gift anonymous. I clicked that box again and again. When my phone finally rang, I leaned back and answered. "Hello."

"I need an anagram of the word *naked*." There was a hum of energy to Jameson's voice.

"No, you don't." I rolled over onto my side. "How's Tuscany?"

"The birthplace of the Italian Renaissance? Full of winding roads, hills and valleys, where a morning mist rolls out in the distance, and the forests are littered with leaves so golden red that the entire world feels like it's on fire in the very best way? That Tuscany?"

"Yes," I murmured. "That Tuscany."

"I've seen better."

"Jameson!"

"What do you want to hear about first, Heiress: Siena, Florence, or the vineyards?"

I wanted *all of it*, but there was a reason Jameson was using the standard Hawthorne gap year to travel. "Tell me about the villa." *Did you find anything?*

"Your Tuscan villa was built in the seventeenth century. It's supposedly a farmhouse but looks more like a castle, and it's surrounded by more than a hundred acres of olive orchard. There's a pool, a wood-fired pizza oven, and a massive stone fireplace original to the house."

I could picture it. Vividly—and not just because I had a binder of photos. "And when you checked the fireplace?" I didn't have to ask if he *had* checked the fireplace.

"I found something."

I sat up, my hair falling down my back. "A clue?"

"Probably," Jameson replied. "But to what puzzle?"

My entire body felt electric. "If you don't tell me, I will *end* you, Hawthorne."

"And I," Jameson replied, "would very much enjoy being ended." My traitorous lips threatened a smile. Tasting victory, Jameson gave me my answer. "I found a triangular mirror."

Just like that, my brain was off to the races. Tobias Hawthorne had raised his grandsons on puzzles, riddles, and games. The mirror was probably a clue, but Jameson had been right: There was no telling what game it was meant to be a part of. In any case, it wasn't what he was traveling the world looking for.

"We'll figure out what the disk was." Jameson as good as read my mind. "The world is the board, Heiress. We just have to keep rolling the dice."

Maybe, but this time we weren't following a trail or playing one of the old man's games. We were feeling around in the dark, hoping that there might be answers out there—answers that would tell us why a small coinlike disk engraved with concentric circles was worth a fortune.

Why Tobias Hawthorne's namesake and only son had left that disk for my mother.

Why Toby had snatched it back from me before he'd disappeared, off to play dead again.

Toby and that disk were my last connections to my mother, and they were gone. It hurt to think about that for too long. "I found another entry to the passageways today," I said abruptly.

"Oh, really?" Jameson replied, the verbal equivalent of holding out a hand at the beginning of a waltz. "Which one did you find?"

"Circular library."

On the other end of the phone line, there was a brief but unmistakable silence.

Realization dawned on me. "You didn't know about that one."

Victory was so very sweet. "Would you like me to tell you where it is?" I crooned.

"When I get back," Jameson murmured, "I'll find it myself."

I had no idea when he was coming back, but soon my year at Hawthorne House would be up. I would be free. I could go anywhere, do anything—and *everything.*

"Where are you headed next?" I asked Jameson. If I let myself think too much about *everything*, I would drown in it—in wanting, in longing, in believing we could have it all.

"Santorini," Jameson replied. "But say the word, Heiress, and—"

"Keep going. Keep looking." My voice went hoarse. "Keep telling me everything."

"Everything?" Jameson repeated in a rough, low tone that made me think of what the two of us could be doing if I were there with him.

I rolled over onto my stomach. "The anagram you were looking for? It's *knead.*"

CHAPTER 3

Weeks passed in a blur of charity galas and prep school exams, nights talking to Jameson and too much time spent wondering whether Grayson would ever pick up a damn phone.

Focus. Pushing everything from my mind, I took aim. Looking down the barrel of the gun, I breathed in and out and took the shot—then another and another.

The Hawthorne estate had everything, including its own shooting range. I wasn't a gun person. This wasn't my idea of fun. But neither was being defenseless. Forcing my jaw to unclench, I lowered my weapon and took off my ear protection.

Nash surveyed my target. "Nice grouping, kid."

Theoretically, I'd never need a gun—or the knife in my boot. In theory, the Hawthorne estate was impenetrable, and when I went out into the world, I would always have armed security with me. But since being named in Tobias Hawthorne's will, I'd been shot at, nearly blown up, and kidnapped. *Theory* hadn't kept the nightmares away.

Nash teaching me to fight back had. "Your lawyer bring you that trust paperwork yet?" he asked casually.

My lawyer was his ex, and he knew her far too well. "Maybe," I replied, Alisa's explanation ringing in my ears. *Typically, with an heir your age, there would be certain safeguards in place. Since Mr. Hawthorne didn't see fit to erect them, it's an option you should consider yourself.* Per Alisa, if I put the money in a trust, there would be a trustee in charge of safeguarding and growing the fortune on my behalf. Alisa and the partners at McNamara, Ortega, and Jones would, of course, be willing to serve as trustees, with the understanding that I would be denied nothing I requested. *A revocable trust will simply minimize the pressure on you until you're ready to fully take the reins.*

"Remind me again," Nash told me, bending to capture my gaze with his. "What's our rule about fightin' dirty?"

He wasn't nearly as subtle as he thought he was when it came to Alisa Ortega, but I still answered the question. "There's no such thing as fighting dirty," I told Nash, "if you win."

CHAPTER 4

The morning of my eighteenth birthday—and the first day of fall break at the vaunted Heights Country Day School—I woke up to see an unspeakably gorgeous ball gown hanging in my doorway. It was a deep midnight green, floor-length, with a bodice marked by tens of thousands of tiny black jewels in a dark, delicate, mesmerizing pattern.

It was a stop-and-stare dress. A gasp-and-stare-again dress.

The kind one would wear to a headline-grabbing, hashtag-exploding black-tie event. *Damn it, Alisa.* I stalked toward the gown, feeling mutinous—then saw the note dangling from the hanger: *WEAR ME IF YOU DARE.*

That wasn't Alisa's handwriting.

I found Jameson at the edge of the Black Wood. He was wearing a white tuxedo that fit his body far too well and standing next to an honest-to-God hot-air balloon.

Jameson Winchester Hawthorne. I ran like the ball gown wasn't weighing me down, like I didn't have a knife strapped to my thigh.

Jameson caught me, our bodies colliding. "Happy birthday, Heiress."

Some kisses were soft and gentle—and some were like fire.

Eventually, the realization that we had an audience managed to penetrate my brain. Oren was discreet. He wasn't looking *at* us, but my head of security clearly wasn't about to let Jameson Hawthorne fly off with me alone.

Reluctantly, I pulled back. "A hot-air balloon?" I asked Jameson dryly. "Really?"

"I should warn you, Heiress..." Jameson swung himself up onto the edge of the basket, landing in a crouch. "I am dangerously good at birthdays."

Jameson Hawthorne was dangerously good at a lot of things.

He held his hand down to me. I took it, and I didn't even try to pretend that I had grown used to this—all of it, any of it, *him*. In a million years, the life Tobias Hawthorne had left me would still take my breath away.

Oren climbed into the balloon after me and fixed his gaze on the horizon. Jameson cast off the ropes and hit the flame.

We surged upward.

Airborne, with my heart in my throat, I stared down at Hawthorne House. "How do you steer?" I asked Jameson as everything but the two of us and my very discreet bodyguard got smaller and farther away.

"You don't." Jameson's arms curved around my torso. "Sometimes, Heiress, all you can do is recognize which way the wind is blowing and plot a course."

The balloon was just the beginning. Jameson Hawthorne didn't do anything halfway.

A hidden picnic.

A helicopter ride to the Gulf.

Speeding away from the paparazzi.

Slow dancing, barefoot, on the beach.

The ocean. A cliff. A wager. A race. A dare. *I'm going to remember this.* That was my overwhelming feeling on the helicopter ride home. *I'm going to remember it all.* Years from now, I'd still be able to *feel* it. The weight of the ball gown, the wind in my face. Sun-warmed sand on my skin and chocolate-covered strawberries melting on my tongue.

By sundown, we were almost home. It had been the perfect day. No crowds. No celebrities. No..."Party," I said as the helicopter approached the Hawthorne estate, and I took in the view below. The topiary garden and adjacent lawn were lit by thousands of tiny lights—and that wasn't even the worst of it.

"That had better not be a dance floor," I told Jameson darkly.

Jameson took the helicopter in for a landing, threw his head back, and smiled. "You're not going to comment on the Ferris wheel?"

No wonder he'd needed to get me out of the House. "You're a dead man, Hawthorne."

Jameson cut the engine. "Fortunately, Heiress, Hawthorne men have nine lives."

As we disembarked and walked toward the topiary garden, I glanced at Oren and narrowed my eyes. "You knew about this," I accused.

"I may have been presented with a guest list to vet for entrance onto the estate." My head of security's expression was absolutely unreadable...until the party came into full view. Then he *almost* smiled. "I also may have vetoed a few names on that list."

And by *a few*, I realized a moment later, he meant almost all of them.

The dance floor was scattered with rose petals and lit by strings of delicate lights that crisscrossed overhead, softly glowing like fireflies in the night. A string quartet played to the left of the kind of cake I would have expected to see at a royal wedding. The Ferris wheel turned in the distance. Tuxedo-clad waiters carried trays of champagne and hors d'oeuvres.

But there were no guests.

"Do you like?" Libby appeared beside me. She was dressed like something out of a goth fairy tale and grinning from ear to ear. "I wanted black rose petals, but this is nice, too."

"What *is* this?" I breathed.

My sister bumped her shoulder into mine. "We're calling it the introvert's ball."

"There's no one here." I could feel my own smile building.

"Not true," Libby replied cheerfully. "I'm here. Nash turned his nose up at the fancy food and put himself in charge of the grill. Mr. Laughlin's running the Ferris wheel, under Mrs. Laughlin's supervision. Thea and Rebecca are stealing a *super*-stolen moment back behind the ice sculptures. Xander's keeping an eye on your surprise, and here's Zara and Nan!"

I turned just in time to be poked with a cane. Jameson's great-grandmother glowered at me while his aunt looked on, austerely amused.

"You, girl," Nan said, which was basically her version of my name. "The neckline on that dress makes you look like a floozy." She wagged her cane at me, then grunted. "I approve."

"So do I," a voice piped up from my left. "Happy faxing birthday, you beautiful beach."

"Max?" I stared at my best friend, then glanced back at Libby.

"Surprise!"

Beside me, Jameson smirked. "Alisa may have been under the impression that there was going to be a much larger party."

But there wasn't. It was just... *us*.

Max threw an arm around me. "Ask me how college is!"

"How's college?" I asked, still absolutely floored.

Max grinned. "Not nearly as entertaining as Ferris Wheel Leapfrog Death Match."

"Ferris Wheel Leapfrog Death Match?" I repeated. That had Xander written all over it. I knew for a fact the two of them had stayed in touch.

"Who's winning?" Jameson cocked his head to one side.

Max replied, but before I could process what she was saying, I saw movement out of the corner of my eye—or maybe I sensed it. Sensed *him*. Clad entirely in black, wearing a ten-thousand-dollar tuxedo the way other guys wore ratty sweatshirts, Grayson Hawthorne stepped onto the dance floor.

He came home. That thought was accompanied by a memory of the last time I'd seen him: *Grayson, broken. Me, beside him*. Back in the present, Grayson Hawthorne let his eyes linger on mine for just a moment, then swept them over the rest of the party. "Ferris Wheel Leapfrog Death Match," he said calmly. "This never ends well."

CHAPTER 5

The next morning, I woke to the sight of my ball gown strewn over the end of my bed. Jameson was asleep beside me. I pushed back the urge to trail my fingertips across his jawline, to lightly touch the scar that ran down his chest.

I'd asked him a dozen times how he'd gotten that scar, and he'd given me a dozen different answers. In some versions, the culprit was a jagged rock. A steel rod. A windshield.

Someday, I'd get the real answer.

I allowed myself one more moment beside Jameson, then slipped from my bed, picked up my Hawthorne pin, got dressed, and headed downstairs.

Grayson was in the dining room, alone.

"I didn't think you would make it home," I said, somehow managing to take the seat opposite his.

"Technically, it isn't *my* home anymore." Even at low volume, Grayson's voice washed over the room like a tide coming in. "In a very short time, everything in this place will officially be yours." That wasn't a condemnation or a complaint. It was a fact.

"That doesn't mean anything has to change," I said.

"Avery." Piercing pale eyes met mine. "It has to. *You* have to." Before I'd come along, Grayson had been the heir apparent. He was practically an expert in what one *had* to do.

And I was the only one who knew: Beneath that invincible, controlled exterior, he was falling apart. I couldn't say that, couldn't let on I was even thinking it, so I stuck to the topic at hand. "What if I can't do this on my own?" I asked.

"You aren't on your own." Grayson let his eyes linger on mine, then carefully and deliberately broke eye contact. "Every year, on our birthdays," he said, after a moment, "the old man would call us into his study."

I'd heard this before. "*Invest. Cultivate. Create,*" I said. From the time they were kids, each year on their birthdays, the Hawthorne brothers had been given ten thousand dollars to invest. They'd also been told to choose a talent or an interest to cultivate, and no expense had been spared in that cultivation. Finally, Tobias Hawthorne had issued a birthday challenge: something they were to invent, create, perform, or will into being.

"*Invest*—you'll soon have covered. *Cultivate*—you should pick something you want for yourself. Not an item or an experience but a skill." I waited for Grayson to ask me what I was going to choose, but he didn't. Instead, he removed a leather book from the inside of his suit jacket and slid it across the table. "As for your birthday challenge, you'll need to create a plan."

The leather was a deep, rich brown, soft to the touch. The edges of the pages were slightly uneven, as though the book had been bound by hand.

"You'll want to start with a firm grasp of your financials. From there, think about the future and map out your time and financial commitments for the next five years."

I opened the book. The thick off-white pages were blank.

"Write it all down," Grayson instructed. "Then tear it apart and rewrite it. Over and over again until you have a plan that works."

"You know what you would do in my position." I would have bet my entire fortune that somewhere, he had a journal—and a plan—of his own.

Grayson's eyes found their way back to mine. "You aren't me."

I wondered if there was anyone at Harvard—a single person—who knew him even a tenth as well as his brothers and I did. "You promised you would help me." The words escaped before I could stop them. "You said you would teach me everything I needed to know."

I knew better than to remind Grayson Hawthorne of a broken promise. I didn't have the right to ask this of him, to ask anything of him. I was with Jameson. I *loved* Jameson. And, Grayson's entire life, everyone had expected too damn much.

"I'm sorry," I said. "This isn't your problem."

"Don't," Grayson ordered roughly, "look at me like I'm broken."

You are not broken. I'd said those words to him. He hadn't believed me then. He wouldn't now, either. "Alisa wants me to put the money in a trust," I said, because the least I owed him was a subject change.

Grayson responded with an arch of his brow. "Of course she does."

"I haven't agreed to anything yet."

A slight smile pulled at the edges of his lips. "Of course you haven't."

Oren appeared in the doorway before I could reply. "I just got a call from one of my men," he told me. "There's someone at the gates."

A warning sounded in my mind because Oren was perfectly capable of taking care of unwanted visitors himself. *Skye? Or*

Ricky? Grayson's mother and my deadbeat of a father were no longer in prison for an attempt on my life that, remarkably, they *hadn't* orchestrated. That didn't mean they weren't still threats.

"Who is it?" Grayson's expression went blade-sharp.

Oren held my gaze as he answered the question. "She says her name is Eve."

CHAPTER 6

For months, I'd kept the existence of Toby's daughter a secret from everyone but Jameson. Because Toby had asked me to—but not *just* because Toby had asked me to.

"I need to take care of this," I said with a calm that I in no way felt.

"I assume my assistance is not required?" Grayson's tone was cool, but I knew him. I knew he would take my declining help as evidence that I was treating him with kid gloves.

Hawthornes aren't supposed to break, his voice whispered in my memory. *Especially me.*

I didn't have the luxury right now of trying to convince Grayson Hawthorne that he wasn't *weak* or *broken* or *damaged* to me. "I appreciate the offer," I told him, "but I'll be fine."

The last thing Grayson needed was to see the girl at the gates.

As Oren drove me out there, my mind raced. *What is she doing here? What does she want?* I tried to prepare myself, but the moment I saw Toby's daughter outside the gates, a wall of emotion crashed into me. Her amber hair blew in a gentle breeze. Even from behind, even wearing a threadbare white dress smudged with stains, this girl was luminescent.

She's not supposed to be here. Toby had been clear: He couldn't save me from the legacy Tobias Hawthorne had left behind, but he *could* save Eve. From the press. From the threats. *From the poisoned tree,* I thought, stepping out of the SUV.

Eve turned. She moved like a dancer, with equal parts grace and abandon, and the moment her eyes met mine, I stopped breathing.

I'd known that Eve was a dead ringer for Emily Laughlin.

I'd known that.

But seeing her was like looking up to see a tsunami bearing down. She had Emily's strawberry-blond hair, Emily's emerald eyes. The same heart-shaped face, the same lips and delicate dusting of freckles.

Seeing her would kill Grayson. It might hurt Jameson, but it would *kill* Grayson.

I have to get her out of here. That thought pounded through my head, but as I reached the gates, my instincts sent up another warning. I scanned the road.

"Let her in," I told Oren. I didn't see any paparazzi, but experience had taught me the dangers of telescopic lenses, and the last thing Jameson or Grayson needed was to see this girl's face plastered all over every gossip site on the internet.

The gates opened. Eve took a step toward me. "You're Avery." She took a jagged breath. "I'm—"

"I know who you are." The words came out harsher than I'd meant them to—and that was the exact moment I saw blood crusted on her temple. "Oh, hell." I stepped closer. "Are you okay?"

"I'm fine." Eve's fingers wound tightly around the strap of her beat-up messenger bag. "Toby isn't."

No. My mind rebelled. My mom had loved Toby. He'd watched out for me once she was gone. *He has to be okay.* A breath trapped in my chest, I let Oren escort the two of us behind the SUV—away from prying eyes and ears.

"What happened to Toby?" I demanded urgently.

Eve pressed her lips together. "He told me that if anything happened to him, I should come to you. And, look, I'm not naive, okay? I know you probably don't want me here." She said those words like a person used to not being wanted. "But I didn't have anywhere else to go."

When I'd found out about Eve, I'd offered to bring her to Hawthorne House. Toby had vetoed that idea. He hadn't wanted anyone to know about her. *So why would he send her to me?* Every muscle in my jaw and stomach tight, I forced myself to concentrate on the only thing that mattered.

"What happened to Toby?" I said again, my voice low and guttural.

The wind caught Eve's hair. Her pink lips parted. "They took him."

Air whooshed out of my lungs, my ears ringing, my sense of gravity distorted. "Who?" I demanded. "Who took him?"

"I don't know." Eve's arms curved protectively around her torso. "Toby found me months ago. He told me who he was. Who *I* was. We were doing fine, just the two of us, but then last week something happened. Toby saw someone."

"Who?" I asked again, the word torn out of me.

"I don't know. Toby wouldn't tell me. He just said that he had to leave."

Toby does that, I thought, my eyes stinging. *He leaves.* "You said someone took him."

"I'm getting to that," Eve said tersely. "Toby didn't want to take me with him, but I didn't give him a choice. I told him that if he tried to leave me behind, I would go to the press."

Despite a leaked photograph and some tabloid rumors, no media outlet had yet been able to substantiate claims that Toby was alive. "You blackmailed him into taking you with him?"

"If you were me," Eve replied, something almost beseeching in her tone, "you would have done the same." She looked down, impossibly long lashes casting shadows on her face. "Toby and I went off the grid, but someone was tracking us, stalking us like prey. Toby wouldn't tell me who we were running from, but on Monday, he said that we had to split up. The plan was for us to meet back up three days later. I waited. I stayed off the grid, just like he'd taught me. Yesterday, I showed up at our meeting place." She shook her head, her green eyes glistening. "Toby didn't."

"Maybe he had second thoughts," I said, wanting that to be true. "Maybe—"

"No," Eve insisted desperately. "Toby never lied to me. He never broke a promise. He wouldn't—" She cut herself off. "Someone took him. You don't believe me? I can prove it."

Eve pulled her hair away from her face. The dried blood I'd seen was just the tip of the iceberg. The skin around the cut was mottled, a sickening mix of black and blue.

"Someone hit you." Until Oren spoke, I'd almost forgotten he was there. "With the butt of a gun, I'm guessing."

Eve didn't even look at him. Her bright green eyes stayed locked on mine. "Toby didn't show up at our meeting place, but someone else did." She let her hair fall back over the bruise. "They grabbed me from behind and told me that if I knew what was good for me, I would forget all about Toby Hawthorne."

"They used his real name?" I managed to form the question.

Eve nodded. "That's the last thing I remember. They knocked me out. I woke up to find they'd stolen everything I had on me. They even went through my pockets." Her voice shook slightly, and then she steeled herself. "Toby and I had stashed a bag for emergencies: a change of clothes for each of us, a little cash." I wondered if she realized how tightly she was holding that bag now. "I bought a bus ticket, and I came here. To you."

You have a daughter, I'd told Toby when we found out about Eve, and he'd replied, *I have two.* Swallowing back the twisted bramble of emotions inside me, I turned to Oren. "We should call the authorities."

"No." Eve caught my arm. "You can't report a dead man missing, and Toby didn't tell me to go to the police. He told me to come to *you*."

My throat tightened. "Someone attacked you. We can report that."

"And who," Eve bit out, "is going to believe a girl like me?"

I'd grown up poor. I'd been *that girl*—the one nobody expected much from, the one who was treated as less than because I had less.

"Bringing the authorities in could tie our hands," Oren told me. "We should prepare for a ransom demand. In the event that we get no such demand..."

I didn't even want to think about what it meant if the person who'd taken Toby wasn't after money. "If Eve tells you where she was supposed to meet Toby, can you send a team to do recon?" I asked Oren.

"Consider it done," he said—then his gaze shifted abruptly to something or someone behind me. I heard a sound from that direction, a strangled, almost inhuman sound, and I knew, even before I turned around, what I would see there. *Who* I would see there.

"Emily?" Grayson Hawthorne was staring at a ghost.

CHAPTER 7

Grayson Davenport Hawthorne was a person who valued control—of every situation, of every emotion. When I took a step toward him, he stepped back.

"Grayson," I said softly.

There were no words for the way he was staring at Eve—like she was a dream, every hope and every torment, *everything*.

Silvery gray eyes closed. "Avery. You should..." Grayson forced a breath in, out. He straightened and squared his shoulders. "I'm not safe to be around right now, Avery."

It took me a moment to realize that he thought he was hallucinating. *Again.* Breaking down. *Again.*

Tell me again that I'm not broken.

Closing the space between us, I took Grayson by the shoulders. "Hey," I said softly. "*Hey.* Look at me, Gray."

Those light eyes opened.

"That's not Emily." I held his gaze and wouldn't let him look away. "And you aren't hallucinating."

Grayson's eyes flickered over my shoulder. "I see—"

"I know," I said, bringing my hand to the side of his face and forcing his eyes back to mine. "She's real. Her name is Eve." I couldn't be sure he was hearing me, let alone processing what I was saying. "She's Toby's daughter."

"She looks..."

"I know," I said, my hand still on his jaw. "Emily's mom was Toby's biological mother, remember?" Newborn Toby had been adopted into the Hawthorne family in secret. Alice Hawthorne had faked a pregnancy to hide the adoption, passing him off as her own. "That makes Eve a Laughlin by blood," I continued. "There's a family resemblance."

"I thought—" Grayson cut off the words. A Hawthorne did not admit weakness. "You knew." Grayson looked down at me, and I finally let my hand fall away from his face. "You aren't surprised to see her, Avery. You knew."

I heard what he wasn't saying: *That night in the wine cellar—I knew.*

"Toby wanted her existence kept secret," I said, telling myself *that* was why I hadn't told him. "He didn't want this life for Eve."

"Who else knows?" Grayson demanded in that heir-apparent tone, the one that made questions sound perfunctory, like he was doing the person he was questioning a courtesy by asking instead of wresting the answer from their mind himself.

"Just Jameson," I replied.

After a long, torturous moment, Grayson looked past me to Eve, emotion etched in every muscle of his jaw. I wasn't sure how much of his torment was because he thought I considered him weak and how much of it was her. Either way, Grayson didn't hide from his pain this time. He walked toward Eve, letting it come, like a shirtless man stepping out into freezing rain.

Eve stared at him. She must have felt the intensity of the moment—*of him*—but she shook it off. "Look, I don't know what *this* is." She gestured in the vicinity of Grayson's face. "But it has been a really long week. I'm filthy. I'm scared." Her voice broke, and she turned to me. "So are you going to invite me inside and let your security goons figure out what happened to Toby, or are we just going to stand here?"

Grayson blinked, like he was seeing her—*Eve*—for the first time. "You're hurt."

She looked at him again. "I'm pissed."

I swallowed. Eve was right. Every second we spent out here was a second that Oren and his team were focused on safeguarding me instead of finding Toby.

"Come on," I said, the words like rocks in my throat. "Let's go back to the House."

Oren opened the back passenger door of the SUV. Eve climbed in, and as I followed, I wondered if this was what Pandora had felt like the moment she opened the box.

CHAPTER 8

I let Eve use my shower. Given the number of bathrooms in Hawthorne House, I recognized that decision for what it was: I wanted her where I could keep an eye on her.

I neglected to consider the fact that Jameson was still in my bed. Eve didn't seem to notice him on her way to my en suite, but Grayson did—and Jameson definitely noticed Eve. The moment the bathroom door closed behind her, he swung his feet over the side of the bed.

Shirtless. "Tell me everything, Heiress."

I searched his expression for some hint of what he was feeling, but Jameson Hawthorne was the consummate poker player. Seeing Eve had to have provoked some kind of emotion in him. The fact that he was hiding it hit me every bit as hard as the way that Grayson couldn't tear his eyes from the bathroom door.

"I don't know where to start," I said. I couldn't make myself say the words *It's Toby.*

Jameson crossed to me, his strides long. "Tell me what you need, Heiress."

Grayson finally pried his gaze away from the bathroom door. He bent, snatched an undershirt off the floor, and tossed it at his brother's face. "Put on a shirt."

Somehow, the comically disgruntled look that Jameson shot Grayson was *exactly* what I needed. I told the two of them everything that Eve had told me. "Eve wasn't able to give Oren a lot of details," I finished. "He's putting together a team to run recon on the abduction site, but—"

"They're unlikely to find much at this point," Grayson finished.

"Convenient, that," Jameson commented. "What?" he said when Grayson's icy eyes narrowed. "I'm just saying that all we have right now is the story of a stranger who showed up on our doorstep and talked her way inside."

He was right. We didn't know Eve.

"You don't believe her?" Grayson wasn't normally the type to ask questions when the answers were already apparent, so this one came with an undercurrent of friction.

"What can I say?" Jameson shrugged again. "I'm a suspicious bastard."

And Eve looks just like Emily, I thought. Jameson wasn't unaffected by that. Not by a long shot.

"I don't think she's lying," I said. *That wound.*

"You wouldn't," Jameson told me softly. "And neither," he told Grayson in a very different tone, "would you."

That was clearly a reference to Emily. She'd played them both, manipulated them both, but Grayson had loved her to the end.

"You knew." Grayson stalked toward Jameson. "You knew she was out there, Jamie. You knew that Toby had a daughter, and you didn't say a word."

"Are you really going to lecture *me* about secrets, Gray?"

What's he talking about? I'd never said a word to Jameson about the things that his brother had admitted to me in the dark of night.

"At a minimum," Grayson enunciated, his voice soft and deadly, "we owe that girl our protection."

"Because of the way she looks?" Jameson threw down the gauntlet.

"Because she's Toby's daughter," Grayson replied, "and that makes her one of us."

My fingers went to my pin. *Eve's a Hawthorne.* That shouldn't have hurt. It wasn't news. Eve was Toby's daughter—but it was already clear to me that Grayson didn't see her as a cousin. *She isn't related to them by blood. They didn't grow up together.* So when Grayson said that she was one of them, that they owed her protection, all I could think was that he'd once spoken similar words about me.

Est unus ex nobis. Nos defendat eius.

"Can we please just focus on Toby?" I said. Grayson must have heard something in my tone because he stepped back.

Stepped down.

I turned to Jameson. "Pretend for a second that you trust Eve. Pretend she looks nothing like Emily. Pretend she's telling the truth. Other than Oren's search, what's our next move?"

This was what Jameson and I did: questions and answers, looking for what other people missed. If he wouldn't do this with me, if seeing Eve had thrown him off that much...

"Motive," Jameson supplied finally. "If we want to find out who took Toby, we need to know *why* they took him."

Logically, I could think of three broad possibilities. "They want something from him. They want to use him as leverage." I swallowed. "Or they want to hurt him."

They knew his real name. Somehow, they knew how to find him.

"There has to be something we're missing," I said. I needed this to be a puzzle. I needed there to be clues.

"You mentioned that Eve said the person who knocked her out went through her pockets." Jameson had a way of playing with the facts of a situation, turning them over like a coin spun from finger to finger. "So what were they looking for?"

What did Toby have that someone else might want badly enough to kidnap him to get it? What could possibly be worth that kind of risk?

What fits in a pocket? My heart nearly exploded in my chest.

What mystery had Jameson and I spent the last nine months trying to solve?

"The disk," I breathed.

The door to the bathroom opened. Eve stood there, wrapped in a white towel, wet hair trailing down the sides of her neck. She wore a locket and nothing else except the towel. Grayson tried very hard not to look at her.

Jameson looked at me.

"Did you need something?" I asked Eve. Her hair was darker wet, less remarkable. Without it to distract from her face, her eyes looked bigger, her cheekbones higher.

"Bandage," Eve replied. If she was self-conscious about standing there in a towel, she didn't show it. "My cut split open in the shower."

"I'll help you," I volunteered before Grayson could. The sooner I tended to Eve, the sooner I could get back to Jameson and the possibility I'd just breathed into being.

What if the person who took Toby was after the disk? My mind racing, I led Eve back into the bathroom.

"What disk?" she asked behind me. I pulled out a first aid kit and handed it to her. She took it from me, her fingers brushing mine. "When I came into the room, you were talking about what happened to Toby," she said stubbornly. "You mentioned a disk."

I wondered how much else she'd heard and whether she'd meant to eavesdrop. Maybe Jameson was right. Maybe we couldn't trust her.

"It might be nothing," I said, brushing off the question.

"What might be nothing?" Eve pressed. When I didn't answer, she dropped another question like a bomb. "Who's Emily?"

I swallowed. "A girl." That wasn't a lie, but it was so far from the truth that I couldn't leave it there. "She died. The two of you—you're related."

Eve chose a bandage and pushed her wet hair back from her face. I almost offered to help her, but something held me back. "Toby told me he was adopted," she said, fixing the bandage in place. "But he wouldn't tell me anything about his biological family—or the Hawthornes."

She waited, like she expected me to tell her something. When I didn't, she looked down. "I know that you don't trust me," she said. "I wouldn't trust me, either. You have everything, and I have nothing, and I know how that looks."

So did I. From experience, *so did I.*

"I never wanted to come here," Eve continued. "I never wanted to ask you for anything—or them." Her voice strained. "But I want Toby back. I want my *father* back, Avery." Her emerald eyes locked on mine, radiating an intensity that was nearly Hawthorne. "And I will do anything—*anything*—to get what I want, even if that means begging for your help. So please, Avery, if you know something that could help us find Toby, just tell me."

CHAPTER 9

I didn't tell Eve about the disk. I justified it to myself because, for all I knew, there was nothing to tell. Not every mystery was an elaborate puzzle. The answer wasn't always elegant and carefully designed. And even if Toby's abduction did have something to do with the disk, where did that leave us?

Feeling like I owed Eve *something,* I asked Mrs. Laughlin to prepare her a room. Tears overflowed the moment the older woman laid eyes on her great-granddaughter. There was no hiding who Eve was.

No hiding that she belonged here.

Hours later, I was alone in Tobias Hawthorne's study. I told myself that I was doing the right thing, giving Jameson and Grayson space. Seeing Eve had dredged up trauma. They needed to process, and I needed to think.

I triggered the hidden compartment in the old man's desk and reached for the folder that Jameson and I kept inside. Flipping it open, I stared at a drawing I'd made: a small coinlike disk the size of a quarter, engraved with concentric circles. The last time I'd seen this bit of metal, Toby had just snatched it from my hands. I'd asked him what it was. He hadn't answered. All I really knew was what I'd read in a message Toby had once written to my mother: that if she ever needed anything, she should go to Jackson. *You know what I left there*, Toby had written. *You know what it's worth.*

I stared at the drawing. *You know what it's worth*. Coming from the son of a billionaire, that was almost unfathomable. In the months since Toby had left, Jameson and I had scoured books on art and ancient civilizations, on rare coins, lost treasures, and great archeological finds. We'd even researched organizations like the Freemasons and the Knights Templar.

Spreading that research out on the desk, I looked for something, anything we'd missed, but there was no record of the disk anywhere, and Jameson's globe-trotting search of Hawthorne vacation properties hadn't turned up anything meaningful, either.

"Who knows about the disk?" I let myself think out loud. "Who knows what it's worth and that Toby had it?"

Who even knew for certain that Toby was alive, let alone where to find him?

All I had were questions. It felt wrong that Jameson wasn't here asking them with me.

Without meaning to, I reached back into the hidden compartment, to another file, one that billionaire Tobias Hawthorne had assembled on me. *Did the old man know about Eve?* I couldn't shake the feeling that if Tobias Hawthorne *had* known about Toby's daughter, I wouldn't be here. The billionaire had chosen me largely for the effect it would have on his family. He'd used me to force the boys to confront their issues, to pull Toby back onto the board.

It should have been her.

A creak sounded behind me. I turned to see Xander stepping out of the wall. One look at his face told me that my BHFF had seen our visitor.

"I come in peace," he announced gravely. "I come with pie."

"He comes with me." Max stepped into the room behind Xander. "What the ever-faxing elf is going on, Avery?"

Xander set the pie down on the desk. "I brought three forks."

I read meaning into his grim tone. "You're upset."

"About sharing this pie?"

I looked away. "About Eve."

"You knew," Xander told me, more injury than accusation in his tone.

I forced myself to meet his eyes. "I did."

"All those times playing Cookie Golf together, and you didn't think this was worth mentioning?" Xander pulled off a piece of pie crust and brandished it in the air. "This might have escaped your attention, but I happen to excel at keeping secrets! I have a mouth like a steel trap."

Max snorted. "Isn't the expression 'a mind like a steel trap'?"

"My mind is more like a roller coaster inside a labyrinth buried in an M. C. Escher painting that is riding on another roller coaster." Xander shrugged. "But my *mouth* is a steel trap. Just ask me about all the secrets I'm keeping."

"What secrets are you keeping?" Max asked obligingly.

"I can't tell you!" Xander triumphantly dug his fork into the pie.

"So if I'd told you that Toby had a daughter out there who looked exactly like Emily Laughlin, you *wouldn't* have told Rebecca?" I said, referring to Emily's sister and Xander's oldest friend.

"I definitely, one hundred percent, entirely... *would* have told Rebecca," Xander admitted. "In retrospect, good on you for not telling me. Excellent call, shows solid judgment."

My phone rang. I looked down at it, then back up at Xander and Max. "It's Oren." My heart beating in my ears, I answered. "What do we know?"

"Not much. Not yet. I sent a team to the rendezvous point where Eve said she was supposed to meet Toby. There was no physical evidence of an altercation, but with a little digging, we did find record of a nine-one-one call, placed hours before Eve said she showed up."

My hand tightened around the phone. "What kind of nine-one-one call?"

"Shots fired." Oren didn't soften the words. "By the time a patrol unit got there, the scene was clear. They put it down to fireworks or a car backfiring."

"Who called nine-one-one?" I asked. "Did anyone see anything?"

"My team is working on it." Oren paused. "In the meantime, I've assigned one of my men to shadow Eve for the duration of her stay at Hawthorne House."

"Do you think she's a threat?" My hand went reflexively, again, to my Hawthorne pin.

"My job is to treat everyone like a threat," Oren replied. "Right now, what I need is for you to promise that you'll stay put and do nothing." My gaze went to the research spread across the desk. "My team and I will find out everything we can as quickly as we can, Avery. Toby might be the target here, but he also might not be."

I frowned. "What's that supposed to mean?"

"Give us twenty-four hours, and I'll let you know."

Twenty-four hours? I was just supposed to sit here, doing nothing, for twenty-four hours? I hung up the phone.

"Does Oren think Eve is a threat?" Max asked in a dramatic stage-whisper.

Xander made a face. "Note to self: Cancel the welcome festivities."

I thought about Oren telling me to let him handle it, then about Eve swearing that all she wanted was to find Toby. "No," I told

Xander. "Don't cancel anything. I want to get a feel for Eve." I needed to know if we could trust her because if we could, maybe she knew something I didn't. "Got any particular festivities in mind?" I asked.

Xander pressed his hands together. "I believe that our best option for assessing the truth of the mysterious Eve's character is... Chutes and Ladders."

CHAPTER 10

The Hawthorne version of Chutes and Ladders wasn't a board game. Xander promised he would explain further once I got Eve to agree to play. Focused on that task, I made my way to the Versailles wing. At the top of the east staircase, I found Grayson standing statue-still outside the wing, dressed in a silver three-piece suit, his blond hair wet from the pool.

A poolside cocktail party. The memory hit me and wouldn't let go. *Grayson is expertly deflecting every financial inquiry that comes my way. I glance toward the pool. There's a toddler balanced precariously on the edge. She leans forward, topples over, goes under, and doesn't come up. Before I can move or even yell, Grayson is running.*

In one liquid motion, he dives into the pool, fully clothed.

"Where's Jameson?" Grayson's question drew me back to the present.

"Probably somewhere he's not supposed to be," I answered honestly, "making very bad decisions and throwing caution to the wind."

I didn't ask Grayson what he was doing outside the Versailles wing.

"I see that Oren put a man on Eve." Grayson almost managed to sound like he was commenting on the weather, but a comment never felt like just a comment coming from him.

"It's Oren's job to make sure I stay safe." I didn't point out that under other circumstances, Grayson would have considered that his job, too.

Est unus ex nobis. Nos defendat eius.

"Oren shouldn't be worried about *me*." Eve stepped into the hall. Her hair was dry and fell in gentle waves. "Your security team should be focusing everything on Toby." Eve let her vibrant green eyes go from me to Grayson, and I wondered if she recognized the effect she had on him. "What do I have to do to convince you that I am not a threat?"

She was looking at Grayson, but I was the one who answered the question. "How about a game?"

"Hawthorne Chutes and Ladders," Xander boomed, standing in front of a pile of pillows, rope ladders, grappling hooks, suction cups, and nylon rope. "The rules are fairly simple." The list of complicated things that Xander Hawthorne considered to be "fairly simple" was lengthy. "Hawthorne House has three chutes—entrances to the passageways that involve, let's say, a drop," Xander continued.

I smiled. I'd already found all three.

"There are slides built into the walls of your mansion?" Max snorted. "Mother-foxing rich people."

Xander did not take offense. "Some chutes are more advantageous than others. If another player beats you to a chute, that chute is frozen for three minutes, so everyone will need one of these." Xander picked one up a pillow and gave it a gentle, but somehow menacing, swing. "Battles must be waged."

"Hawthorne Chutes and Ladders involves pillow fights?" Max asked in a tone that made me think she was picturing all four Hawthorne brothers swinging pillows at one another. Possibly shirtless.

"Pillow *wars*," Xander corrected. "Once you successfully claim your chute and make it to the ground floor, you exit the House, and it's a race to climb to the roof from the outside."

I surveyed the climbing supplies spread out at our feet. "We get to choose a ladder?"

"One does not," Xander corrected me austerely, "simply *choose* a ladder."

Grayson broke the silence he'd adopted the moment Eve had stepped into the hall. "Our grandfather liked to say that every choice worth anything came with a cost."

Eve assessed him. "And the cost for climbing supplies is..."

Grayson answered her assessing look with one of his own. "A secret."

Xander elaborated. "Each player confesses a secret. The person with the best secret gets to pick their climbing supplies first, and so on and so forth. The person with the least impressive secret goes last." I was starting to see why Xander had chosen this game. "Now," he continued, rubbing his hands together. "Which brave soul wants to go first?"

I eyed Eve, but Grayson intervened. "I'll go." He fixed his silvery eyes straight ahead. I wasn't sure what to expect, but it definitely wasn't him saying, with absolutely no intonation, "I kissed a girl at Harvard."

He...No, I wasn't going to finish that thought. What Grayson Hawthorne did with his lips was none of my business.

"I got a tattoo." Max offered up her own secret with a grin. "It's very nerdy and in a location I will not disclose. My parents can *never* find out."

"Tell me more," Xander said, "about this nerdy tattoo."

Grayson arched a brow at his brother, and I tried to think of something that would make Eve feel like she had to open up.

"Sometimes," I said quietly, "I feel like Tobias Hawthorne made a mistake." Maybe that wasn't a secret. Maybe it was obvious. But the next part was harder to say. "Like he should have chosen someone else."

Eve stared at me.

"The old man didn't make mistakes," Grayson said in one of those tones that dared you to argue—and strongly advised against it.

"My turn." Xander raised his hand. "I figured out who my father is."

"You *what*?" Grayson whipped his head toward his brother. Skye Hawthorne had four sons, each with a different father, none of whom she'd identified. Nash and Grayson had discovered their fathers within the last year. I'd known that Xander was looking for his.

"I don't know if he knows about me." Xander rushed the words. "I haven't made contact. I'm not sure I'm going to, and by the sacred rules of Chutes and Ladders, none of you can *ever* mention this again unless I bring it up first. Eve?"

With the rest of us still focused on Xander, Eve bent and picked up a grappling hook. As I turned to look at her, she trailed her finger along its edge. "Almost twenty-one years ago, my mom got drunk and cheated on her husband, and I was the result." She didn't meet a single person's eyes. "Her husband knew I wasn't his, but they stayed married. I used to think that if I could be good enough—smart enough, sweet enough, *something* enough—the man we all pretended was my father would stop blaming me for being born." She tossed the grappling hook back down. "The worst part was my mom blamed me, too."

Grayson leaned toward her. I wasn't even sure he knew he was doing it.

"As I got older," Eve continued, her voice quiet but raw, "I realized that it didn't matter how perfect I was. I was never going to be good enough because they didn't want me to be *perfect* or *extraordinary.* They wanted me to be invisible." Whatever emotions Eve was feeling were buried too deep to see. "And that is the one thing that I will never be."

Silence.

"What about your siblings?" I asked. Up until now, I'd been so focused on Eve's resemblance to Emily, on the fact that she was Toby's daughter, that I hadn't thought about her other family members—or what they'd done.

"Half-siblings," Eve said with absolutely no intonation.

Technically, the Hawthorne brothers were half-siblings. Technically, Libby and I were. But there was no mistaking Eve's tone: It meant something different to her.

"Eli and Mellie came here under false pretenses," I said. "For you."

"Eli and Mellie never did a damn thing for me," Eve replied, her voice hoarse, her head held high. "Christmas morning when I was five, when they had presents under the tree and I didn't? The family reunions that everyone got to go to but me? Every time I got grounded for existing just a little too loudly? Every time I had to beg a ride home from something because no one bothered to pick me up?" She looked down. "If my *siblings* came to Hawthorne House, it sure as hell wasn't for me. I haven't spoken a word to either of them in two years." Shining emerald eyes made their way back to mine. "Is that personal enough for you?"

I felt a needle's stab of icy guilt. I remembered what it was like coming to Hawthorne House as an outsider, and I thought suddenly about my mom and the way she would have welcomed Toby's daughter with open arms.

About what she would say if she could see me cross-examining her now.

Ballots were passed out. Secrets were ranked. Supplies were chosen.

And then the race was on.

CHAPTER 11

This was what I discovered about Eve during the remainder of Chutes and Ladders: She was competitive, she wasn't afraid of heights, she had a high tolerance for pain, and she definitely recognized the effect she had on Grayson.

She fit here, at Hawthorne House, with the Hawthornes.

That was the thought at the top of my mind as my fingers latched on to the edge of the roof. A hand reached down and closed around my wrist. "You're not first," Jameson told me in a tone that clearly communicated that he knew how I felt about *that*. "But you're not last."

That honor would eventually go to Xander and Max, who had spent far too long pillow fighting each other. I looked past Jameson to the part of the roof that flattened out.

To Grayson and Eve.

"On a scale from boring to brooding," Jameson quipped, "how's he holding up?"

Heaven forbid Jameson Hawthorne get caught openly *caring* about his brother.

"Honestly?" I bit my lip, catching it between my teeth for a moment too long, then pitched my voice low. "I'm worried. Grayson isn't okay, Jameson. I don't think your brother has been okay for a very long time."

Jameson moved toward the edge of the roof—the *very* edge—and looked out at the sprawling estate. "Hawthornes aren't, as a general rule, allowed to be anything else."

He was hurting, too, and when Jameson Hawthorne hurt, he took risks. I knew him, and I knew there was only one way to make him admit to the pain and purge the poison.

"Tahiti," I said.

That was a code word I didn't use lightly. If Jameson or I called *Tahiti*, the other one had to metaphorically strip.

"Your birthday was the second anniversary of Emily's death." Jameson's shoulders and back were taut beneath his shirt. "I almost succeeded in not thinking about it, but now wouldn't be the worst time for you to tell me I didn't kill her."

I stepped up beside him, right on the edge of the roof, heedless of the sixty-foot drop. "What happened to Emily wasn't your fault."

Jameson turned his head toward me. "It also wouldn't be the worst time to tell me that you aren't jealous of Eve standing that close to Grayson."

I'd wanted to know what he was feeling. This was part of it, part of what thinking about Emily did to him.

"I'm not jealous," I said.

Jameson looked me right in the eyes. *"Tahiti."*

He'd shown me his. "Okay," I said roughly. "Maybe I am, but it's not just about Grayson. Eve is Toby's daughter. I wanted to be. I thought I was. But I'm not, and she is, and now, suddenly, she's here, and she's connected to this place, to all of you—and no, I don't like it, and I feel petty for feeling that way." I stepped back from the edge. "But I'm going to tell her about the disk."

Whether or not I could fully trust Eve, I trusted that we wanted the same thing. I understood better now what it must have meant to her to meet Toby, to be *wanted*.

Before Jameson could question my decision about the disk, Max hauled herself up onto the roof and collapsed. "*Faaaaaaax.*" She drew out the word. "I am never doing that again."

Xander pulled himself up behind her. "How about tomorrow? Same time?"

Their appearance pulled Grayson and Eve toward us.

"So?" Eve said, her expression flecked with vulnerability, her voice tough. "Did I pass your little test?"

In response, I withdrew my drawing of the disk from my pocket and handed it to Eve. "The last time I saw Toby," I said slowly, "he took this disk from me. We don't know what it is, but we know it's worth a fortune."

Eve stared at the drawing, then her eyes found mine. "How do you know that?"

"He left it for my mother. There was a letter." That was as much as I could bring myself to tell her. "Did he ever say anything to you about any of this? Do you have any idea where he was keeping the disk?"

"No." Eve shook her head. "But if someone did take Toby to get this..." Her breath hitched. "What are they going to do to him if he won't give it to them?"

And, I thought, feeling sick, *what will they do to him once they have it?*

CHAPTER 12

That night, the only thing that kept me from nightmares was Jameson's body next to mine. I dreamed about my mom, about Toby, about fire and gold. I woke to the sound of shouting.

"I'm going to throttle him!" There was a grand total of one person who could get a rise out of my sister.

As Jameson began to stir, I slipped out of bed and padded out of my room to the hall. "Another cowboy hat?" I guessed. For the past two months, Nash had been buying cowboy hats for Libby. A veritable rainbow of colors and styles. He liked to leave them where my sister would find them.

"Look at this!" Libby demanded. She held up a cowboy hat. It was black with a bejeweled skull and crossbones in the center and metal spikes down the side.

"It's very you," I told her.

"It's perfect!" Libby said, outraged.

"Face it, Lib," I told her. "You're a couple."

"We're not a couple," Libby insisted. "This isn't my life, Ave. It's yours." She looked down, her hair, dyed black with rainbow tips, falling into her face. "And experience has taught me that I am utterly deficient when it comes to love. So." Libby thrust the cowboy hat at me. "I am not in love with Nash Hawthorne. We are not a couple. We are not dating. And he is definitely not in love with me."

"Avery." Oren announced his presence. I turned to face him, and my pulse jumped.

"What is it?" I asked. *"Toby?"*

"This arrived by courier in the dead of night." Oren held out an envelope with my name written across the front in elegant script. "I screened it—no trace of poison, explosives, or recording devices."

"Is it a ransom demand?" I asked. If it was a ransom demand, I could call Alisa, have her pay it.

Not waiting for a reply, I took the envelope from Oren. It was too heavy to just be a letter. My senses heightened, the world around me falling into slow motion, I opened it.

Inside, I found a single sheet of paper—and a familiar golden disk.

What the hell? I looked up. "Jameson!" He was already on his way to me. *We were wrong.* The words died, trapped in my throat. *The person who kidnapped Toby wasn't after the disk.*

I stared at it, my mind racing.

"Why would Toby's abductor send that to you?" Jameson asked. "Proof of life?"

"Proof that they have him." I didn't want to be making the correction, but this wasn't proof of *life*. "And the fact that they sent it," I continued, steeling myself, "means that either the person who took Toby doesn't know what the disk is worth…"

"Or they don't care." Jameson laid a hand on my shoulder.

Toby's okay. He has to be. He has to. The disk burning my palm like a brand, I closed my fist around it and made myself read the accompanying message. The paper was linen, expensive. Letters had been scripted onto it in a deep blood red.

A
RE
ANCE
A R

"That's it?" Jameson said. "There was nothing else?"

I checked the envelope again. "Nothing." I brought my fingertip to the writing—and the red ink. My stomach twisted. "That *is* ink, isn't it?"

Blood red.

"I don't know," Jameson replied intensely, "but I do know what it says."

I stared at the letters scattered across the page.

A
RE
ANCE
A R

"It's a simple trick," Jameson told me. "One of my grandfather's favorites. You decode the message by inserting the same sequence of letters into every blank. Five letters, in this case."

My heart brutalizing the inside of my rib cage, I tried to focus. What five letters could go after *A* or *RE* and before *ANCE*?

After a few seconds, I saw it. Slowly, painstakingly, my brain ticked off the answer, letter by letter. "*V. E. N.*" I took a sharp breath. "*G. E.*"

Venge. Completed, the message was anything but comforting. "Avenge," I made myself say out loud. "Revenge. Vengeance." Decoded, the last line seemed more like a signature.

My eyes flashed to Jameson's, and he said it for me. "Avenger."

CHAPTER 13

I texted Grayson and Xander. When they met us in the circular library, Eve was with them. Wordlessly, I held up the disk. Hesitantly, Eve took it from me, and the room went silent.

"How much did you say it was worth?" she asked, her voice a jagged whisper.

I shook my head. "We don't know, not exactly—but a lot." It was another four or five seconds before Eve reluctantly handed the disk back to me.

"There was a message?" Grayson asked, and I passed the paper over. "They didn't demand a ransom," he noted, his voice almost too calm.

My chest burned like I'd been holding a breath for far too long, even though I hadn't. "No," I said. "They didn't." The day before, I'd come up with three motives for kidnapping. *The kidnapper wanted something from Toby. The kidnapper wanted to use Toby as leverage.*

Or the kidnapper wanted to hurt him.

One of those options seemed much more likely now.

Xander craned his neck over Grayson's shoulder to get a closer look at the note. He decoded the message as quickly as Jameson had. "Revenge themed. Cheery."

"Revenge for what?" Eve asked desperately.

The obvious answer had occurred to me the moment I'd decoded the message, and it hit me again now with the force of a shovel swung at my gut. "Hawthorne Island," I said. "The fire."

More than two decades earlier, Toby had been a reckless, out-of-control teenager. The fire that the world presumed had taken his life had also taken the lives of three other young people. *David Golding. Colin Anders Wright. Kaylie Rooney.*

"Three victims." Jameson began circling the room like a panther on the prowl. "Three families. How many suspects does that give us in total?"

Eve moved, too, toward Grayson. "What fire?"

Xander popped between them. "The one that Toby accidentally-but-kind-of-on-purpose set. It's a long, tragic story involving daddy issues, inebriated teenagers, premeditated arson, and a freak lightning strike."

"Three victims." I repeated what Jameson had said, but my eyes went to Grayson's. "Three families."

"One yours," Grayson replied. "And one mine."

My mom's sister had died in the fire on Hawthorne Island. Billionaire Tobias Hawthorne had saved his own family's reputation by pinning the blame for the fire on her. Kaylie Rooney's family—my mom's family—was full of criminals. The violent kind.

The kind who hated Hawthornes.

I turned and walked toward the door, my stomach heavy. "I have to make a call."

Out in one of Hawthorne House's massive, winding corridors, I dialed a number that I had only called once before and tried to ignore the memory that threatened to overwhelm me.

If my worthless daughter had taught you the first damn thing about this family, you wouldn't dare have dialed my number. The woman who'd birthed and raised my mother wasn't exactly the maternal type. *If that little bitch hadn't run, I would have put a bullet in her myself.* The last time I'd called, I'd been told to forget my grandmother's name and that, if I was lucky, she and the rest of the Rooney family would forget mine.

Yet there I was, calling again.

She picked up. "You think you're untouchable?"

I took the greeting as evidence that she'd recognized my number, which meant that I didn't need to say anything but "Do you have him?"

"Who the hell do you think you are?" Her rough, throaty voice lashed at me like a whip. "You really think I can't get to you, Miss High and Mighty? You think you're safe in that castle of yours?"

I'd been told that the Rooney family was small-time, that their power paled compared to that of the Hawthorne family—and the Hawthorne heiress. "I think that it would be a mistake to underestimate you." I balled my left hand into a fist as my right hand's grip on the phone went viselike. *"Do. You. Have. Him."*

There was a long, calculating pause. "One of those pretty little Hawthorne grandsons?" she said. "Maybe I do—and maybe he won't be quite so pretty when you get him back."

Unless she was playing me, she'd just tipped her hand. I knew where the Hawthorne grandsons were. But if the Rooneys didn't know that Toby was missing—if they didn't know or believe that he was *alive*—I couldn't afford to let on that she'd guessed wrong.

So I played along. "If you have Jameson, if you lay a finger on him—"

"Tell me, girl, what do they say happens if you lie down with dogs?"

I kept my voice flat. "You wake up with fleas."

"Around here, we have a different saying." Without warning, the other end of the line exploded into vicious barks and growls, five or six dogs at least. "They're hungry, and they're mean, and they have a taste for blood. You think about that before you call this number again."

I hung up, or maybe she did. *The Rooneys don't have Toby.* I tried to concentrate on that.

"You okay there, kid?" Nash Hawthorne had a gentle manner and remarkable timing.

"I'm fine," I said, the words a whisper.

Nash pulled me into his chest, his worn white T-shirt soft against my cheek.

"I've got a knife in my boot," I mumbled into his shirt. "I'm an excellent shot. I know how to fight dirty."

"You sure do, kid." Nash stroked a hand over my hair. "You want to tell me what this is about?"

CHAPTER 14

Back in the library, Nash examined the envelope, the message, and the disk.

"The Rooneys don't have Toby," I announced. "They're ruthless, and if they knew for sure Toby was alive, they would probably be making a real effort to feed his face to a pack of dogs, but I'm almost certain they don't have him."

Xander raised his right hand. "I have a question about faces and dogs."

I shuddered. "You don't want to know."

Grayson took up a perch on the edge of the tree-trunk desk, unbuttoning his suit jacket. "I can likewise clear the Graysons."

Eve gave him a look. "The *Graysons*?"

"My sire and his family," Grayson clarified, his face like stone. "They're related to Colin Anders Wright, who died in the fire. Sheffield Grayson abandoned his wife and daughters some months back."

That was a lie. Sheffield Grayson was dead. Eve's half sister had killed him to save me, and Oren had covered it up. But Eve gave no sign that she knew that, and based on what she'd told us about her siblings, that tracked.

"Rumors place my so-called father somewhere in the Caymans,"

Grayson continued smoothly. "I've been keeping an eye on the rest of the family in his absence."

"Does the Grayson family know about you?" Jameson asked his brother. No banter, no sarcasm. He knew what *family* meant to Grayson.

"I saw no need for them to," came the reply. "But I can assure you that if Sheffield Grayson's wife, sister, or daughters had a hand in this, I would know."

"You hired someone." Jameson's eyes narrowed. "With what money?"

"Invest. Cultivate. Create." Grayson didn't offer any more explanation than that before he stood. "If we've ruled out the families of Colin Anders Wright and Kaylie Rooney, that leaves only the family of the third victim: David Golding."

"I'll have someone look into it." Oren didn't even step out of the shadows to speak.

"Seems like you do that a lot." Eve leveled a gaze in his direction.

"Heiress." Jameson suddenly stopped pacing. He picked up the envelope the message had come in. "This was addressed to *you*."

I heard what he was saying, the possibility he'd seen. "What if Toby isn't the target of revenge?" I said slowly. "What if I am?"

"You have a lot of enemies?" Eve asked me.

"In her position," Grayson murmured, "it's hard not to."

"What if we're looking at this wrong?" When Xander paced, it wasn't in straight lines or in circles. "What if it's not about the message? What if we should be focusing on the code?"

"The game," Jameson translated. "We all recognized that word trick."

"Sure did." Nash hooked his thumbs in the pockets of his worn jeans. "We're looking for someone who knows how the old man played."

"What do you mean *how the old man played*?" Eve asked.

Grayson answered and kept it brief. "Our grandfather liked puzzles, riddles, codes."

For years, Tobias Hawthorne had laid out a challenge for his grandsons every Saturday morning—a game to play, a multi-step puzzle to be solved.

"He liked testing us," Nash drawled. "Making the rules. Watching us dance."

"Nash has granddaddy issues," Xander confided to Eve. "It's a tragic yet engrossing tale of—"

"You don't want to be finishing that sentence, little brother." There wasn't anything explicitly dangerous or threatening in Nash's tone, but Xander was no dummy.

"Sure don't!" he agreed.

My thoughts raced. "If we're looking for someone who knows Tobias Hawthorne's games, someone dangerous and bitter with a grudge against me…"

"Skye." Jameson and Grayson said their mother's name at once. Trying to kill me hadn't worked out too well for her. But given that Sheffield Grayson had framed her for a murder attempt she hadn't committed, *not* trying to kill me hadn't worked out too well for Skye Hawthorne, either.

What if this was her next play?

"We need to confront her," Jameson said immediately. "Talk to her—in person."

"I'm going to have to veto that idea." Nash strolled toward Jameson, his pace unhurried.

"How does that classic proverb go?" Jameson mused. "*You're not the boss of me*? It's something like that. No, wait, I remember! It's *You're not the boss of me, wanker*."

"Excellent use of British slang," Xander commented.

Jameson shrugged. "I'm a man of the world now."

"Jamie's right." Grayson managed to say that without grimacing. "The only way we'll get anything out of Skye is face-to-face."

No one could hurt Grayson, hurt any of them, like Skye could. "Even if she is behind this," I said, "she'll deny everything."

That was what Skye did. In her mind, she was always the victim, and when it came to her sons, she knew just how to twist the knife.

"What if you show her the disk?" Eve suggested quietly. "If she recognizes it, maybe you can use it to get her talking."

"If Skye had any idea what that disk was worth," I replied, "she definitely wouldn't have sent it to me." Skye Hawthorne had been almost entirely disinherited. No way was she parting with anything valuable.

"So if she makes a play for the disk," Grayson stated archly, "we'll know that she's aware of its value, and ergo, not behind the abduction."

I stared Grayson down. "I'm not letting any of you do this without me."

"Avery." Oren stepped out of the shadows and gave me a look that was part paternal, part military commander. "I strongly advise against any kind of confrontation with Skye Hawthorne."

"I've found duct tape more effective than advice, myself," Nash told Oren conversationally.

"It's settled, then!" Xander said brightly. "Family reunion, Hawthorne style!"

"Uh, Xander?" Max appeared in the doorway, looking rumpled. She held up a phone. "You left this on your nightstand."

Nightstand? I shot Max a look. I'd known that she and Xander were friends, but that was *not* a friendly kind of rumple. "Rebecca texted," Max told Xander, conspicuously ignoring my look. "She's on her way here."

I was distracted enough by the idea of Max and Xander spending the night together that it took a moment for the rest to penetrate. *Rebecca.* Seeing Eve would destroy Emily's sister.

"New plan," Xander announced. "I'm skipping family reunion. The rest of you can report back."

Eve frowned. "Who's Rebecca?"

CHAPTER 15

Oren drove, and Nash sat shotgun. Two additional bodyguards piled into the back of the SUV, which left me in the middle row with Jameson on one side and Grayson on the other.

"Aren't you supposed to be on a flight back to Harvard right about now?" Jameson leaned forward, past me, to shoot his brother a look.

Grayson arched an eyebrow. "Your point?"

"Tell me I'm wrong," Jameson said. "Tell me that you're not staying because of Eve."

"There's a threat," Grayson snapped. "Someone moved against our family. Of course I'm staying."

Jameson reached around me to grab Grayson by his suit. "She's not Emily."

Grayson didn't flinch. He didn't fight back. "I know that."

"Gray."

"I *know* that!" The second time, Grayson's words came out louder, more desperate.

Jameson let go of him.

"Despite what you seem to believe," Grayson bit out, "what you *both* seem to believe, I can take care of myself." Grayson was the Hawthorne who had been raised to lead. The one who was never allowed to need anything or anyone. "And you're right, Jamie—she's *not* Emily. Eve is vulnerable in ways that Emily never was."

The muscles in my chest tightened.

"That must have been a really illuminating game of Chutes and Ladders," Jameson said.

Grayson looked out the window, away from both of us. "I couldn't sleep last night. Neither could Eve." His voice was controlled, his body still. "I found her wandering the halls."

I thought about Grayson kissing a girl at Harvard. Grayson seeing a ghost.

"I asked her if the bruise on her temple was paining her," Grayson continued, the muscles in his jaw visible and hard. "And she told me that some boys would want her to say yes. That some people want to think that girls like her are weak." He went silent for a second or two. "But Eve isn't weak. She hasn't lied to us. She hasn't asked for a damn thing except help finding the one person in this world who sees her for who she is."

I thought of Eve talking about how hard she'd tried as a child to be *perfect*. And then I thought about Grayson. About the impossible standards he held himself to.

"Maybe I'm not the one who needs a reminder that this girl is her own person," Grayson said, his voice taking on a knifelike edge. "But go ahead, Jamie, tell me I'm compromised, tell me that my judgment can't be trusted, that I'm so easily manipulated and fragile."

"Don't," Nash warned Jameson from the front seat.

"I'll be happy to discuss all of your personal shortcomings," Jameson told Grayson. "Alphabetically and in great detail. Let's just get through this first."

This took us to a neighborhood full of McMansions. Once, the sheer size of the lots and the houses that sat on them would have astounded me, but compared to Hawthorne House, these enormous homes seemed absolutely ordinary.

Oren parked on the street, and as he began rattling off our security protocol, all I could think was *How did Skye Hawthorne end up here?*

I hadn't kept track of what happened to her after the DA had dropped the murder and attempted murder charges, but on some level, I had expected to find her in either dire straits or the utter lap of luxury—not suburbia.

We rang the doorbell, and Skye answered the door wearing a loose aquamarine dress and sunglasses. "Well, this is a surprise." She looked at the boys over her sunglasses. "Then again, I drew a change card this morning. The Wheel of Fortune, followed by the Eight of Cups, inverted." She sighed. "And my horoscope did say something about forgiveness."

The muscles in Grayson's jaw tensed. "We're not here to forgive you."

"Forgive *me*? Gray, darling, why would I need anyone's forgiveness?" This, from the woman whose charges had been dropped only because they had arrested her for the wrong attempt on my life. "After all," Skye continued, retreating into the house and graciously allowing us to follow, "I didn't throw *you* out onto the streets, now did I?"

Grayson had forced Skye to leave Hawthorne House—for me. "I made sure you had a place to go," he said stiffly.

"I didn't let *you* rot away in prison," Skye continued dramatically. "I didn't force you to grovel to friends for decent legal counsel. Really! Don't you boys talk to me about forgiveness. I'm not the one who abandoned you."

Nash raised an eyebrow. "Debatable, don't you think?"

"Nash." Skye made a *tsk*ing sound. "Aren't you a bit old to be holding on to childish grudges? You of all people should understand: I wasn't made to be stationary. A woman like me can absolutely die of inertness. Is it really so hard to understand that your mother is also a person?"

She could shred them without even trying. Even Nash, who'd had years to get over Skye's lack of motherly impulses, wasn't immune.

"You're wearing a ring." Jameson cut in with a shrewd observation.

Skye offered him a coy smile. "This little thing?" she said, brandishing what had to be a three-carat diamond on her left ring finger. "I would have invited you boys to the wedding, but it was a small courthouse affair. You know how I detest spectacle, and given how Archie and I met, a courthouse wedding seemed appropriate."

Skye Hawthorne *lived* for spectacle.

"'A courthouse wedding seemed appropriate'," Grayson repeated, digesting her meaning and narrowing his eyes. "You married your defense attorney?"

Skye gave an elegant little shrug. "Archie's children and grandchildren are always after him to retire, but my darling husband will be practicing criminal defense until he dies of old age." In other words: Yes, she'd married her lawyer, and yes, he was significantly older than she was—and quite possibly not long for this world. "Now, if you're not here to beg for my forgiveness..." Skye eyed each of her three sons in turn. "Then why are you here?"

"A package was delivered to Hawthorne House today," Jameson said.

Skye poured herself a glass of sparkling wine. "Oh?"

Jameson withdrew the disk from his pocket. "You wouldn't happen to know what this is, would you?"

For a split second, Skye Hawthorne froze. Her pupils dilated. "Where did you get that?" she asked, moving to take it from him, but like a magician, Jameson made the "coin" disappear.

Skye recognized it. I could see the hunger in her eyes.

"Tell us what that is," Grayson ordered.

Skye looked at him. "Always so serious," she murmured, reaching out to touch his cheek. "And the shadows in those eyes..."

"Skye." Jameson drew her attention away from Grayson. *"Please."*

"Manners, Jamie? From you?" Skye dropped her hand. "Color me shocked, but even so, there's not much I can tell you. I've never seen that before in my life."

I listened closely to her words. She'd never *seen* it. "But you know what it is," I said.

For a moment, Skye let her eyes meet mine, like we were two players shaking hands before a match.

"Sure would be a shame if someone got to your husband," Nash piped up. "Warned him about a few things."

"Archie won't believe a word you say," Skye responded. "He's already defended me against bogus charges once."

"I'd wager I know a thing or two he'd find interesting." Nash leaned back against a wall, waiting.

Skye looked back to Grayson. Of all of them, she still had the tightest hold on him. "I don't know much," she hedged. "I know that coin belonged to my father. I know that the great Tobias Hawthorne cross-examined me for hours when it went missing, describing it again and again. But I wasn't the one who took it."

"Toby was." I said what we were all thinking.

"My little Toby was so angry that summer." Skye's eyes closed, and for a moment, she didn't seem dangerous or manipulative or even coy. "I never really knew why."

The adoption. The secrecy. The lies.

"Ultimately, my darling little brother ran off and took *that* as a parting gift. Based on our father's reaction, Toby chose his revenge very well. To get that kind of response out of someone with my father's means?" Skye opened her eyes again. "It must be *very* precious."

Go to Jackson. Toby's instructions to my mother echoed in my mind. *You know what I left there. You know what it's worth.*

"You don't have Toby." Jameson cut to the chase. "Do you?"

"Are you admitting," Skye said cannily, "that my brother is alive?"

Anything we told her, she might well sell to the press.

"Answer the question," Grayson ordered.

"I don't really *have* any of you anymore, now do I? Not Toby. Not you boys." Skye looked almost mournful, but the glint in her eyes was a little too sharp. "Really, what exactly are you accusing me of, Grayson?" Skye took a drink. "You act like I'm such a monster." Her voice was still high and clear, but intense. For the first time, I could see a resemblance between her and her sons—but especially Jameson. "All of you do, but the only thing that I have ever wanted was to be loved."

I had the sudden sense that this was Skye's truth, as she saw it.

"But the more I needed love, the more I craved it, the more indifferent the world became. My parents. Your fathers. Even you boys." Skye had told Jameson and me once that she left men after she got pregnant as a test: If they really wanted her, they would follow.

But no one ever had.

"We loved you," Nash said in a way that made me think of the little boy he must have been. "You were our mother. How could we not?"

"That's what I told myself, each time I got pregnant." Skye's eyes glistened. "But none of you stayed mine for long. No matter what I did, you were your grandfather's first and mine second." Skye helped herself to another sip, her voice becoming more cavalier. "Daddy never really considered me a player in the grand game, so I did what I could. I gave him heirs." She turned her gaze on me. "And look how that turned out." She gave a little shrug. "So I'm done."

"You really expect us to believe that you're just throwing in the towel?" Jameson asked.

"Darling, I don't particularly care what you believe. But I'd rather rule my own kingdom than settle for scraps of *hers*."

"So you're just stepping back from it all?" I stared at Skye Hawthorne, trying to divine some truth. "Hawthorne House? The money? Your father's legacy?"

"Do you know what the real difference is between millions and billions, Ava?" Skye asked. "Because at a certain point, it's not about the money."

"It's about the power," Grayson said beside me.

Skye raised her glass to him. "You really would have made a wonderful heir."

"So that's it?" Nash asked, looking around the massive foyer. "This is your kingdom now?"

"Why not?" Skye replied airily. "Daddy never saw me as a power player anyway." She gave another elegant little shrug. "Who am I to disappoint?"

CHAPTER 16

The walk down the lengthy driveway was tense.

"Well, I for one found that refreshing," Jameson declared. "Our mother *isn't* the villain this time." He could act like he was bulletproof, like Skye's callousness couldn't touch him, but I knew better. "My favorite part, personally," he continued grandly, "was being blamed for never loving her enough, though I must say the reminder that we were conceived in a vain attempt to get a lock on those sweet, sweet Hawthorne billions never goes astray."

"Shut up." Grayson removed his suit jacket and hung a sharp right.

"Where are you going?" I called after him.

Grayson turned back. "I'd prefer to walk."

"Eighteen miles?" Nash drawled.

"I will assure you—all of you—once again..." Grayson rolled up his shirtsleeves, the motion practiced, emphatic. "I can take care of myself."

"Say that again," Jameson encouraged, "but try to sound even *more* like an automaton this time."

I gave Jameson a look. Grayson was hurting. They both were.

"You're right, Heiress," Jameson said, holding up his hands in defeat. "I'm being horribly unfair to automatons."

"You're spoiling for a fight," Grayson commented, his voice dangerously neutral.

Jameson took a step toward his brother. "An eighteen-mile walk would do."

For several seconds, the two of them engaged in a silent staring contest. Finally, Grayson inclined his head. "Don't expect me to talk to you."

"Wouldn't dream of it," Jameson replied.

"You're both being ridiculous," I said. "The two of you can't walk back to Hawthorne House." I really should have known better by now than to tell a Hawthorne he couldn't do something.

I turned to Nash. "Aren't you going to say anything?" I asked him.

In response, Nash opened the back door of the SUV for me. "I call shotgun."

Alone in the middle row, I spent the drive back to Hawthorne House in silence. Skye had definitely gotten to her sons. Grayson would turn that inward. Jameson would act out. I could only hope they both made it home unscathed. Aching for them, I wondered who had made Skye so desperate to be the center of someone's world that she couldn't even love her own children, for fear they wouldn't love her back enough.

On some level, I knew the answer. *Daddy never really considered me a player in the grand game.* I thought back further, to a poem that Toby had written in code. *The tree is poison, don't you see? It poisoned S and Z and me.*

"Skye loved being pregnant." Nash broke the silence in the SUV, glancing back at me from the front seat. "I ever tell you that?"

I shook my head.

"The old man doted on her. She stayed at Hawthorne House for the entirety of each pregnancy, nested even. And when she had a new baby, it was like magic, those first few days. I remember standing in the doorway, watching her feeding Gray right after they got home from the hospital. All she did was stare at him, softly crooning. Baby Gray was a real quiet little guy, solemn. Jamie was a screamer. Xander wiggled." Nash shook his head. "And every time, those first few days, I thought, *Maybe she'll stay.*"

I swallowed. "But she never did."

"The way Skye tells it, the old man stole us away. Truth is, she's the one who put my brothers in his arms. She *gave* them to him. Problem was never that she didn't love us—she just wanted the rest of it more."

Her father's approval. The Hawthorne fortune. I wondered how many babies Nash had seen his mother give away before he'd decided he didn't want a part of any of it.

"If you had a baby...," I said.

"When I have a baby," came the deep, heart-shattering reply, "she'll be my whole world."

"She?" I repeated.

Nash settled back into his seat. "I can picture Lib with a little girl."

Before I could respond to *that*, Oren got a call. "What have you got?" he asked the moment he answered. "Where?" Oren brought the SUV to a stop outside the gates. "There's been a breach," he told the rest of us. "A sensor was tripped in the tunnels."

Adrenaline flooded my bloodstream. I reached for the knife in my boot—not to draw it, just to remind myself: I wasn't defenseless. Eventually, my brain calmed enough for me to remember the circumstances in which we'd left Hawthorne House.

"I want teams coming in from both sides," Oren was saying.

"Stop." I cut him off. "It's not a security breach." I took a deep breath. "It's Rebecca."

CHAPTER 17

The tunnels that ran beneath the Hawthorne estate had fewer entrances than the secret passageways. Years ago, Tobias Hawthorne had shown those entrances to a young Rebecca Laughlin. The old man had seen a girl living in the shadows of her sick older sister. He'd told Rebecca that she deserved something of her own.

I found her in the tunnel beneath the tennis courts. Guided only by the light on my phone, I made my way toward the place where she stood. The tunnel dead-ended into a concrete wall. Rebecca stood facing it, her red hair wild, her lithe body held stiff.

"Go away, Xander," she said.

I stopped a few feet shy of her. "It's me."

I heard Rebecca take in a shaky breath. "Go away, Avery."

"No."

Rebecca was good at wielding silence as a weapon—or a shield. After Emily's death, she'd isolated herself, wrapped in that silence.

"I have all day," I said.

Rebecca finally turned to look at me. For a beautiful girl, she cried ugly. "I met Eve. We told her the truth about Toby's adoption." She sucked in a gulp of air. "She wants to meet my mom."

Of course she did. Rebecca's mother was Eve's grandmother. "Can your mom handle that?" I asked.

I'd only met Mallory Laughlin a few times, but *stable* wasn't a word I would have used to describe her. As a teenager, she'd given baby Toby up for adoption, unaware that the Hawthornes were the ones who had adopted him. Her baby had been so close, for years, and she hadn't known—not back then. When she'd finally had another child two decades later, Emily had been born with a heart condition.

And now Emily was dead. As far as Mallory knew, Toby was, too.

"*I'm* not handling this," Rebecca told me. "She looks so much like her, Avery." Rebecca sounded beyond angry, beyond gutted, her voice a mosaic of far too many emotions to be contained in one body. "She even sounds like Emily."

Rebecca's entire life growing up had been about her sister. She'd been raised to make herself small.

"Do you need me to tell you that Eve *isn't* Emily?" I asked.

Rebecca swallowed. "Well, she doesn't seem to hate me, so..."

"Hate you?" I asked.

Rebecca sat and pulled her knees tight to her chest. "The last thing Em and I ever did was fight. Do you know how hard she would have made me work to be forgiven for that? For being *right*?" They'd fought about Emily's plans for that night—the plans that had gotten her killed. "Hell," Rebecca said, fingering the ends of her choppy red hair, "she'd hate me for this, too."

I sat down beside her. "Your hair?"

Some of the tightness in Rebecca's muscles gave way, and her entire body shuddered. "Emily liked our hair long."

Our hair. The fact that Rebecca could say that without realizing how screwed up it was, even now, made me want to hit someone on her behalf. "You're your own person, Rebecca," I told her, willing her to believe that. "You always have been."

"What if I'm not good at being my own person?" Rebecca had been different these last few months. She looked different, dressed different, went after what she wanted. She'd let Thea back in. "What if this whole thing is just the universe telling me that I don't *get* to move on? *Ever.*" Rebecca's chin trembled. "Maybe I'm a horrible person for wanting to."

I'd known that seeing Eve would hurt her. I'd known that it would dredge up the past, the same way it had for Jameson—for Grayson. But this was Rebecca, cut to the bone.

"You are not a horrible person," I said, but I wasn't sure that *I* could make her believe that. "Have you told Thea about Eve?" I asked.

Rebecca stood and dug the toe of her beat-up combat boot into the ground. "Why would I?"

"Bex."

"Don't look at me like that, Avery."

She was hurting. This wasn't going to *stop* hurting any time soon. "What can I do?" I asked.

"Nothing," Rebecca said, and I could hear her breaking. "Because now I have to go and figure out how to tell my mother that she has a grandchild who looks exactly like the daughter she would have chosen to keep, if the universe had given her a choice between Emily and me."

Rebecca was here. She was alive. She was a good daughter. But her mother could still look right at her and sobbingly say that all her babies died.

"Do you want me to go with you to tell your mom?" I asked.

Rebecca shook her head, the choppy ends of her hair catching in a draft. "I'm better at wanting things now than I used to be, Avery." She straightened, an invisible line of steel running down her spine. "But I don't get to want you with me for this."

CHAPTER 18

I stayed in the tunnels after Rebecca was gone, debating, then wound my way back toward Hawthorne House and exited up a hidden staircase into the Great Room. Once I had cell phone reception again, I pulled the trigger and made the call.

"To what do I owe this rather dubious honor?" Thea Calligaris had perfected the art of the verbal smirk.

"Hello to you, too, Thea."

"Let me guess," she said pertly. "You're in desperate need of fashion assistance? Or maybe one of the Hawthornes is having a meltdown?" I didn't reply, and she amended her guess. "More than one?"

A year ago, I never would have imagined the two of us as anything even remotely resembling friends, but we'd grown on each other—more or less. "I need to tell you something."

"Well," Thea replied coyly, "I don't have all day. In case you missed the memo, my time is *very* valuable." Over the summer, Thea had gone viral. Somewhere between Saint Bart's and the Maldives, she'd become an Influencer with a capital *I*. Then she'd come back, to Rebecca.

No matter how long it takes, Thea had told me once. *I'm going to keep choosing her.*

I told her everything.

"When you say this girl looks exactly like—"

"I mean *exactly*," I reiterated.

"And Rebecca—"

Rebecca was going to kill me for this. "They just met. Eve wants to meet Bex's mom."

For a full three seconds, Thea was uncharacteristically silent. "This is messed up, even by Hawthorne and Hawthorne-adjacent standards."

"Are *you* okay?" I asked. Emily had been Thea's best friend.

"I don't do vulnerable," Thea retorted. "It clashes with my bitch aesthetic." She paused. "Bex didn't want you to tell me, did she?"

"Not exactly."

I could practically *hear* Thea shrugging that off—or trying to. "Just out of curiosity," she said lightly, "exactly how many Hawthornes *are* having meltdowns right now?"

"Thea."

"It's called schadenfreude, Avery. Though really, the Germans should come up with a word that more precisely captures the emotion of getting petty satisfaction out of knowing that the world's most arrogant bastards have itty-bitty feelings, too." Thea wasn't as cold as she liked to pretend to be, but I knew better than to call her on it where Hawthornes were concerned.

"Are you going to call Rebecca?" I asked instead.

"And let her avoid my call?" Thea replied tartly. There was a beat. "Of course I am." She'd let Rebecca go once. She wasn't going to again. "Now, if that's everything, I have an empire to build and a girl to chase."

"Take care of her, Thea," I said.

"I will."

CHAPTER 19

Oren waited until I was off the phone with Thea to make his presence known. He stepped into view, and I forced my brain to focus.

"Anything yet?" I asked him.

"No luck tracing the courier service, but the team I sent to the rendezvous point where Toby was supposed to meet Eve reported in again."

The memory of two words rang in my mind: *shots fired*. "Did you figure out who placed the nine-one-one call?" I asked, holding on to my calm the way a person dangling over a forty-foot drop holds on to whatever they can reach.

"The call was placed from a neighboring warehouse. My men tracked down the owner. He has no idea who placed the call, but he did have something for us."

Something. The way Oren said that made my stomach feel like it had been lined with lead. "What?"

"Another envelope." Oren waited for me to process before he continued. "Sent last night via courier, untraceable. The warehouse owner was paid cash to give it to anyone who came asking about a nine-one-one call. Payment came with the package, so it's likewise untraceable." Oren held out the envelope. "Before you open it—"

I wrenched it out of his hands. Inside, there was a picture of Toby, his face bruised and swollen, holding a newspaper with yesterday's date. *Proof of life.* I swallowed and turned the picture over. There was nothing on the back, nothing else in the envelope.

As of yesterday, he was alive. "No ransom demand?" I choked out.

"None."

I looked back at Toby's bruises, his swollen face. "Were you able to find out anything about the family of David Golding?" I asked, trying to get a grip on myself.

"Currently out of the country," Oren replied. "And their financials are clear."

"What now?" I asked. "Do we know where Eli and Mellie are? What about Ricky? Is Constantine Calligaris still in Greece?" I hated how frantic I sounded and the way my mind was jumping from possibility to possibility with no segue: Eve's half-siblings, my father, Zara's recently estranged husband, *who else?*

"I've been tracking all four of the individuals you just mentioned for more than six months," Oren reported. "None were within two hundred miles of the location of interest when Toby was taken, and I have no reason to suspect any kind of involvement from any of them." Oren paused. "I also did some checking into Eve."

I thought about Eve slicing herself open for that game of Chutes and Ladders, about what Grayson had said about her in the car. "And?" I asked quietly.

"Her story checks out," Oren told me. "She moved out the day she hit eighteen, went no contact with her entire family, siblings included. That was two years ago. She had a waitress job that she showed up to regularly until she and Toby went dark last week. From age eighteen until she met Toby a couple of months ago, she was living hand to mouth with what seemed to be some truly awful roommates. Digging deeper and going back a few more years, I found a record of an incident at her high school involving Eve and an apparently beloved male teacher. *He said, she said.*" Oren's expression hardened. "She has reason to distrust authority."

And who, Eve had asked me, *is going to believe a girl like me?*

"What else?" I asked Oren. "What aren't you telling me?" I knew him well enough to know that there was *something.*

"Nothing regarding Eve." Oren stared at me for a long moment, then reached into his shirt pocket and handed me a square of paper. "This is a list of members of your security team and our close associates who have been approached with job offers in the past three weeks."

I did a quick count. *Thirteen.* This couldn't be normal. "Approached by whom?" I asked.

"Private security firms, mostly," Oren replied. "Far too many of them for comfort. There's no common denominator in ownership between the different companies, but something like this doesn't just happen unless someone is *making* it happen."

Someone who wanted holes in my security. "You think this is related to Toby's abduction?" I asked.

"I don't know." Oren clipped the words. "My men are loyal and well-paid, so the attempts failed, but I don't like this, Avery—any of it." He gave me a look. "Your friend Max is scheduled to return to college tomorrow morning. I would like to send a security detail back with her, but she seems . . . *resistant* to the idea."

I swallowed. "You think that Max is in danger?"

"She could be." Oren's voice was steady. *He* was steady. "I would be negligent at this point to assume that you weren't the target of a concentrated and multipronged assault. Maybe you are. Maybe you aren't. But until we know otherwise, I have no choice but to proceed like there's a major threat—and that means assuming that anyone close to you could be the next target."

CHAPTER 20

I wasn't sure which was going to be harder: convincing Max to let Oren assign a bodyguard to her or showing that picture of Toby to Eve. I ended up going in search of Max first and found her *and* Eve in the bowling alley with Xander, who had a bowling ball in each hand.

"I call this move *the helicopter*," he intoned, lifting his arms to the side.

Even in the darkest of times, Xander was Xander. "You're going to drop one of those on your foot," I said.

"That's okay," Xander responded cheerfully. "I have two feet!"

"Did Skye know anything about the disk?" Eve brushed past Xander and Max. "Is she involved?"

"No to the second question," I said. "And the first doesn't matter right now." I swallowed, my plan of confronting the Max situation first evaporating. "This does." I handed Eve the picture of Toby and looked away.

I couldn't watch, but not watching didn't help. I could *feel* Eve beside me, staring at the picture. Her breathing was audible and uneven. She *felt* this, the way I did.

"Get rid of it." Eve dropped the photograph. Her voice rose. "*Get it out of here.*"

I bent to pick up the photo, but Xander ditched the bowling balls and beat me to it. He took out his phone. As I watched, he turned it to flashlight mode and ran it behind the photo.

"What are you doing?" Max asked.

I was the one who answered. "He's looking to see if there's a message embedded in the paper's grain." If some parts of the page were denser than others, the light wouldn't penetrate as well. I hadn't *wanted* to look that closely at the photograph, at Toby's face, but now that Xander had turned on flashlight mode, my brain shifted gears. *What if there's more to this message?*

"We're going to need a black light," I said. "And a heat source." If we were dealing with someone familiar with Tobias Hawthorne's games, then invisible ink was a definite possibility.

"On it!" Xander said. He handed me the photo, then bounded out of the room.

"What are you doing?" Eve asked me, her words coming out hollow.

I was scanning the photo, looking past Toby's injuries this time. "The newspaper," I said suddenly, forcefully. "The one Toby's holding." I took out my own phone and took a photo of the photo, so I could zoom in. "The front-page article." Adrenaline flooded my bloodstream. "Some of the letters are blacked out. See this word? You can tell from context that it should be *crisis*, but the first *I* is blacked out. Same for the *A* in this word. Then *L*, *W*. Another *A*."

Sliding over to the bowling computer, I hit the button to enter a new player and typed in the five letters I'd already read off, then kept going. In total, there were eighteen letters blacked out in the article.

D. I typed the last one, then went back and added spacing. I hit

Enter, and the message flashed across the scoring screen overhead. ***I ALWAYS WIN IN THE END.***

I'd known that someone was playing with us, with me. But this made it so much clearer that Toby's abductor wasn't just playing *with* me. They were playing *against* me.

When Xander came back carrying a black light in one hand and a Tiffany lamp in the other, he took one look at the words on the screen and set them down. "A bold choice of name," he said. He gave me a hopeful look. "Yours?"

"No." I refused to give in to the darkness that wanted to come and instead turned to Max. "I'm going to need you to agree to take a bodyguard back with you tomorrow."

Max opened her mouth, probably to object, but Xander poked her shoulder. "What if we can get you someone dark and mysterious with a tragic backstory and a soft spot for puppies?" he said in a wheedling tone.

After a long moment, Max poked him back. "Sold."

When things settled down even a little, she and I were going to be having a long talk about poking, nightstands, and her *friendship* with Xander Hawthorne. But for now...

I turned to Oren, a new fear hitting me far too late. "What about Jameson and Grayson? They're still not home." If anyone close to me could be a target, then—

"I have a man on each of them," Oren replied. "Last I heard, the boys were still together, and things were getting ugly. Hawthorne ugly," he clarified. "No external threats."

Given their emotional states after that conversation with Skye, *Hawthorne ugly* was probably the best we could hope for.

They're safe. For now. Feeling claustrophobic, I turned back to the words on the screen. ***I ALWAYS WIN IN THE END.***

"Single first-person pronoun," I said, because it was easier to dissect the message than to wonder what *winning* looked like to the person who had Toby. "That suggests we're dealing with an individual, not a group. And the words *in the end,* those seem to imply that there might have been losses along the way." I breathed, and I thought, and I willed myself to see more than that in the words. "What else?"

Two and a half hours later, Jameson and Grayson still weren't home, and I was spinning my wheels. I'd been over and over the message, and then the photo itself again and the envelope, in case there was something else there. But nothing I did seemed to matter.

Avenge. Revenge. Vengeance. Avenger. I always win in the end.

"I hate this," Eve said, her voice quiet and reedy. "I *hate* feeling helpless."

I did, too.

Xander looked from Eve to me. "Are you two brooding?" he asked. "Because, Avery, I am, as ever, your BHFF, and you *know* the penalty for brooding!"

"I am not playing Xander Tag," I told him.

"What's Xander Tag?" Max asked.

"What *isn't* Xander Tag?" Xander replied philosophically.

"Is this all a joke to you?" Eve asked sharply.

"No," Xander said, his voice suddenly serious. "But sometimes a person's brain starts cycling. No matter what you do, the same thoughts just keep repeating, over and over. You get stuck in a loop, and when you're inside that loop, you can't see past it. You'll keep coming up with the same possibilities, to no end, because the answers you need—they're outside the loop. Distractions aren't just distractions. Sometimes they can break you out of the loop, and once you're out, once your brain stops cycling—"

"You see the things you missed before." Eve stared at Xander for a moment. "Okay," she said finally. "Bring on the distractions, Xander Hawthorne."

"That," I warned her, "is a very dangerous thing to say."

"Pay no attention to Avery!" Xander instructed. "She's just a little gun-shy from The Incident."

Max snorted. "What incident?"

"That doesn't matter," Xander said, "and in my defense, I didn't expect the zoo to send an *actual* tiger. Now..." He tapped his chin. "What are we in the mood for? The Floor Is Magma? Sculpture Wars? Jell-O Assassins?"

"I'm sorry." Eve's voice was stilted. She turned toward the door. "I can't do this."

"Wait!" Xander called after her. "What are your thoughts on fondue?"

CHAPTER 21

In Hawthorne House, *fondue* involved twelve fondue pots accompanied by three full-sized chocolate fountains. Mrs. Laughlin had it all set up in the chef's kitchen within the hour.

Distractions aren't just distractions, I reminded myself. *Sometimes, you need them to break the loop.*

"In terms of cheese fondue," Xander orated, "we've got your gruyère-based, your gouda-based, your beer cheddar, your fontina, your chällerhocker—"

"Okay," Max cut in. "Now you're just making up words."

"Am I?" Xander said in his most dashing voice. "For dipping, we've got your baguettes, your sourdough, breadsticks, croutons, bacon, prosciutto, salami, sopressata, apples, pears, and various vegetables, grilled or raw. Then there's the dessert fondues! For the purists among us, dark chocolate, milk chocolate, and white chocolate fountains. More inventive dessert combinations are in the pots. I *highly* recommend the salted caramel double chocolate."

Surveying the vast array of options for dessert dippers, Max picked up a strawberry in one hand and a graham cracker in the other.

"Hit me," Xander yelled, jogging backward. "I'm going wide!"

Max tossed the graham cracker. Xander caught it in his mouth. Grinning, Max dipped the strawberry in one of the dessert pots, took a bite, then moaned. "Fax me, this is good."

Break the loop, I thought, so I began to make my way through the spread myself, dying with every bite. Beside me, Eve slowly started to do the same.

With a mouth full of bacon, Xander picked up a spare fondue fork and brandished it like a sword. "En garde!"

Max armed herself. The result was chaos. The kind of chaos that ended with Max and Xander both drenched from the fountains and Eve taking a dark chocolate banana to the chest.

"I beg your chocolatey pardon," Xander said. Max whapped him with a breadstick.

Eve looked down at the mess that was her shirt. "This was my only top."

I glanced at Max. *You and I will be talking very soon.* Then I turned to Eve. "Come on," I said. "I'll get you a new shirt."

"*This* is your closet?" Eve was stunned. Racks, cabinets, and shelves stretched twelve feet overhead, all of them full.

"I know," I told her, remembering how I'd felt when they'd brought the clothes in. "You should see the closet in the bedroom that used to be Skye's. It's nineteen hundred square feet, two stories tall, and has its own champagne bar."

Eve stared at the clothes.

"Help yourself," I told her, but she didn't move.

"Really," I said. "Take whatever you want."

She reached for a pale green shirt but froze when she felt the fabric. I wasn't a fashion person, but the incredible softness of expensive clothes, the *feel* of them—that was what still got me, too.

"Toby didn't want me to be a part of this." Eve just kept looking at that shirt. "The mansion. The food. The clothes." She took a breath, the sharp intake of air audible. "He hated this place. *Hated* it. And when I asked why, all he would say was that the Hawthorne family wasn't what they appeared to be, that this family had secrets." She finally pulled the green shirt off the hanger. "Dark secrets. Maybe even dangerous ones."

I thought about all the Hawthorne secrets I'd learned since coming here—not just the truth about Toby's adoption or his role in the fire on Hawthorne Island, but everything else, too.

Nan killed her husband. Zara cheated on both of hers. Skye named her sons after their fathers, and at least one of them was a dangerous man. Tobias Hawthorne bribed Nash's dad to stay away. Jameson watched Emily Laughlin die.

And that wasn't even taking into account the secrets I'd had a hand in creating since I got here. I'd allowed Grayson to cover up his mother's involvement in an attempt on my life and pin all the blame on Libby's abusive ex. I'd looked the other way when Toby and Oren had decided that Sheffield Grayson's body needed to disappear.

Across from me, Eve was still waiting for me to say something.

"I'll let you get dressed," I told her.

Back in my bedroom, I found myself wondering what other Hawthorne secrets I still didn't know. I went back to the photo of Toby, and this time, I let myself look directly at his eyes. *Is this about you or me or this family? How many enemies do we have?*

A knock broke into my thoughts. I opened my door to find Mr. Laughlin standing there—and Oren, along with Eve's guard, positioned down the hall.

"Pardon the interruption, Avery. I've got something for you." The old groundskeeper had a cart with him, filled with long rolls of paper.

Another special delivery? My heart rate ticked up. "Did these come by courier service?"

"I dug these out for you myself." As gruff as Mr. Laughlin's manner was, there was something almost gentle in his moss-colored eyes. "You just had a birthday. Each year following *his* birthday, Mr. Hawthorne had plans drawn up for the next expansion on the House."

Tobias Hawthorne had never finished Hawthorne House. He'd added on every year.

"These are the blueprints." Mr. Laughlin nodded to the cart as he wheeled it into the room. "One set for each year since we broke ground on the House. Thought you might want to see them if you're planning an addition of your own."

"Me?" I said. "Add on to Hawthorne House?"

Eve stepped into the room, wearing the green silk shirt, and for a moment she stared at the blueprints the way she'd stared at the clothes in my closet. Then a figure appeared in the doorway.

Jameson. His face and body were drenched in mud. His shirt was torn, his shoulder bleeding.

Mr. Laughlin put an arm around Eve's shoulder. "Come on, missy. We should go."

CHAPTER 22

"You're bleeding," I told Jameson.

He showed his teeth in a wicked smile. "I'm also dangerously close to getting mud on . . . everything."

There was mud on his face, in his hair. His clothes were drenched in it, his shirt clinging to his abdomen, letting me see every line of the muscles underneath.

"Before you ask," Jameson murmured. "I'm fine, and so is Gray."

I wondered if Grayson Hawthorne had even a fleck of mud on him.

"Oren said things got Hawthorne ugly." I gave Jameson a look.

He shrugged. "Skye has a way of messing with our heads." Jameson did not elaborate on the mud, the blood, or what exactly he and Grayson had gotten up to. "At the end of the day, we all learned what we needed to know. Skye's not involved in the kidnapping."

I'd learned a lot more than that since. The words tumbling out, I told Jameson everything: the picture of Toby, the message the kidnapper had hidden in it, Eve's comment about dark and dangerous secrets, what Oren had told me about the attempts to hire my security team away.

The more I talked, the closer Jameson moved toward me, the closer I needed to be to him.

"No matter what I do," I said, our bodies brushing, "I don't feel like I'm getting anywhere."

"Maybe that's the point, Heiress."

I recognized the tone in his voice, knew it as well as I knew each of his scars. "What are you thinking, Hawthorne?"

"This second message changes things." Jameson's arms curved around me. I could feel mud soaking into my shirt, feel the heat of his body from underneath his. "We were wrong."

"About what?" I asked.

"The person we're dealing with—they're not playing a Hawthorne game. In the old man's games, the clues are always sequential. One clue leads you to the next, if only you can solve it."

"But this time," I said, picking up his train of thought, "the first message didn't lead us anywhere. The second message just came."

Jameson reached one hand up to touch my face, smearing my jawline with mud. "Ergo, the clues in this game aren't sequential. Working one isn't going to magically lead you to the next, Heiress, no matter what you do. Either Toby's captor just wants you scared, in which case, these are vague warnings with no greater design."

I stared at him. "Or?" He'd said *either*.

"Or," Jameson murmured, "it's all part of the same riddle: one answer, multiple clues."

His hip bones pressed lightly into my stomach. "A riddle," I repeated, my voice rough. "Who took Toby—and why?"

Avenge. Revenge. Vengeance. Avenger. I always win in the end.

"An incomplete riddle," Jameson elaborated. "Delivered piece by piece. Or a story—and we're at the mercy of the storyteller."

The person doling out hints, clues that went nowhere in

isolation. "We don't have what we need to solve this," I said, hating what I was saying and how defeated I sounded saying it. "Do we?"

"Not yet."

I wanted to scream, but I looked up at him instead. I saw a jagged cut on the underside of his jaw and reached for his chin. "This looks bad."

"On the contrary, Heiress, bleeding is a devastatingly good look for me."

Xander wasn't the only Hawthorne who specialized in distractions.

Needing this and not liking the look of that cut on his jaw, I allowed myself to be distracted. "Let's make this a game," I told Jameson. "I bet that you can't shower and wash off all that mud before I find what we need from the first aid kit."

"I have a better idea." Jameson lowered his lips to mine. My neck arched. More mud on my face, my clothes. "I bet," he countered, "that *you* can't wash all this mud off before I..."

"Before you what?" I murmured.

Jameson Winchester Hawthorne smiled. "Guess."

CHAPTER 23

"Your move."

I'm back in the park, playing chess opposite Harry. Toby. *The second I think the name, his face changes. The beard is gone, his face bruised and swollen.*

"Who did this to you?" I ask, my voice echoing and echoing until I can barely hear myself think. "Toby, you have to tell me."

If only I can get him to tell me, I'll know.

"Your move." Toby thunks the black knight into a new position on the board.

I look down, but suddenly, I can't see any of the pieces. There's only shadows and fog where each of them should be.

"Your move, Avery Kylie Grambs."

I whip my head up because it's not Toby's voice that says the words this time.

Tobias Hawthorne stares back at me from across the table. "The thing about strategy," he says, "is that you always have to be thinking seven moves ahead." He leans across the table.

The next thing I know, he has me by the neck.

"Some people kill two birds with one stone," he says, strangling me. "I kill twelve."

I woke up frozen, locked in my own body, my heart in my throat, unable to breathe. *Just a dream.* I managed to suck in oxygen and roll sideways off my bed, landing in a crouch. *Breathe. Breathe. Breathe.* I didn't know what time it was, but it was still dark outside. I looked up at the bed.

Jameson wasn't there. That happened sometimes when his brain wouldn't stop. The only question tonight was *stop what?*

Trying to shake off the last remnants of the dream, I strapped on my knife then went to look for him, making my way to Tobias Hawthorne's study.

The study was empty. No Jameson. I found myself staring at the wall of trophies the Hawthorne grandsons had won—and not just trophies. Books they'd published, patents they'd been granted. Proof that Tobias Hawthorne had made his grandsons extraordinary.

He'd made them in his own image.

The dead billionaire *had* always thought seven moves ahead, always killed twelve birds with one stone. How many times had the boys told me that? Still, I couldn't help feeling like my subconscious had just served up a warning—and not about Tobias Hawthorne.

Someone else was out there, strategizing, thinking seven steps ahead. A storyteller telling a story—and making moves all the while.

I always win in the end.

Frustration building inside me, I pushed open the balcony doors. I let the night air hit my face, breathed it in. Down below, Grayson was in the pool, swimming in the dead of night, the pool lit just enough that I could make out his form. The moment I saw him, memory took me.

A crystal glass sits on the table in front of him. His hands lay on either side of the glass, the muscles in them tensed, like he might push off at any moment. I didn't let myself sink into the memory, but another slice of it hit me anyway as I watched Grayson swimming down below.

"You saved that little girl," I say.

"Immaterial." Haunted silver eyes meet mine. "She was easy to save."

Another outdoor light turned on below. *The motion sensor by the pool.* My hand went to my knife, and I was on the verge of calling out for security when I saw the person who had tripped the sensor.

Eve was wearing a nightgown, one of mine that I didn't remember her taking. It hit her mid-thigh. A breeze caught the material the second before Grayson saw her. From this distance, I couldn't make out the expressions on their faces. I couldn't hear what either of them said.

But I saw Grayson pull himself from the pool.

"Avery."

I turned. "Jameson. I woke up, and you weren't there."

"Hawthorne insomnia. I had a lot on my mind." Jameson pushed past me and looked down. I took that as permission to look again, too. To see Grayson placing an arm around Eve. *He's wet. She doesn't care.*

"How long would you have stood here, watching them, if I hadn't come?" Jameson asked, an odd tone in his voice.

"I already told you, I'm worried about Grayson." My mouth felt like cotton.

"Heiress." Jameson turned back to me. "That's not what I meant."

A ball rose in my throat. "You're going to have to be more specific."

Slowly, deliberately, Jameson pushed me up against the wall. He waited, as he always did, for my nod, then obliterated the space between us. His lips crushed mine. My legs wrapped around him as his body pinned mine to the wall.

Jameson Winchester Hawthorne.

"That was very...specific," I said, trying to catch my breath. He was still holding on to me, and I couldn't pretend that I didn't know why he'd needed to kiss me like that. "I'm with you, Jameson," I said. "I want to be with *you*."

Then why do you care how Grayson looks at her? The question was alive in the air between us, but Jameson didn't ask it.

"It was always going to be Grayson," he said, letting go of me.

"No," I insisted. I reached for him, pulled him back.

"For Emily," Jameson told me. "It was always going to be Grayson. She and I—we were too much alike."

"You are *nothing* like Emily," I said fiercely. Emily had used them, both of them. She'd played them against each other.

"You didn't know her," Jameson told me. "You didn't know me back then."

"I know you now."

He looked at me with an expression that made me ache. "I know about the wine cellar, Heiress."

My heart stilled in my chest, my throat closing in around a breath I couldn't expel. I pictured Grayson on his knees in front of me. "What is it you think you know?"

"Gray was in a bad place." Jameson's tone was a perfect match for that expression on his face—cavernous and full of *something*. "You went down to check on him. And..."

"And what, Jameson?" I stared at him, trying to anchor myself to this moment, but unable to completely banish memories I had no right to hold.

"And the next day, Grayson couldn't look at you. Or me. He left for Harvard three days early."

Comprehension washed over me. "No," I insisted. "Whatever you're thinking, Jameson—I would *never* do that to you."

"I know that, Heiress."

"Do you?" I asked, because his voice had gone hoarse. He wasn't acting like he knew.

"It's not *you* who I don't trust."

"Grayson wouldn't—"

"It's not my brother, either." Jameson gave me a look, dark and twisted, full of longing. "Trustworthiness has never really been *my* thing, Heiress."

That sounded like something Jameson would have said when we first met. "Don't say that," I told him. "Don't talk about yourself that way."

"Gray has always been so perfect," Jameson said. "It's inhuman how good he was at just about everything. If we were competing—at anything, really—and I wanted to win, I couldn't do it by being better. I had to be *worse*. I had to cross lines that he wouldn't, take risks—the bigger and more unfathomable to him the better."

I thought about Skye and the way she'd told me once that Jameson Winchester Hawthorne was *hungry*.

"I never learned how to be good or honorable, Heiress." Jameson placed a hand on either side of my face, pushed his fingers back into my hair. "I learned how to be bad in the most strategic ways. But now? With you?" He shook his head. "I want to be better than that. *I do*. I don't ever want for you—for us, for *this*—to become a game." He trailed his thumb down my jawline, his fingers lightly skimming my cheekbone. "So if you decide you're not sure about this, Heiress, about me—"

"I *am* sure," I told him, capturing his hands in mine. I pressed his knuckles to my mouth and realized they were swollen. "I am, Jameson."

"You have to be." There was an urgency to Jameson's words, a *need*. "Because I'm terrible at hurting, Heiress. And if what we have now—if *everything* we have now—starts to feel like another competition between Grayson and me, like a game? I don't trust myself not to play."

CHAPTER 24

The next morning, I awoke to an empty bed and someone rapping on my door.

"I'm coming in," Alisa called. She tried to open the door, but Oren stopped her from the hallway.

"I could be naked in here," I grumbled loudly, hastily throwing on designer sweatpants before telling Oren to let her in.

"And you could count on my discretion if you were," Alisa replied briskly. "Attorney-client privilege."

"Was that an actual joke?" I asked. In response, Alisa placed a leather satchel on my dresser. "If that's more paperwork for me to look over," I told her, "I don't want it."

I had enough on my plate right now without thinking about the trust paperwork—or the journal Grayson had given me, its pages still blank.

"That's not paperwork." Alisa didn't clarify what the bag *was*. Instead, she fixed me with what I had termed the Alisa Look. "You should have called me. The moment someone showed up claiming to be Toby Hawthorne's daughter, you should have called."

I glanced at Oren, wondering if he'd changed his mind and told her about Eve. "Why?" I asked Alisa. "The will is through probate. Eve isn't a legal threat."

"This isn't just about the will. That threatening note you received—"

Notes, plural. I glanced at Oren, and he gave a slight shake of his head—he wasn't the one who had tipped her off to any of this.

Alisa rolled her eyes at the two of us. "This is the part where you tell me—erroneously—that you have everything under control."

"I advised against calling you," Oren told her point-blank. "This was a security issue, not a legal one."

"Really, Oren?" For a split second, Alisa looked hurt, then she converted that to extreme professional annoyance. "Let's address the elephant in the room, shall we?" she said. "Yes, I took a chance when Avery was in that coma, but if I hadn't moved her back to Hawthorne House when I did, she wouldn't *have* a security team. The terms of the will were ironclad. Do you understand that, Oren? If I hadn't done what I did, Avery wouldn't be entitled to live at Hawthorne House with all its fancy security. You wouldn't be able to pay your men." Alisa stared at him, hard. "She would be out there with *nothing*, so, yes, I took a calculated risk, and thank God I did." She turned to me. "Since I am the *only* one in this room who can claim to make the good, smart decision under fire—when things start going up in flames, *you damn well pick up the phone*."

I winced.

"As it was," Alisa muttered, "I had to hear about this from Nash."

That startled a response out of me. "Nash called you?"

"He can't even stand to be in the same room with me," Alisa said softly, "but he called. Because *he* knows I am good at my job." She walked toward me, her heels clicking against the wood floor. "I can't help you if you won't let me, Avery, not with this and not with everything you're about to have on your plate."

The money. She was talking about my inheritance—and the trust.

"What happened, Alisa?" Oren crossed his arms over his chest.

"What makes you think something happened?" Alisa asked coolly.

"Instinct," my head of security replied. "And the fact that someone has been trying to chip away at Avery's security team."

I could practically see Alisa filing that piece of information away. "I've become aware of a smear campaign," she said, giving Oren tit for tat. "Gossip websites, mostly. Nothing you need to concern yourself with, Avery, but one of my connections in the press has informed me that the going rate for pictures of you with any of the Hawthornes has inexplicably tripled. Meanwhile, at least three companies that Tobias Hawthorne owned a significant stake in are experiencing... turbulence."

Oren's eyes narrowed. "What kind of turbulence?"

"CEO turnover, sudden scandal, FDA investigations..."

Avenge. Revenge. Vengeance. Avenger. I always win in the end.

"On the business end of things, what are we looking for?" Oren asked Alisa.

"Wealth. Power. Connections." Alisa set her jaw. "I'm on it."

She was on it. Oren was on it. But we weren't any closer to an answer or to getting Toby back, and there was nothing I could do about it. *An incomplete riddle. A story—and we're at the mercy of the storyteller.*

"I'll let you know as soon as I find something," Alisa said. "In the meantime, we need to keep Eve happy, away from the press, and under surveillance until the firm can assess the best course of action. I suspect a modest settlement, in exchange for an NDA, may be in order." In full-on lawyer mode, Alisa didn't even pause before moving on to the next item on her agenda. "If, at any point, a ransom needs to be arranged, the firm can handle that as well."

Was that where this was headed? The end of this story, once the riddle was complete? Was Toby's captor just waiting until he had me where he wanted me to make demands?

"I'll have my team keep you in the loop," Oren told Alisa briskly.

My lawyer nodded like she expected nothing less, but I got the sense that Oren letting her back in mattered to her. "I suppose the only business that remains is *that*." Alisa nodded toward the leather satchel she'd placed on my dresser. "When I updated the partners on the current situation, I was given this bag and its contents to pass along to you, Avery."

"What is it?" I asked, walking toward my dresser.

"I don't know." Alisa sounded perturbed. "Mr. Hawthorne's instructions were that it was to remain secure and unopened, unless certain conditions were met, in which case it was to be delivered promptly to you."

I stared at the bag. Tobias Hawthorne had left me his fortune, but the only message I'd ever received from him was a grand total of two words: *I'm sorry*. I reached out to touch the leather bag. "What conditions?"

Alisa cleared her throat. "We were to deliver this to you in the event that you ever met Evelyn Shane."

I remembered vaguely that *Eve* was short for *Evelyn*—but then another realization took over. *The old man knew about Eve.* That revelation hit me like splinters to my lungs. I'd assumed that the dead billionaire hadn't known about Toby's *actual* daughter. At some point, I'd started believing, deep down, that I'd only been chosen to inherit because Tobias Hawthorne hadn't realized there was someone out there who suited his purposes better than I did.

A stone that killed at least as many birds. A more elegant glass ballerina. A sharper knife.

But he knew about Eve all along.

CHAPTER 25

Alisa left. Oren took up position in the hall, and all I could do was stare at the bag. Even without opening it, I knew in my gut what I would find inside. *A game.*

The old man had left me a game.

I wanted to call Jameson, but everything he'd said the night before lingered, ghostlike in my mind. I didn't know how long I stood there staring at my last bequest from Tobias Hawthorne before Libby poked her head into my room.

"Cupcake pancakes?" My sister held out a plate, piled high with her latest concoction, then followed the direction of my gaze. "New laptop bag?" she guessed.

"No," I said. I took the pancakes from Libby and told her about the leather satchel.

"Are you going to…open it?" my sister prodded innocently.

I wanted to see what was in that bag. I wanted—*so badly*—to play a game that actually *went* somewhere. But opening the satchel without Jameson here felt like admitting that there was something wrong.

Libby handed me a fork, and my gaze caught on the inside of her left wrist. A few months ago, she'd gotten a tattoo, a single word inked from wrist bone to wrist bone, just under the heel of her hand. *SURVIVOR*.

"Still thinking about what you want for the other wrist?" I asked.

Libby looked down at her arm. "Maybe, for my next tattoo, I should go with . . . *open the bag, Avery!*" The enthusiasm in her voice reminded me of the moment when we'd first found out that I'd been named in Tobias Hawthorne's will.

"How about *love*?" I suggested.

Libby narrowed her eyes. "If this is about me and Nash . . ."

"It's not," I said. "It's just about you, Lib. You're the most loving person I know." Enough of the people she'd loved had hurt her that, these days, it seemed like she saw her giant heart as a point of weakness, but it wasn't one. "You took me in," I reminded her, "when I had no one."

Libby stared at both of her wrists. "Just open the darn bag."

I hesitated again, then got annoyed with myself. This was *my* game. For once, I wasn't a part of the puzzle, a tool. I was a player.

So, play.

I reached for the bag. The leather was supple. I let my fingers explore the bag's strap. It would have been just like the old man to leave a message etched in the leather. When I found nothing, I unclasped the flap and flipped it open.

In the main pouch, I found four things: a handheld steamer, a flashlight, a beach towel, and a mesh bag filled with magnetic letters. On the surface, that collection of objects seemed random, but I knew better. There was always a method to the old man's madness. At the beginning of each Saturday-morning challenge for the boys, the billionaire had laid out a series of objects. *A fishing hook, a price tag, a glass ballerina, a knife.* By the end of the game, all of those objects would have served a purpose.

Sequential. The old man's games are always sequential. I just have to figure out where to start.

I searched the side pouches and was rewarded with two more objects: a USB drive and a circular piece of blue-green glass. The latter was the size of a dinner plate, as thick as two stacked quarters, and just translucent enough that I could see through it. As I held up the glass and peered through it, my mind went to a piece of red acetate that Tobias Hawthorne had left taped to the inside cover of a book.

"This could serve as a decoder," I told Libby. "If we can find something written in the same blue-green shade as the glass..." My head swam with the possibilities. Was this the way it was for the Hawthorne boys after so many years of playing the old man's games? Did every clue call to mind one they'd solved before?

Libby darted to my desk and grabbed my laptop. "Here. Try the USB."

I plugged it in, feeling like I was on the verge of something. A single file popped up: **AVERYKYLIEGRAMBS.MP3**. I stared at my name, mentally rearranging the letters. *A very risky gamble.* I clicked on the file. After a brief delay, I was hit with a blast of sound, undecipherable, verging on white noise.

I pushed down the urge to cover my ears.

"Should we turn it down?" Libby asked.

"No." I hit Pause, then pulled the audio track back to the start. Bracing myself, I turned the volume *up*. This time, when I hit Play, I didn't just hear noise. I heard a voice, but there was no way I could make out actual words. It was like the file had been corrupted. I felt like I was listening to someone who couldn't get a full sound out of their mouth.

I played the full clip six, seven, eight times—but repeating it didn't help. Playing it at different speeds didn't help. I downloaded an app that let me play it backward. Nothing.

I didn't have what I needed to make sense of the USB. *Yet.*

"There has to be something here," I told my sister. "A clue that starts things off. We might not be able to make out the audio file now, but if we follow the trail the old man left, the game might tell us how to restore the audio."

Libby gave me a wide-eyed look. "You sound exactly like them. The way you just said *the old man*, it's like you knew him."

In some ways, I felt like I did. At the very least, I knew how Hawthornes thought, so this time, I didn't just trail my fingers over the leather of the satchel. I gave the entire bag a thorough inspection, looking for anything I'd missed, then went through the objects one by one.

I started with the steamer, plugging it into the wall. I released the compartment that would hold water. After verifying that it was empty, I added water, half expecting some kind of message to appear on the sides when I did.

Nothing.

I clicked the compartment back into place and waited until the ready light came on. Holding the steamer away from my body, I gave it a try. "It works," I said.

"Should we try it on that bag, which probably costs ten thousand dollars and undoubtedly should not be steamed?" Libby asked.

We did, to no effect—at least, none related to the puzzle. I turned my attention to the flashlight next, turning it on and off, then checking the battery chamber to ensure that it contained nothing but batteries. I unfolded the beach towel and stood up so I could get an eagle's-eye view of the design.

Black-and-white chevron, no unexpected breaks in the pattern.

"That just leaves this," I told Libby, picking up the mesh bag. I opened it, spilling dozens of magnetic letters onto the floor. "Maybe it spells out the first clue?"

I began by sorting the letters: consonants in one pile, vowels in another. I hit a 7 and started a third pile for numbers.

"Forty-five pieces in total," I told my sister once I was done. "Twelve numbers, five vowels, twenty-eight consonants." Moving as I spoke, I pulled out the five vowels—one each of *A*, *E*, *I*, *O*, and *U*. That didn't strike me as a coincidence, so I started pulling out consonants, too—one of each letter, until I had the whole alphabet represented, with seven letters left behind.

"These are the extras," I told Libby. "One *B*, three *P*'s, and three *Q*'s." I did the same thing for the numbers, pulling out each digit from one to nine and turning my attention to the leftovers. "Three *fours*," I said. I stared at what I had. "*B*, *P*, *P*, *P*, *Q*, *Q*, *Q*, four, four, four."

I repeated that a few times. A phrase came into my head: *Mind your P's and Q's*. I lingered on it for a moment, then dismissed it. What wasn't I seeing?

"I'm not exactly a rocket scientist," Libby hedged, "but I don't think you're going to get words out of those letters."

No vowels. I considered starting over again, playing with the letters in a different way, but couldn't bring myself to do it. "There's three of each," I said. "Except for the *B*."

I picked up the *B* and rubbed my thumb over its surface. What wasn't I seeing? *P*, *P*, *P*, *Q*, *Q*, *Q*, *4*, *4*, *4—but only one B*. I closed my eyes. Tobias Hawthorne had designed this puzzle for me. He must have had reason to believe not just that it could be solved, but that *I* could solve it. I thought about the file folder the billionaire had kept on me. Pictures of me doing everything from working at a diner to playing chess.

I thought of my dream.

And then I saw it—first in my mind's eye, and once my eyelids flew open, right in front of me. *P*, *Q*, *4*. I pulled those three down, then repeated the process. *P*, *Q*, *4*. When I saw what I had left, my heart jumped into my throat, pounding like I was standing at the edge of a waterfall.

"*P, Q, B*, four," I told Libby breathlessly.

"Cream cheese frosting and black velvet corsets!" Libby replied. "We are just saying random combinations of things now, right?"

I shook my head. "The code—it's not words," I explained. "These are chess notations—descriptive, not algebraic."

After my mother had died, long before I'd ever heard the name Hawthorne, I'd played chess in the park with a man who I'd known as Harry. *Toby Hawthorne.* His father had known that—known that I played, known who I played with.

"It's a way of keeping track of your moves and your opponent's," I told Libby, a rush of energy thrumming through my veins. "This one—P-Q4—is short for pawn to Queen four. It's a common opening move, which is often countered by black making the same move—pawn to Queen four. Then the white pawn goes to Queen's Bishop four."

P-QB4.

"So," Libby said sagely, "chess."

"Chess," I repeated. "The move—it's called the Queen's Gambit. Whoever's playing white puts that second pawn in a position to be sacrificed, which is why it's considered a gambit."

"Why would you sacrifice a piece?" Libby asked.

I thought about billionaire Tobias Hawthorne, about Toby, about Jameson, Grayson, Xander, and Nash. "To take control of the board," I said.

It was tempting to read more meaning into that, but I couldn't linger. I had the first clue now. It would lead me to another. I started walking.

"Where are you going?" Libby called after me. "And do you want me to have Jameson meet us there? Or Max?"

"The game room." I made it to the door before I answered the second half of that question, my stomach twisting. "And yes to Max."

CHAPTER 26

Built-in shelves lined the walls, all of them overflowing with games.

"Do you think the Hawthornes have played all of them?" Max asked Libby and me.

There were hundreds of boxes on those shelves, maybe a thousand. "Every single one," I said. There was nothing more Hawthorne than winning.

If what we have now—if everything *we have now—starts to feel like another competition between Grayson and me, like a game? I don't trust myself not to play.*

I slammed that door in my mind. "We're looking for chess sets," I said, focusing on that. "There is probably more than one. And while we're looking..." I shot my best friend a pointed look. "Max can catch us up on the Xander situation."

Better her romantic drama taking center stage than mine.

"Everything involving Xander is a situation," Max hedged. "He specializes in situations!"

I scanned the boxes on the closest shelf, checking for chess sets. "True." I waited, knowing that she would break.

"It's . . . *new.*" Max squatted to stare at the lower shelves. "Like, really new. And you know I hate labels."

"You love labels," I told her, skimming my fingers across game after game. "You literally own multiple label makers."

Chess set! Victorious, I pulled the box from the shelf and kept looking.

"The situation—Xander, me. It's . . . *fun.* Are relationships supposed to be fun?"

I thought about hot-air balloons and helicopters and dancing barefoot on the beach.

"I mean, I've never actually been friends with a guy first," Max continued. "Like, even in fiction, *friends to lovers*? Never my thing. I'm more *star-crossed tragedy, supernatural soul mates, enemies to lovers.* Epic, you know?"

"You don't get much more epic than Hawthornes," Libby told her, and then, as if she'd caught herself, she straightened, turned her attention back to the shelf, and pulled out chess set number two.

"Do you know what Xander did when I had my first college test?" Max was rambling now. "Before things even got romantic? He sent me a book bouquet."

"What's a book bouquet?" Libby replied.

"*Exactly!*" Max said. "*Mother-faxing exactly.*"

"You like him," I translated. "A lot."

"Let's just say I am definitely reconsidering my favorite tropes." Max popped up to standing, a wooden box held in her hand. "Number three."

Ultimately, there were six. I scoured the boxes, looking for anything scribbled onto cardboard, etched into metal, or carved into wood. *Nothing.* I verified that no pieces were missing, then reached into my leather satchel and pulled out the flashlight. As far as I could tell, it was just a normal flashlight, but I'd been Hawthorne-adjacent long enough to know that there were dozens of kinds of invisible ink. That thought in mind, I shined the light on each of the six chessboards. After that, I inspected the individual pieces. *Nothing.*

Frustrated, I looked up—and saw Grayson in the doorway, backlit. In my mind, I could still see him putting an arm around Eve. *He's wet. She doesn't care.*

I stood.

"Xander's looking for you," Grayson told Max dryly. "I suggested he text, but he claims that's cheating."

Max turned to me. "Xander's my ride to the airport."

I hated this. "Are you sure you have to go?" I asked, dread heavy in the pit of my stomach.

"Do you want me to fail out of college, thereby ruining my chances at grad-school-slash-med-school-slash-law-school?"

I let out a long huff of air. "Oren assigned someone to go with you?"

"I have been assured that my new bodyguard is exceptionally broody with hidden layers." Max hugged me. "Call me. Constantly. And you!" she said as she turned and walked past Grayson. "Watch where you're aiming those cheekbones, buddy."

And just like that, my best friend was gone.

Grayson stayed in the doorway, like there was an invisible line just over the threshold. "What's all of this?" he asked, looking at the mess spread out in front of me.

Your grandfather left me a game. I didn't tell Grayson that. I couldn't. I needed to find Jameson and tell *him* first.

Libby took my silence as her cue to exit, squeezing past Grayson as she did.

“I talked to Eve last night.” Grayson must have decided not to push me on the chess sets. “She’s struggling.”

So was I. So was Jameson. So was *he*.

“I think it would help her,” Grayson said, “to see Toby’s old wing.”

I remembered Eve’s comment about Hawthorne secrets. If there was one place in Hawthorne House rife with secrets, it was the deserted wing that Tobias Hawthorne had kept bricked up for years.

“I know that Toby means something to you, Avery.” Grayson stepped toward me, across that invisible line into the room. “I can imagine that letting Eve see his wing might feel like an intrusion on something that was just yours until now.”

I looked away and sat back down among the chess pieces. “It’s fine.”

Grayson moved forward again and crouched beside me, his forearms braced against his knees, his suit jacket falling open. “I know you, Avery. And I know what it feels like to have a stranger show up at Hawthorne House and threaten the very ground beneath your feet.”

I’d been that stranger for him.

Pushing back against what felt like a lifetime of memories, I focused on Grayson in the here and now. “I’ll make you a deal,” I said. Jameson was wagers; Grayson was deals. “I’ll show Eve Toby’s wing if you tell me how you’re doing. How you’re *really* doing.”

I expected him to look away, but he didn’t. Silvery gray eyes stayed locked on mine, never blinking, never wavering. “Everything hurts.” Only Grayson Hawthorne could say that and still sound utterly bulletproof. “It hurts all the time, Avery, but I know the man I was raised to be.”

CHAPTER 27

I told Grayson that he could take Eve to Toby's wing, and he informed me that that wasn't the deal. I'd said that *I* would show Eve Toby's wing. I deeply suspected he was headed for the pool.

Packing up the satchel and taking it with me, I held up my end of the bargain.

Eve's pace slowed as Toby's wing came into view. There was still rubble visible from the brick wall that the old man had erected decades ago.

"Tobias Hawthorne closed off this wing the summer that Toby disappeared," I told Eve. "When we found out that Toby was still alive, we came here looking for clues."

"What did you find?" Eve asked, something like awe in her tone as we stepped through the remains of bricks and into Toby's foyer.

"Several things." I couldn't blame Eve for wanting to know. "For starters, this." I knelt to trigger the release on one of the marble tiles. Beneath, there was a metal compartment, empty but for a poem engraved on the metal.

"'A Poison Tree,'" I said. "An eighteenth-century poem written by a poet named William Blake."

Eve dropped to her knees. She trailed her hand over the poem, reading it silently without so much as taking or expelling a breath.

"Long story short," I said, "teenaged Toby seemed to identify with the feeling of wrath—and what it cost to hide it."

Eve didn't respond. She just stayed there, her fingers on the poem, her eyes unblinking. It was like I'd ceased to exist for her, like the entire world had.

It was at least a minute before she looked up. "I'm sorry," she said, her voice wavering. "It's just, what you just said about Toby identifying with this poem—you could have been describing me. I didn't even know he liked poetry." She stood and turned three-sixty, taking in the rest of the wing. "What else?"

"The title of the poem led us to a legal text on Toby's bookshelf," I said, the air thick with memories. "In a section on the fruit of the poisonous tree doctrine, we found a coded message that Toby left behind before he ran away—another poem, one he wrote himself."

"What did it say?" Eve asked, her tone almost urgent. "Toby's poem?"

I'd been over the words often enough that I knew them by heart. "*Secrets, lies, all I despise. The tree is poison, don't you see? It poisoned S and Z and me. The evidence I stole is in the darkest hole. Light shall reveal all, I writ upon the*..."

I trailed off, the way the poem had. I expected Eve to finish it for me, to fill in the word that both Jameson and I had known went at the end. *Wall.*

But she didn't. "What does he mean, the evidence he stole?" Eve's voice rang through Toby's empty suite. "Evidence of what?"

"His adoption, I'm guessing," I said. "He kept a journal on his walls, written in invisible ink. There are still some black lights in this room from when we read them. I'll turn them on and kill the lights."

Eve reached out to stop me before I could. "Could I do this part alone?"

I hadn't been expecting that, and my knee-jerk reaction was *no.*

"I know you have just as much right to be here as I do, Avery—or more. It's your house, right? But I just..." Eve shook her head, then looked down. "I don't look like my mom." She fingered the ends of her hair. "When I was a kid, she kept my hair short—these ugly, uneven bowl cuts she'd do herself. She said it was because she didn't want to have to mess with it, but when I got older, when I started taking care of my hair myself and grew it out, she let it slip that she'd kept it short because no one else in our family had hair like mine." Eve took a breath. "No one had eyes like mine. Or a single one of my features. No one thought the way I did or liked the things I liked or felt things the same way." She swallowed. "I moved out the day I hit eighteen. They probably would have kicked me out if I hadn't. A few months later, I convinced myself that maybe I had family out there. I did one of those mail-in DNA tests. But...no matches."

No one even remotely Hawthorne-adjacent would have handed over their DNA to one of those databases. "Toby found you," I reminded Eve gently.

She nodded. "He doesn't really look like me, either. And he's a hard person to get to know. But *that poem*..."

I didn't make her say anything else. "I get it," I told her. "It's fine."

On my way out the door, I thought about my mom and all the ways we were alike. She'd given me my resilience. My smile. The color of my hair. The tendency to guard my heart—and the ability, once those guards were down, to love fiercely, deeply, unapologetically.

Unafraid.

CHAPTER 28

I found Jameson on the climbing wall. He was at the top, where the angles became treacherous, his body held to the wall through sheer force of will.

"Your grandfather left me a game," I said. My voice wasn't loud, but it carried.

Without a moment's hesitation, Jameson dropped from the wall.

He was too high up. In my mind, I saw him landing wrong. I *heard* bones shattering. But just like the first time I'd met him, he landed in a crouch.

When he stood up, he gave no signs of being worse for wear.

"I hate it when you do that," I told him.

Jameson smirked. "It's possible that I was deprived of maternal attention as a child unless I was bleeding."

"Skye noticed if you were bleeding?" I asked.

Jameson gave a little shrug. "Some of the time." He hesitated, just for a fraction of a second, then stepped forward. "I'm sorry about last night, Heiress. You didn't even call *Tahiti*."

"You don't have to apologize," I told him. "Just ask me about the game your grandfather designed to be delivered to me if and when Eve and I ever met."

"He knew about her?" Jameson tried to wrap his mind around that. "The plot thickens. How far through the game are you?"

"Solved the first clue," I said. "Now I'm looking for a chess set."

"There are six in the game room," Jameson replied automatically. "That's how many it takes to play Hawthorne chess."

Hawthorne chess. Why was I not surprised? "I found all six. Do you know if there's a seventh somewhere else?"

"I don't *know* of one." Jameson gave me a look: part trouble, part challenge. "But do you still have that binder Alisa made for you, detailing your inheritance?"

I found an entry in the binder's index: *Chess set, royal.* I flipped to the page indicated and read, tearing through the description as fast as I could. The set was valued at nearly half a million dollars. The pieces were made of white gold, encrusted with black and white diamonds—nearly ten thousand of them. The pictures were breathtaking.

There was only one place *this* chess set could be.

"Oren," I called out to the hallway, knowing he'd be somewhere within earshot. "I need you to take us to the vault."

The last time I'd been to the Hawthorne vault, I'd jokingly asked Oren if it contained the crown jewels, and his very serious response had been *To what country?*

"If what you're looking for isn't here," Oren told Jameson and me as we surveyed the steel drawers lining the walls, "some pieces are kept in an even more secure location off-site."

Jameson and I got to work gingerly opening drawer after drawer. I managed not to gawk at anything until I came to a scepter made of shining gold interwoven with another lighter metal. *White gold? Platinum?* I had no idea, but it wasn't the materials that caught my eye. It was the design of the scepter. The metalwork was impossibly intricate. The effect was delicate, but dangerous. *Beauty and power.*

"Long live the Queen," Jameson murmured.

"The Queen's Gambit," I said, my mind racing. Maybe we weren't looking for a chess set.

But before I could follow that thought any further, Jameson opened another drawer and spoke again. "Heiress." There was something different in his tone this time.

I looked at the drawer he'd opened. *So this is what ten thousand diamonds looks like.* Each chess piece was magnificent; the board looked like a jewel-encrusted table. According to the binder, forty master artisans had spent more than five thousand hours bringing this chess set to life—and it looked it.

"You want to do the honors, Heiress?"

This was my game. A familiar, electric feeling coming over me, I examined each piece, starting with the white pawns and working my way up to the king. Then I did the same thing with the black pieces, glittering with black diamonds.

The bottom of the black queen had a seam. If I hadn't been looking for it, I wouldn't have seen it. "I need a magnifying glass," I told Jameson.

"How about a jeweler's loupe?" he countered. "There has to be one around here somewhere."

Eventually, he found one: a small lens with no handle, just a cylindrical rim. Using the loupe to look at the bottom of the black queen told me that what I'd seen as a seam was actually a gap, like someone had cut a paper-thin line into the bottom of the piece. And peeking through that gap, I saw something.

"Were there any other jeweler's tools with the loupe?" I asked Jameson.

Even the smallest file he brought me couldn't fully fit into the gap, but I managed to wedge the tip through—and it caught on something.

"Tweezers?" Jameson offered, his shoulder brushing mine.

File. Tweezers. Loupe.

File. Tweezers. Loupe.

Sweat was pouring down my temples by the time I finally managed to lock the tweezers onto the edge of something. *A strip of black paper.*

"I don't want to tear it," I told Jameson.

His green eyes met mine. "You won't."

Slowly, painstakingly, I pulled the strip out. It was no bigger than a fortune tucked inside a fortune cookie. Golden ink marked the page—with handwriting I recognized all too well.

The only message Tobias Hawthorne had ever left me before was that he was sorry. Now, to that, I could add two more words.

I turned to Jameson and read them out loud: *"Don't breathe."*

CHAPTER 29

A person stopped breathing when they were awestruck or terrified. When they were hiding and any sound could give them away. When the world around them was on fire, the air thick with smoke.

Jameson and I scoured every single smoke detector in Hawthorne House.

"You're smiling," I told him, disgruntled when the last one turned up nothing.

"I like a challenge." Jameson gave me a look that reminded me that I'd *been* a challenge for him. "And maybe I'm feeling nostalgic for Saturday mornings. Say what you will about my childhood, but it was never boring."

I thought back to the balcony. "You didn't mind being set against your brothers?" I asked. *Against Grayson?* "Being forced to compete?"

"Saturday mornings were different," Jameson said. "The puzzles, the thrill, the old man's attention. We *lived* for those games. Maybe not Nash, but Xander and Grayson and me. Hell, Gray even let loose sometimes because the games didn't reward perfection. He and I used to team up against Nash, at least until the end. Everything else our grandfather did—everything he gave us, everything expected of us—was about molding the next generation of Hawthornes to be something extraordinary. But Saturday mornings, those games—they were about showing us that we already *were*."

Extraordinary, I thought. *And a part of something*. That was the siren call of Tobias Hawthorne's games.

"Do you think that's why your grandfather left me this game?" I asked.

The billionaire had set my game to start if and only if I met Eve. Had he known that I would start questioning his almighty judgment in choosing me the moment she showed up? Had he wanted to show me what I was capable of?

That I was extraordinary?

"I think," Jameson murmured, relishing the words, "that my grandfather left three games when he died, Heiress. And the first two both told us something about why he chose you."

Don't breathe. We didn't solve the clue that night. The next day was Monday. Oren cleared me to go to school so long as he stuck to my side. I could have called out sick and stayed home, but I didn't. My game had proven an effective distraction, but Toby was still in danger, and nothing could keep my mind off that for long.

I went to school because I wanted the paparazzi—that my opponent had so kindly set on me like dogs—to take a picture of me with my head held high.

I wanted the person who had taken Toby to realize that I wasn't down.

I wanted him to make his next damn move.

I spent my free mods in the Archive—prep school for *library*. I was almost done with the calculus homework I'd ignored over the long weekend when Rebecca came in. Oren allowed her past.

"You told Thea." Rebecca stalked toward me.

"Is that such a bad thing?" I asked—from a safe distance.

"She is *relentless*," Rebecca muttered.

Proving the point, Thea appeared in the doorway behind her. "I was under the impression that you *liked* relentless." Only Thea could make that sound flirty in these circumstances.

Rebecca grudgingly met her girlfriend's eyes. "I kind of do."

"Then you're going to *love* this part," Thea told her. "Because it's the part where you stop fighting this, stop fighting me, stop running away from this conversation, and let go."

"I'm fine, Thea."

"You're not," Thea told her achingly. "And you don't have to be, Bex. It's not your job to be *fine* anymore."

Rebecca's breath hitched.

I knew when my presence wasn't necessary. "I'm going to go," I said, and neither one of them even seemed to hear me. In the hallway, I was informed by an office aid that the headmaster's office was looking for me.

The headmaster's office? I thought. *Not the headmaster?*

On the way there, I made conversation with Oren. "Think someone tipped the school off about my knife?" I wondered how seriously private schools took their weapons policies when it came to students who were on the verge of inheriting billions. But when Oren and I got to the office, the secretary greeted me with a sunny smile.

"Avery." She held out a package—not an envelope, but a box. My name was scripted on the top in familiar, elegant writing. "This was delivered for you."

CHAPTER 30

Oren commandeered the package. It was hours before I got it back—and by the time I did, I was safely ensconced inside the walls of Hawthorne House, and Eve, Libby, and all the Hawthorne brothers had joined me in the circular library.

"No note this time," Oren reported. "Just this."

I stared at what looked to be a jewelry box: square, a little bigger than my hand, possibly antique. The wood was a dark cherry color. A thin line of gold rimmed the edges. I went to open the lid, then realized the box was locked.

"Combination lock." Oren nodded toward the front edge of the box, where there were six dials, grouped in pairs. "Added recently, I would guess. I was tempted to force it open, but given the circumstances, preserving the integrity of the jewelry box seemed like a priority."

After two envelopes, the fact that Toby's abductor had sent a package this time felt like an escalation. I didn't want to think about what I might find inside that jewelry box. The first envelope had contained the disk, the second, a picture of a beaten Toby. As far as proof went, as far as a reminder of the stakes, a reminder of who held the power here...

How long until the kidnapper starts sending pieces?

"The combination might be just a combination." Jameson stared at the box like he could see through it—into it. "But there's also the possibility that the numbers themselves are a clue."

"The package was sent to the school?" Grayson's gaze was sharp. "And it made it all the way to the headmaster's office? Whoever sent it knows how to get around Country Day security protocols."

That seemed like a message in and of itself: The person who'd sent this wanted me to know that they could get to me.

"It would be best," Oren stated calmly, "if you planned to stay home from school for a few days, Avery."

"You, too, Xan," Nash added.

"And just let someone make us run and hide?" I looked from Oren to Nash, furious. "No. I'm not going to do that."

"Tell you what, kid." Nash cocked his head to the side. "We'll spar for it. You and me. Winner makes the rules, and loser doesn't whine about it."

"Nash." Libby gave him a reproachful look.

"If you don't like that, Lib, you ain't gonna love my thoughts about *your* safety."

"Oren and Nash are right, Heiress." Jameson's hand found its way to mine. "It's not worth the risk."

I was fairly certain Jameson Hawthorne had never said those words before in his life.

"Can you all just stop arguing?" Eve demanded, her voice high and terse. "We have to open it. Right now. We have to get inside that box as quickly as humanly possible and—"

"Evie," Grayson murmured. "We need to be careful."

Evie?

"For once," Jameson declared, "I agree with Gray. Caution isn't the worst idea here."

That wasn't like Jameson, either.

Xander turned to Oren. "How certain are we that this box won't explode the second we open it?"

"Very," Oren replied.

I made myself ask the next question—*the* question—even though I didn't want to. "Any idea what's inside?"

"From the looks of the X-rays," Oren replied, "a phone."

Just a phone. Relief rolled over me slowly, like feeling coming back to a limb that had gone numb. "A phone," I said out loud. Did that mean Toby's captor was planning to call?

What happens if I don't answer?

I didn't let myself linger on that question. Instead, I turned my attention back to the boys. "You're Hawthornes. Who knows how to crack a combination lock?"

The answer was all of them. Within ten minutes, they had the combination: *fifteen, eleven, thirty-two.* Once it clicked open, Oren took the box, inspected its contents, and turned the whole thing back over to me.

The inside of the box was lined with deep red velvet. A cell phone sat nestled in the fabric. I picked the phone up and turned it over, looking for anything out of the ordinary, then I turned my attention to the touch screen. I tried the same combination that had opened the box as a passcode. *Fifteen. Eleven. Thirty-two.*

"I'm in," I said. I clicked through the icons on the phone one by one. The photo roll was empty. The weather app was set to local weather. There were no notes, no text messages, no locations saved in the map function. Under the clock app, I found a timer counting down.

12 HOURS, 45 MIN, 11 SEC...

I looked up at the others, feeling each tick of the timer in the pit of my stomach. Eve said what I was thinking. "What happens when it hits zero?"

My stomach clenching, I thought of Toby, of what I *hadn't* found in this box. Jameson stepped in front of me, green eyes steady on mine. "Forget the timer for now, Heiress. Go back to the main screen."

I did and, fury building, checked out the rest of the phone. There was no music loaded onto it. The internet browser's home screen was a search engine—nothing special there. I clicked on the calendar. There was an event set to begin on Tuesday at six in the morning. *When the timer hits zero*, I realized.

All the calendar entry said was *Niv.* I turned the phone so the others could read it.

"Niv?" Xander said, wrinkling his forehead. "A name, maybe? Or the last two letters could be a roman numeral."

"N-four." Grayson took out his own phone and executed a search. "The first two things that come up when I search the letter and the numeral are a federal form and a drug called phentermine hydrochloride—an appetite suppressant, apparently."

I rolled that over in my mind but couldn't make sense of it. "What kind of federal form?"

"A financial one," Eve replied, reading over Grayson's shoulder. "Securities and Exchange Commission. It looks like it might have something to do with investment companies?"

Investment. There could be something there.

"What else?" Nash threw the words out. "There's *always* something else."

This wasn't a Hawthorne game, not exactly, but the tricks were the same. I clicked on the icon for email, but that just brought up a prompt with instructions for setting up that function. Finally, I navigated to the phone's call log. *Empty.* I clicked over to voicemail messages. *None.* One more click took me to the phone's contacts.

There was exactly one number stored on this phone. The name it was stored under was CALL ME.

I sucked in a breath.

"Let me do it," Jameson said. "I can't protect you from everything, Heiress, but I can protect you from this."

Jameson wasn't the Hawthorne I usually associated with protection.

"No," I told him. The package had been sent to *me*. I couldn't let anyone do this for me—not even him. I hit Call before anyone could stop me and set it to speakerphone. My lungs refused to breathe until the second someone picked up.

"Avery Kylie Grambs." The voice that answered was male, deep and smooth with an intonation that sounded almost aristocratic.

"Who is this?" I asked, the words coming out tight.

"You can call me Luke."

Luke. The name reverberated through my mind. The person on the other end of the line didn't sound particularly young, but it was impossible to place his age. All I knew was that I'd never spoken to him before. If I had, I would have recognized that voice.

"Where's Toby?" I demanded. In response, I received only a chuckle. "What do you want?" No answer. "At least tell me that you still have him." *That he's still okay.*

"I have many things," the voice said.

Holding the phone so tightly that my hand started to throb, I clung to my last shreds of control. *Be smart, Avery. Get him talking.* "What do you want?" I asked again, more calmly this time.

"Curious, are you?" Luke played with the words like a cat playing with a mouse. "Fine word, *curious*," he continued, his voice like velvet. "It can mean that you're eager to learn or know something, but also, *strange* or *unusual*. Yes, I think that description fits you very well."

"So this is about me?" I asked through gritted teeth. "You want me curious?"

"I'm just an old man," came the reply, "with a fondness for riddles."

Old. How old? I didn't have time to dwell on that question—or the fact that he'd referred to himself in the same way that Tobias Hawthorne's grandsons referred to the dead billionaire.

"I don't know what kind of sick game you're playing," I said harshly.

"Or maybe you know exactly what kind of sick game I'm playing."

I could practically hear his lips curving into a knife-sharp smile.

"You have the box," he said. "You have the phone. You'll figure the next part out."

"What next part?"

"Tick tock," the old man replied. "The timer's counting down to our next call. You won't like what happens to your Toby if you don't have an answer for me by then."

CHAPTER 31

W*hat did we learn?* I tried to concentrate on that, not the threat, not the timer counting down.

Toby's captor had referred to himself as old.

He'd called me by my full name.

He played with words—and with people. "He likes riddles," I said out loud. "And games."

I knew someone who fit that description, but billionaire Tobias Hawthorne was dead. He'd been dead for a year.

"What precisely are we supposed to figure out?" Grayson asked crisply.

I looked reflexively toward Jameson. "There must be something to find or decode," I said, "just like there was in the earlier deliveries."

"The next part of the same riddle," Jameson murmured, our minds in sync.

Eve looked between the two of us. "What riddle?"

"*The* riddle," Jameson said. "Who is he? Why is he doing this? The first two clues were straightforward enough to decode. He's upped his ante with this installment."

"We must be missing something," I said. "A detail about the box or the package or—"

"I recorded the phone call." Xander held up his phone. "In case there's a clue in something he said. Beyond that..."

"We have the combination," Jameson finished. "And the calendar entry."

"Niv," I said out loud. Moving on instinct, I checked the box for hidden compartments. There weren't any. There was nothing else on the phone, nothing that popped out when we listened to my exchange with Toby's captor a second time. Or a third.

"Can your team trace the call?" I asked Oren, trying to think ahead, trying to come at this problem from all sides. "We have the number."

"I can try," Oren replied evenly, "but unless our opponent is far less intelligent than he appears, the number is unregistered, and the call was routed through the internet, not a phone tower, with the signal split across a thousand IP addresses, bouncing all over the world."

My throat tightened. "Could the police help pin it down?"

"We can't call the police," Eve whispered. "He could *kill* Toby."

"Discreet inquiries could potentially be made to a trusted police contact without providing details," Oren said. "Unfortunately, my three most trusted contacts have been recently transferred."

There was no way that was a coincidence. Attacks on my business interests. Attempts to chip away at my security team. Paparazzi set on my every move. Police contacts transferred. I thought about what Alisa had said we were looking for. *Wealth. Power. Connections.*

"Play the recording again," I told Xander.

My BHFF did as I asked, and this time, as the conversation

ended, Jameson looked to Grayson. "He said that Avery could *call* him Luke. Not that his name *was* Luke."

"Does that matter?" I asked.

Grayson held Jameson's gaze. "It could."

Eve started to say something, but the sound of a ringing phone silenced her. It wasn't the burner phone. It was mine. My eyes darted to the caller ID. *Thea.*

I answered. "I'm kind of busy right now, Thea."

"In that case, do you want the bad news first or the really bad news?"

"Is Rebecca—"

"Someone got a picture of Eve standing outside the gates of Hawthorne House. It just went live."

I winced. "Was that the bad news or—"

"It went live," Thea continued, "on the internet's biggest gossip site, alongside a picture of Emily and an exposé on rumors that Emily Laughlin was killed by Grayson and Jameson Hawthorne."

CHAPTER 32

I texted Alisa first. Handling scandals like this was part of her job. Breaking the news to the boys and Eve was harder. Forcing my mouth to say the words felt like breaking my ankle. *A moment of wrongness. A sick* crunch. *The shock.* Then the shock wore off.

"This is bullshit," Nash bit out. He took a breath, then turned discerning eyes on his brothers. "Jamie? Gray?"

"I'm fine." Grayson's face was like stone.

"And in keeping with my general superiority in our sibling relationship," Jameson added with a sardonic smile that was just a little too sharp, "I am better than fine."

This was Luke's doing. It had to be.

Eve pulled the gossip site up on her phone. She stared at it. Her own picture. Emily's.

I flashed back to that moment in Toby's wing when she'd told me that she didn't look like anyone in her family.

"Why does it say you killed her?" Eve asked, her voice reedy. She didn't look up from her phone, but I knew who she was addressing that question to.

"Because," Grayson replied, his voice blade-edged, "we did."

"Like hell you did," Nash swore. He looked around at the rest of us. "What's the rule about fightin' dirty?" he asked. No one answered. "Gray? Jamie?" He swiveled his gaze to me.

"There's no such thing as fighting dirty," I said lowly, "if you win." I wanted to win. I wanted to get Toby back. I wanted to take the bastard who had kidnapped him—the bastard who had just done this to Jameson and Grayson and Eve—*down*.

"Fighting dirty?" Eve asked, finally looking up from the website. "Is that what you call this? My face is going to be everywhere."

This was exactly what Toby *hadn't* wanted.

"Glitter cannon," Xander said.

I shot him a look. This really wasn't the time for levity—or sparkles.

"This right here is a glitter cannon," Xander reiterated. "Detonate one in the middle of a game, and it makes a huge mess. The kind that gets everywhere, sticks to everything."

Grayson's expression hardened. "And runs down the clock while you clean it up."

"While you *try* to clean it up," Libby said gently. She'd been quiet in all of this, but my sister had empathy in spades, and she didn't have to know Grayson or Jameson or even Eve as well as I did to know how hard they'd been hit.

"Some things don't clean easy," Nash agreed in a slow, steady drawl, his eyes finding Libby's like it was the most natural thing in the world. "You'll think you've finally got it all. Everything's fine. And then five years later..."

"There's still glitter in Grayson's bathroom," Xander finished. I got the feeling that wasn't a metaphor.

"Luke did this," I said. "He set this up. He detonated the blast. He wants us distracted." *He wants to run down the clock. He wants us to lose.*

Tick tock.

Eve turned her phone off and tossed it roughly onto the desk. "Screw the glitter," she said. "I don't want to figure out what happens to Toby if that timer hits zero."

None of us did.

Xander played the conversation with Luke back again, and we got to work.

CHAPTER 33

6 HOURS, 17 MIN, 9 SEC...

It was getting to the point where I didn't even need to look at the time. I just knew. We weren't getting anywhere. I tried to clear my head, but fresh air didn't help. Giving money anonymously to people who needed it didn't help.

When I went back inside, I arrived in the circular library just in time to hear Xander's phone go off. He was the only person I knew who used the first twelve digits of pi as a ringtone. After an uncharacteristically muted conversation, he brought the phone to me.

"Max," he mouthed.

I took the phone. "Let me guess," I said, holding it to my ear. "You've seen the news?"

"What makes you think that?" Max responded. "I was just calling to catch you up on my bodyguard situation. Piotr stubbornly refuses to choose a theme song, but otherwise, our bodyguard-and-bodyguard-ee relationship is working out quite well."

Leave it to Max to make light of needing security. *Because of me.* I couldn't help feeling responsible, any more than I could help feeling like Eve had been outed to the world only because she'd made the poor choice of coming to *me* for help.

My name was the one on the envelopes, the one on the box. I was the one in Luke's sights, but anyone close to me could end up in the crosshairs.

"I'm sorry," I told Max.

"I know," my best friend replied. "But don't worry. I'll choose a theme song for him." She paused. "Xander said something about... a cannon?"

The whole story burst out, like water demolishing a broken dam: the package delivery, the box, the phone, the call with "Luke"—and his ultimatum.

"You sound like a person who needs to think out loud," Max opined. "Proceed."

I did. I just kept talking and talking, hoping my brain would find something different to say this time. I got to the event in the calendar and said, "We thought *Niv* might be a reference to an SEC form, N-four. We've spent hours trying to track down Tobias Hawthorne's filings. I guess *Niv* could be a name, or initials, but—"

"Niv," Max repeated. "Spelled *N-I-V*?"

"Yes."

"N-I-V," she repeated. "As in *New International Version*?"

I tilted my head to the side. "New international version of what?"

"The B-I-B-L-E—and now, I am officially going to have Sunday school songs running on a loop all night."

"The Bible," I repeated, and suddenly, it clicked. "Luke."

"My second-favorite Gospel," Max noted. "I'll always be a John girl at heart."

I barely heard her. My brain was going too fast, images flashing through my mind, slices of memory piling up one after the other. "The numbers."

The combination might be just a combination, Jameson had said. *But there's also the possibility that the numbers themselves are a clue.*

"What numbers?" Max asked.

My heart beat viciously against my rib cage. "Fifteen, eleven, thirty-two."

"Are you faxing kidding me?" Max was delighted. "Am I about to solve a Hawthorne riddle?"

"Max!"

"The book of Luke," she said, "chapter fifteen, verses eleven through thirty-two. It's a parable."

"Which one?" I asked.

"The parable of the prodigal son."

CHAPTER 34

None of us slept more than three hours that night. We read every version of Luke 15:11–32 that we could find, every interpretation of it, every reference to it.

Nine seconds left on the timer. Eight. I watched it count down. Eve was sitting beside me, her feet curled under her body. Libby was on my other side. The boys were standing. Xander had the recorder ready.

Three. Two. One—

The phone rang. I answered it and set it to speaker so everyone could hear. "Hello."

"Well, Avery Kylie Grambs?"

The use of my full name did not go unnoticed. "Luke, chapter fifteen, verses eleven through thirty-two." I kept my voice calm, even.

"What about Luke, chapter fifteen, verses eleven through thirty-two?"

I didn't want to perform for him. "I solved your puzzle. Let me talk to Toby."

"Very well."

There was silence, and then I heard Toby's voice. "Avery. Don't—"

The rest of that sentence was cut off. My stomach sank. I felt fury snaking its way through my body. "What did you do to him?"

"Tell me about Luke, chapter fifteen, verses eleven through thirty-two."

He has Toby. I have to play this his way. All I could do was hope my adversary would eventually tip his hand. "The prodigal son demanded his inheritance early," I said, trying not to let any of the emotions I was feeling into my voice. "He abandoned his family and squandered the fortune he'd been given. But despite all of this, his father embraced him upon his return."

"A wasteful youth," the man said, "wandering the world—ungrateful. A benevolent father, ready to welcome him home. But if memory serves correctly, there were three characters in that story, and you've only mentioned two."

"The brother." Eve came to stand beside me and spoke before I could. "He stayed and worked alongside his father for years for no reward."

There was silence on the other end of the phone line. And then, the slash of a verbal knife: "I will talk only to the heiress. The one Tobias Hawthorne *chose*."

Eve shrank in on herself, like she'd been struck, her eyes wet, her expression like stone. On the other end of the line, there was silence.

Had he hung up?

Panicked, my grip on the phone tightened. "I'm here!"

"Avery Kylie Grambs, there are three characters in the parable of the prodigal son, are there not?"

Breath left my lungs. "The son who left," I said, sounding calmer than I felt. "The son who stayed. And the father."

"Why don't you ruminate on that?" There was another long pause, and then: "I'll be in touch."

CHAPTER 35

R*uminating* looked like this: Libby went to make coffee, because when things got bad, she took care of other people. Grayson stood, straightened his suit jacket, and turned his back on the rest of us. Jameson began pacing like a panther on the prowl. Nash took off his cowboy hat and stared at it, an ominous expression on his face. Xander darted out of the room, and Eve lowered her head into her hands.

"I shouldn't have said anything," she said hoarsely. "But after he cut Toby off—"

"I understand," I told her. "And it wouldn't have mattered if you'd stayed silent. We would have ended up in the exact same place."

"Not *exactly*." Jameson came to a stop directly in front of me. "Think about what he said after Eve interrupted—and the way he referred to you."

"As *the heiress*," I replied, and then I remembered the rest of it. "The one Tobias Hawthorne chose." I swallowed. "The prodigal son is a story about inheritance and forgiveness."

"Everyone who thinks that Toby was kidnapped as part of a giant *forgiveness* plot," Nash said, his drawl doing nothing to soften the words, "raise your hand."

All our hands remained down. "We already know this is about revenge," I said harshly. "We know it's about winning. This is just another piece of the same damn riddle that we aren't meant to solve."

Now I was the one who couldn't stand still. Rage didn't simmer. It burned.

"He wants us driving ourselves crazy, going over and over it," I said, striding toward the massive tree trunk desk and bracing my hands against it, *hard*. "He wants us *ruminating*. And what's even the point?" I was so close to punching the wood. "He's not done yet, and he's not going to give us what we need to solve this until he wants it solved."

I'll be in touch. Our adversary was like a cat that had a mouse by the tail. He was batting at me, then letting me go, creating the illusion that maybe, if I was very clever, I could slip his grasp, when he wasn't the least afraid I would.

"We have to try," Eve said with quiet desperation.

"Eve's right." Grayson turned back toward us—toward her. "Just because our opponent *thinks* this is beyond our capabilities to figure out doesn't mean that it is."

Jameson placed his hands next to mine on the desk. "The other two clues were vague. This one, less so. Even partial riddles can sometimes be solved."

As futile as it felt, as angry as I was, they were right. We had to try. For Toby, we had to.

"I'm back!" Xander burst into the room. "And I have props!" He thrust his hand out. In his palm, there were three chess pieces: a king, a knight, and a bishop.

Jameson reached for the chess pieces, but Xander smacked his hand away. "The father." Xander brandished the king and set it down on the desk. "The prodigal son." He plunked down the knight. "And the son who stayed."

"The bishop as the son who kept faith," I commented as Xander placed the final piece on the desk. "Nice touch." I stared at the three pieces. *A wasteful youth, wandering the world—ungrateful.* The memory of that voice stuck to me like oil. *A benevolent father, ready to welcome him home.*

I picked up the knight. "*Prodigal* means wastrel. We all know what teenage Toby was like. He slept and drank his way across the country, was responsible for a fire that killed three people, and allowed his family to think he was dead for decades."

"And through all of that," Jameson mused, picking up the king, "our grandfather wanted nothing more than to welcome his prodigal son home."

Toby, the prodigal. Tobias, the father.

"That just leaves the other son," Grayson said, walking over to join us as the desk. Nash circled up, too, leaving only a muted Eve on the outskirts. "The one who toiled faithfully," Grayson continued, "and was given nothing."

He managed to say those words like they held no meaning to him, but this part of the story had to hit close to home for him—for all of them. "We already talked to Skye," I said, picking up the bishop, the faithful son. "But Skye isn't Toby's only sibling."

I hated to even say it because I hadn't seen Tobias Hawthorne's older daughter as an enemy in months.

"It's not Zara," Jameson said with the kind of intensity I associated with him and only him. "She's Hawthorne enough to pull it off, if she wanted to, but unless we believe that the man on that phone call was an actor—a front—we *know* who the third player in this story is."

Avenge. Revenge. Vengeance. Avenger.

I always win in the end.

The three characters in the story of the prodigal son.

Each piece of the riddle told us something about our opponent. "If Toby is supposed to be the unworthy prodigal," I said, my entire body wound tight, "and Tobias Hawthorne is the father who forgave him, the only role left for Toby's abductor is the other son."

Another son. My body went utterly still as that possibility sank in.

Xander raised his hand. "Anyone else wondering if we have a secret uncle out there no one knows about? Because at this point, *secret uncle* just kind of feels like it belongs on the Hawthorne bingo card."

"I don't buy it." Nash's voice was steady, sure, unhurried. "The old man wasn't exactly scrupulous, but he *was* faithful—and damn possessive of anyone or anything he considered his. Besides, we don't have to go lookin' for *secret* uncles."

I registered his meaning at the exact same time that Jameson did. "That wasn't Constantine on the phone," he said. "But—"

"Constantine Calligaris wasn't Zara's first husband," I finished. Tobias Hawthorne might have had only one son, but he'd had more than one *son-in-law.*

"No one ever talks about the first guy," Xander offered. "Ever."

A son, cut from the family, ignored, forgotten. I looked to Oren. "Where's Zara?"

That question was loaded, given their history, but my head of security answered like the professional he was. "She wakes up early in the mornings to tend the roses."

"I'll go." Grayson wasn't asking permission or volunteering.

Eve finally joined the rest of us at the desk. She looked up at Grayson, tear tracks on her face. "I'll go with you, Gray."

He was going to take her up on the offer. I could tell that just by looking at him, but I didn't object. I didn't let myself say a single word.

But Jameson surprised me. "No. You go with Grayson, Heiress."

I had no idea what to read into that—if he still didn't trust Eve, if he didn't trust Grayson around Eve, or if he was just trying to fight his demons, set aside a lifelong rivalry, and trust me.

CHAPTER 36

Grayson and I found Zara in the greenhouse. She wore white gardening gloves that fit her hands like a second skin and held a pair of shears so sharp they probably could have cut through bone.

"To what do I owe this pleasure?" Zara angled her head toward us, the look in her eyes coolly advertising the fact that she was a Hawthorne and, by definition, missed nothing. "Out with it, both of you. You want something."

"We just want to talk," Grayson said evenly.

Zara ran her finger lightly over a thorn. "No Hawthorne has ever just wanted to talk."

Grayson didn't argue that point. "Your brother Toby has been abducted," he said, with that uncanny ability to say things that *mattered* as if they were simply facts. "There's been no demand for ransom, but we've received several communications from his kidnapper."

"Is Toby alright?" Zara took a step toward Oren. "John—is my brother alright?"

He gently met her gaze and gave her what he could. "He's alive."

“And you haven’t found him yet?” Zara demanded. Her tone was pure ice. I could see the exact moment she remembered who she was talking to and realized that if *Oren* couldn’t find Toby, there was a very good chance he couldn’t be found.

“We think there might be a family connection between Toby and the person who took him,” I said.

Zara’s expression wavered, like ripples across the water. “If you came here to make accusations, I suggest you stop beating around the bush and make them.”

“We’re not here to accuse you of anything,” Grayson said with absolute, unerring calm. “We need to ask you about your first husband.”

“Christopher?” Zara arched a brow. “I assure you, you don’t.”

“Toby’s abductor has been sending clues,” I said, rushing the words. “The most recent involves the biblical story of the prodigal son.”

“We’re looking,” Grayson stated, “for someone who viewed Tobias Hawthorne as a father and felt as though he got a raw deal. Tell us about Christopher.”

“He was everything that was expected of me.” Zara lifted the shears to clip a white rose. *Off with its head.* “Wealthy family, politically connected, charming.”

Wealth, Alisa had said. *Power. Connections.*

Zara set the white rose in a black basket, then clipped three more. “When I filed for divorce, Chris went to my father and played the dutiful son, fully expecting the old man to talk some sense into me.”

It was Grayson’s turn now to arch a brow. “How thoroughly was he destroyed?”

Zara smiled. “I assure you, the divorce was civil.” In other words:

utterly. "But it hardly matters. Christopher died in a boating accident not long after everything was finalized."

No, I thought, a visceral, knee-jerk reaction. *Not another dead end*. "What about his family?" I asked, unwilling to let this go.

"He was an only child, and his parents are likewise deceased."

I felt like the mouse I'd imagined earlier, like I'd been made to think I had a chance when I never really had. But I couldn't give up. "Is it possible that your father had another son?" I asked, going back to that possibility. "Besides Toby?"

"A pretermitted heir who *didn't* come crawling out of the woodwork after the will was read?" Zara responded archly. "With billions at stake? Hardly likely."

"Then what are we missing?" I asked, more desperation in my tone than I wanted to admit.

Zara considered the question. "My father liked to say that our minds have a way of tricking us into choosing between two options when there are really seven. The Hawthorne gift has always been seeing all seven."

"Identify the assumptions implicit in your own logic," Grayson said, clearly citing a dictate he'd been taught, "then negate them."

I thought about that. What assumptions had we made? *That Toby is the prodigal son, Tobias the father*. It was the obvious interpretation, given Toby's history, but that was the thing about riddles. The answer *wasn't* obvious.

And on that first phone call, Toby's captor had referred to himself as an *old man*.

"What happens if we take Toby out of the story?" I asked Grayson. "If your grandfather *isn't* the father in the parable?" My heart drummed in my chest. "What if he's one of the sons?"

Grayson looked to his aunt. "Did the old man ever talk to you about his family? His parents?"

"My father liked to say that he didn't have a family, that he came from nothing."

"That was what he *liked* to say," Grayson confirmed.

In my mind, all I could picture were the three chess pieces. If Tobias Hawthorne was the bishop or the knight...who the hell was the king?

CHAPTER 37

"We need to find Nan," Jameson said immediately, once Grayson and I had reported back. "She's probably the only person alive who could tell us if the old man had family that Zara doesn't know about."

"Finding Nan," Xander explained to Eve, in what appeared to be an attempt to cheer her up, "is a bit like a game of Where's Waldo, except Waldo likes to jab people with her cane."

"She has favorite places in the House," I said. *The piano room. The card room.*

"It's Tuesday morning," Nash commented wryly.

"The chapel." Jameson looked at each of his brothers. "I'll go." He turned to me. "Feel like a walk?"

The Hawthorne chapel—located beyond the hedge maze and due west of the tennis courts—wasn't large, but it was breathtaking. The stone arches, hand-carved pews, and elaborate stained-glass windows looked like they'd been the work of dozens of artisans.

We found Nan resting in a pew. "Don't let in a draft," she barked without so much as turning around to see who she was barking at.

Jameson shut the chapel door, and we joined her in the pew. Nan's head was bowed, her eyes closed, but somehow, she seemed to know exactly who had joined her. "Shameless boy," she scolded Jameson. "And you, girl! Forget about our weekly poker game yesterday, did you?"

I winced. "Sorry. I've been distracted." That was an understatement.

Nan opened her eyes for the sole purpose of narrowing them at me. "But now that you *want* to talk, it doesn't matter if I'm in the middle of something?"

"We can wait until you're finished praying," I said, properly chastened—or at least trying to look that way.

"Praying?" Nan grumbled. "More like giving our Maker a piece of my mind."

"My grandfather built this chapel so Nan would have someplace to yell at God," Jameson informed me.

Nan harrumphed. "The old coot threatened to build me a mausoleum instead. Tobias never thought I'd outlive him."

That was probably as close to an opening as we were going to get. "Did your son-in-law have any family of his own?" I asked. "Parents?"

"As opposed to what, girl? Springing forth fully formed from the head of Zeus?" Nan snorted. "Tobias always did have a God complex."

"You loved him," Jameson said gently.

A breath caught in Nan's throat. "Like my own child." She closed her eyes for a second or two, then opened them and continued. "He had parents, I suppose. From what I remember, Tobias said they had him older and didn't much know what to do with a boy like him." Nan gave Jameson a look. "Hawthorne children can be trying."

“So he was a late-in-life baby,” I summarized. “Did they have any other children?”

“After having Tobias, I doubt they would have dared.”

“What about older siblings?” Jameson asked.

One father, two sons…

“None of those, either. By the time Tobias met my Alice, he was well and truly alone. Father died of a heart attack when Tobias was a teenager. Mother only outlasted the father by about a year.”

“What about mentors?” Jameson asked. I could practically see him playing out a dozen different scenarios in his mind. “Father figures? Friends?”

“Tobias Hawthorne was never in the business of making friends. He was in the business of making money. He was a single-minded bastard, wily and brutal.” Nan’s voice shook. “But he was good to my Alice. To me.”

“Family first,” Jameson said softly beside me.

“No man has ever built an empire without doing a thing or two they aren’t proud of, but Tobias didn’t let that follow him home. His hands weren’t always clean, but he never once raised them—not to Alice or their children or you boys.”

“You would have killed him if he had,” Jameson said affectionately.

“The mouth on you,” Nan chided.

His hands weren’t always clean. That single phrase sent me back to the first message we’d received from Toby’s kidnapper. At the time, it had seemed likely that the target of revenge was either Toby or me. But what if it was Tobias Hawthorne himself?

What if this—all of it—had always been about the old man? *What if I’m just the one* he *chose? What if Toby is just* his *lost son?* The possibility took hold of my mind, gripped it like fingernails digging into flesh.

"What did your son-in-law do?" I asked. "Why weren't his hands clean?"

Nan offered no reply to that question.

Jameson reached out and took her hand. "If I told you that someone wanted revenge against the Hawthorne family—"

Nan patted the side of his face. "I'd tell that person to get in line."

CHAPTER 38

Identify your assumptions. Question them. Negate them. As I stepped out of the chapel, I felt like a shell over my brain had been cracked wide open, and now possibilities were streaming in from every side.

What would I have done from the very beginning if I'd assumed that Toby had been taken as revenge for something that his father had done? I thought about Eve talking about Hawthorne secrets—*dark secrets, maybe even dangerous ones*—and then about Nan and her talk of empires and dirty hands.

What had Tobias Hawthorne done on his way to the top? Once he'd amassed all that money and all that power, what had he used it to do? *And to whom?*

My brain sorting through possible next moves at warp speed, I turned to Oren. "You tracked threats against Tobias Hawthorne, back when you were his head of security. He had a List, like mine."

List, capital L, threats. People who required watching.

"Mr. Hawthorne had a List," Oren confirmed. "But it was a bit different than yours."

My List was heavy on strangers. From the moment I'd been

named Tobias Hawthorne's heir, I'd been thrust into the kind of worldwide spotlight that automatically came with online death threats and would-be stalkers, people who wanted to be me and people who wanted to hurt me.

It was always worse right after a new story broke. *Like now.*

"Would my grandfather's List happen to be a list of people he screwed over?" Jameson asked Oren.

He saw what I did: If Toby's captor was telling a story about envy, revenge, and triumphing over an old enemy, Tobias Hawthorne's List was a hell of a place to start.

Jameson and I caught the others up to speed, and Oren had the List delivered to the solarium. The room had glass walls and a glass ceiling, so no matter where you stood, you could feel the sun on your skin. After our near all-nighter, the seven of us were going to need all the help staying awake that we could get.

Especially because this was going to take a while.

Tobias Hawthorne hadn't just had a list of names. He'd had file folders like the one he'd assembled on me, but for hundreds of people. Hundreds of *threats.*

"You tracked all these people?" I asked Oren, staring at the stack and stacks of files.

"It wasn't a matter of actively tracking so much as knowing what they looked like, knowing their names, keeping an eye out." Oren's expression was smooth, unreadable, *professional.* "The files were Mr. Hawthorne's doing, not mine. I was only allowed to look at them if the person started popping up."

Right now, we didn't have a face. We didn't have a name, so I focused on what we did have. "We're looking for an older man," I told the others quietly. "Someone who was bested and betrayed by Tobias Hawthorne." I wanted there to be more than that for us to go on. "There might be a family connection or a family-like connection or maybe even just a story focused on three people."

"Three *men*," Eve said, seeming to have recovered her voice, her grit, and her poise. "In the parable, they're all *men*. And this guy took Toby, not Zara or Skye. He took the *son*."

She'd clearly been thinking about this. I stole a look at Grayson, and the way he was looking at Eve made me think that she hadn't been *thinking* alone.

"Well," Xander said, in an attempt at cheer. "That's not nothing to go on!"

I turned my attention back to the folders—stacks and stacks of them that left a heavy feeling in my stomach. "Whoever this man is," I said, "whatever his history with Tobias Hawthorne, whatever he lost—he's wealthy, powerful, and connected now."

CHAPTER 39

By the time we'd each made it through three or four folders, even the sunlight streaming in from all sides couldn't banish the dark pall that had settled over the room.

This was what I'd known before reading the files: Tobias Hawthorne had filed his first patents in the late sixties and early seventies. At least one had turned out to be valuable, and he'd used the profits from that to fund the land acquisitions that had made him a major player in Texas oil. He'd eventually sold his oil company for upward of a hundred million dollars, and after that, he'd diversified with a Midas touch for turning millions to billions.

All of that was public information. The information in these files told the parts of the story that the myth of Tobias Hawthorne glossed over. *Hostile takeovers. Competitors run out of business. Lawsuits filed for the sole purpose of bankrupting the other party.* The ruthless billionaire had a habit of zeroing in on a market opportunity and moving into that space with no mercy, buying up patents and smaller corporations, hiring the best and the brightest and using them to destroy the competition—only to pivot to a new industry, a new challenge.

He paid his employees well, but when the wind changed or the profits dried up, he laid them off without mercy.

Tobias Hawthorne was never in the business of making friends. I'd asked Nan exactly what her son-in-law had done that he wasn't proud of. The answer was all around us, and it was impossible to ignore the details in any of the files just because they didn't match what we were looking for.

I stared down at the folder in my hand: *Seaton, Tyler.* It appeared that Mr. Seaton, a brilliant biomedical engineer, had been caught up in one of Tobias Hawthorne's pivots after seven years of loyal—and lucrative—service. Seaton was downsized. Like all Hawthorne employees, he'd been given a generous severance package, including an extension of his company insurance. But eventually, that extension had run out, and a noncompete clause in the fine print of his contract had made it nearly impossible for him to find other employment.

And insurance.

Swallowing, I forced myself to stare at the pictures in this file folder. Pictures of a little girl. *Mariah Seaton.* She'd been diagnosed with cancer at age nine, just before her father lost his job.

She was dead by twelve.

Feeling sick to my stomach, I forced myself to continue paging through the file. The final sheet contained financial information about a transaction—a generous donation the Hawthorne Foundation had made to St. Jude Children's Research Hospital.

This was Tobias Hawthorne, billionaire, balancing his ledger. *That's not balance.*

"Did you know about this?" Grayson said, his voice low, his silver eyes targeting Nash.

"Which 'this' might we be talkin' about, little brother?"

"How about buying patents from a grieving widow for one one-hundredth of what they were worth?" Grayson threw down the file, then picked up another one. "Or posing as an angel investor when what he really wanted was to incrementally acquire enough of the company to be able to shut it down to clear the way for *another* of his investments?"

"I'll take *boilerplate contracts that give him control of his employees' IP* for two thousand, Alex." Jameson paused. "Whether that IP was created on the clock or not."

Across the room, Xander swallowed. "You really don't want to read about his foray into pharmaceuticals."

"Did you know?" Grayson asked Nash again. "Is that why you always had one foot out the door? Why you couldn't stand to be under the old man's roof?"

"Why you save people," Libby said quietly. She wasn't looking at Nash. She was looking at her wrists.

"I knew who he was." Nash didn't say more than that, but I could see tension beneath the rough stubble on his jaw. He angled his head down, the rim of his cowboy hat obscuring his face.

"Do you remember the bag of glass?" Jameson asked his brothers suddenly, an ache in his tone. "It was the puzzle with the knife. We had to break a glass ballerina to find three diamonds inside. The prompt was *Tell me what's real*, and Nash won because the rest of us focused on the diamonds—"

"And I handed the old man a real bag of shattered glass," Nash finished. There was something in his voice that made Libby stop looking at her wrists and walk to put one hand silently on his arm.

"The shattered glass," Grayson said, a wave of tension rippling through his body. "That lecture he gave us about how, to do what he had done, sacrifices had to be made. Things got broken. And if you didn't clean up the shards…"

Xander finished the sentence, his Adam's apple bobbing, "People got hurt."

CHAPTER 40

Thirty-six hours passed—no word from Toby's captor, an ever-growing hoard of paparazzi outside the gates, and too much time spent in the solarium with files on Tobias Hawthorne's enemies. His many, many enemies.

I finished the files in my stack. Each of the four Hawthorne brothers finished theirs. So did Libby. So did Eve. Nothing matched. Nothing fit. But I didn't want to admit that we'd hit another wall. I didn't want to feel cornered or outmatched or like everyone around me had taken repeated shots to the gut for *nothing*.

So I kept going back to the solarium, rereading files the others had already gone through, even though I knew the Hawthornes hadn't missed a damn thing. That these files were burned into them now.

The moment Jameson had finished his stack, he'd disappeared into the walls. The only reason I knew he hadn't taken off for parts unknown halfway around the world was that the bed was warm beside me when I woke in the morning. Grayson took to the pool, pushing himself past the point of human endurance again and again, and after Nash had finished, he'd dodged the press at the gates, snuck out to a bar, and came back at two in the morning with a split lip and a trembling puppy tucked into his shirt. Xander was barely eating. Eve seemed to think that she didn't need sleep and that if she could just memorize every detail of every file, an answer would present itself.

I understood. The two of us didn't talk about Toby, about the silence from his captor, but it fueled us on.

I'll be in touch.

I reached for another file—one of the few I hadn't made it through myself yet—and opened it. *Empty.* "Have you read this one?" I asked Eve, my heart whamming against my rib cage with sudden, startling force. "There's nothing here."

Eve looked up from the file she'd been scouring for the past twenty minutes. The desperate hope in *her* eyes flickered and died when she saw which file I was referring to. "Isaiah Alexander? There was a page in there before. Just one. Short file. Another disgruntled employee, fired from a Hawthorne lab. *PhD, rising star*—and now the guy has nothing."

No wealth. No power. No connections. *Not what we're looking for.*

"So where's the page?" I asked, the question gnawing at me.

"Does it matter?" Eve said, her tone dismissive, annoyance marring her striking features. "Maybe it got mixed in with another file."

"Maybe," I said. I closed the file, and my gaze caught on the tab. *Alexander, Isaiah.* Eve had said the name, but I hadn't processed it—not until now.

Grayson's father was Sheffield *Grayson.* Nash's father was named Jake *Nash.* And Xander's name was short for *Alexander.*

I found my BHFF in his lab. It was a hidden room filled with the most random assortment of items imaginable. Some people did found art, turning everyday objects into artistic commentary. Xander was more of a found *engineer.* As far as Hawthorne-brother coping mechanisms went, it was probably the healthiest one in the House.

"I need to talk to you about something," I said.

"Can it be about off-label uses for medieval weaponry?" Xander requested. "Because I have some ideas."

That was concerning on many levels, and it was so Xander that I wanted to cry or hug him or do anything except hold up that file and make him talk to me about something he'd made it very clear during Chutes and Ladders that he didn't want to talk about.

"Is this your father?" I said gently. "Isaiah Alexander?"

Xander turned to look at me. Then, as if coming to a very serious decision, he lifted his hand and pressed one finger to the end of my nose. "Boop."

"You're not going to distract me," I told him, the exasperation I might have normally felt replaced by something more tender and painful. "Come on, Xan. I'm your BHHFF. Talk to me."

"Double boop." Xander pressed my nose again. "What's the extra *H* for?"

"Honorary," I told him. "You guys made me an honorary Hawthorne, and that makes me your Best Honorary Hawthorne Friend Forever. So *talk*."

"Triple boo—" Xander started to say, but I ducked before he could touch my nose. I straightened, caught his hand gently in mine, and squeezed.

This was *Xander*, so there wasn't a hint of accusation in my voice when I asked my next question. "Did you take the page that was in this file?"

Xander gave an emphatic shake of his head. "I didn't even know Isaiah was on the List. I can probably tell you what his file says, though. I kind of spent the past several months making a file of my own."

This time, I didn't push down the urge to hug him. Hard. "Eve said he was a PhD who got fired from a Hawthorne lab," I said, once I'd pulled back.

"That about covers it," Xander replied, his cheery tone a copy of a copy of the real thing. "Except for timing. It's possible that Isaiah was fired around the time I was conceived. Maybe because I was conceived? I mean, maybe not! But maybe?"

Poor Xander. I thought about what he'd said in Chutes and Ladders. "Is that why you haven't contacted him?"

"I can't just call him." Xander gave me a plaintive look. "What if he hates me?"

"No one could possibly hate you, Xander," I told him, my heart twisting.

"Avery, people have hated me my whole life." There was something in his tone that made me think that very few people understood what it was like to be Xander Hawthorne.

"Not anyone who knows you," I said fiercely.

Xander smiled, and something about it made me want to cry. "Do you think it's okay," he said, sounding younger than I'd ever heard him, "that I loved playing those Saturday morning games? Loved growing up here? Loved the great and terrible Tobias Hawthorne?"

I couldn't answer that for him—for any of them. I couldn't make these past few days hurt less. But there was one thing I could say. "You didn't love the great and terrible Tobias Hawthorne. You loved the old man."

"I was the only one who knew that he was dying." Xander turned to pick up what looked like a tuning fork, but he didn't make a single move to add it to whatever contraption he was building. "He kept it a secret from everyone else for weeks. He wanted me with him at the end, and do you know what he said to me—the very last thing?"

"What?" I asked quietly.

"By the time this is over, you'll know what kind of man I was—and what kind of man you want to be."

CHAPTER 41

I headed back to the solarium empty-handed, having hit yet another dead end. *I'll be in touch.* That sinister promise echoed in my mind as I rounded the corner and saw Eve's guard. I nodded to him, glanced briefly back at Oren, then pushed opened the solarium door.

Inside, Eve was sitting with a file laid out on the ground in front of her and a phone in her hand. *Taking pictures.*

"What are you doing?" I asked, startled.

Eve looked up. "What do you think I'm doing?" Her voice broke. "I need sleep. I know I need sleep, but I can't stop. And I can't take these files out of this room, so I thought..." She shook her head, her eyes tearing, amber hair falling into her face. "Never mind. It's dumb."

"It's not dumb," I told her. "And you do need sleep."

We all did.

I checked Jameson's wing before I returned to my own. He wasn't in either. I remembered what it had been like when I'd discovered that my mom wasn't who I'd thought she was. I'd felt like I was mourning her death all over again, and the only thing that had helped was Libby reminding me of the kind of person my mom had been, proving to me that I *had* known her in every way that mattered.

But what could I say to Jameson or Xander or any of them about Tobias Hawthorne? That he really *was* brilliant? Strategic? That he'd had some small shreds of conscience? That he'd cared for his family, even if he'd disinherited all of them for a stranger?

By the time this is over, you'll know what kind of man I was—and what kind of man you want to be. I thought about the billionaire's last words to Xander. By the time *what* was over? By the time Xander had found his father? By the time all the games that Tobias Hawthorne had planned before his death had been played?

That thought drew my gaze to the leather satchel on my dresser. For two days, I'd been consumed with Toby's captor's sick riddle and the hope, however thin, that we were getting closer to solving it. But the truth was that all the *ruminating* we'd done had gotten us nowhere. It had probably been *designed* to lead us nowhere—until the riddle was complete.

I'll be in touch.

I hated this. I needed a win. I needed a distraction. *By the time this is over, you'll know what kind of man I was.* Slowly, I walked over to my dresser, thought about Tobias Hawthorne and those files, and picked up the satchel.

Moving methodically, I laid out the objects I hadn't yet used. *The steamer. The flashlight. The beach towel. The glass circle.* I said the last clue Jameson and I had uncovered out loud. *"Don't breathe."*

I cleared my mind. After a moment, my gaze locked on the towel, then on the blue-green circle. *That color. A towel. Don't breathe.*

With sudden, visceral clarity, I knew what I had to do.

A person stopped breathing when they were terrified, surprised, awed, trying to be quiet, surrounded by smoke—or underwater.

CHAPTER 42

A motion-sensor light came on as I stepped onto the patio. In my mind, in the span of a single heartbeat, I saw the pool the way it looked in daytime, with light reflecting off the water, the tiles on the bottom making it look as breathtakingly blue-green as the Mediterranean.

The same shade as the piece of glass I carried in my right hand. I held the beach towel in my left. Clearly, this was going to require getting wet.

At night, the water was darker, shadowy. I heard Grayson swimming before I saw him and felt the exact moment he became aware of my presence.

Grayson Davenport Hawthorne's hand slapped the edge of the pool. He pulled himself upright. "Avery." His voice was quiet, but in the still of the night, it carried. "You shouldn't be here." *With me* went unsaid. "You should be asleep."

Grayson and his *ought*s and *should*s. *Hawthornes aren't supposed to break.* His voice spoke deep in my memory. *Especially me.*

I shook off the memory as much as I could. "Is there a light out here?" I asked. I didn't want to have to deal with things going dark every time I stood too still—and I couldn't bring myself to look at Grayson, look at his light, piercing eyes, the way I had that night.

"There's a control panel under the portico."

I managed to find it and turn the pool lights on but ended up accidentally turning a fountain on, too. Water sprayed upward in a magnificent arc as the pool light cycled through colors: pink, purple, blue, green, violet. It felt like watching fireworks. Like magic.

But I hadn't come down here for magic. One touch turned off the fountain. Another stopped the cycle of colors in the light.

"What are you doing?" Grayson asked me, and I knew that he was asking why I was *here*, with him.

"Did Jameson tell you about the bag your grandfather left me?" I asked.

Grayson pushed off the wall, treading water as he measured his response. "Jamie doesn't tell me everything." The silences in Grayson's sentences always spoke volumes. "In fairness, there's quite a bit that I don't tell him."

That was the closest he'd ever come to mentioning that night in the wine cellar, the things he'd confessed to me.

I held up the glass circle. "This was one of several items in a bag that your grandfather instructed be delivered to me if Eve and I ever met. There was also—"

"What did you say?" Without warning, Grayson pulled himself out of the water. It was October and cool enough at night that he had to be freezing, but he did a very good impression of someone utterly incapable of feeling cold.

"When I met Eve, it triggered one of your grandfather's games."

"The old man knew?" Grayson was standing so still that if the pool light hadn't been on, he would have disappeared into the darkness. "My grandfather knew about Eve? He knew that Toby had a daughter?"

I swallowed. "Yes."

Every muscle in Grayson's body had gone tight. "He knew," he repeated savagely. "And he left her there? He knew, and he didn't say a damn word to any of us?" Grayson strode toward me—then past me. He braced himself against the portico wall, his palms flat, the muscles in his back so tense that it looked like his shoulder blades might split the skin.

"Grayson?" I didn't say more than that. I wasn't sure what else to say.

"I used to tell myself that the old man loved us," Grayson stated with all the precision of a surgeon slicing through good flesh to get to bad. "That if he held us to impossible standards, it was for the noble purpose of forging his heirs into what we needed to be. And if the great Tobias Hawthorne was harder on me than on my brothers, I told myself that it was because I needed to be more. I believed that he taught me about honor and duty because *he* was honorable, because he felt the weight of *his* duty and wanted to prepare me for it."

Grayson slammed his hand down onto the wall hard enough for the rough surface to tear into his palm.

"But the things he did? The dirty little secrets in those file folders? Knowing about Eve and letting her be raised by people who treated her as less than? Pretending that our family owed Toby's daughter nothing? There's nothing *honorable* about that." Grayson shook. *"Any of it."*

I thought about Grayson never allowing himself to break because he knew the man he'd been raised to be. I thought about Jameson saying that Grayson had always been so *perfect*. "We don't know how long your grandfather knew about Eve," I said. "If it was a recent discovery, if he knew that she looked like Emily, maybe he thought it would be too painful—"

"Maybe he thought I was too weak." Grayson turned to face me. "That's what you're saying, Avery, as hard as you try to make it mean something else."

I took a step toward him. "Grief doesn't make you weak, Grayson."

"Love does." Grayson's voice went brutally low. "I was supposed to be the one who was above it all. Emotion. Vulnerability."

"Why you?" I asked. "Why not Nash? He's the oldest. Why not Jameson or Xan—"

"Because it was supposed to be me." Grayson took in a ragged breath. I could practically see him fighting to slam the cage door closed on his emotions once more. "My whole life, Avery, it was supposed to be me. That was why I had to be better, why I had to sacrifice and be honorable and put family first, why I could *never* lose control—because the old man wasn't going to be around forever, and *I* was the one who was supposed to take the reins once he was gone."

It was supposed to be Grayson. I thought. *Not me.* A year on, and part of Grayson still couldn't let go of that, even knowing that the old man had never really intended to leave him the fortune.

"And I understood, Avery—*I did*—why the old man might have looked at this family, looked at *me*, and decided that we were unworthy of *his* legacy." Grayson's voice shook. "I understood why he thought I wasn't good enough—and you were. But if the great Tobias Hawthorne *wasn't* honorable? If he never met a line he wouldn't cross for his own selfish gain? If 'family first' was just some bullshit lie he fed to me? Then why?" Grayson brought his eyes to mine. "What's the point, Avery, of any of this?"

"I don't know." My voice sounded just as raw as his. Hesitantly, I raised the glass circle again. "But maybe there's more to it, a piece of the puzzle that we don't know. . . ."

"More games." Grayson slammed his hand against the wall again. "The old bastard has been dead a year, and he's still pulling strings."

My right hand holding the blue-green glass, I dropped the towel with my left and reached for him.

"Don't," Grayson breathed. He turned to walk past me. "I told you once before, Avery: I'm broken. I won't break you, too. Go back to bed. Forget about that piece of glass and whatever else was in that bag. Stop playing the old man's games."

"Grayson—"

"Just stop."

That felt final in a way that nothing else between us ever had. I didn't say anything. I didn't go after him. And when the way he'd told me to stop rang in my mind, I thought about Jameson, who never stopped.

About the person I was with Jameson.

I walked over to the water. I took off my pants and my shirt, laid the glass gingerly on the side of the pool, and dove in.

CHAPTER 43

I barreled through the water with my eyes open. The blue-green mosaic at the bottom of the pool beckoned me, illuminated by the lights I'd turned on. I swam closer, then ran my hand over the tiles, taking everything in: *that* color, the smoothness, the variation in the cut and size of the tiny tiles, the way they'd been laid, almost in a swirl.

I kicked off the bottom, and when I broke the surface, I paddled to the side. Taking the glass circle in one hand, I pulled myself along the edge to the shallow end with the other. Standing, I submerged the glass, then went under myself. *Don't breathe.*

Filtered through the glass, the blue-green tiles disappeared. Beneath them, I could see a simpler design: squares, some of them light, some dark. *A chessboard.*

There was always a moment in these games when I was hit with the almost physical realization that nothing Tobias Hawthorne had ever done had been without layers of purpose. All those additions to Hawthorne House, and how many of them contained one of his tricks just waiting for the right game?

Traps upon traps, Jameson had told me once. *And riddles upon riddles.*

I came back up for air, the image of the chessboard burned into my mind. I thought about Grayson telling me not to play, about Jameson, who should have been playing alongside me. And then I cleared my mind of all of that. I thought about the clues that had preceded this one: the Queen's Gambit, leading to the royal chess set to *Don't breathe*. I went down again, held up the glass again, and mentally populated the squares with pieces.

I played out the Queen's Gambit in my mind. *P-Q4. P-Q4. P-QB4.*

Refusing to blink, I memorized the locations of the squares involved in those moves, then came up for air. Setting the glass back on the side of the pool, I pulled myself out, the night air a brutal shock to my system.

P-Q4, I thought. With single-minded purpose, I dove for the bottom. No matter how I pushed or prodded at the mosaic of tiles that made up the first square, nothing happened. I swam to the second—still nothing, then went up for air again, swam to the side again, pulled myself out again, shivering, shaking, *ready*.

I drew in air, then dove again. *P-QB4.* The location of the last move in the Queen's Gambit. This time, when I pushed against the tiles, one turned, hitting the next and the next, like some kind of clockwork marvel.

I watched the chain reaction go, piece by piece, afraid to even blink, terrified that whatever this was, it would only last a moment. A final tile turned, and the entire section—the square I'd seen through the glass—popped up. My lungs starting to burn, I wedged my fingers underneath. They brushed something.

Almost. Almost.

My body was telling me to go to the surface—*screaming* at me to go to the surface—but I shoved my fingers under the tile again. This time, I managed to pull a flat package out, an instant before the compartment began to close.

I pushed off, kicked, then exploded past the surface of the water. I gasped and couldn't stop gasping, sucking in the night air again and again. I swam for the side of the pool. This time, when my hand reached for the edge, another hand grabbed mine.

Jameson pulled me out of the water. "*Don't breathe*," he murmured.

I didn't ask him where he'd been or even if he was okay. I just held up the package I'd retrieved from the bottom of the pool.

Jameson bent to pick up the beach towel and wrapped it around me. "Well done, Heiress." His lips brushed mine, and the world felt charged, brimming with anticipation and the thrill of the chase. This was the way he and I were supposed to be: no running, no hiding, no recriminations, no regrets.

Just *us*, questions and answers and what we could do when we were together.

I went to open the package and found it vacuum sealed. Jameson held out a knife. I recognized it. *The* knife—from the shattered glass game.

Taking it from him, I sliced the package open. Inside, there was a fireproof pouch. I unzipped it and found a faded photograph. Three figures—all women—stood in front of an enormous stone church.

"Do you recognize them?" I asked Jameson.

He shook his head, and I turned the photograph over. On the back, written in Tobias Hawthorne's familiar scrawl, was a place and a date. *Margaux, France, December 19, 1973.*

I'd been playing the billionaire's games long enough for my brain to latch immediately onto the date. *12/19/1973.* And then there was the location. "Margaux?" I said out loud. "Pronounced like Margo?"

That could mean we were looking for a person with that name—but in a Hawthorne game, it could also mean so many other things.

CHAPTER 44

Jameson got me into a hot shower, and my mind raced. Decoding a clue required separating meaning from distraction. There were four elements here: the photograph; the name *Margaux*; the location in France; and the date, which could have been an actual date or could have been a number in need of decoding.

In all likelihood, some combination of those four elements was meaningful, and the rest were just distractions, but which were which?

"Three women." Jameson hung a towel, warm from the towel heater, over the shower's glass door. "A church in the background. If we scan the photograph, we could try a reverse image search—"

"—which would only help," I filled in, the water white-hot against my chilled skin, "if a copy of this exact photograph exists online." Still, it was worth a try. "We should try to locate the church, figure out its name," I murmured, steam growing thicker in the air around me. "And we can talk to Zara and Nan. See if they recognize any of these women."

"Or the name Margaux," Jameson added. Through the steam on the glass door, he was a blur of color: long, lean, familiar in ways that made me ache.

I turned off the rain shower spray. I wrapped my towel around my body and stepped out onto the bathroom rug. Jameson met my eyes, his face moonlit through the window, his hair a mess my fingers wanted to touch. "There's also the date to consider," he murmured. "And the rest of the objects in the bag."

"A steamer, a flashlight, a USB," I rattled off. "We could try the steamer and the flashlight on the photograph—and the pouch it came in."

"Three objects left." Jameson's mouth ticked upward at the ends. "And three already used. That puts us halfway through, and my grandfather would say that's a good point to step back. Go back to the beginning. Consider the framing and your charge."

I felt my own lips parting and tilting up at the ends. "There were no instructions given. No question, no prompt."

"No question, no prompt." Jameson's voice was low and silky. "But we know the trigger. You met Eve." Jameson chewed on that for a moment, then turned. His green eyes looked like they were focused on something no one but him could see, as if a multitude of possibilities suddenly stretched out before him like constellations in the sky. "The start of the game was triggered when you met Eve, which means this game might tell us something about you or something about Eve, something about why my grandfather chose you instead of Eve, or..."

Jameson turned again, caught up in a web of his own thoughts. It was like everything else had ceased to exist, even me.

"*Or*," he repeated, like that was the answer. "I didn't see it at the beginning," he said, his voice low and struck through with electric energy. "But now that it seems like the old man might be at the center of the current onslaught?" Jameson's gaze snapped back to the real world. "What if..."

Jameson and I lived for those two words. *What if?* I *felt* them now. "You think there could be a connection," I said, "between the game your grandfather left me and everything else?"

Toby's abduction. The old man with a fondness for riddles. Someone coming at me from all sides.

My question grounded Jameson, and his gaze leapt to mine. "I think that this game was delivered to you because Eve showed up here. And the *only* reason that Eve came here was because there was trouble. No trouble, no Eve. If Toby hadn't been abducted, she wouldn't be here. My grandfather always thought seven steps ahead. He saw dozens of permutations in how things could play out, planned for every eventuality, strategized for each and every possible future."

Sometimes, when the boys talked about the old man, they made him sound more than mortal. But there were limits to what a person could foresee, limits to even the most brilliant mind's strategy.

Jameson caught my chin in his hand and tilted my head gently backward, angling it up toward him. "Think about it, Heiress. What if the information we need to find out who took Toby is really in *this* game?"

My throat tightened, my entire body feeling the shot of hope with physical force. "Do you really think it could be?" I asked, my voice breaking.

Shadows fell across Jameson's eyes. "Maybe not. Maybe I'm stretching. Maybe I'm just seeing what I want to see, seeing him the way I want to see him."

I thought about the files, about Jameson disappearing into the walls of Hawthorne House. "I'm here," I told him softly. "I am right here with you, Jameson Hawthorne." *Stop running.*

He shuddered. "Say *Tahiti*, Heiress."

I brought my hand to the side of his neck. *"Tahiti."*

"Do you want to know the worst part? Because the worst part

isn't knowing what my grandfather would do—and has done—to win. It's knowing in my gut and in my bones, with every fiber of my being, *why*. It's knowing that everything he's done in the name of winning, I would have done, too."

Jameson Winchester Hawthorne is hungry. That was what Skye had told me during my first few weeks at Hawthorne House. Grayson was dutiful and Xander was brilliant, but Jameson had been the old man's favorite because Tobias Hawthorne had been born *hungry*, too.

It hurt me to see them as alike. "Don't say that, Jameson."

"It was all just strategy to him," Jameson said. "He saw connections that other people missed. Everyone else played chess in two dimensions, but Tobias Hawthorne saw the third, and when he recognized a winning move, he took it."

There's nothing more Hawthorne than winning.

"Just because you *could* do it," I told Jameson fiercely, "doesn't mean you would have."

"Before you, Heiress? I *absolutely* would have." His voice was intense. "I can't even hate him now. He's a part of me. He's in me." Jameson's fingers lightly touched my hair, then curled into it. "But mostly, I can't hate him, Avery Kylie Grambs, because he brought me you."

He needed me to kiss him, and I needed it, too. When Jameson finally pulled away—*just one centimeter, then two*—my lips ached for his. He brought his mouth to my ear. "Now, back to the game."

CHAPTER 45

We worked until almost dawn, slept briefly, woke intertwined. We talked to Nan and Zara, played with the numbers, identified the church, which wasn't even in France, let alone in Margaux. We went back to the unused objects in the bag: a steamer, a flashlight, the USB.

By midmorning, we were stuck in a loop.

As if he'd divined the need for something to snap us out of it, Xander texted Jameson's phone. Jameson held it out for me to see. *911.*

"An emergency?" I asked.

"More like a summons," Jameson told me. "Come on." We made it as far as the hallway before we ran into Nash, who was leaving Libby's room in the clothes he'd worn the day before, holding a small, wiggling ball of chaos and brown fur.

"I really hope you didn't try to give that incredibly adorable puppy to my sister," I told him.

"He didn't." Libby padded into the hallway wearing an I EAT MORNING PEOPLE shirt and black pajama pants. "He knows better. That is a Hawthorne dog." Libby reached out to stroke the puppy's ear. "Nash found her in an alley. Some drunk assholes were poking at her with a stick." Knowing Nash as I did, I doubted that had turned out well for the drunk assholes. "He saved her," Libby continued, letting her hand drop. "That's what he does."

"I don't know, darlin'," Nash said, giving the pup a scratch, his eyes on my sister. "I was in pretty rough shape. Maybe she saved me."

I thought about little Nash watching Skye with his baby brothers, watching her give them away. And then I thought about Libby taking me in.

"You get Xander's nine-one-one?" Jameson asked his brother.

"Sure did," Nash drawled.

"Nine-one-one?" Libby frowned. "Is Xander okay?"

"He needs us," Nash told my sister, allowing the puppy to lick his chin. "We each only get one a year. A text like that comes in, it doesn't matter where you are or what you're doing. You drop everything and go."

"Xander just hasn't told us where to go yet," Jameson added.

Right on cue, Jameson's phone buzzed; Nash's, too. A series of texts came through in quick succession. Jameson angled his phone toward me so that I could see.

Xander had sent four photographs, each containing a little drawing. The first was a heart with the word *CARE* written in the middle of it. I scrolled to the second picture and frowned. "Is that a monkey riding a bicycle?"

Libby moved toward Nash and took his phone from his pocket. There was something intimate about the action—the way he let her, the way she knew he would. "The monkey appears to be saying *EEEEEE!*" Libby commented

Nash looked at the picture. "Could be a lemur," he opined.

I shook my head and looked at the third picture: Xander had drawn a tree. The fourth picture was an elephant jumping on a pogo stick, also saying *EEEEEE!*

I looked at Jameson. "Do you have any idea what this means?"

"As previously established, nine-one-one means Xander is calling us in," Jameson said. "By Hawthorne rules, this summons cannot be ignored. As for the pictures... work it out for yourself, Heiress."

I looked at the pictures again. The *care* heart. The animals yelling *Eeee.*

"Tree's an oak, if that helps," Nash told me. The puppy barked.

Care. Eee. Oak. Eee. I thought—and then I put it all together. "You've got to be kidding me," I told Jameson.

"What?" Libby asked.

Jameson smirked. "Hawthornes never kid about karaoke."

CHAPTER 46

Five minutes later, we were in the Hawthorne theater. Not to be confused with the Hawthorne *movie* theater, this one had a stage, a red velvet curtain, stadium and box seating—the whole shebang.

Xander stood on the stage, holding a microphone. A screen had been set up behind him, and there must have been a projector somewhere because "911!" danced on the screen.

"I need this," Xander said into the microphone. "You need this. We all need this. Nash, I've cued up the Taylor Swift for you. Jameson, get ready to break out those dance moves because this stage is calling your name, and we all know that your hips are utterly incapable of falsehood. And as for Grayson..." Xander paused. "Where *is* Gray?"

"Grayson Hawthorne skipping out on karaoke?" Libby said. "I'm shocked, I tell you. *Shocked.*"

"Gray has a voice so deep and smooth that you will shed literal tears as he sings something so old school that you will come to believe he spent the 1950s wearing the most dapper of suits and hanging out with his bestie, Frank Sinatra," Xander swore. He swung his gaze to his brothers. "But Gray's not here."

Jameson glanced at me. "You don't ignore a nine-one-one text," he told me. "No matter what."

"Where *is* Grayson?" Nash asked. And that was when I heard it—a sound halfway between a crash and the shattering of wood.

Jameson jogged out to the hallway. There was another crash. "Music room," he told us.

Xander jumped off the stage. "My duet will have to wait!"

"Who were you going to duet with?" Libby asked.

"Myself!" Xander yelled as he ran for the door, but Nash caught him.

"Hold on there, Xan. Let Jamie go." Nash looked toward me. "You go, too, kid."

I wasn't sure what Nash thought was going on here—or why he seemed so sure that Jameson and I were the ones Grayson needed.

"In the meantime," Nash told Xander, "give me the mic."

As Jameson and I made our way down the corridor, the sound of achingly beautiful violin music began drifting into the hall. The music room door was open, and when I stepped through it, I saw Grayson poised in front of open bay windows, wearing a suit without the jacket, his shirt unbuttoned, a violin pressed to his chin. His posture was perfect, each movement smooth.

The floor in front of him was covered with shards of wood.

I couldn't remember how many ultra-expensive violins Tobias Hawthorne had purchased in pursuit of *cultivating* his grandson's musical ability, but it looked like Grayson had destroyed at least one.

The song reached a final note, so high and sweet it was almost unbearable. Then there was silence as Grayson lowered the violin, took a step away from the windows, and then raised the instrument again—over his head.

Jameson caught his brother's forearm. "Don't." For a moment, the two of them grappled, sorrow and fury. "*Gray*. You're not hurting anyone but yourself." That had no effect, so Jameson went for the jugular. "You're scaring Avery. And you missed Xander's nine-one-one."

I wasn't scared. I could never be scared of Grayson—but I could ache for him.

Grayson slowly lowered the violin. "I apologize," he told me, his voice almost too calm. "It's your property I've been destroying."

I didn't care about my *property*. "You play beautifully," I told Grayson, pushing back the urge to cry.

"Beauty was expected," Grayson replied. "Technique without artistry is worthless." He looked down at the remains of the violin he'd destroyed. "Beauty is a lie."

"Remind me to mock you for saying that later," Jameson told him.

"Leave me," Grayson ordered, turning his back on us.

"If I'd known we were having a party," Jameson half sang, "I would have ordered food."

"A party?" I asked.

"A pity party." Jameson smirked. "I see you dressed for the occasion, Gray."

"You're right." Grayson walked toward the door. "This is self-indulgent. Thoroughly beneath me."

Jameson reached out to trip him, and then it was on. I understood now why Nash had sent Jameson. Sometimes Grayson Davenport Hawthorne needed a fight—and Jameson was only too happy to oblige.

"Let it all out," Jameson said, ramming his head into Grayson's stomach. "Poor baby."

Tobias Hawthorne hadn't just expected *beauty*. The four Hawthorne grandsons were also damn near lethal.

Grayson flipped Jameson onto his back, then went in for the kill. I knew Jameson well enough to realize that he'd just *let* himself be pinned.

Every muscle in Grayson's body was tight. "I thought that *we* failed *him*," he said, his voice low. "I thought we weren't enough. *I* wasn't enough, wasn't worthy. But you tell me, Jamie: What the hell is there for us to be worthy *of*?"

"He played to win," Jameson gritted out beneath his brother. "Always. You can't tell me that comes as a surprise."

"You're right." Grayson didn't loosen his grip. "He was ruthless. He raised us to be the same. Especially me."

Jameson locked his eyes onto his brother's. "To hell with what he wants. What do you want, Gray? Because we both know that you haven't let yourself want anything in a very long time."

The two of them were sucked into a staring contest: silvery gray eyes and deep green ones, one set narrowed and one wide open.

Grayson looked away first, but he didn't remove his forearm from Jameson's neck. "I want to get Toby back. For Eve." There was a pause, and then Grayson's head turned toward mine, the light reflecting off his blond hair in a near-halo. "For you, Avery."

I closed my eyes, just for a moment. "Jameson thinks—we both think—that there might be a connection between Toby's kidnapping and the game your grandfather left me. That it might tell us something."

Grayson angled his gaze back toward his brother's, then dropped his hold and abruptly stood.

I continued, "I know you didn't want to play—"

"I will," Grayson said, the words cutting through the air. He reached a hand down to Jameson and pulled him to his feet, leaving the two of them standing just inches apart. "I'll play, and I'll win," Grayson said, with the force of absolute law, "because we are who we are."

"We always will be," Jameson said. No matter how close I got to the Hawthorne brothers, there would always be things they shared that I could barely fathom.

"Here, Heiress." Jameson broke eye contact with his brother, removed the photograph from his pocket, and handed it to me. "You're the one who found this clue. You're the one who should explain it."

It felt significant: Jameson bringing me closer to Grayson instead of pushing me away.

I held the picture out, and Grayson's fingers brushed mine as he took it.

"We don't know who those three women are," I said. "There's a date on the back. And a caption. We can take you through what we've already done."

"That won't be necessary." Grayson's gaze was sharp. "What else was in the bag that our grandfather left you?"

I went to get it, and when I came back, Grayson and Jameson were standing farther apart. Both of them were breathing heavily, and the expressions on their faces made me wonder what had passed between them while I was gone.

"Here," I said, ignoring the tension in the room. I laid out the remaining three objects in the game, naming them as I did. "A steamer, a flashlight, a USB drive."

Grayson set the photograph down next to them. After what felt like a small eternity, he flipped the photograph over to read the caption once more.

"The date gives us numbers," Jameson said. "A code or—"

"Not a code," Grayson murmured, picking up the steamer. "A vintage." His gaze found its way slowly and inexorably to mine. "We need to go down to the wine cellar."

CHAPTER 47

As I pulled open the door to the wine cellar, so much of that night came back to me: the cocktail party, the way Grayson had deftly deflected every person who *just wanted a minute* of my time to tell me about *a unique financial opportunity*, the little girl in the pool, Grayson diving in to save her.

I could remember the way he'd looked climbing out of the water, dripping wet in an Armani suit. Grayson hadn't even asked for a towel. He'd acted like he wasn't even wet. I remembered people talking to him, the little girl being returned to her parents. I remembered the brief glimpse I caught of his face—his *eyes*—right before he disappeared down these stairs.

I'd known that he wasn't okay, but I'd had no idea why.

Focus on the game. I tried to stay in the moment—here, now, with both of them. Jameson went first down the spiraling stone steps. I was a step behind him, walking where he walked, not daring to look back over my shoulder at Grayson.

Just find the next clue. I let that be my beacon, my focus, but the moment we hit the bottom of the stone staircase, the landing came into view: a tasting room with an antique table made of the darkest cherry wood. Chairs sat on either side of the table, their arms carved so that the ends became lions: one set watchful, one set roaring.

And just like that, I was taken back.

The lines of Grayson's body are like architecture: his shoulders even, his neck straight, though his head and eyes are cast down. A crystal glass sits on the table in front of him. His hands lay on either side of the glass, the muscles in them tensed, like he might push off at any moment.

"You shouldn't be here." Grayson doesn't pull his eyes from the glass—or the amber liquid he's been drinking.

"And it's your job to tell me what I should and shouldn't do?" I retort. The question feels dangerous. Just being here does, for reasons I can't even begin to explain.

"Did someone say something to you?" I ask. "At the party—did someone upset you?"

"I do not upset easily," Grayson says, the words sharp. He still hasn't looked away from the glass, and I can't shake the feeling that I'm not supposed to be seeing this.

That no one is supposed to see Grayson Hawthorne like this.

"The child's grandfather." Grayson's tone is modulated, but I can see the tension in his neck, like the words want to come roaring out of him, ripping their way from his throat. "Do you know what he told me?" Grayson lifts his glass and drains what remains—every last drop. "He said that the old man would have been proud of me."

And there it is, the thing that has Grayson down here drinking alone. I cross to sit in the chair opposite his. "You saved that little girl."

"Immaterial." Haunted silver eyes meet mine. "She was easy to save." He picks up the bottle, pours exactly two fingers into the glass, those icy eyes of his watchful. There's tension in his fingers, his wrists, his neck, his jaw. "The true measure of a man is how many impossible things he accomplishes before breakfast."

I understand suddenly that Grayson is gutted because he doesn't believe that Tobias Hawthorne was or would be proud of him—not for saving that girl or anything else.

"Being worthy," he continues, "requires being bold." He lifts the glass to his mouth again and drinks.

"You are worthy, Grayson," I tell him, reaching for his hands and holding them in mine.

Grayson doesn't pull back. His fingers curl into fists beneath my hands. "I saved that girl. I didn't save Emily." That's a statement of fact, a truth carved into his soul. "I didn't save you." He looks up at me. "A bomb went off, and you were lying on the ground, and I just stood there."

His voice vibrates with intensity. Beneath my touch, I can feel his body doing the same.

"It's okay. I'm fine," I say, but it's clear he doesn't hear it—won't hear it. "Look at me, Grayson. I am right here. I am fine. We are fine."

"Hawthornes aren't supposed to break." His chest rises and falls. "Especially me."

I stand and make my way to his side of the table without ever letting go of his hands. "You're not broken."

"I am." The words are swift and brutal. "I always will be."

"Look at me," I say, but he won't. I bend down toward him. "Look at me, Grayson. You are not broken."

His eyes catch on mine. Our chests rise and fall in unison now.

"Emily was in my head." There's something hushed and barely restrained in his voice. "I heard her after the bomb went off, like she was right there. Like she was real."

This is a confession. I'm standing, and he's sitting, back straight, head bowed.

"For weeks, I hallucinated her voice. For weeks, she whispered to me." Grayson looks up at me. "Tell me again that I'm not broken."

I don't think. I just take his head in my hands. "You loved her, and you lost her," I start to say.

"I failed her, and she will haunt me until the day I die." Grayson's eyes close. "I'm supposed to be stronger than this. I wanted to be stronger than this. For you."

Those last two words nearly undo me. "You don't have to be anything for me, Grayson." I wait until he opens his eyes, until he's looking at me. "This," I say. "You. It's enough."

He drops from the chair to his knees, his eyes closing again, the enormity of this moment all around us. I kneel, wrap my arms around him.

"You're enough," I say again.

"It will never be enough."

The memory was everywhere. I could feel Grayson curling in on himself, into me. I could feel his shudder. And then he'd told me to go, and I'd fled because deep down, I knew what he meant when he said that it would never be enough. He meant *us*. What we were—and what we weren't. What had shattered in those weeks when Emily had been whispering in his ear.

What might have been.

What *could* have been.

What couldn't be, now.

The next day, Grayson had left for Harvard without even saying good-bye. And now he was back, right there behind me, and we were doing this.

Grayson, Jameson, and me.

"This way." Grayson nodded to a clear glass door to our right. When he opened it, a burst of cold air hit my face. Stepping through the doorway, I let out a long, slow breath, half expecting to see it, wispy and white in the chilly air.

"This place is enormous." I stayed in the present through sheer force of will. *No more flashbacks. No more what-ifs.* I focused on the game. That was what was needed. What I needed and what both of them needed from me.

"There are technically *five* cellars, all interconnected," Jameson narrated. "This one's for white wine. Through there is red. If you keep wrapping around, you'll hit scotch, bourbon, and whiskey."

There had to be a fortune down here in alcohol alone. *Think about that. Nothing but that.*

"We're looking for a red wine." Grayson's voice cut into my thoughts. "A Bordeaux."

Jameson reached for my hand. I took it, and he stepped away, allowing his fingers to trail down mine—an invitation to follow as he wound into the next room. I did.

Grayson pushed past me, past Jameson, snaking his way through aisle after aisle, scanning rack after rack. Finally, he stopped. "Chateau Margaux," he said, pulling a bottle out of the closest rack. "Nineteen seventy-three."

The caption on the photograph. Margaux. 1973.

"You want to guess what the steamer's for?" Jameson asked me.

A bottle of wine. A steamer. I took the Chateaux Margaux from Grayson, turning it over in my hand. Slowly, the answer took hold. "The label," I said. "If we try to tear it off, it might rip. But steam will loosen the adhesive. . . ."

Grayson held the steamer out to me. "You do the honors."

CHAPTER 48

On the back of the label of the lone bottle of Chateau Margaux 1973 in Tobias Hawthorne's collection, there was a drawing. A pencil sketch of a dangling, tear-drop crystal.

"Jewelry?" Grayson ventured a guess, but I'd already been in the vault.

"No," I said slowly, picturing the crystal in the drawing and thinking back. *Where have I seen something like that before?* "I think we're looking for a chandelier."

There were eighteen crystal chandeliers in Hawthorne House. We found the one we were looking for in the Tea Room.

"Are we going up?" I asked, craning my neck at the twenty-foot ceilings. "Or is that thing coming down?"

Jameson strolled over to a wall panel. He hit a button, and the chandelier slowly lowered to eye level. "For dusting purposes," he told me.

Even the thought of trying to dust this monstrosity gave me palpitations. There had to be at least a thousand crystals on the chandelier. One wrong move, and they could all shatter.

"What now?" I breathed.

"Now," Jameson told me, "we take it one by one."

Examining the individual crystals took time. Every few minutes, I brushed against Jameson or Grayson, or one of them brushed against me.

"This one," Grayson said suddenly. "Look at the irregularities."

Jameson was on top of him in a heartbeat. "Etching?" he asked.

Instead of responding to his brother, Grayson turned and handed the crystal to me. I stared at it, but if there was a message or clue contained in this crystal, I couldn't make it out with my naked eye.

We could use a jeweler's loupe, I thought. *Or—*

"The flashlight," I breathed. I reached inside the leather satchel. Locking my hand around the flashlight, I took a quick breath. I held out the crystal, then shined the light through. The irregularities caused the light to refract just so. At first, the result was incomprehensible, but then I flipped the crystal over and tried again.

This time, the flashlight's beam refracted to form a message. As I stared at the light projected onto the floor, there was no missing the words—the warning.

DON'T TRUST ANYONE.

CHAPTER 49

A chill hit the base of my neck, like the feeling of being watched from behind or standing knee-deep in long grass and hearing the rattle of a snake. My grip tightening around the crystal, I couldn't look away.

DON'T TRUST ANYONE.

"What is that supposed to mean?" I said, my stomach lined with dread as I finally looked to Jameson and Grayson in quick succession. "Is it a clue?"

We still had one object left in the bag. This wasn't over. Maybe the letters of this warning could be rearranged, or the first letter in every word made out initials, or—

"Can I see the crystal?" Jameson asked. I gave it to him, and he slowly rotated it under the flashlight's beam until he found what he was looking for. "There, at the top. Three letters, too small and faint to make out without the light."

"*Fin*?" Grayson said, an edge to the question.

"*Fin.*" Jameson placed the crystal back in my hand, then brought his dark green eyes to mine. "As in *finished*, Heiress. The end. This isn't a clue. This is *it*."

My game. Quite possibly the last bequest of Tobias Hawthorne.

And this was it? *Don't trust anyone.* "But what about the USB?" I said. The game couldn't be over. This couldn't be all that Tobias Hawthorne had left us with.

"Misdirection?" Jameson tossed out. "Or maybe the old man left you a game *and* a USB. Either way, this started with the delivery of the bag, and it ends here."

Setting my jaw, I righted the crystal in the flashlight's beam, and the words reappeared on the floor. *DON'T TRUST ANYONE.*

After everything, that was all the billionaire had for me? *My grandfather always thought seven steps ahead,* I could hear Jameson saying. *He saw dozens of permutations in how things could play out, planned for every eventuality, strategized for each and every possible future.*

What kind of strategy was this? Was I supposed to think that Toby's captor was closer than he appeared? That his reach was long, and anyone could be in his pocket? Was I supposed to question *everyone* around me?

Take a step back, I thought. *Go back to the beginning. Consider the framing and your charge.* I stopped. I breathed. And I thought. *Eve.* This game had been triggered when we met. Jameson had theorized that his grandfather had foreseen something about the trouble that had brought Eve here, but what if it was simpler than that?

Much, much simpler.

"This game started because Eve and I met." I said the words out loud, each leaving my mouth with the force of a shot, though I barely spoke over a whisper. "She was the trigger."

My thoughts jumped to the night before. To the solarium, the files, and Eve with her phone. "What if 'Don't trust anyone,'" I said slowly, "really means 'Don't trust her'?"

Until I said the words, I hadn't realized how much I'd let my guard down.

"If the old man had intended for you to be wary only of Eve, the message wouldn't have said *don't trust anyone*. It would have said *don't trust her*." Grayson spoke like someone who couldn't possibly be anything less than correct, let alone *wrong*.

But I thought about Eve asking to be left alone in Toby's wing. The way she'd looked at the clothes in my closet. How quickly she'd gotten Grayson on her side.

If Eve hadn't looked so much like Emily, would he be defending her now?

"*Anyone* includes Eve by definition," I pointed out. "It has to. If she's a threat—"

"*She. Is. Not. A. Threat.*" Grayson's vocal cords tensed against his throat. In my mind's eye, I could still see him on his knees in front of me.

"You don't want her to be one," I said, careful not to let myself feel too much.

"Do *you*, Heiress?" Jameson asked suddenly, his eyes searching mine. "Do you want her to be a threat? Because Gray's right. The message wasn't 'Don't trust her.'"

Jameson was the one who'd mistrusted Eve from the start! *I'm not jealous. That's not what this is.* "Last night," I said, my voice hitching, "I caught Eve taking pictures of the files in the solarium. She had an excuse. It sounded plausible. But we don't know her."

You don't know her, Grayson.

"And your grandfather never brought her here," I continued. "*Why?*" I brought my eyes back toward Jameson, willing him to latch on to the question. "What did he know about Eve that we don't?"

"Avery." Oren saying my name from the doorway was the only warning I got.

Eve walked into the Tea Room, her hair damp, wearing the

white dress she'd worn the day she arrived. "He knew about me?" She looked from me to Grayson, a portrait of devastation. "Tobias Hawthorne knew about me?"

I was a good poker player, in large part because I could spot a bluff, and this—her chin trembling, her voice hardening, the aching look in her eyes, the set of her mouth, like she wouldn't *let* her lips turn down—didn't feel like a bluff.

But a voice in the back of my head said three words. *Don't trust anyone.*

The next thing I knew, Eve was walking toward me. Oren moved to stand between us, and Eve's eyes angled upward, like she was taking a moment to steel herself. *Trying not to cry.*

She held out her phone. "Take it," Eve spat out. "Passcode three eight four five."

I didn't move.

"Go ahead," Eve told me, and this time, her voice sounded deeper, rougher. "Look at the photos. Look at anything you want, Avery."

I felt a stab of guilt, and I glanced at Jameson. He was watching me intently. I didn't let myself react—at all—when Grayson came to stand beside Eve.

Looking down, wondering if I'd made a mistake, I plugged the passcode Eve had given me into her phone. It unlocked the screen, and I navigated to her photo roll. She hadn't deleted the one I'd seen her taking, and this time, I identified which file she'd photographed.

"Sheffield Grayson." I brought my eyes back up to Eve's, but she wouldn't even look at me.

"I'm sorry," she told Grayson, her voice quiet. "But he's the wealthiest person in any of those files. He has motive. He has means. I know you said it wasn't him, but—"

"*Evie.*" Grayson gave her a look, the kind of Grayson Hawthorne look that burned itself into your memory because it said everything he wouldn't. "It's not him."

Sheffield Grayson was dead, but Eve didn't know that. And she was right: He *had* come after Toby. *Just not now.*

"If it's not Sheffield Grayson," Eve said, her voice cracking, "then we have *nothing.*"

I knew that feeling: the desperation, the fury, the frustration, the sudden loss of hope. But I still looked back down at Eve's phone and scrolled backward through her photo reel. *Don't trust anyone.* There were three more photos of Sheffield Grayson's file and a few of Toby's room, and that was it. If she'd taken photos of any other files—or anything else—they'd been deleted. I scrolled back further and found a picture of Eve and Toby. He looked like he was trying to swat the camera away, but he was smiling—and so was she.

There were more pictures of the two of them, going back months. Just like she'd said.

If the old man had intended for you to be wary only of Eve, the message wouldn't have said don't trust anyone. *It would have said* don't trust her.

Doubt shot through me, but I pulled up her call log. There were a lot of incoming calls, but she hadn't picked up a single one. She hadn't placed any, either. I went to her texts and quickly realized why she'd been getting so many calls. *The story. The press.* When I'd been in a similar situation, I'd had to get a new phone. I kept clicking through texts, needing to know if there was more, and then I came to one that said simply: *We have to meet.*

I looked up. "Who's this from?" I asked, angling the phone toward her.

"Mallory Laughlin," Eve shot back. "She left voicemails, too. You can verify the number." She looked down. "I guess she's seen the pictures of me. Rebecca must have given her my number. I turned my phone off once the story broke so I could concentrate on Toby, but look at all the good that did." Eve drew in a ragged breath. "I am done with this sick bastard's twisted little games." Her chin came up, and her emerald eyes went diamond hard. "And I am not going to stay where I'm not wanted. *I can't.*"

I could feel this entire situation getting away from me, like sand slipping through my fingers.

"Don't go," Grayson told Eve, the words soft. And then he turned to me, and that softness fell away. "Tell her not to go." This was the tone he'd used with me right after I'd inherited, the one made for warnings and threats. "I mean it, Avery." Grayson looked at me. I expected his eyes to be icy or blazing, but they were neither. "I have never asked for anything from you."

It was palpable in his voice: the many, many things he had never asked for.

I could feel Jameson watching me, and I had no idea what he wanted or expected me to do. All I knew was that if Eve left, if she walked out of Hawthorne House and past the gates, into the line of fire, and something happened to her, Grayson Hawthorne would never forgive me.

"Don't go," I told Eve. "I'm sorry."

I was, and I wasn't. Because those words just wouldn't leave me alone: *Don't trust anyone.*

"I want to meet Mallory." Eve lifted her chin. "She's my grandmother. And at least *she* didn't know about me."

"I'll take you to see her," Grayson said quietly, but Eve shook her head.

"Either Avery takes me," she said, equal parts challenge and injury in her tone, "or I walk."

CHAPTER 50

Oren wasn't happy about me leaving Hawthorne House, but when it became clear that I wasn't going to be dissuaded, he ordered security teams to all three SUVs. When we departed, a trio of identical vehicles pulled out past the gates, leaving the paparazzi hoarde with no way of knowing which one Eve and I were in.

Xander was the only Hawthorne with us. He'd come for Rebecca's sake, not Eve's, and Eve had allowed it. We'd left Grayson and Jameson behind.

"What's she like?" Eve asked Xander, once we were clear of the paparazzi. "My grandmother?"

"Rebecca's mom was always... intense." Xander's response pulled my attention away from the heavily tinted window. "She used to be a surgeon, but once Emily was born and they found out about her heart, Mallory quit to devote herself to managing Em's condition full-time."

"And then Emily died," Eve said softly. "And..."

"Kablooey." Xander made an exploding motion with his fingers. "Bex's mom started drinking. Her dad goes on these monthlong business trips."

"And now I'm here." Eve looked at her hands: her fingers were thin, her nails uneven. "So this is going to go really well," she muttered.

That was probably an understatement. I texted Thea to give her a heads-up. No response. I pulled up her social media and found myself staring at the last four photos she'd posted. Three of them were black-and-white self-portraits. In one, Thea stared directly at the camera, wearing heavy mascara, her face streaked black with tears. In the second, she was curled into a ball, her hands fisted, almost no clothing visible on her body. In the third, Thea was flipping off the camera with both hands.

Beside me, Eve looked at my phone. "I think I might like those even better than poetry." That sounded like the truth. Everything she said did. That was the problem.

I focused on Thea's fourth picture, the most recently uploaded, the only color photo in this set. There were two people in the picture, both laughing, their arms around each other: Thea Calligaris and Emily Laughlin. That picture was the only one with a caption: *She was MY best friend, and YOU don't know what you're talking about.*

I goggled at the enormous number of responses the picture had, then glanced at Xander. "Thea's doing damage control." I couldn't fight the gossip sites, but she could.

Xander angled his phone to me. "She posted a video, too." He hit Play.

"You may have heard certain . . . rumors." Thea's voice was coy. "About her." The picture of Thea and Emily flashed across the screen. "And them." A picture of all four Hawthorne brothers. "And her." The picture of Eve. "This. Is. A. Mess." Thea moved her body with each word, a captivating dance that made all of this seem less calculated. "But," she continued, "they're *my* mess. And those rumors about Grayson and Jameson Hawthorne and my dead best friend? They aren't true." Thea leaned toward the camera, until her face took up the whole screen. "And I know they're not true because I'm the one who started them."

The video ended abruptly, and Xander leaned his head back against the seat. "She is by far the most magnificent and terrifying individual I have ever fake dated."

Eve gave him a look. "You fake date a lot?"

She seemed so normal. I hadn't found anything on her phone. But I had to keep my guard up.

Didn't I?

CHAPTER 51

Rebecca answered the door before we even had a chance to knock. "My mom's right through there," she told Eve quietly. Taking a deep breath, Eve walked past Rebecca.

"On a scale of one to pi," Xander murmured, "how bad is it?"

Rebecca pulled her hand from his and laid three fingers on his palm. Her normally creamy skin was red and chapped around her nailbeds and knuckles.

Three, on a scale of one to pi. Given the value of pi, that definitely wasn't good.

Rebecca led Xander and me from the small entryway into the living room, where Eve and her mother were. The first thing I noticed were the snow globes sitting on a shelf. They looked like they had been polished until they gleamed. In fact, everything that I could see looked freshly cleaned, like it had been scrubbed and scrubbed again.

Rebecca's hands. I wondered if the cleaning had been her idea—or her mother's.

"Rebecca, this was supposed to be a family affair." Mallory Laughlin didn't take her eyes off Eve, even once Xander and I came into view.

Rebecca looked down, ruby-red hair falling into her face. She always looked like the kind of person an artist would want to paint. Even partially obscured, there was something fairy-tale beautiful about the pain on her face.

Eve reached out to take her grandmother's hand. "I'm the one who asked Avery to come with me. Toby... he considers her family, too."

Ouch. If Eve had meant that as a guilt trip, it was both brutal and effective.

"That's ridiculous." Mallory sat, and when Eve did the same, Mallory leaned toward her, drinking in her presence like a woman gulping down sand in a desert mirage. "Why would my son pay that girl any attention when you're right here?" She lifted a hand to the side of Eve's face. "When you're so perfect."

Beside me, Rebecca sucked a breath in around her teeth.

"I know I look like your daughter," Eve murmured. "This must be difficult."

"You look like me." Rebecca's mom smiled. "Emily did, too. I remember when she was born. I looked at her, and all I could think was that she *was* me. Emily was mine, and nobody was ever going to take her away from me. I told myself that she would never want for anything."

"I'm sorry for your loss," Eve said quietly.

"Don't be sorry," Mallory replied, a sob in her voice. "You've come back to me now."

"Mom." Rebecca cut in without ever looking up from the floor. "We talked about this."

"And I've told you that I don't need you or anyone else to infantilize me." Mallory's reply was sharp enough to slice through glass. "The world is like that, you know." The woman oriented back toward Eve, sounding more maternal. "You have to learn to take what you want—and never, ever let someone take what you don't want to give." Mallory laid a hand on Eve's cheek. "You're strong. Like me. Like Emily was."

This time, there was no audible response from Rebecca. I bumped my shoulder gently against hers, a silent, deliberate *I'm here.* I wondered if Xander felt as useless as I did standing there, watching her oldest scars seeping.

"Can I ask you something?" Eve said to Mallory.

Mallory smiled. "Anything, sweet girl."

"You're my grandmother. Is your husband here? Is he my grandfather?"

Mallory's reply was controlled. "We don't need to talk about that."

"All I've ever wanted is to know where I come from," Eve told her. "Please?"

Mallory stared at her for the longest time. "Could you call me Mom?" she asked softly. I saw Rebecca shake her head—not at her mother or at Eve or at anyone. She was just shaking it because this was not a good idea.

"Tell me about Toby's father?" Eve asked. "Please, Mom?"

Mallory's eyes closed, and I wondered what dead places inside of her had seized with life when Eve had uttered that one little word.

"Eve," I said sharply, but Rebecca's mother spoke over me.

"He was older. Very attractive. Very mysterious. We used to sneak around the estate, up to the House, even. I had free rein of it all in those days, but I was forbidden to bring guests. Mr. Hawthorne valued his privacy. He would have lost his mind if he'd known what I was getting up to, what we did in his hallowed halls." Mallory opened her eyes. "Teenage girls and the forbidden."

"What was his name?" Rebecca asked, taking a step toward her mother.

"This really doesn't concern you, Rebecca," Mallory snapped.

"What *was* his name?" Eve co-opted Rebecca's question. Maybe it was supposed to be a kindness, but it felt cruel because *she* got an answer.

"Liam," Mallory whispered. "His name was Liam."

Eve leaned forward. "What happened to him? Your Liam?"

Mallory stiffened like a marionette whose strings were suddenly pulled tight. "He left." Her voice was calm—too calm. "Liam left."

Eve took both of Mallory's hands in hers. "Why did he leave?"

"He just did."

The doorbell rang, and Oren strode to the door. I followed him to the foyer. As his hand closed over the knob, he gave an order, doubtless to one of his men outside.

"Close in." Oren glanced over his shoulder at me. "Stay put, Avery."

"Why is Avery staying put?" Xander asked, coming into the foyer beside me. Rebecca took one step to follow him, then hesitated, frozen in her own personal purgatory, caught between us and the words being murmured between Eve and her mother.

My brain got to the answer to Xander's question before Oren could articulate it. "This is the first time I've left the estate since the last package was delivered," I noted. "You're expecting another delivery."

In reply, my head of security answered the door with his gun drawn.

"Hello to you, too," Thea said dryly.

"Don't mind Oren." Xander greeted her. "He mistook you for a threat of the less passive-aggressive variety."

The sound of Thea's voice shattered the ice that had frozen Rebecca's feet to the ground. "Thea. I wanted to call, but my mom took my phone."

"And someone turned mine off," Thea said. She looked from Rebecca to me. "While I was in the shower, someone came into my house, into my bedroom, turned off my phone, and left *this* beside it, with handwritten instructions to bring it here."

Thea held out an envelope. It was a deep golden color, shining and reflective.

"Someone broke into your house?" I asked, my voice hushed.

"Into your bedroom?" Rebecca was beside Thea in a heartbeat.

Oren took possession of the envelope. He'd set a trap for the courier *here*, but the message had been delivered elsewhere—to Thea.

Did you see her photos? That video? I asked Toby's captor silently. *Is this what she gets, for helping me?*

"I had a guard on your house," Oren told Thea. "He didn't report anything unusual."

I stared at the envelope in Oren's hand, at my full name written across the front. *Avery Kylie Grambs.* Something in me snapped, and I snatched the envelope, turning it over to see a wax seal holding it closed.

The design of the seal took my breath away. *Rings of concentric circles.*

"It's like the disk," I said, the words catching in my throat.

"Don't open it," Oren told me. "I need to make sure—"

The rest of his words were lost to the roar in my mind. My fingers tore into the envelope, like my body had been set to autopilot at full throttle. Once I'd broken the seal, the envelope unfolded, revealing a message written on the interior in shining silver script.

363-1982.

That was it. Just those seven digits. *A phone number?* There was no area code, but—

"Avery!" Rebecca yelped, and I realized the paper I was holding had caught fire.

Flames devoured the message. I dropped it, and seconds later, the envelope and the numbers were nothing but ashes. "How..." I started to say.

Xander came to stand beside me. "I could rig an envelope to do that." He paused. "Honestly? I *have* rigged an envelope to do that."

"I told you to wait, Avery." Oren gave me what I could only describe as a Dad Look. I was clearly on very thin ice with him.

"What did the message say?" Rebecca asked me.

Xander produced a pen and a sheet of paper shaped like a scone, seemingly out of nowhere. "Write down everything you remember," he told me.

I closed my eyes, picturing the number—and then wrote: *363-1982.*

I turned the paper around so that Xander could see it. "Nineteen eighty-two." Xander latched on to the numbers after the dash. "Could be a year. The three-hundred-and-sixty-third day of which was December twenty-ninth."

December 29, 1982.

"Looks like a phone number to me," Thea scoffed.

"That was my first thought, too," I murmured. "But no area code."

"Was there anything that could indicate location?" Xander asked. "If we could derive an area code, that would give us a number to call."

A number to call. A date to check. And who knew how many other possibilities there were? It could be a cipher, coordinates, a bank account...

"I recommend we return to Hawthorne House immediately,"

Oren cut in. His expression was downright stony. "That is, if you're still interested in letting me do my job, Avery."

"I'm sorry," I said. I trusted Oren with my life, and I owed him better than making his job harder than it had to be. "I saw the seal on the envelope, and something in me snapped."

Rings of concentric circles. When Toby was taken, I'd thought that the disk might have something to do with why, but when his captor had sent it back, I'd assumed that I was wrong.

But what if I wasn't?

What if the disk had always been part of the riddle?

"The number could be a misdirection," Xander said, bouncing lightly on the balls of his feet. "The seal might *be* the message."

"Out!"

I turned back toward the living room. Mallory Laughlin was stalking toward us.

"I want all of you out of my house!"

Our presence here had never been welcome, and now there'd been *fire*.

"Ma'am." Oren held up a hand. "I'm recommending that we *all* return to Hawthorne House."

"What?" Thea asked, her honey-brown eyes narrowing.

Oren flicked his gaze toward her. "You should plan for an extended stay. Call it a slumber party."

"You think Thea's in danger." Rebecca looked around the room. "You think we all are."

"Breaking and entering is an escalation." Oren's tone was measured. "We're dealing with an individual who has proved that he is willing to go through intermediaries to get to Avery. He used Thea to send a message this time—and not just in the literal sense."

I can get to anyone. You can't protect them. That was the message.

"This is ridiculous," Rebecca's mom spat. "I won't be accompanying you anywhere, Mr. Oren, and neither will my daughters."

"Daughter," Rebecca said quietly. I felt my heart twist in my chest.

Oren was not dissuaded. "I'm afraid that even if you weren't already at risk, this visit would put you on our villain's radar. As much as you don't want to hear it, Ms. Laughlin—"

"It's *doctor,* actually," Rebecca's mother snapped. "And I don't care about the risk. The world can't take any more from me than it already has."

I moved closer to Rebecca, whose arms were wrapped around her middle, like all she could do was stand there and just keep taking the blows.

"That isn't true," Thea said quietly.

"Thea." Rebecca's voice was strangled. "Don't."

Mallory Laughlin spared a fond look for Thea. "Such a nice girl." She turned to Rebecca. "I don't know why you have to be so nasty to your sister's friends."

"I am not," Thea said, steel in her voice, "a nice girl."

"You need to come with us," Eve told Mallory. "I need to know you're safe."

"*Oh.*" Mallory's expression softened. There was something tragic about the moment the tension gave way, like it was the only thing that had kept her from crumbling. "You need a mother," she told Eve. The tenderness in her voice was almost painful.

"Come to Hawthorne House," Eve said again. "For me?"

"For you," Mallory agreed, not even sparing a look for Rebecca. "But I'm not setting a foot in the mansion. All these years, Tobias Hawthorne let me think my boy was dead. He never told me that I had a granddaughter. It was bad enough that he stole my baby, bad enough that those boys killed my Emily—*I am not stepping foot in the House.*"

“You can stay at Wayback Cottage,” Oren said soothingly. “With your parents.”

“I’ll stay with you,” Rebecca said quietly.

“No,” her mother snapped. “You love Hawthornes so much, Rebecca? Stay with them.”

CHAPTER 52

Oren called in one of the decoy SUVs to bring Mallory, Rebecca, and Thea back to the estate. Eve opted to ride with them instead of Xander and me, and when the second SUV pulled up to the House, neither she nor Mallory were in it.

"Eve said to tell you she's staying at the cottage." Rebecca looked down. "With my mom."

I am not going to stay where I'm not wanted, I could hear Eve saying. *I can't.* I felt another stab of guilt, then wondered if that was the point.

"She said she'll try to figure out what the number means herself," Thea added. "Just not here."

If Eve was trustworthy, I'd hurt her. Badly. But if she wasn't…

I turned to Oren. "You still have a man on Eve?"

"One for her," my head of security confirmed, "one for Mallory, six securing the gates, four more guarding the immediate perimeter here, and three besides me in the House."

That should have made me feel safer, but all I could think was *don't trust anyone.*

Alisa was waiting for me in the foyer. Oren must have known, but he hadn't warned me.

Before I could say a thing, a small barking blur rounded the corner.

An instant later, Libby followed, giving chase. "House too big!" she huffed. "Puppy too fast! I hate cardio!"

"Have you named her yet?" Xander called as the puppy closed in on us.

Libby stopped running and bent over, her hands on her knees. "I told you to name her, Xander. She's—"

"A Hawthorne dog," Xander finished. "As you wish." He picked the puppy up and snuggled her to his chest. "We shall call you Tiramisu," he declared.

"This is Nash's doing, I presume?" Alisa reached out to stroke the puppy's ear. "Fair warning," she told the pup softly, "Nash Hawthorne has never loved anything he didn't leave."

Libby stared at Alisa for a moment, then pushed her sweaty hair out of her kohl-rimmed eyes. "Would you look at that," she said in a deadpan. "It's time for my cardio."

As my sister stalked off, I narrowed my eyes at Alisa. "Was that really necessary?"

"We have bigger problems right now." Alisa held out her phone. There was a news article on the screen.

"People Are Getting Very Nervous": Hawthorne Heiress on Verge of Taking the Reins.

Apparently, *Market Watch* did not have a high opinion of my capabilities. All ventures in which Tobias Hawthorne had been a major investor were being flagged with caution.

"The onslaught continues," I muttered. "I don't have time for this."

"And you won't have to be the one to deal with things like this," Alisa replied, "if you establish a trust."

Don't trust anyone. Suddenly, I heard that warning in a different way. Had Tobias Hawthorne meant it to have a double meaning?

The closer I got to the year mark, the harder Alisa pushed, and the closer she and her firm got to losing the reins.

"Leave her alone, Alisa."

I looked up to see Jameson striding toward us. He was wearing a crisp white dress shirt, cuffed to his forearms. "A trust isn't necessary. Avery can make do with financial advisors."

"Financial advisors won't calm anyone's nerves about the idea of an eighteen-year-old calling the shots with one of the world's biggest fortunes." Alisa offered Jameson a closed-lipped, *the defense rests* kind of smile. "Perception matters." She turned back to me. "And to that end, there's something else you should see."

She took her phone from me, toggled to a new page, then passed it back to me. This time, I found myself looking down at the celebrity gossip site that had broken the story about Emily and Eve.

Switching Hawthornes? Hawthorne Heiress and Her Swinging New Lifestyle.

Beneath that *lovely* headline, there was a series of pictures. *Jameson in his tuxedo and me in my ball gown, dancing on the beach. A still frame taken from an interview I'd done months ago with Grayson—when he'd kissed me.* The last picture was of me with Xander, standing on the porch at Rebecca's house less than an hour earlier.

I hadn't realized the paparazzi had caught us there. *Then again, maybe it wasn't the paparazzi.* It was getting harder not to feel like our adversary was everywhere.

"Let's look at the positives here," Xander suggested. "I look dashing in that photo."

"There's no reason for Avery to see something like this," Jameson said forcefully.

Jameson Winchester Hawthorne in protective mode was a thing to behold.

"Perception matters," Alisa reiterated.

"Right now," I replied, handing her phone back to her, "other things matter more. Tell me you've found something, Alisa. Who's pulling the strings?"

She'd said that she was on it days ago—and then I hadn't heard a word.

"Do you know how many people there are out there with a net worth of at least two hundred million dollars?" Alisa said calmly. "About thirty thousand. There are eight hundred billionaires in the United States alone, and this wouldn't take billions."

"It would take connections."

I looked up to the stairs—and Grayson. He walked down them to join us but stopped short of looking at me. He was wearing all black, but not a suit.

"Whatever you have," Grayson told Alisa, "send it to me." Finally—*finally*—his eyes made their way to mine. "Where's Eve?"

I felt like he'd struck me.

"The cottage." Rebecca answered. "With my mom and grandpa."

"If we find anything," I said, trying not to let Grayson's cutting look cut me, "we'll call her."

"Find anything..." Jameson's eyes laser-locked on mine. "About what?"

"The person who took Toby is getting more aggressive," Oren said.

"More aggressive how?" Alisa pressed.

Xander held Tiramisu up to his face and spoke in the puppy's voice. "Don't worry. The fire was very small."

"What fire?" Jameson demanded, and he closed the space between us taking my hand. "Tell us, Heiress."

"Another envelope. The message caught fire when it hit the air. Seven numbers."

Jameson's thumb traced the heel of my hand. "Well then, Heiress. Game on."

CHAPTER 53

We had two potential clues: the seal and the number. Given that we were no closer to identifying the disk than Jameson and I had been for months, I opted to concentrate on the number.

Divide and conquer wasn't a Hawthorne family motto, but it might as well have been. Grayson took financials: bank records, investment accounts, transactions. Xander, Thea, and Rebecca took the date angle: *December 29, 1982*. That left a myriad of possibilities for Jameson and me, among them the phone number. If we really were missing an area code, then filling in the blank would accomplish two things: First, it would give us a number to try calling. Second, it would give us a location.

A hint to where Toby was being held? Or another piece of the riddle?

"There are more than three hundred area codes in the United States," Jameson said from memory.

"I'll print out a list," I told him, but what I really wanted to say was *Are we okay?*

Thirty minutes into making phone calls—each area code, followed by *363-1982*—I hadn't had a single call go through. Taking a break, I plugged the number into an internet search and skimmed the results. *A court case involving discriminatory housing practices. A baseball card valued at over two thousand dollars. A hymn from the 1982 Hymnal in the Episcopal Church.*

A phone rang. I looked up. Thea held up her phone. "Blocked number," she said, and because she was Thea Calligaris and didn't know the meaning of the words *hesitation* or *second-guess*, she answered.

Two seconds later, she passed the phone to me. I pressed it to my ear. "Hello?"

"Who am I?" a voice—*that* voice—said.

That question didn't just *get* under my skin; it had been living there for days, and I wondered if he'd called Thea's phone for the sole purpose of reminding me that he'd gotten to her.

"You tell me," I replied. He wasn't going to get a rise out of me. Not now.

"I already did." His voice was as smooth as ever, his cadence distinct.

Jameson grabbed the list with the area codes, then scrawled a message on it. *ASK ABOUT THE DISK.*

"The disk," I said. "You knew what it was." I paused to allow for a response that never came. "When you sent it back to me as proof that you had Toby, you knew what it was worth."

"Intimately."

"And you want me to guess? What it is, what all of this means?"

"Guessing," Toby's captor said silkily, "is for those too weak in mind or spirit to *know*."

That sounded like something Tobias Hawthorne would have said.

"I had a program installed on your little friend's cell phone. I've been tracking you, listening to you. You're there, in his inner sanctum, aren't you?"

Tobias Hawthorne's study. That was what he meant by inner sanctum. He *knew* where we were. The phone in my hand felt dirty, threatening. I wanted to hurl it out a window, but I didn't.

"Why does it matter where I am?" I asked.

"I tire of waiting." Somehow, that sounded more threatening than any words I'd ever heard this man speak. *"Look up."*

The line went dead. I handed the phone to Oren. "He had someone install a program to let him spy on us." So why had he given it up?

Because he wants me to know that he's everywhere.

Oren dropped the phone and stamped his heel down on it, hard. Thea's outraged squeal was drowned out by the cacophony of thoughts in my head.

"*Look up.*" I repeated the words. My eyes traveled toward Jameson's. "He asked me if I was in your grandfather's inner sanctum, but I think he knew the answer. And he told me to *look up.*"

I angled my head toward the ceiling. It was high, with mahogany beams and custom moldings. If *look up* had been part of one of Tobias Hawthorne's riddles, I would have been fetching a ladder right now, but we weren't dealing with Tobias Hawthorne.

"He's been listening to us," I said, feeling that like oil on my skin. "But even if he hacked Thea's camera, he wouldn't have been able to see me. So where would someone picture me in this room if they didn't know where I was sitting?"

I walked toward Tobias Hawthorne's desk. I knew he'd spent hours sitting there, working, strategizing. Putting myself in his position, I took a seat behind the desk. I looked down at it, like I was working, and then I looked up. When that didn't work, I thought about the way that neither Jameson nor Xander could think sitting down. Standing, I walked to the other side of the desk. *Look up.*

I did and found myself staring at the wall of trophies and medals that the Hawthorne grandsons had won: national championships in everything from motocross to swimming to pinball; trophies for surfing, for fencing, for riding bulls. These were the talents that Tobias Hawthorne's grandsons had cultivated. These were the kind of results he'd expected.

There were other things on the wall, too: comic books written by Hawthornes; a coffee table book of Grayson's photographs; some patents, most of them in Xander's name.

The patents, I realized with a start. Each certificate had a number on it. *And each number,* I thought, the world around me suddenly crisp and in hyperfocus, *has seven digits.*

CHAPTER 54

We looked up US Patent number 3631982. It was a utility patent issued in 1972. There were two patent holders: Tobias Hawthorne and a man named Vincent Blake.

Who am I? the man on the phone had said. And when I'd told him to tell me, he'd said that he already had.

"Vincent Blake," I said, turning to the boys. "Did your grandfather ever mention him?

"No," Jameson replied, energy and intensity rolling off him like a storm rolling in. "Gray? Xan?"

"We all know the old man had secrets." Grayson's voice was tight.

"I got nothing," Xander admitted. He wedged himself in front of me to get a better look at the computer screen, then scrolled through the patent information and stopped on a drawing for the design. "It's a mechanism for drilling oil wells."

That rang a bell. "That's how your grandfather made his money—at least at first."

"Not with this patent," Xander scoffed. "Look. Right here!" He pointed at the drawing, at some detail I couldn't even make out. "I'm not exactly an expert at petroleum engineering, but even I can see that right there is what one would call a fatal flaw. The design is supposed to be more efficient than prior technology, but..." Xander shrugged. "Details, details, boring things—long story short is that this patent is worthless."

"But that's not the only patent the old man filed in nineteen seventy-two." Grayson's voice was like ice.

"What was the other patent?" I asked.

A few minutes later, Xander had it pulled up. "The goal of this mechanism is the same," he said, looking at the design, "and you can see some elements of the same general framework—but this one *works*."

"Why would anyone file two patents in the same year with such similar designs?" I asked.

"Utility patents cover the creation of new or improved technologies." Jameson came to stand behind me, his body brushing mine. "Breaking a patent isn't easy, but it can be done if you can weasel your way around the claims to uniqueness made by the prior patent. You have to break each claim individually."

"Which this patent does," Xander added. "Think of it like a logic puzzle. This design changes just enough that the infringement case isn't there—and *then* it adds the new piece, which forms the basis of *its* claims. And it's that new piece that made this patent valuable."

This patent had only one holder: Tobias Hawthorne. My mind raced. "Your grandfather filed a bad patent with a man named Vincent Blake. He then immediately filed a better and non-infringing patent by himself, one that made the first completely worthless."

"And made our grandfather millions," Grayson added. "Before that, he was working on oil rigs and playing inventor at night. And afterward..."

He became Tobias Hawthorne.

"Vincent Blake." My chest tightened around my racing heart. "That's who we're dealing with. That's who has Toby. And this is why he wants revenge."

"A patent?"

I looked up to see Eve. "I texted her," Grayson told me, preempting any suspicions I might have had about her sudden appearance.

"All of this," Eve continued, emotion palpable in her tone, "because of a *patent*?"

Who am I? Vincent Blake had asked me. But that wasn't the end of this. It couldn't be. I'd thought the riddle was who took Toby—and why. But what if there was a third element, a third question?

What does he want?

"We need to know who we're dealing with." Grayson sounded nothing like the shattered boy from the wine cellar. He sounded more than capable of *dealing with* threats.

"You've really never heard of this guy?" Thea asked. "He's rich and powerful and hates your family's guts, and you've never even heard his name?"

"You know as well as I do," Grayson replied, "that there are different kinds of rich."

Jameson tossed me his phone, and I skimmed the information he'd pulled up on Vincent Blake. "He's from Texas," I noted. This state suddenly felt much smaller. "Net worth just under half a billion dollars."

"Old oil money." Jameson met Grayson's gaze. "Blake's father hit liquid gold in the Texas oil boom of the nineteen thirties. By the late nineteen fifties, a young Vincent had inherited it all. He spent two more decades in oil, then pivoted to ranching."

That didn't tell us anything about what the man was *really* capable of—or what he wanted. "He must be in his eighties now," I said, trying to stick to the facts.

"Older than the old man," Grayson stated, his tone balanced on a knife's edge between icy and cool.

"Try adding your grandfather's name to the search terms," I told Jameson.

Besides the patent, we got one other hit: a magazine profile from the eighties. Like most coverage of Tobias Hawthorne's meteoric rise, it mentioned that his first job had been working on an oil rig. The difference was that this article also mentioned the name of the man who had owned that rig.

"So Blake was his boss," Jameson spitballed. "Picture this: Vincent Blake owns the whole damn company. It's the late sixties, early seventies, and our grandfather is nothing but a grunt."

"A grunt with big ideas," Xander added, tapping his fingers rapidly against his thigh.

"Maybe Tobias takes one of those ideas to the boss," I suggested. "The gutsy move pays off, and they end up collaborating on the design for a new kind of drilling technology."

"At which point," Grayson continued with deadly calm, "our grandfather double-crosses a rich and powerful man to claim a fortune in intellectual property for himself."

"And said powerful man doesn't sue him into oblivion?" Xander was dubious. "Just because the second patent doesn't infringe the first doesn't mean that a wealthy man couldn't have buried a nobody from nowhere in legal fees."

"So why didn't he?" I asked, my body buzzing with the adrenaline that always accompanied finding the kind of answer that raised a thousand more questions.

We knew who had Toby.

We knew what this was about.

But there were still details that ate at me, pulling at the edges of my mind. The disk. The *three* characters in the story. *What's his endgame here? What does he want?*

"Someone must know more about Blake's connection to your grandfather." Eve looked at each of the Hawthorne brothers in turn.

I thought through our next move. Tobias Hawthorne had married Alice in 1974—just two years after the patent was filed. And when Jameson had asked Nan about friends and mentors, her response had been that Tobias Hawthorne had never been in the business of making friends.

She hadn't said a word about mentors.

CHAPTER 55

This time, I went to see Nan alone. "Vincent Blake." I placed the metallic disk on the dining room table, where Nan was having tea.

She snorted in my general direction. "That supposed to be a bribe?"

Either Nan had no more idea what the disk was than we did, or she was bluffing. "Tobias Hawthorne worked for a man named Vincent Blake in the early seventies. It might have been before he and Alice started dating—"

"It wasn't," Nan grunted. "Long courtship. The fool insisted he wanted to make something of himself before he gave my Alice his ring."

Nan was there. She remembers.

"Tobias and Vincent Blake collaborated on a patent," I said, trying to tune out the incessant pounding of my heart. "And then your son-in-law cheated Blake out of a development that was worth millions."

"Did he now?" For a moment, it seemed like that was all Nan was going to say, then she scowled. "Vincent Blake was rich and fancied himself more powerful than God. He took a liking to Tobias, brought him into the fold."

"But?" I prompted.

"Not everyone was happy about it. Mr. Blake liked to pit his protégés against each other. His son was too young to be a factor back then, but Mr. Blake had made it very clear to his nephews that being family didn't get you a free pass. Power had to be earned. It had to be *won*."

"Won," I repeated. I thought of that first phone call with Blake. *I'm just an old man with a fondness for riddles.* All this time, we'd thought that Toby's captor was playing one of Tobias Hawthorne's games. But what if Tobias Hawthorne had taken his cue from Vincent Blake? What if, before he'd been the orchestrator of those Saturday morning games, he'd been a player?

"What happened?" I pressed Nan. "If Tobias was in Blake's inner circle, why double-cross him?"

"Those nephews I mentioned? They wanted to send a message. Mark their territory. Put Tobias in his place."

"What did they do?" I asked.

"There was no Mrs. Blake in those days," Nan grunted. "She passed away when their little boy was born, and the child couldn't have been more than fifteen when Mr. Blake started inviting Tobias over for dinner. Eventually, Tobias started bringing my Alice along. Mr. Blake took a liking to her, too, but he was of a certain type." She gave me a look. "The type who believed that boys would be boys."

"Did he..." I couldn't even finish the sentence. "Did they..."

"If you're thinking the worst, the answer is *no*. But if you're thinking that the nephews came at Tobias through Alice, that they harassed her, manhandled her, and one went so far as to pin her down, force his lips to hers—*well, then*."

Nan had strongly implied on more than one occasion that she'd killed her first husband, a man who'd broken her fingers for playing the piano a little too well. I deeply suspected she would have castrated Vincent Blake's nephews if she'd had even half a chance.

"And Blake didn't do anything?" I asked.

Nan didn't reply, and I remembered how she'd characterized the man: as the type who believed that boys would be boys. "And that's when your son-in-law decided to get out," I guessed, the picture becoming clearer.

"Tobias stopped dreaming of working for Blake and set his sights on becoming him. A better version. A better *man*."

"So he filed two patents," I said. "One that they'd worked on together and then a different one—a better one. Why didn't Blake sue him?"

"Because Tobias beat him, fair and square. Oh, it was a little underhanded, maybe, and a betrayal, certainly, but Vincent Blake appreciated someone who could play the game."

A rich and powerful man had let a young Tobias Hawthorne go, and in return, Tobias Hawthorne had eclipsed him—billions to his millions.

"Is Blake dangerous?" I asked.

"Men like Vincent Blake and Tobias—they're always dangerous," Nan replied.

"Why didn't you tell Jameson and me this earlier?"

"It was more than forty-five years ago," Nan scoffed. "Do you know how many enemies this family has made since then?"

I thought about that. "Your son-in-law had a list of threats. Blake wasn't on it."

"Then Tobias must not have considered Blake a threat—that, or he thought the threat was neutralized."

“Why would Blake take Toby?” I asked. “Why now?”

“Because my son-in-law isn’t here anymore to hold him at bay.” Nan took my hand and held it tight. The expression on her face grew tender. “You’re the one playing the piano now, girl. Men like Vincent Blake—they’ll break every one of those fingers of yours if you let them.”

CHAPTER 56

As I made my way back to the others, I thought about the fact that Vincent Blake had addressed every one of his missives to *me*. And he'd made it clear on the phone that he wouldn't speak to anyone but "the heiress."

You're the one playing the piano now, girl.... Nan's words were still echoing in my mind when I stepped into the foyer and heard a hushed conversation, bouncing off the walls of the Great Room.

"Don't do this." That was Thea, her voice low and intense. "Don't fold in on yourself."

"I'm not." *Rebecca.*

"Don't be *sad*, Bex."

Rebecca read meaning in that emphasis. "Be angry."

"Hate your mom, hate Emily and Eve, hate me if you have to, but don't you dare disappear."

The second he saw me, Jameson crossed the foyer. "Anything?"

I swallowed. "Vincent Blake brought your grandfather into his inner circle. Treated him like family—or his version of family, anyway."

"The prodigal son." Jameson's eyes lit on mine.

"Eve?" That was Grayson—and he was yelling. I scanned the

foyer. *Oren, Xander, Thea and Rebecca stepping in from the Great Room. But no Eve.*

Grayson burst into view. "Eve's gone. She left a note. She's going after Blake."

"What about her guard?" I asked Oren.

Grayson was the one who answered. "She went to the bathroom, gave him the slip."

"Should we be worried?" Xander threw that question out there.

Men like Vincent Blake and Tobias, I could hear Nan warning me, *they're always dangerous*.

"I'm going after her." Grayson viciously cuffed his sleeves, like he was preparing for a fight.

"Grayson, stop," I said urgently. "Think." Eve bolting made no sense. Did she think she could just show up on Vincent Blake's door and demand Toby back?

Jameson stepped between Grayson and me. He held my gaze for a second or two, then turned to his brother. "Stand down, Gray."

Grayson looked like someone who didn't know the meaning of the words. He was stone: unmovable, the muscles in his jaw rock hard. "I can't fail her again, Jamie."

Again. My heart twisted. Jameson placed a hand on his brother's shoulder. "I invoke *On Spake*."

Grayson swore. "I don't have time—"

"*Make. Time*." Jameson leaned forward and said something—I couldn't hear what—directly into Grayson's ear. *On Spake* was a Hawthorne rite; it meant that Grayson couldn't speak until Jameson was done.

As Jameson finished whispering furiously in his ear, Grayson stood very still. I waited for him to call for a fight, to exercise his right to respond to what Jameson had said in a physical way. But instead, Grayson Davenport Hawthorne parted with two and only two words. "I waive."

"Waive what?" Rebecca asked.

Thea snorted derisively. "Hawthornes."

"Heiress?" Jameson turned back to me. "I need to speak to you. Alone."

CHAPTER 57

Jameson led me to the third floor, to a hobby room filled with model trains. There were dozens of them and twice as many tracks set up on glass tables. Jameson pressed a button on the side of one of the trains. At his touch, the wall behind us split in two, revealing a hidden room the size and shape of an old-fashioned phone booth. Its walls were made entirely out of gemstone slabs—a shining, metallic black for half the room and iridescent white for the other.

"Obsidian," Jameson told me. "And agate crystal."

"What are we doing here, Jameson?" I asked. "What do you need to tell me?"

It felt like we were on the verge of something. *A secret? A confession?* Jameson nodded toward the gemstone room. I stepped inside. The ceiling overhead glimmered in a rainbow of colors—more gems.

I realized too late that Jameson hadn't followed me into the room.

The wall behind me closed. It took me a second to process what had just happened. *Jameson trapped me in here.* "What are you doing?" I banged on the wall. "Jameson!" My phone rang. "Let me out of here," I demanded the second I hit Answer.

"I will," Jameson promised on the other end of the line. "When we get back."

We. Suddenly, I understood why Grayson had waived his right to fight, post–*On Spake*. "You promised him you'd go after Eve together."

Jameson didn't tell me I was wrong.

"What if she's dangerous?" I asked. "Even if all she wants is to get Toby back, can you honestly say that she wouldn't trade you or Grayson to get him? We barely know her, and your grandfather's message said—"

"Heiress, have you ever known me to shy away from danger?"

My fingers curled into a fist. Jameson Winchester Hawthorne lived for danger. "If you don't let me out of here, Hawthorne, I will—"

"Do you want to know how I got my scar?" Jameson's voice was softer than I'd ever heard it. I knew immediately what scar he was talking about.

"I want you to open the door," I said.

"I went back." He let those words linger. "To the place where Emily died—*I went back.*"

Emily's heart had given out after cliff jumping. "Jameson..."

"I jumped from dangerously high up, the way she did. Nothing happened the first time. Or the second. But the third..."

I could picture the scar in my mind, running the full length of Jameson's torso. How many times had I dragged my fingers along its edges, feeling the smooth skin of his stomach on either side?

"There was a fallen tree, submerged in the water. I could only see one branch. I had no idea what was underneath. I thought I'd cleared the whole thing, but I was wrong."

I pictured Jameson barreling down from the top of a cliff, hitting the water. I pictured a jagged branch catching his flesh, barely slowing him down.

"I didn't feel pain, not at first. I saw blood in the water—and *then* I felt it. Like my skin was on fire. I made my way to the shore, my body screaming. Somehow, I managed to pull myself to my feet. The old man was standing there. He didn't bat an eye at the blood, didn't ask me if I was okay, didn't yell. All he said, looking my bleeding body up and down, was *Got that out of your system, did you?*"

I leaned against the wall of my gemstone cage. "Why are you telling me this now?"

I could hear the sound of his footstep on the end of the line. "Because Gray is going to keep jumping until it hurts. He's always been the solid one, Heiress. The one who never trembles, never backs down, never doubts. And now, he's lost his mooring, and I have to be the strong one."

"Take me with you," I told Jameson.

"Just this once," he said, an aching tone in his voice, "let *me* be the one who protects you, Avery."

He'd used my actual name. "I don't need you to protect me. You can't just leave me here, Jameson!"

"Can't. Shouldn't. Have to. This is my family's mess, Heiress." For once, there was nothing wicked in Jameson's tone, no innuendo. "It's up to us to clean it up."

"And what about Eve?" I asked. "You know what your grandfather said. *Don't trust anyone.* Grayson isn't thinking straight, but you—"

"I'm thinking more clearly than I ever have. I don't trust Eve." His voice was low and aching. "The only person I trust with all that I am and all that could be, Heiress, is you."

And just like that, Jameson Winchester Hawthorne hung up the phone.

CHAPTER 58

I was going to throttle Jameson. The two of us were races and wagers and dares, not this.

I tried calling Oren, but it went to voicemail. Libby didn't pick up, either, which probably meant her phone wasn't charged. I tried Xander, then Rebecca. I was halfway to calling Thea before I remembered her phone had been destroyed. Trying to calm myself, I took out my knife, plotted murder, then gave away ten thousand dollars to strangers struggling to pay rent.

Finally, I texted Max. *Jameson locked me in the world's most expensive dungeon,* I wrote. *He's got some asinine idea about protecting me.*

Max's reply didn't take long. *THAT GREEN-EYED BASTARD.*

I grinned despite myself and typed back: *You cursed.*

Max replied in rapid-fire: *Would you prefer "smirking, paternalistic ship-head who can shove his mother-faxing paternalism up his mother-faxing asp"?*

I snorted, then finally calmed down enough to take in the three-hundred-and-sixty-degree view of the gemstone room. *Two walls made of obsidian,* I thought. *Two walls made of white agate.* Probing the walls didn't lead me to an exit switch but did reveal that the gemstones had been formed into bricks, and if you pressed at the top or bottom of any of those bricks, they rotated. Rotating a black brick turned it white. Rotating a white brick turned it black.

I thought about all the times I'd seen Xander fiddling with a handheld puzzle, then craned my neck, taking in every detail of the walls, the ceiling, the floor. Jameson hadn't locked me in a dungeon.

He'd locked me in an *escape room*.

Three hours in, I still hadn't hit on the right pattern, and with each passing minute, I wondered if Jameson and Grayson had caught up to Eve. Warnings of all kinds swirled in my mind.

Don't trust anyone.

Anyone close to you could be the next target.

I tire of waiting.

In my darkest moments, I thought about how Eve had sworn that she would do anything—*anything*—to get Toby back.

Don't think about her. Or them. Or any of it. I stared at the glittering room around me—the opulence, the beauty—and tried not to feel like the walls were closing in. "Glittering," I muttered. "Opulence. What about diamonds?"

I'd already tried dozens of designs: *the letter H; a chessboard, a key*...

Now I tried a black diamond on each of the white walls, a white diamond on each of the black ones. *Nothing.* Frustrated, I swept my hand over one of the diamonds, wiping it away.

Click.

My eyes went wide at the sound. *Two black diamonds, one white one, nothing on the other obsidian wall.* With a second click, a panel on the floor popped up. I squatted to get a better look. *Not a panel. A trapdoor.* "Finally!"

No thinking, no hesitation, I dropped down into darkness. I grabbed my phone and switched on the flashlight, then followed the twists and turns of the winding passageway until I hit a ladder. I climbed it and came to a ceiling—and another trapdoor.

Laying my palms flat against it, I pushed until it gave, then pulled myself up into a bedroom, though not one I'd seen before. A beat-up six-string guitar leaned against the wall in front of me; a king-sized bed made of what looked to be repurposed driftwood sat to my left. I turned around to see Nash perched on a metal stool next to a large wooden workbench that seemed to be doubling as a dresser.

He was blocking the door.

I walked toward him. "I'm leaving," I said, my temper simmering. "Don't try to stop me. I'm going after Jameson and Grayson."

"That right?" Nash didn't move from the stool. "I taught you to fight because I trust you to *think*, kid." He stood, his expression mild. "That trust misplaced?" Nash gave me a second to chew on that question, then stepped aside, clearing the way to the door.

Damn it, Nash. I blew out a long breath. "No."

I thought past my fury and worry and the dark, looping thoughts. I was three hours behind, and it wasn't like Oren would have let Jameson and Grayson run off alone.

"If you want to borrow some duct tape when the knuckleheads get back," Nash drawled, "I could be persuaded."

"Thanks, Nash." A little calmer, I stepped into the hall and saw Oren. "Jameson, Grayson, and Eve," I said immediately, an edge in my voice. "What's their status?"

"Safe and accounted for," Oren reported. "Eve made it to the Blake compound but wasn't allowed admittance. The boys got there shortly thereafter and talked her down. They're all on their way back now."

Relief hit, clearing the way for my annoyance to surge. "You let Jameson lock me up!"

"You were safe." Oren's lips twitched. "Secured."

"Behold!" boomed a voice from the other side of Oren. "The heroes ride into battle! Avery will be liberated!"

I looked past Oren to see Xander, Thea, and Rebecca incoming. Xander was holding an enormous metal shield that looked like it had been lifted straight off the arm of a medieval knight.

"I swear to all that is good and holy," Thea said under her breath, "if you say one more word about LARPing right now, Xander—"

I stepped around Oren. "I appreciate the 'rescue,' Xan, but you couldn't answer your phone?" I looked to Rebecca. "You, either?"

"Sorry," Rebecca said. "My phone was on silent. We were blowing off some steam." Her green eyes slid to Thea's. "Playing pool."

I glanced at Thea. Her sweater was ripped at the shoulder, her hair markedly less than perfect. The two of them might have been in the billiards room or arcade, but there was no way in hell they'd been *playing pool.* But at least Rebecca didn't look like a shell of herself anymore.

"What's your excuse?" I asked Xander.

He held his shield to the side. "Step into my office."

I rolled my eyes but joined him.

Xander used the shield to block us off from Oren, then led me around the corner. "I went down the rabbit hole of doing a deep dive on Vincent Blake's holdings, current and past," Xander admitted. "Blake was the sole funder of the VB Innovation Lab." Xander paused, steeling himself. "I recognized the name. VB is where Isaiah Alexander worked right after he was fired."

Xander's father worked for Vincent Blake. That thought was like a domino in my mind, knocking down another and another. *There are three characters in the parable of the prodigal son, are there not?*

The king, the knight, and the bishop. The son who'd stayed faithful.

"Does Isaiah Alexander still work for Blake?" I asked Xander, my mind whirring.

"No," Xander said emphatically. "Not for fifteen years. And I know what you're thinking, Avery, but there's no way Isaiah had any involvement in Toby's abduction. He's a mechanic who owns his own garage, and the other mechanic who works for him is out on maternity leave, so he's been pulling double shifts for weeks." Xander swallowed. "But still...he might know something that could give us the upper hand. Or know someone who knows something. Or know someone who knows someone who knows—"

Thea placed a hand helpfully over Xander's mouth.

The file. The domino chain in my mind hit its conclusion, and I sucked in a breath. *Isaiah Alexander's file was empty, and Xander didn't take the page.*

What were the chances that the missing page had mentioned Vincent Blake?

Eve took it. That might have been a leap. It might not have been fair. I couldn't even tell anymore.

My entire body buzzing, I stepped around Xander's shield and looked to Oren, who—not surprisingly—had followed us around the corner. "Jameson, Grayson, and Eve are on their way back here?" I asked, clipping the words. "They're secured, under the watchful eyes of your men, and will be for the next three hours?"

Oren's eyes narrowed with suspicion. "What are you going to do if I say yes?"

That gives us three hours. I looked to Xander. "I think we need to talk to Isaiah. But if you're not ready—"

"I was born ready!" Xander brandished his shield. He smiled a very Xander Hawthorne smile, then let his bravado falter. "But before we go, group hug?"

CHAPTER 59

An hour later, we were parked outside a small-town mechanic shop with a large security team in tow, having given the paparazzi the slip on the highway. There was only one man working inside the shop. He was under a car when we walked in.

"You'll have to wait." Isaiah Alexander's voice was neither low nor high.

I hoped, for Xander's sake, that he really wasn't involved in any of this.

"Need a hand?" Xander offered. When some people got nervous, they clammed up. Xander babbled. "I'm pretty good with mechanical things, unless or maybe especially if they're flammable."

That got a chuckle. "Spoken like someone with too much time on their hands." Isaiah Alexander rolled out from underneath the car and stood. He was tall like Xander but broader through the shoulders. His skin was a darker brown, but their eyes were the same.

"You looking for a job?" he asked Xander, like wayward teenagers showed up here all the time with a trio of teenage girls and several bodyguards in tow.

"I'm Xander." Xander swallowed. "Hawthorne."

"I know who you are," Isaiah said, his tone no-nonsense but somehow gentle. "Looking for a job?"

"Maybe." Xander shifted his weight from foot to foot and then resumed nervous babbling. "I should probably warn you that I've dismantled four and a half Porsches past the point of no return in the last two years. But in my defense, they had it coming, and I needed the parts."

Isaiah took that in stride. "Like to build things, do you?"

The question—and the slight upward curve of his lips—almost undid me, so I couldn't imagine how hard it hit Xander.

"You're not surprised to see me." Xander sounded stunned—this from a person who could *literally* stun himself and proceed without missing a beat. "I thought you would be," he blurted out. "Surprised. Or that you wouldn't know who I was. I prepared a mental flowchart that geared my reaction toward your exact level of surprise and knowledge."

Isaiah Alexander looked at his son, his expression steady. "Was it three-dimensional?"

"My mental flowchart?" Xander threw his hands up in the air. "Of course it was three-dimensional! Who makes two-dimensional flowcharts?"

"Nerds?" Thea suggested, and then she stage-whispered, "Ask me who makes three-dimensional flowcharts, Xander."

"Thea." Rebecca nudged her.

"I'm helping," Thea insisted, and sure enough, Xander seemed to steady a little.

"You knew about me?" he asked Isaiah, quiet but more intense than I'd ever seen him.

Isaiah met Xander's eyes. "Since before you were born."

Then why weren't you there? I thought with a ferocity that stole my breath. My own father had been mostly absent, but this was *Xander*, king of distractions and chaos, BHFF, who'd known about this man for *months* but had only come here for me.

I couldn't bear the idea of him getting hurt.

"Do you want me to go?" Xander asked Isaiah hesitantly.

"Would I have asked you if you wanted a job," Isaiah replied, "if I did?"

Xander blinked. Repeatedly. "I came here because we need to talk to you about Vincent Blake," he said, like that was the one thing he *could* say of the thousands pounding through his brain.

Isaiah cocked an eyebrow. "Sounds like a want more than a need to me."

"That's what people say about second lunch," Xander replied, reverting to babble mode, "and it's a dirty lie."

"On the lunch bit," Isaiah told him, "we agree." Then he turned, eyeing a nearby car. "I worked for Blake for just over two years, beginning shortly after you were born."

Xander took a deep breath. "Right after you worked for my grandfather?"

Isaiah seemed to steel himself at the mention of Tobias Hawthorne. "The entire time I worked for Hawthorne, competitors tried to steal me away. Each time, your grandfather would sweeten my contract. I was twenty-two, a prodigy, on the top of the world—and then I wasn't." Isaiah popped the hood of the car. "After Hawthorne fired me, the offers dried up pretty damn quick. I went from young, rash, and flying high with a mid-six-figure salary to untouchable overnight."

"Because of Skye," Xander bit out.

Isaiah looked up from the engine to pin Xander with a look. "I made my own decisions where your mother was concerned, Xander."

"And the old man punished you for them," Xander replied, like a kid pushing on a bruise to see how much it hurt.

"It wasn't a punishment." Isaiah returned his attention to the car. "It was strategy. I was a twenty-two-year-old who'd been so flush with cash that I'd never imagined it would stop coming. I'd blown through most of what I'd made, so once I was fired and blacklisted, I conveniently didn't have the resources to put up much of a fight for custody."

It wasn't about Skye. I realized with a start what Isaiah Alexander was saying. *Tobias Hawthorne fired Isaiah because of Xander.* Not because the old man had been unhappy about his youngest grandson's conception but because he'd refused to share him.

"So you just gave up on your son?" Rebecca asked Isaiah sharply. She wasn't a person who knew how to fight for herself, but she'd fight for Xander every time.

"I managed to scrape together enough for a third-rate lawyer to file suit when Xander was born. The court ordered a paternity test. But wouldn't you know, it came back negative."

So said the man with Xander's eyes. Xander's smile. The man who heard the word "flowchart" and asked if Xander built them in three dimensions.

"Skye named me Alexander." Xander wasn't, by nature, a quiet person, but his voice was barely audible now. "They faked the DNA test."

"I couldn't prove it," Isaiah told him. "I couldn't get near you." He tweaked something, then slammed the hood of the car. "And I couldn't get a job. Enter Vincent Blake."

"I don't want to talk about Vincent Blake," Xander said with enough intensity that I half expected him to start yelling. Instead, his voice dropped to a whisper. "You're saying that you *wanted* me?"

I thought about how badly I'd wanted Toby to be my father

instead of Ricky Grambs, about Rebecca growing up invisible and Eve moving out the day she turned eighteen. I thought about Libby, whose mother had taught her she deserved a partner that degraded and controlled her, about Jameson's *hunger* and Grayson's punishing perfection, both of them competing for approval that was always just out of reach.

I thought about Xander and how scared he'd been to come here.

You're saying that you wanted *me?* The question echoed all around us.

Isaiah responded: "Still do."

Xander bolted. One second, he was there, and the next, he was out the door.

"We'll go after him," Rebecca told me, taking Thea with her. "You ask whatever you need to, Avery, because Xander can't. He shouldn't have to."

The door slammed behind Rebecca and Thea, and I looked up at Isaiah Alexander. *Your son is amazing,* I thought. *You can't ever hurt him.* But I forced myself to focus on the reason we'd come here and the questions Xander couldn't ask. "So after you were fired and blacklisted, Vincent Blake just came out of nowhere and offered you a job?"

Isaiah assessed me for so long that I felt about four years old and five inches tall. But whatever he saw in my face earned me an answer. "Blake came to me at my lowest point, told me that he wasn't scared of Tobias Hawthorne, and if I wasn't, either, we could do great things together. He offered me a position as the head of his new innovation lab. I had free rein to invent whatever I wanted, as long as I did it in his name. I had money again. I had freedom."

"So why did you quit?" I asked. That was a guess, but my gut said it was a good one.

"I started noticing things I wasn't supposed to notice," Isaiah said calmly. "The pattern's there if you look for it. People who stand in Vincent Blake's way—they aren't standing for long. Accidents were had. People disappeared. Nothing anyone could prove. Nothing that could be tied to Blake, but once I saw the pattern, I couldn't unsee it. I knew who I was working for."

We'd come here in part to find out what Vincent Blake was capable of. And now I knew.

"So I quit," Isaiah said. "I took the money I'd earned—and saved this time—and I bought this place so I'd never have to work for another Vincent Blake or Tobias Hawthorne again."

What had happened to Isaiah wasn't right. None of this was right.

Rebecca and Thea reappeared. Xander wasn't with them. "There's a doughnut shop down the street," Rebecca told me, out of breath. "We have a twelve-jelly-and-cream situation."

I looked back at Isaiah.

"Sounds like you're needed," he said, calmly returning his attention to the car he'd been working on. "I'll be here."

CHAPTER 60

Rebecca and Thea led me to a doughnut shop, then waited outside. I found Xander sitting at a table by himself, stacking doughnuts one on top of the other. By my count, there were five.

"Behold!" Xander declared. "The Leaning Tower of Bavarian Cream-a!"

"Where are the other seven doughnuts?" I asked him, taking his cue and not pushing this too much too soon.

Xander shook his head. "I have so many regrets."

"You literally just picked up another doughnut," I pointed out.

"I couldn't possibly regret *this* doughnut," Xander stated emphatically.

I softened my voice. "You just found out that the Hawthorne family faked a paternity test to keep your father, who *wanted* you, out of your life. It's okay to be angry or devastated or…"

"I don't super excel at anger, and devastation is really more for people who slow down long enough to let their brains focus on the sadness. My expertise falls more squarely in the Venn diagram overlap between unbridled enthusiasm and infinite—"

"Xander." I reached across the table and laid my hand on top of his. For a moment, he just sat there, looking down at our hands.

"You know I love you, Avery, but I don't want to talk to you about this." Xander removed his hand from underneath mine. "I don't want to have to explain to you what I don't want to explain to you. I just want to finish this doughnut and eat his four best doughnut-y friends and congratulate myself for probably not vomiting."

I didn't say another word. I just sat there with him until Oren appeared in my peripheral vision. He inclined his head to the right. Xander and I had been spotted—by a local, I was guessing, but when it came to the Hawthorne family and the Hawthorne heiress nothing stayed *local* for long.

We went back to Isaiah's garage. "Do you want us to wait outside?" I asked Xander.

"No. I just want you to give me that little metal disk," Xander replied. "I'm assuming you have it on you?"

I did, and I handed it to him because right now, I would have done anything Xander wanted.

He pushed open the door and walked slowly back to the car Isaiah was working on. "I need to ask you two things. First, what are your thoughts on Rube Goldberg machines?"

"Never made one." Isaiah met Xander's gaze. "But I tend to think they should have catapults."

Xander nodded, like that was an acceptable answer. "Second, have you ever seen something like this before?" He held the disk out to Isaiah, the two of them towering over everyone else present.

Isaiah took the disk from Xander. "Where the hell did you kids get this?"

"You do know what it is," Xander said, his eyes lighting up. "Some kind of artifact?"

"Artifact?" Isaiah shook his head, handing the disk back to Xander, who handed it to me. "No. *That* is Mr. Blake's calling card. He always called it the family seal."

I thought about the wax seal on the envelope of the last message, bearing the same symbol.

"I think he had, what, five of those coins?" Isaiah continued. "If you had one of the seals, it meant you had Blake's blessing to play in his empire as you wished—until you displeased him. If that happened, you were stripped of the seal and the status and power that came with it. It's how Blake kept his family on a very short string. Every person with a drop of his blood or his dead wife's fought tooth and nail to have one of the seals."

I considered the implications. "Only family?"

"Only family," Isaiah confirmed. "Nephews, great-nephews, cousins once removed."

"What about Blake's son?" I asked. Nan had mentioned a son.

"I heard there was a son," Isaiah replied. "But he took off years before I came into the picture."

The prodigal son, I thought suddenly, and adrenaline rushed into my veins.

"What do you mean when you say Vincent Blake's son *took off*?" I asked Isaiah.

"I meant what I said." Isaiah fixed me with a look. "The son took off at some point and didn't come back. It's part of what made the seals so valuable. There was no direct heir to the family fortune. Rumor had it, when Blake dies, anyone holding one of *those*—" Isaiah nodded toward the disk. "Gets a stake."

Isaiah had said that there were five seals. That meant the disk I was holding in my hand was worth somewhere in the neighborhood of a hundred million dollars. I thought of Toby and the instructions he'd left my mother about going to Jackson if she needed anything. *You know what I left there*, he'd written. *You know what it's worth.*

"More than twenty years ago, Toby Hawthorne stole this from his father." I stared at the seal, at the layers of concentric rings. "But why did Tobias Hawthorne have one of the Blake family seals? There's no way Blake was planning to leave one-fifth of his fortune to a billionaire who betrayed him."

Isaiah gave a shrug, but there was something hard about it, like he refused to give Tobias Hawthorne or Vincent Blake any space in his mind. "I've told you what I know," he said. "And I should be getting back to work." His gaze went to Xander. "Unless..."

For a moment, I heard the same uncertainty in his tone that I'd heard in Xander's when I asked him about his father's file.

"I do want to talk," Xander said, rushing the words. "I do, I mean, if you do."

"Okay, then," Isaiah said.

The rest of us were almost out the door when Rebecca stopped and turned around. "What was the name of Vincent Blake's son?" she asked, an odd tone in her voice.

"It's been a long time," Isaiah said, but then he glanced back at Xander and sighed. "Just let me think for a minute.... Will." Isaiah snapped his fingers. "The son's name was Will Blake."

Will Blake. For a split second, I wasn't standing there in Isaiah's shop. I was in Toby's wing of Hawthorne House, reading a poem inscribed on metal.

William Blake. "A Poison Tree."

CHAPTER 61

What if Toby hadn't chosen that poem just for the emotions it conveyed? What if the secrets and lies he'd written about himself went beyond his hidden adoption?

Why did Tobias Hawthorne have that seal?

Rebecca, Thea, and I gave Xander time with his father. The rest of us waited in the SUV. I had Oren pull around the block so that if the paparazzi showed up at the doughnut shop, they'd focus on my SUVs, not Isaiah's garage. While we waited, my mind raced. *William Blake. The Blake family seal. Revenge. Avenge. Vengeance. Avenger.*

When Xander climbed into the SUV, he didn't say a word about his father. "Hit me with all those thinky thoughts," he told me.

I studied him for a moment. His brown eyes were steady and bright, so I obliged. "What Vincent Blake is doing now—kidnapping Toby, playing games with me—I don't think any of that is really about a patent filed fifty years ago." The patent number had told us who we were dealing with. We'd *assumed* that it also gave us motive, but we were wrong. "I think this is about Vincent Blake's son."

"The prodigal son," Xander murmured. "Will Blake."

A wasteful youth. Vincent Blake's distinctive voice rang in my mind. *Wandering the world—ungrateful. A benevolent father, ready to welcome him home. But if memory serves correctly, there were three characters in that story...*

Everything pointed to the third person in this story being Tobias Hawthorne—and if that was the case, maybe Xander had it wrong. "What if Will isn't the prodigal?" I said. "On the phone, Blake emphasized that there were three characters in the parable of the prodigal son. The father—"

"Vincent Blake," Thea filled in.

I nodded. "The son who betrayed his family, took the money, and ran—what if that's not Vincent Blake's *actual* son? What if it's a man he'd brought into the family fold? Young Tobias Hawthorne. Nan said that Blake's son was younger at the time, fifteen when your grandfather would have been..." I did the math. "Twenty-four."

"At fifteen, Vincent Blake's son might not have been old enough to have one of those seals," Xander said, thinking out loud, "but he was plenty old to witness the betrayal."

My entire body felt alive and alert, horrified and entranced. "Witness the betrayal," I echoed, "and wonder why his father let some nobody from nowhere get away with screwing him out of millions?"

That put Will Blake in the position of the son who had stayed—the good son, upset that the prodigal's betrayal was rewarded instead of punished.

There are three characters in the parable of the prodigal son, are there not?

Avenge. Revenge. Vengeance. Avenger.

I always win in the end.

"The question is," Xander said, "why did Toby leave a poem by a poet named *William Blake* hidden in his wing, way back when?"

"And what are the chances," I added, one thought leaping to the forefront of my mind, "that Will *did* have one of the Blake family seals with him when he disappeared?"

If the seal in Tobias Hawthorne's possession had belonged to Vincent Blake's son…

It felt like we were barreling toward the edge of a cliff.

"How long ago did Will Blake go missing?" Rebecca wasn't looking at any of us. Light from the window hit her hair. Her tone was throaty and intense.

I got out my phone and did a search. And then another. Eventually, I was sure: The last time that Vincent Blake had been publicly photographed with his son, Will had been in his early twenties. "Forty years ago?" I estimated. "Plus or minus. Rebecca—"

"Will is one nickname for William," Rebecca said, sucking every last molecule of oxygen out of the car. "But another one is Liam."

CHAPTER 62

Mallory Laughlin hadn't revealed much about the man who'd gotten her pregnant. She'd said that he was older, very charming. She'd said that his name was *Liam*. And when Eve had asked what had happened to Liam, all she would say was that he had left.

If Liam was Will Blake...

If he'd sought out a sixteen-year-old girl living on the Hawthorne estate...

If he got that girl pregnant...

And if Will really hadn't been seen for more than forty years... *plus or minus*...

Questions piled up in my head. Did Toby know or suspect that Will Blake was his biological father? Did Vincent Blake know that Toby was his grandson? *Is that why he took him?* And if the seal that Toby had stolen from his father really did belong to Vincent Blake's son—how had it come to be in Tobias Hawthorne's possession in the first place?

What happened to Will Blake?

If we'd been barreling toward the edge of the cliff before, I was in the free fall now.

The moment we arrived back at Hawthorne House and I burst out of the SUV, Jameson was there. He stopped, inches from me, intensity radiating off his body. Everything we'd learned was about to come pouring out of my mouth when he spoke.

"What the hell is wrong with you, Heiress?"

I stared at him, disbelief giving way to anger that bubbled up in me and exploded out. "What's wrong with *me*? You're the one who locked me in the world's most bejeweled escape room!"

"To keep you safe," Jameson emphasized. "Vincent Blake is powerful, and he's connected, and he's going to keep coming for *you*, Avery, because you're the one holding the keys to this kingdom. And I don't know if he wants what you have, or if he wants to burn it down, but either way, how am I supposed to keep you safe if you won't let me?"

I knew that Jameson loved me—and that pissed me off because our love wasn't supposed to be like this. "You're not supposed to *keep* me anything!" I burst out. He tried to look away, but I wouldn't let him. "Ask me what we found."

He didn't.

"Just ask me, Jameson."

I could see him wanting to, warring with himself. "Promise me first."

"Promise you what?" I asked.

"That you'll be more careful. That I won't come home to find you gone again."

I wasn't sure how to say this to make him believe it, so I put both my hands flat on his chest and stared into green eyes that I knew better than anyone else's. "I'm not going to stay locked up here, and it is not your place to lock me up. I don't need your protection."

"This is what you want!" Jameson sounded like the words had been ripped out of him. Breathing heavily, he curled his fingers around mine. "It's what you've always wanted. An arrogant, duty-bound asshole who tries to be honorable and would die to protect the girl he loves."

I froze. Logically, I knew that my heart was still beating. I was still breathing. But it didn't feel like it. I could see the others in my peripheral vision, but I couldn't move, couldn't ask Jameson to lower his voice, couldn't focus on anything but the green of his eyes, the lines of his face.

"I'm not Grayson," he told me, ravaged by the words.

"I don't want you to be," I said, pleading—for what, I wasn't even sure.

"Yes, you do," Jameson insisted quietly. "And it doesn't even matter because I'm not putting on a show here, Heiress. I'm not playing at being overprotective or pretending that, for once in my life, I want to do the right thing." He brought his hands to the side of my face, then the back of my neck, and I felt his touch through every square inch of my body. "I love you. I *would* die to protect you. I would make you hate me to keep you safe because *damn it, Avery*—some things are too precious to gamble."

Jameson Winchester Hawthorne loved me. He *loved* me, and I loved him. But I didn't know how to make him believe that when I said I didn't want him to be Grayson, I meant it.

"This is who I want to be," Jameson said, his voice hoarse, "for you."

I wished suddenly that neither one of us was standing on the lawn of Hawthorne House. That it was my birthday again or that the year mark had passed and we were halfway around the world, seeing everything, doing everything, having it all. I wished that Toby had never been taken, that Vincent Blake didn't exist, that Eve had never come here—

Eve, I thought suddenly, and then I realized something that I should have realized much sooner. If Vincent Blake's son was Toby's father, that made Eve the man's great-granddaughter.

Eve and Vincent Blake are family. The words exploded in my mind like shrapnel. I thought about Eve telling me about doing a mail-in DNA test, about the way that she'd first earned my trust because I'd thought I understood what Toby meant to her, how it must have felt for her to finally be wanted, to finally have *family* who wanted her.

But what if that family *wasn't* Toby?

What if someone else had found her first?

I thought back to showing her Toby's wing, to the moment when I'd mentioned "A Poison Tree" and said the poet's name: William Blake. Eve had dropped to her knees, reading the poem over and over again. *She recognized the name.*

"Heiress." Jameson was still looking at me, and I knew, just from the way he let his thumbs skim lightly over my cheekbones, that he knew my mind had taken flight. He didn't blame me for it. He didn't ask me for anything else. All he said was "Tell me."

So I did.

And then he told me that Eve was at Wayback Cottage—with Grayson.

CHAPTER 63

Oren and two of his men drove Jameson and me to Wayback Cottage. Rebecca didn't come with us, didn't *want* to come with us. Thea and Xander stayed with her.

I rang the bell—again and again until Mrs. Laughlin answered.

"Grayson and Eve," I said, trying to sound calmer than I felt. "Are they here?"

Mrs. Laughlin pinned me with a look that had probably been used on generations of Hawthorne children. "They're in the kitchen with my daughter."

I made my way there, Jameson on my heels, Oren directly to my left, his men only steps behind him. We found Eve sitting across a worn wooden table from Mallory. Grayson stood behind Eve like a wayward angel keeping watch.

Eve swiveled her gaze toward us, and I wondered if I was imagining the canny look in her eyes, imagining her assessing the situation, assessing me, before speaking. "Any updates?"

One, I thought. *I know that you're related to Vincent Blake.*

"I tried to get to Toby," Eve continued intently, "but I couldn't. *Someone* brought me back."

That someone was standing so close to her now.

"Grayson," I said. "I need to talk to you."

Eve turned to look at him. There was something delicate about the way her hair fell off her shoulder, something almost mesmerizing about the way she lifted her eyes to his.

"Grayson," I said again, my voice urgent and low.

Jameson didn't give me the opportunity to say his brother's name a third time. "Avery found out something that you need to know. Outside, Gray. Now."

Grayson walked toward us. Eve came, too. "What did you find out?" she asked.

"What is it you're hoping I'll find out—or hoping I won't?" I hadn't meant to say that out loud, but now that I had, I marked her reaction.

"What is that supposed to mean?" Eve snapped, something like hurt flickering over her face.

Was that an act? *This whole time—has it all been an act?* My gaze landed on the chain around her neck, and I flashed back to the moment she'd stepped out of my bathroom wearing nothing but a towel and a locket. Why would Eve, who'd insisted she'd spent her whole life with no one, wear a locket?

What was inside?

A small metal disk. Isaiah had said that there were five, that Vincent Blake gave them exclusively to family—and Eve was family.

"Open your locket," I said sharply. "Show me what's inside."

Eve stood very still. I moved, reaching for it—but Grayson caught my hand. He gave me a look like a shard of ice. "What are you doing, Avery?"

"Vincent Blake had a son," I said. I hadn't wanted to do this here, in front of Mallory and Mrs. Laughlin, but so be it. "His name was Will. I think he was Toby's father. And *this*?" I withdrew the Blake family seal, the one that had been in Toby's possession when he disappeared. "It was almost certainly Will's. Blake gave them to family members who held his favor." I could feel Eve watching me. Her face was blank—so carefully blank. "Isn't that right, Eve?"

"You have no right," Mallory Laughlin snapped shrilly, "to come in here and say any of this. *Any of it.*" She looked past me to Mrs. Laughlin. "Are you going to just stand there and let her do this?" she demanded, her voice going up an octave. "This is your home!"

"I think it would be best," Mrs. Laughlin told me stiffly, "if you left."

I'd spent a year making inroads with her and the rest of the staff. I'd gone from being an outsider and an enemy to being accepted. I didn't want to lose that, but I couldn't back down.

"He called himself Liam," I said quietly, my gaze going to Mallory's. "He didn't tell you who he really was—or why he was here."

Mrs. Laughlin took a step toward me. "You need to go."

"Will Blake sought out your daughter," I said, turning back toward the woman who'd served as a steward of the Hawthorne estate for most of her life. "He would have been in his twenties. She was only sixteen. She snuck him onto the estate—up to Hawthorne House, even." I didn't stop. "It was probably his idea."

A pained expression forced Mrs. Laughlin's eyes closed. "Stop this," she begged me. "Please."

"I don't know what happened," I said, "but I do know that Will Blake hasn't been seen since. And for some reason, you and your husband let the Hawthornes adopt your grandson and pass him off as their own flesh and blood, even to the baby's mother."

A high-pitched mewling sound escaped Mallory's throat.

"You were trying to protect them, weren't you?" I asked Mrs. Laughlin softly. "Your daughter *and* Toby. You were trying to protect them from Vincent Blake."

"What is she talking about?" Eve glided back toward Mallory, then ducked down, angling her head so that her eyes were looking directly into Mallory's. "You have to tell me the truth," she continued. "All of it. Your Liam . . . he didn't *leave*, did he?"

I saw then what she was doing—what she had been doing. "That's why you're here," I realized. "What did Vincent Blake offer you if you brought him answers?"

"That's enough," Grayson told me sharply.

"It really, really isn't," Jameson replied, blazing by my side.

"You know what this necklace means to me, Grayson," Eve said, her fist covering the locket. "You know why I wear it. *You know, Grayson.*"

"*Don't trust anyone*," I said, my tone a match for hers. "That was the old man's message. His final message, Gray. Because if Eve's here, Vincent Blake might not be far behind."

Eve turned her body into Grayson's, her every movement a study in grace and fury. "Who cares about Tobias Hawthorne's final message?" she asked, her voice shattering at the end of that question. "He didn't want me, Grayson. He chose Avery. I was *never* going to be enough for him. You know what that's like, Gray. Better than anyone—you know."

I could feel him slipping through my fingers, but I couldn't stop fighting. "You pushed us to ask Skye about the seal," I said, staring Eve down. "You've been asking around about deep, dark Hawthorne family secrets. You pressed and pressed for answers on Toby's father—"

A single tear rolled down Eve's cheek.

"*Avery*." Grayson's tone was one I recognized. This was the boy who'd been raised as the heir apparent. The one who didn't have to dirty his hands to put an adversary in their place.

Am I the enemy again, Gray?

"Eve has done nothing to you." Grayson's voice cut into me like a surgeon's knife. "Even if what you're saying about Toby's parentage is true, Eve is not to blame for her family."

"Then get her to open the locket," I said, my mouth dry.

Eve walked toward me. When she got within three feet, Oren shifted. "That's close enough."

Without a word to him, or to anyone, Eve opened her locket. Inside, there was a picture of a little girl. *Eve*, I realized. Her hair was cut short and uneven, her little cheeks gaunt. "No one ever cherished her. No one ever would have put her picture in a locket." Eve met my gaze, and though she looked vulnerable, I thought I saw something else underneath that vulnerability. "So I wear this as a reminder: Even if no one else loves you, you can. Even if no one else ever puts you first, *you can*."

She was standing there admitting that she was going to put herself first, but it was like Grayson couldn't see that. "Enough," he ordered. "This isn't you, Avery."

"Maybe, Gray," Jameson countered, "you don't know her as well as you think."

"Out!" Mrs. Laughlin boomed. "All of you, out!"

Not one of us moved, and the older woman's eyes narrowed.

"This is my house. Mr. Hawthorne's will granted us lifelong, rent-free tenancy." Mrs. Laughlin looked at her daughter, then at Eve, and finally she turned back to me. "You can fire me, but you can't evict me, and you *will* leave my home."

"Lottie," Oren said quietly.

"Don't you *Lottie* me, John Oren." Mrs. Laughlin glared at him. "You take your girl, you take the boys—and you get out."

CHAPTER 64

"What is wrong with you?" Grayson exploded as soon as we were outside.

"Did you hear a word I said in there?" I asked, my heart breaking like cracking glass, bit by jagged bit. "Did you hear what *she* said? She's going to put herself first, Grayson. She *hates* your grandfather. We aren't her family. *Blake* is."

Grayson stopped walking toward the SUV. He went stiff, attending to the cuffs of his dress shirt and brushing an imaginary speck off the lapel of his suit. "Clearly," he said, his tone almost regal, "I was wrong about you."

I felt like he'd just thrown ice-cold water in my face. Like he'd hit me.

And then I watched Grayson Hawthorne walk away.

A guy who thinks he knows everything, I could hear myself saying what felt like a lifetime ago.

A girl with a razor-sharp tongue.

I could hear Grayson telling me that I had an expressive face, telling Jameson that I was one of them, in Latin, so I wouldn't understand it. I could feel Grayson correcting my grip on a longsword, see him catching my Hawthorne pin before it could hit the ground. I saw him sliding a hand-bound journal across the dining room table to me.

"Oren can post men to watch the cottage." Jameson spoke beside me. He knew how much I was hurting but did me the courtesy of pretending he didn't. "If Eve is a threat, we can keep her contained."

I turned to look at him. "You know that this isn't about Grayson and me," I said, forcing the image of Grayson walking away out of my mind. "Tell me you know that, Jameson."

"I know," he replied, "that I love you, and despite all odds, you love me." Jameson's smile was smaller but no less crooked than usual. "I also know that Gray's the better man. He always has been. The better son, the better grandson, the better Hawthorne. I think that's why I wanted so badly for Emily to choose me. For once, I wanted to be the one. But it was always him, Heiress. I was a game to her. She loved *him*."

"No." I shook my head. "She didn't. You don't treat people you love like that."

"*You* don't," Jameson replied. "You're honorable, Avery Kylie Grambs. Once you were with me, you were *with me*. You love me, scars and all. I know that, Heiress. *I do*." Jameson said those words, and he meant them. He believed them. "Is it so awful," he continued, "that I want to be a better man for you?"

I thought about our fight. "*Better* is being my friend and my partner and realizing that you don't get to make decisions for me. *Better* is the way you make me see myself as a person who's capable of anything. I would jump out of a plane with you, Jameson, snowboard down the side of a volcano with you, bet everything that I have on *you*—on us, against the world. You don't get to run off and take risks and expect me to stay behind in a gilded cage of your making. That isn't who you are, and it's *not* what I want." I didn't know how to say this so that he would really hear me. "You," I told him, taking a step closer, "have always made me bold. You're the one who pushes me out of my comfort zone. You don't get to box me back in now."

Jameson looked at me like he was trying to memorize every detail of my face. "I moved on from Emily," he said. "Gray didn't. And I know in my soul that if he had, he could have loved you. He would have. With everything you are, Heiress, what other choice would he have had?"

"It was always going to be you," I told Jameson. He needed to hear it. I needed to say it, even though *always* painted over so much.

In response, Jameson gave me another crooked smile. "It's times like this, Heiress, that I wish I'd fallen in love with a girl who wasn't quite so good at bluffing."

Jameson left, the way Grayson had.

"Let's get you back up to the House," Oren said. He didn't offer any commentary on what had just happened.

I didn't let myself think about Jameson or Grayson. I thought about the rest of it instead, about Vincent Blake's missing son and *vengeance* and the games that Blake was never going to stop playing with me. The stories in the tabloids, the paparazzi, financial assaults from every side, trying to chip away at my security team, and the entire time, taunting me that he had Toby.

Clue after clue.

Riddle after riddle.

I was sick of it. When I got back to the House, I went to get the phone Blake had sent me. I called the only number I had for him, and when he didn't answer, I started placing other calls from my real phone—to every person who had received a coveted invitation to the owner's suite of *my* NFL team, to every player in Texas society who had tried to cozy up to me at a charity gala, every person who'd wanted my buy-in for a *financial opportunity*.

Money attracted money. Power attracted power. And I was done waiting for the next clue.

It took some time, but I found someone who had Vincent Blake's cell phone number and was willing to give it to me, no questions asked. My heart beat with the force of punch after punch in my chest as I dialed the number.

When Blake answered, I didn't bother with pretense. "I know about Eve. I know about your son."

"Do you?"

Questions and riddles and games. *No more.* "What do you *want*?" I asked. I wondered if he could hear my anger—and every ounce of emotion buried underneath.

I wondered if that made him think he was winning.

"What do I want, Avery Kylie Grambs?" Vincent Blake sounded amused. "Guess."

"I'm done guessing."

Silence greeted me on the other end of the line—but he was still there. He didn't hang up. And I wasn't going to be the one to break the silence first.

"Isn't it obvious?" Blake said at long last. "I want the truth that Tobias Hawthorne hid from me all these years. I want to know what happened to my son. And I want you, Avery Kylie Grambs, to dig up the past and bring me his body."

CHAPTER 65

Vincent Blake believed his son was dead. He believed the body was *here*. I thought about the Blake family seal, the fact that Toby had stolen it, his father's reaction when he had.

You know what I left there, Toby had written my mother long ago. *You know what it's worth.* A teenage Toby had stolen the seal—and left a hidden copy of "A Poison Tree" by William Blake for his father to find.

"He wanted you to know that he knew the truth." It felt right somehow to be addressing Tobias Hawthorne. This was his legacy.

All of it.

"What did you do," I whispered, "when you found Vincent Blake's son on your property?"

When he'd realized that a man had come at him through a sixteen-year-old girl. That girl might have fancied herself in love, but Tobias Hawthorne wouldn't have seen it that way. Will Blake was in his twenties. Mallory was only sixteen.

And unlike Vincent Blake, Tobias Hawthorne didn't believe that *boys would be boys.*

What happened to him? I could hear Eve asking. *Your Liam.* And all Mallory Laughlin had said was *Liam left.*

Why did he leave?

He just did.

I started walking and ended up in Toby's old wing, reading the lines of "A Poison Tree" and the diary that Toby had kept in invisible ink on his walls. I understood young Toby's anger now, in a way I hadn't before. *He knew something.*

About his father.

About the reason the adoption was kept secret.

About Will Blake and the decision to hide a dangerous man's only grandchild in plain sight. I thought about Toby's poem, the one we'd decoded months ago.

Secrets, lies,
All I despise.
The tree is poison,
Don't you see?
It poisoned S and Z and me.
The evidence I stole
Is in the darkest hole.
Light shall reveal all
I writ upon the...

"*Wall*," I finished now, the way I had then. But this time my brain was seeing all of it through a new lens. If Toby had known what the seal was when he stole it, that meant he knew who Will Blake was, who Vincent Blake was. And if Toby knew that...

What else had he known?

The evidence I stole

Is in the darkest hole.

When I'd recited this poem for Eve, she'd asked me, *Evidence of what?* She'd been looking for answers, for proof. *For a body,* I thought. *Or more realistically at this point, for bones.* But Eve hadn't found any of it yet. If she had, Blake wouldn't have laid this task before me.

I want the truth that Tobias Hawthorne hid from me all these years. I want to know what happened to my son.

Hawthorne House was full of dark places: hidden compartments, secret passages, buried tunnels. Maybe all Toby had ever found was the seal. *Or maybe he found human remains.* That thought was insidious because some part of me had suspected, deep down, that that was what we were looking for, before Vincent Blake had ever told me as much.

His son had come here. He'd targeted a child under Tobias Hawthorne's protection. In his *home.*

Where would a man like Tobias Hawthorne hide a body?

Oren had disposed of Sheffield Grayson's body—how, I wasn't sure. But Vincent Blake's son had disappeared long before Oren had come to work for the old man. Back then, the Hawthorne fortune was new and considerably smaller. Tobias Hawthorne probably hadn't even had security.

Back then, Hawthorne House was just another mansion.

Tobias Hawthorne added onto it every year. That thought wound its way through my mind; my heart pumped it through my veins.

And suddenly, I knew where to start.

I pulled out the blueprints that Mr. Laughlin had given me. Each one detailed an addition that Tobias Hawthorne had made to Hawthorne House over the decades since it was built. *The garage. The spa. The movie theater. The bowling alley.* I unrolled sheet after sheet, plan after plan. *The rock-climbing wall. The tennis court.* I found plans for a gazebo, an outdoor kitchen, a greenhouse, and so much more.

Think, I told myself. There were layers of purpose in everything

Tobias Hawthorne had ever done—everything he'd *built*. I thought about the compartment at the bottom of the swimming pool, about the secret passages in the House, the tunnels beneath the estate, all of it.

There were a thousand places that Tobias Hawthorne could have hidden his darkest secret. If I came at this randomly, I'd get nowhere. I had to be logical. Systematic.

Lay the plans out in chronological order, I thought.

Only a handful of blueprints were marked with years, but each set showed how the proposed addition would be integrated with the House or surrounding property. I needed to find the earliest plan—the one in which the House was the smallest, the simplest—and work forward from there.

I went through page after page until I found it: the original Hawthorne House. Slowly, painstakingly, I put the rest of the blueprints in order. By dawn, I'd made it halfway through, but that was enough. Based on the few sets that had dates on them, I could calculate years for the rest.

I'd been focused on the wrong question in Toby's wing. *Not where Tobias Hawthorne would have hidden a body—but when?* I knew the year that Toby had been born, but not the month. That let me narrow it down to two sets of plans.

The year before Toby's birth, Tobias Hawthorne had erected the greenhouse.

The year of Toby's birth had been the chapel.

I thought about Jameson saying that his grandfather had built the chapel for Nan to yell at God—and then I thought about Nan's response. *The old coot threatened to build me a mausoleum instead.*

What if that hadn't been a threat? What if Tobias Hawthorne had just decided it was too obvious?

Where would a man like Tobias Hawthorne hide a body?

CHAPTER 66

Stepping through the stone arches of the chapel, I scanned the room: the delicately carved pews, the elaborate stained-glass windows, an altar made of pure white marble. This early in the day, light streamed in from the east, bathing the room in color from the stained glass. I studied each panel, looking for something.

A clue.

Nothing. I went through the pews. There were only six of them. The woodwork was captivating, but if it held any secrets—hidden compartments, a button, instructions—I couldn't find them.

That left me with the altar. It came up to my chest and was a little over six feet long and maybe three feet deep. On the top of the altar, there was a candelabra; a gleaming, golden Bible; and a silver cross. I carefully examined each one, and then I knelt to look at the script carved into the front of the altar.

A quote. I ran my fingers over the inscription and read it out loud. *"So we fix our eyes not on what is seen, but on what is unseen, since what is seen is temporary, but what is unseen is eternal."*

That sounded biblical. It was too early to call Max, so I typed the quote into the phone and it gave me a Bible verse: 2 *Corinthians 4:18*.

I thought about Blake using a different Bible verse as a combination on a lock. How many of *his* games had a young Tobias Hawthorne played?

"Fix our eyes not on what is seen," I said out loud, *"but on what is unseen."* I stared at the altar. *What is unseen?*

Kneeling in front of the altar, I ran my fingers along it: up and down, left and right, top to bottom. I made my way around to the back, where I found a slight gap between the marble and the floor. I bent to look, but I couldn't see anything, so I slid my fingers into the gap.

Almost immediately, I felt a series of raised circles. My first instinct was to push one, but I didn't want to be rash, so I kept exploring until I had a full count. There were three rows of raised circles, with six in each row.

Eighteen, total. 2 *Corinthians 4:18*, I thought. Did that mean that I needed to press four of the eighteen raised circles? And if so, which four?

Frustrated, I stood. With Tobias Hawthorne, nothing was ever easy. I walked around the altar again, taking in its size. The billionaire had wanted to build a mausoleum, but he hadn't. He'd built this chapel, and I couldn't help but notice that if this giant slab of marble was hollow, there would be room for a body inside.

I can do this. I stared at the verse inscribed on what I suspected was Will Blake's tomb. *"So we fix our eyes not on what is seen,"* I read out loud again, *"but on what is unseen, since what is seen is temporary, but what is unseen is eternal."*

Unseen.

What did it mean to fix your eyes on something that was unseen? I had no way of looking at the raised circles. I couldn't see them. I'd had to feel them. *With my fingers*, I thought, and suddenly, just like that, I knew what this inscription meant—not in a biblical sense, but to Tobias Hawthorne.

I knew exactly how I was supposed to see what was unseen.

I took out my phone, and I looked up how numbers were written in Braille. *Four. One. Eight.*

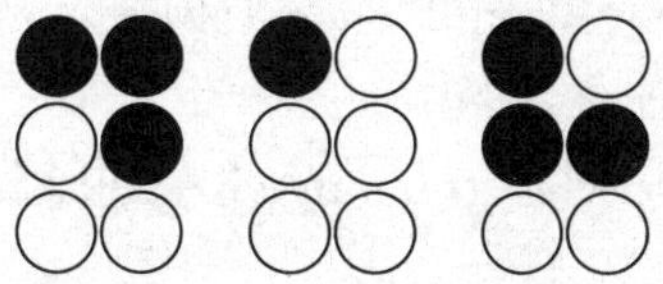

Crouching back down behind the altar, I slid my fingers under the marble and pressed only the raised circles indicated. *Four. One. Eight.*

I heard a creak, and my eyes darted to the top of the altar. A slab of marble had separated from the rest. *Unlocked.*

I moved the candelabra, the Bible, and the cross to the floor. The slab that had released was maybe two inches thick and too heavy for me to move myself.

I looked to Oren, who was standing guard as always. "I need your help," I told him.

He stared at me, long and hard, then cursed under his breath and came to help me. We slid the marble slab, and it didn't take much movement to realize that my instincts had been right. The inside of the altar *had* been hollowed out. There was a space big enough for a body.

But there were no remains. Instead, I found a shroud, the kind that might have once draped a skeleton or a corpse. *By the time the chapel and this altar were finished, would there have been anything left but bones?* I didn't smell death. Stretching to reach in and move the shroud, I saw that the marble inside this makeshift crypt had been defaced with familiar handwriting.

Toby's.

I wondered how long it had taken him to angrily carve six words into the marble. I wondered if this was where he'd found the Blake family seal. I wondered what else he'd found here.

I KNOW WHAT YOU DID, FATHER.

Those were the words he'd left behind—the words that Tobias Hawthorne would have found, once Toby ran away, if he'd checked to see if this secret remained.

And then I saw one last thing in what must have once been Will Blake's tomb.

A USB drive.

CHAPTER 67

I locked my hand around the USB. As I pulled it out, my mind raced. The drive definitely hadn't been sitting in a tomb for twenty years. It looked new.

"You know, Avery, I want to be surprised that you got here first, but I'm not." *Eve.* I whipped my head up to see her standing in the chapel doorway beneath a stone arch. "Some people just have that magic touch," she continued softly. She walked toward me, toward the altar. "What did you find in there?"

She sounded hesitant, vulnerable, but the second Oren stepped into her path, the matching expression on her face flickered like a light bulb a second before it burns out.

"There was supposed to be human remains in there," Eve said calmly. *Too* calmly. "But there weren't, were there?" She cocked her head to the side, her hair falling in gentle amber waves as her gaze landed on the USB in my hand. "I'm going to need you to give me that."

"Are you out of your mind?" I asked. I didn't notice her hands moving until it was too late.

She's got a gun. Eve held her weapon the way that Nash had taught me to hold mine. *Her gun is pointed straight at me.* That thought shouldn't have computed, but I had a knife in my boot. I'd spent all that time training. So when my body should have been panicking, an unnatural calm settled over me instead.

Oren drew his sidearm. "Put the weapon down," he ordered.

It was like Eve didn't even hear him, like the only person in this room she could see or hear was me.

"Where did you even get a gun?" I was stalling for time, assessing the situation. "There's no way you made it onto the estate with one that first morning." Even as I said the words, I thought about Eve bolting the moment she'd "discovered" Vincent Blake's name.

"Put the gun down!" Oren repeated. "I guarantee you that I can get a shot off before you can, and I don't miss."

Eve took a step forward, utterly, beautifully unafraid. "Are you really going to let your bodyguard shoot me, Avery?"

This was a different Eve. Gone were the layers of self-protection, the vulnerability, the raw emotion—all of it.

"You helped Blake abduct Toby, didn't you?" I said, certainty washing over me like a wave of heat.

"I wouldn't have had to," Eve replied, her tone smooth and hard, "if Toby had opened up. If he'd just agreed to bring me here. *But he wouldn't.*"

"This is the last time that I'm going to tell you to put the gun down!" Oren boomed.

"I'm still Toby's daughter," Eve said, adopting a familiar, wide-eyed expression, her gun unwavering. "And honestly, Avery, how do you think Gray will feel if Oren shoots me? What do you think will happen if that beautiful, broken boy walks in here to find me bleeding out on the floor?"

At her mention of Grayson, I instinctively looked for him, but he wasn't there. My body shaking with pent-up rage, I turned to Oren. "Put the gun down," I told him.

My head of security stepped directly in front of me. "She puts hers down first."

A haughty expression on her face, Eve lowered her weapon. Oren was on her in an instant, taking her to the ground, pinning her down.

Eve looked up at me from the chapel floor and smiled. "You want Toby back, and I want whatever you found in that tomb."

She'd called it a tomb. She'd said earlier that there were supposed to be remains in there. I wondered how she'd come to that conclusion, and then I remembered where I'd left her—and with whom. "Mallory," I said.

"She admitted that Liam didn't leave. I believe her exact words were *There was so much blood.*" Eve's gaze went to the altar. "So where's the body?"

"Is that really all you care about?" I asked her. From the very beginning, she'd told me that there was only one thing that mattered to her. I was starting to think that wasn't a lie—it was just that her single-minded purpose had nothing to do with Toby.

It had never been about Toby.

"*Caring* is a recipe for getting hurt, and I haven't let anyone hurt me in a very long time." Eve smiled again, like she was the one who had the upper hand, not the one pinned to the ground. "In all fairness, I did warn you, Avery. I told you that if I were you, I wouldn't trust me, either. I told you that I am a person who will do anything—*anything*—to get what I want. I told you that *invisible* is the one thing that I will never be."

"And Toby," I said, staring at her, sick understanding coming over me, "wanted you to hide."

"Blake wants me by his side," Eve said, zeal in her voice. "I just have to prove myself first."

"You don't have one of the seals yet, do you?" I asked. I thought about Nan saying that Vincent Blake didn't give anyone—not even family—a free ride.

"I'm going to get one," Eve told me, her voice burning with the fury of purpose. "Give me that USB, and maybe you can get what you want, too." She paused, then hit a nail right through my heart. "*Toby*."

I hated even hearing her say his name. "How could you do this?" I said, thinking of the picture Blake had sent, the bruises on his face—and then of the pictures of Toby and Eve on Eve's camera roll. "He trusted you."

"It's easy to make people trust you," Eve commented softly, "if you let them see you bleed." I thought about the bruises she'd shown up here sporting and wondered if she'd *told* someone to hit her. "You can spend your whole life trying not to hurt," Eve continued, her voice high and clear, "but making people hurt *for* you? That's real power."

I thought of Toby telling me that he had two daughters.

"Give me the USB," Eve said again, her eyes still blazing, "and you won't ever have to see me again, Avery. I'll earn my seal, and you can have this place and those boys all to yourself. Win-win."

She was delusional. Oren had her pinned. She'd come at me *with a gun*. She was in no position to negotiate. "I'm not giving you anything," I said.

A flash of movement. I whipped my head toward the chapel door. Grayson stood there, backlit, his eyes locked on Oren, who was still restraining Eve.

"Let her go," Grayson ordered.

"She's a threat." Oren clipped the words. "She pulled a gun on Avery. The only place I am *letting* her go is far, far away from all of you."

"Grayson." I felt sick. "This isn't what it looks like—"

"Help me," Eve begged him. "Get the USB that Avery has. Don't let them take this from me, too."

Grayson stared at her a moment longer, then walked slowly toward me. He took the USB from my hand. I just stood there. Feeling like my insides had been hollowed out, I watched as he turned back to Eve. "I can't let you have this," Grayson said softly.

"Grayson—" Eve and I said his name in unison.

"I heard."

Eve was unabashed. "Whatever you heard, you *know* that I am not the villain here, Grayson. Your grandfather—he owed me better. He owed you better, and you and your family owe Avery *nothing*."

Grayson's eyes met mine. "I owe her more than she realizes."

A dam broke inside me, and all of the hurt I hadn't let myself feel came flooding out, and with it, everything else I felt—and had ever felt—for Grayson Hawthorne.

"You're as bad as your grandfather was," Eve tried. "Look at me, Grayson. *Look at me*."

He did.

"If you let Oren kick me out of here or call the police, if you try to force me to go back to Vincent Blake empty-handed, I swear to you, I will find a cliff to jump off of." There was something fierce and mad and savage in Eve's voice—something that sold that threat completely. "Emily's blood is on your hands. Do you really want mine there, too?"

Grayson stared at her. I could see him reliving the moment he'd found Emily. I could see the effect that Eve's specific threat—a *cliff*—had on him. I could see Grayson Davenport Hawthorne drowning, fighting the undertow in vain. And then I saw him stop fighting and let the memories and the grief and the truth wash over him.

And then Grayson took a breath. "You're a big girl," he told Eve. "You make your own choices. Whatever you do after Oren sends you packing—that's on you."

I wondered if he really meant that. If he believed it.

"This is your chance," Eve said, fighting Oren's grip. "This is redemption, Grayson. I'm yours, and you could be mine. It's your fault Emily's dead. You could have stopped her—"

Grayson took a single step toward her. "I shouldn't have had to." He looked down at the USB in his hand. "And this would be useless to you."

"You can't know that." Eve was a wild thing now, fighting Oren with everything she had.

"Assuming this USB is my grandfather's handiwork," Grayson told her, "you would need a decoder to make sense of any of the files. A Hawthorne never leaves any knowledge of value unprotected."

"So I'll break the encryption," Eve said dismissively.

Grayson arched an eyebrow at her. "Not without a second drive."

A second drive.

"You can't do this to me, Grayson. We're the same, you and I." There was something in the way Eve said that, something in her voice that made me think she believed it.

Grayson didn't blink. "Not anymore."

An instant later, Oren's men came crashing through the door.

Oren turned to me. "How do you want to handle this, Avery?"

Eve had pointed a gun at me. That, at least, was a crime. Lying to us wasn't. Manipulating us wasn't. I couldn't prove anything else. And she wasn't the *real* enemy here.

The real threat.

"Have your men escort Eve off the estate," I told Oren. "We'll deal directly with Vincent Blake from now on."

Eve didn't make them drag her. "You haven't won," she told me. "He'll keep coming—and sooner or later, all of you will wish to God that this had ended with me."

CHAPTER 68

Oren left Grayson and me alone in the chapel.

"I owe you an apology."

I met Grayson Hawthorne's eyes, as light and piercing as they'd been the first time I saw him. "You don't owe me anything," I said—not out of compassion but because it hurt to let myself think about how much I'd expected from him.

"Yes. I do." After a long moment, Grayson looked away. "I," he said, like that one word cost him everything, "have been punishing myself for so long. Not just for Emily's death—for every weakness, every miscalculation, *every*—" He cut off, like his windpipe had closed suddenly around the words. I watched as he forced a jagged breath into his lungs. "No matter what I was or what I did—it was never enough. The old man was always there, pushing for better, for more."

I'd thought once that he had bulletproof confidence. That he was arrogant and incapable of second-guessing himself and utterly sure of his own power.

"And then," Grayson said, "the old man was gone. And then... there was you."

"Grayson." His name caught in my throat.

Grayson just looked at me, his light eyes shadowed. "Sometimes, you have an idea of a person—about who they are, about what you'd be like together. But sometimes that's all it is: an idea. And for so long, I have been afraid that I loved the *idea* of Emily more than I will ever be capable of loving anyone real."

That was a confession and self-condemnation and a curse. "That's not true, Grayson."

He looked at me like the act of doing so was painful and sweet. "It was never just the idea of you, Avery."

I tried not to feel like the ground was suddenly moving underneath my feet. "You *hated* the idea of me."

"But not you." The words were just as sweet, just as painful. "Never you."

Something gave inside me. "Grayson."

"I know," he said roughly.

I shook my head. "You're still so convinced that you know everything."

"I know that Jamie loves you." Grayson looked at me the way you look at art in a glass case, like he wanted to reach out to touch me but couldn't. "And I've seen the way that you look at him, the way the two of you are together. You're in love with my brother, Avery." He paused. "Tell me you're not."

I couldn't do that. He knew I couldn't. "I am in love with your brother," I said, because it was true. Jameson was part of me now—part of who I'd spent the past year becoming. I'd changed. If I hadn't, maybe things could have been different, but there was no going back.

I was who I was *because* of Jameson. I hadn't been lying when I'd told him that I didn't want him to be anyone else.

So why was this so hard?

"I wanted Eve to be different," Grayson told me. "I wanted her to be you."

"Don't say that," I whispered.

He looked at me one last time. "There are so many things that I will never say."

He was getting ready to walk away, and I had to let him—but I couldn't. "Promise me you won't leave again," I told Grayson. "You can go back to Harvard. You can go wherever you want, do whatever you want—just promise me that you won't shut us out again." I lifted my hand to my Hawthorne pin. I knew he had one of his own. I knew that, but I took mine off and pinned it on him anyway. "*Est unus ex nobis.* You said that to Jameson once, do you remember? *She is one of us.* Well, it goes both ways, Gray."

Grayson closed his eyes, and I was hit with the feeling that I would never forget the way he looked standing there in the light from the stained-glass windows. Without his armor. Without pretense. Raw.

"*Scio,*" Grayson told me. *I know.*

I looked down at the USB in his hand.

"I have the other one," I told him. "It was the one object in the leather satchel that we never used, remember?"

Grayson's eyes opened. He stepped out of the light. "Are you going to call my brothers?" he asked me. "Or shall I?"

CHAPTER 69

Xander plugged the first USB into his computer, dragged the audio file onto the desktop, then removed the USB and exchanged it for the USB from the tomb. He dragged the second file to his desktop, too.

"Play the first one," Jameson instructed.

Xander did. Garbled, undecipherable speech filled the air, a blast of white noise.

"And the second?" Nash prompted. For as long as I'd known him, he'd resisted dancing to the old man's tune. But he was here. He was doing this.

The lone file on the second USB was also an audio clip. It was just as messed up as the first.

"What happens if you play them together?" I asked. Grayson had said that to make sense of one file, you needed a decoder. In isolation, the clips were nothing but noise. But if you had both USBs, both files...

Xander opened an audio editing app and dumped the files in. He lined them up, then hit a sequence of buttons that caused them to play.

Combined, the result wasn't garbled. "Hello, Avery," a man's voice said, and I felt the change in the air around me, in all of *them*. "We're strangers, you and I. I imagine that's something you've thought about quite a bit."

Tobias Hawthorne. The one and only time I'd met him, I was six years old. But he was omnipresent in this place. Hawthorne House bore his mark. Every room. Every detail.

The boys bore it, too.

"All great lives should have at least one grand mystery, Avery. I won't apologize for being yours." Tobias Hawthorne was a man who didn't apologize for much. "If you've spent late nights and early mornings asking yourself *Why me?* Well, my dear, you are not the only one. What is the human condition, if not *Why me?*"

I could feel the shift in each of the Hawthorne brothers as they listened to Tobias Hawthorne's words and the cadence of his speech.

"As a young man, I believed myself destined for greatness. I fought for it, I *thought* my way to the top, I cheated, I lied, I made the world bend to my will." There was a pause, and then: "I got lucky. I can admit that now. I'm dying, and not slowly, either. *Why me?* Why is this body giving out? Why am I the one sitting in a palace of my own making when there are others out there with minds like mine? I got lucky. Right place, right time, right ideas, right mind." He let out an audible breath. "If only that were it.

"If you are playing this message, then things have become as dire as I projected. Eve is there, and certain events have led you to finding the tomb that once housed this family's greatest secret. How much, I wonder, have you put together for yourself, Avery?"

Every time he said my name, I felt like he was here in this room. Like he could see me. Like he had been watching me from the moment I'd stepped through Hawthorne House's grand front door.

"But then," he continued, an odd sort of smile in his voice, "you're not alone, are you? Hello, boys."

I felt Jameson shift, his arm brushing mine.

"If you boys are indeed there with Avery, then at least one thing has worked out as I intended. You know quite well that she is not your enemy. Perhaps, if I have chosen as well as I think I have, she has reached a place inside of you that I never could. Dare I even say made you whole?"

"Turn it off," Nash said, but none of us listened. I wasn't even sure he meant it.

"I hope you enjoyed the game I left you. Whether your mother and aunt have found and played theirs, I cannot say. The odds I've calculated suggest it could go either way, which is why, Xander, I left you with the charge I did. I trust that you have looked for Toby. And Avery, I believe in my heart of hearts that Toby has found you."

Each word the dead man said made this entire situation feel that much eerier. How much of what had happened since he'd died had he foreseen? Not just foreseen, but planned, moving us all around like pawns?

"If you are listening to this, then there is a high likelihood that Vincent Blake has revealed himself as a clear and present threat. I'd hoped to outlive the bastard. For years, he and I have had an armistice of sorts. He considered himself magnanimous at first, to let me go. Later, once he began to resent my growing fortune, my power, my status—well, those things kept him in check.

"*I* kept him in check."

There was another pause, and it felt sharper somehow this time, honed.

"But now I am gone, and if Blake knows what I suspect you now know, God help you all. If Eve is there, if Blake knows or even suspects what I have kept from him all these years, then he is coming.

For the fortune. For my legacy. For you, Avery Kylie Grambs. And for that, I do apologize."

I thought of the letter that Tobias Hawthorne had left me. The only explanation I'd been given, back at the start. *I'm sorry.*

"But better you than them." Tobias Hawthorne paused. "Yes, Avery. I really am that much of a bastard. I really did paint a target on your forehead. Even without the truth surfacing, I saw the probabilities for what they were. Once I was no longer there to hold him at bay, Blake was always going to make his move. *Hunting season,* he might call it—playing the game, destroying all opponents, taking what was mine. And that, my dear, is why it is now *yours.*"

I'd known that I was a tool. I'd known he'd chosen me for what he could use me to do. But I hadn't realized, hadn't ever even suspected, that Tobias Hawthorne had named me his heir because I was disposable.

"I met your mother, you know." The billionaire didn't stop. He never stopped. "Once when I believed her to be merely a waitress and once after I had deduced that she was Hannah Rooney, my only son's great love. I thought to use her to get to Toby. I tried my hand at working her—cajoling, threatening, bribing, manipulating. And do you know what your mother told me, Avery? She told me that she knew who Vincent Blake was, knew what had happened to his son, knew where Toby had hidden the Blake family seal, and that if I came near her—or you—again, she would bring the whole house of cards tumbling down."

I tried to picture my mom threatening a man like Tobias Hawthorne.

"Did you know about the seal?" Tobias asked, his tone almost conversational. "Did you know this family's darkest secret? I think not, but I am a man who has made an empire by always, *always* questioning my own assumptions. I excel at nothing if not contingencies. So here we are, Avery Kylie Grambs. The little girl with the funny little name. A skeleton key for so many little locks.

"I had six weeks from my diagnosis until now. Another two, I wager, until my deathbed. Enough time to put the final pieces in place. Enough time to draw up one last game with so very many layers. *Why you*, Avery? To draw the boys in one last time? To bequeath to them a mystery befitting Hawthornes, the puzzle of a lifetime? To bring them back together through you? *Yes*." He said the word *yes* like a man who relished saying it. "To pull Toby out of the shadows? To do in death what I was unable to do in life and force him back onto the board? *Yes*."

The sound of my own body was suddenly overwhelming. The beating of my heart. Each breath I somehow managed to draw. The rush of blood in my ears.

"And," Tobias Hawthorne continued with an air of finality, "to my great shame, to pull Blake's attention and focus—and the attention and focus of all of my enemies, of whom there are doubtlessly many—to you."

Yes. He didn't say it this time, but I thought it, and then I thought about Nan telling me that I was the one playing the piano now—and men like Vincent Blake, they'd break every single one of my fingers if they could.

"Call it misdirection," the dead billionaire said. "I needed someone to draw fire, and who better than Hannah Rooney's daughter, on the off chance that she *had* told you my secret? You'd hardly have motive to reveal it once the money was yours."

Traps upon traps. And riddles upon riddles. The words that Jameson had spoken to me long ago came back to me—followed by something Xander had said. *Even if you* thought *that you'd manipulated our grandfather into this, I guarantee that he'd be the one manipulating you*.

"But take as your consolation this, my very risky gamble: I have watched you. I have come to know you. As you draw fire away from those that I hold most dear, know that I believe there is at least a sliver of a chance that you will survive the hits you take. You may be tested by the flames, but you need not burn.

"If you are listening to this, Blake is coming." Tobias Hawthorne's tone was intense now. "He will box you in. He will hold you down. He will have no mercy. But he will also underestimate you. You're young. You're female. You're nobody—*use that*. My greatest adversary—and yours now—is an honor-bound man. Best him, and he'll honor the win."

Something in Tobias Hawthorne's tone made those words sound not just like advice but also like *good-bye*.

"My boys." Hawthorne sounded like he was smiling again, a crooked smile like Jameson's, a hard one like Grayson's. "If you are indeed listening to this, judge me as harshly as you like. I've made my deals with so very many devils. Find me wanting. Hate me if you must. Let your anger light a fire that the world will never extinguish.

"Nash. Grayson. Jameson. Xander." He said their names one at a time. "You were the clay, and I was the sculptor, and it has been the joy and honor of my life to make you better men than I will ever be. Men who may curse my name but will never forget it."

My hand found its way to Jameson's, and he held on to me for dear life.

"On your marks, boys," Tobias Hawthorne said on the recording. "Get set. *Go*."

CHAPTER 70

Silence had never sounded this loud. I'd never seen the Hawthorne brothers so still—all of them, like they'd been stung with a paralyzing venom. As big an impact as hearing the truth from Tobias Hawthorne's mouth had on me, he wasn't the formative influence of *my* life.

I forced myself to speak because they couldn't. "You always did say that the old man liked to kill ten birds with one stone."

Jameson brought his eyes up from the ground to me, then let out a rough, pained chuckle. "Twelve."

Twelve birds, one stone. I'd been warned. From the moment I'd received a ring holding a hundred keys—from before that, even—I'd been warned by each of the Hawthorne brothers in turn.

Traps upon traps. And riddles upon riddles.

Even if you thought *that you'd manipulated our grandfather into this, I guarantee that he'd be the one manipulating you.*

This family—we destroy everything we touch.

You're not a player, kid. You're the glass ballerina—or the knife.

And then there was the message that Tobias Hawthorne had left me himself, back at the very beginning. *I'm sorry.*

"We did exactly what he thought we would." Xander snapped out of it and began to move—wild gestures, weight on the balls of his feet. "All of us. From the beginning."

"That sonofabitch." Nash let out a long whistle, then leaned back against the wall. "How dangerous do we think Vincent Blake is?" The question sounded casual and calm, but I could imagine Nash strolling up to a rabid bull with that exact expression on his face.

"Dangerous enough to require a decoy." Grayson's calm was a different sort than Nash's—icy and controlled. "We're dealing with a family whose fortune, though significantly smaller, goes back a lot further than ours. There's no telling what people or institutions Blake has in his pocket."

"The old man took the four of us off the board." Jameson swore. "He raised us to fight but never intended this fight for us."

I thought about Skye saying that her father had never considered her a player in the grand game, then about a letter that Tobias Hawthorne had left his daughters. There was a part where he'd said that not one of them would see his fortune. *There are things I have done that I am not proud of, legacies that you should not have to bear.*

The truth had been there, right in front of us, for months. Tobias Hawthorne had left me his fortune so that if and when his enemies descended after his death, they would descend on *me*. He'd picked his target carefully, placed me as a cog in a complicated machine.

Twelve birds, one stone.

If you are listening to this, Blake is coming. He will box you in. He will hold you down. He will have no mercy. I could feel something inside me hardening. Tobias Hawthorne hadn't foreseen exactly *how* Vincent Blake would come at me. Hawthorne hadn't known that Toby would be caught in Blake's plot, but he'd damn well known what the man was capable of. And his only consolation to me had been that he thought there was a *sliver* of a chance that I could survive.

I wanted to despise Tobias Hawthorne—or at least judge him—but all I could think was the other words he'd left me. *You may be tested by the flames, but you need not burn.*

"Where are you going?" Jameson called after me.

I didn't look back over my shoulder, couldn't quite bring myself to look at any of them. "To make a call."

Vincent Blake answered on the fifth ring, a power play in and of itself. "Presumptuous little thing, aren't you?"

You're young. You're female. You're nobody—use that.

"Eve is gone," I said, banishing any hint of emotion from my tone. "You don't have anyone on the inside now."

"You seem very sure of that, little girl." Blake was amused, like my attempt at playing this game was nothing to him but that—an amusement.

He wants me to believe that he has someone else inside Hawthorne House. Staying silent even a moment too long would have been seen as weakness, so I spoke. "You want the truth about what happened to your son. You want his remains found and returned to you." My breathing wanted to go shallow, but I was a better bluffer than that. "What, besides Toby, will you give me if I deliver what you want?"

I didn't know where whatever remained of William Blake was. But a person could only play the cards they'd been dealt. Blake thought that I had something he wanted. Without Eve here, I might be his only way of getting it.

I needed an advantage. I needed leverage. Maybe this was it.

"What will I give you?" Blake's amusement deepened into

something darker, twisted. "What, besides Toby, do I have that you want? I am so very glad you asked."

The line went dead. He'd hung up on me. I stared down at my phone.

A moment later, Oren stepped into my peripheral view. "There's a courier at the gate."

CHAPTER 71

There was no point in cross-examining the person who delivered the package. We knew who it was from. We knew what he wanted.

"Everything okay?" Libby asked me when Oren's man appeared in the foyer with the package. I shook my head. *Whatever this is—it's definitely not okay.*

Oren completed his initial security screen, then handed both the contents and the packaging over to me: one gift box large enough to hold a sweater; inside it, thirteen letter-sized envelopes; inside each envelope, a clear, thin, rectangular sheet of plastic with an abstract black-and-white design inked onto it. Looking at any one sheet in isolation was like doing one of those inkblot tests.

"Stack them," Jameson suggested. I wasn't sure when he'd come into the room, but he wasn't alone. All four of the Hawthorne brothers circled around me. Libby hung back, but only slightly.

I laid sheet on top of sheet, the designs combining to form a single picture—but it wasn't that easy. Of course it wasn't. There were four ways that each sheet could go—*up or down, front or back*.

I felt the sheets with my fingertips, locating the side on which the ink had been printed. Moving with lightning speed, I began matching the sheets in the lower left corner, using the patterns to guide me.

One, two, three, four—no, that one's the wrong way. I kept going, one sheet on top of another on top of another, until a picture emerged. A black-and-white photograph.

And in that photograph, Alisa Ortega lay on a dirt floor, her head lolled to one side, her eyes closed.

"She's alive," Jameson said beside me. "Unconscious. But she doesn't look..."

Dead, I finished for him. *What, besides Toby, do I have that you want?* I could hear Vincent Blake saying. *I am so very glad you asked.*

"Lee-Lee." Nash didn't sound calm, not this time.

I swallowed. "Is there any chance she's in on it?" I asked, hating myself for even giving life to the question, for letting Blake get to me that much.

"*None*," Nash said, biting out the word with almost inhuman ferocity.

I looked to Jameson and Grayson. "Your grandfather said *don't trust anyone*, not just *don't trust her.* He at least considered it possible that Blake would be able to get to someone else in my inner circle." I looked back down at Alisa's seemingly unconscious body. "And right now, Alisa and her firm have a lot to lose if I don't agree to a trust."

The power behind the fortune. The ability to move mountains and make men.

"You can trust Alisa," Nash said roughly. "She's loyal to the old man, always has been." Libby came closer and laid a hand on his back, and he turned his head to look at her. "This ain't what you think, Lib. I don't have feelings for her, but just because things don't work out with a person doesn't mean they stop mattering."

"No one ever stops mattering," Libby said, like the words were a revelation, "to you."

"Nash is right. There's no way Alisa is in on it," Jameson said. "Vincent Blake took her, just like he took Toby."

Because she works for me.

"The bastard can't do this," Grayson swore with a powerful intensity I hadn't seen from him in months. "We'll *destroy* him."

You can't. That was why Tobias Hawthorne had disinherited them, why he'd drawn Blake's focus to me—and the people I cared about. Oren had assigned a bodyguard to Max. He'd brought Thea and Rebecca here. He'd shut down avenue after avenue of using other people to get to me—but Alisa hadn't been on lockdown.

She'd been out there playing games of her own.

With shaking hands, I called her number. Again. And again. She didn't pick up. "Alisa always picks up," I said out loud. I forced my eyes to Oren's. "*Now* can we call the police?"

Toby was a dead man. You couldn't report a dead man missing. But Alisa was very much alive, and we had the picture as proof of foul play.

"Blake will have someone—maybe multiple someones—high up in all the local police departments."

"And I don't?" I said.

"You did," Oren told me, past tense, and I remembered what he'd said about the rash of recent transfers.

"What about the FBI?" I asked. "I don't care if the case is federal or not—Tobias Hawthorne had people, and they're my people now. Right?"

No one replied, because whoever Tobias Hawthorne may or may not have had in his pocket, there was no one in mine. Not without Alisa there to pull the strings.

Check. I could practically see the board, see the moving pieces, see the way that Vincent Blake was boxing me in.

"Lee-Lee wouldn't want us to go to the authorities." Nash seemed to have trouble finding his voice. It came out in a slow, deep rumble. "The optics."

"You don't care about optics," I told him.

Nash took off his cowboy hat, his eyes shadowed. "I care about a lot of things, kid."

"What do we have to do," Libby asked fiercely, "to get Alisa back?"

I was the one who answered the question. "Find a body—or what's left of one after forty years."

Nash's eyes narrowed. "This had better be one hell of an explanation."

CHAPTER 72

The moment I finished explaining, Nash strode off ominously. Libby went with him. Strategizing our next move, I asked Xander where Rebecca and Thea were.

"The cottage." Xander was rarely this solemn. "Bex was ignoring her mom's calls, but then her grandma called, after Eve..."

After Eve got the truth out of Mallory, I finished silently. Forcing my mind to focus on that truth and what it meant for us now, I led the boys to my room and showed them the blueprints.

"These are in chronological order," I said. "I used that chronology to find the construction project erected in the wake of Toby's conception: the chapel. The altar was made of stone and hollow inside." I swallowed. "A tomb—but no body hidden in it, just the USB, which your grandfather must have hidden there shortly before his death, and a message scratched into the stone by Toby way back when."

"Not that you need another nickname," Xander commented, "but I'm liking *Sherlock*. What did the message say?"

I looked past Xander to Jameson and... Grayson wasn't there. I wasn't sure when we'd lost him. I didn't let myself wonder why.

"*I know what you did, Father.*" I answered Xander's question. "I'm taking that to mean that at some point after Toby found out he was adopted and before he ran away at nineteen…"

"He found out about *Liam*," Jameson finished.

I thought about all the messages Toby had left his father: "A Poison Tree," hidden under a floor tile; a poem of his own making, coded into a book of law; the words inside the altar.

The now-empty altar.

"Toby found the body." Saying it out loud made it seem real. "It was probably just bones by then. He stole the seal, moved the remains, left a series of hidden messages for the old man, and went on a self-destructive tear across the country that ended in the fire on Hawthorne Island."

I thought about Toby, about his collision course with my mother and the ways their love might have been different if Toby hadn't been broken by the horrific secrets he carried.

The real Hawthorne legacy.

I saw now why Toby was determined to stay away from Hawthorne House. I could understand why he'd wanted to protect my mother—his *Hannah, the same backward as forward*—and later, once she was dead and I'd already been pulled into this mess, why he had needed to at least try to protect *Eve* from everything that came along with the Hawthorne fortune.

From the truth and the poisonous tree. From Blake.

"*The evidence I stole,*" I said out loud, staring down at the blueprints, "*is in the darkest hole….*"

"The tunnels?" Jameson was behind me—right behind me. I felt his suggestion as much as heard it.

"That's one possibility," I said, and then I pulled four sets of blueprints. "The others are these—the additions made to Hawthorne House during the time span in which Toby must have discovered and moved the remains. He could have taken advantage of the construction somehow."

Toby had been sixteen when he'd discovered that he was adopted, nineteen when he'd left Hawthorne House forever. I pictured crews breaking ground on each of those additions. *The evidence I stole is in the darkest hole. . . .*

"This one," Jameson said urgently, kneeling over the plans. "Heiress, look."

I saw what he saw. "The hedge maze."

Jameson and I made our way to the maze. Xander went for reinforcements. "Start at the outside and work our way in?" Jameson asked me. "Or go to the center of the maze and spiral out?"

It felt right somehow that it was just the two of us. Jameson Winchester Hawthorne and me.

The hedges were eight feet tall, and the maze covered an area nearly as large as the House. It would take days for us to search it all. Maybe weeks. Maybe longer. Wherever Toby had hidden the body, his father either hadn't found it or had chosen not to risk moving it again.

I pictured men planting these hedges.

I pictured nineteen-year-old Toby, in the dead of night, somehow finding a way to bury the bones of the man responsible for half his DNA.

"Start at the center," I told Jameson, my voice echoing in the space all around us, "and spiral out."

I knew the path that would take us to the heart of the maze. I'd been there before, more than once—with Grayson.

"I don't suppose you know where he went, do you, Heiress?" Jameson had a way of making every question sound a little wicked and a little sharp—but I knew, *I knew* what he was really asking.

What he was always trying not to ask himself when it came to Grayson and me.

"I don't know where Grayson is," I told Jameson, and then I hung a left, and the muscles in my throat tightened. "But I do know that he's going to be okay. He confronted Eve. I think he finally let go of Emily, finally forgave himself for being human."

Right turn. Left turn. Left again. Straight. We were almost to the center now.

"And now that Gray is okay," Jameson said close behind me, "now that he's so delightfully *human* and ready to move on from Emily..."

I hit the center of the maze and turned around to face Jameson. "Don't finish that question."

I knew what he was going to ask. I knew he wasn't wrong to ask. But still, it stung. And the only way that he was ever going to stop asking—himself, me, Grayson—was if I gave him the full, unvarnished truth.

The truth I hadn't let myself think too often or too clearly.

"You were right before when you called my bluff," I told Jameson. "I can't say that it was always going to be you."

He walked past me toward the hidden compartment in the ground where the Hawthornes kept their longswords. I heard him opening the compartment, heard him searching.

Because Jameson Winchester Hawthorne was always searching for something. He couldn't stop. He would never stop.

And I didn't want to, either. "I can't say that it was always going to be you, Jameson, because I don't believe in destiny or fate—I believe in choice." I knelt next to him and let my fingers explore the compartment. "You chose me, Jameson, and I chose to open up to you, to all of the possibilities of *us*, in a way that I had never opened up to anyone before."

Max had told me once to picture myself standing on a cliff overlooking the ocean. I felt like I was standing there now, because love wasn't just a choice—it was dozens, hundreds, thousands of choices.

Every day was a choice.

I moved on from the compartment that held the swords, running my hands over the ground at the center of the maze, looking, searching still. "Letting you in," I told Jameson, the two of us crouched feet apart, "becoming *us*—it changed me. You taught me to *want*."

How to want things.

How to want *him*.

"You made me hungry," I told Jameson, "for everything. I want the world now." I held his gaze in a way that *dared* him to look away. "And I want it with you."

Jameson made his way to me—just as my fingers hit something, buried in the grass, wedged into the soil.

Something small and round and metal. *Not the Blake family seal. Just a coin. But the size, the shape . . .*

Jameson brought his hands to my face. His thumb lightly skimmed my lips. And I said the two words guaranteed to take that spark in his eyes and set it on fire.

"Dig here."

CHAPTER 73

My arms were aching by the time the ground caved in, revealing a chamber below—part of the tunnels, but not a part I'd ever seen.

Before I could say a word, Jameson leapt into the darkness.

I lowered myself down more cautiously, landing beside him in a crouch. I stood, shining the light from my phone. The chamber was small—and empty.

No body.

I scanned the walls and saw a torch. Latching my fingers around the torch, I tried to pull it from the wall, to no avail. I let my fingers explore the metal sconce that held the torch in place. "There's a hinge back here," I said. "Or something like it. I think it rotates"

Jameson placed his hand over mine, and together we twisted the torch sideways. There was a scraping sound and then a hiss, and the torch burst into flame.

Jameson didn't let go, and neither did I.

We pulled the flaming torch from the sconce, and as the flame came close to the wall's surface, words lit up in Toby's writing.

"*I was never a Hawthorne*," I read out loud. Jameson let his hand fall to his side, until I was the only one holding the torch. Slowly,

I walked the perimeter of the room. The flame revealed words on each wall.

I was never a Hawthorne.

I will never be a Blake.

So what does that make me?

I saw the message on the final wall, and my heart contracted. *Complicit.*

"Try the floor," Jameson told me.

I brought the torch low, careful of the flame, and one final message lit up. *Try again, Father.*

The body wasn't here.

It had never been here.

A light shone down from up above. *Mr. Laughlin.* He helped us out of the chamber, silent the whole time, his expression absolutely unreadable, right up to the point that I tried to step from the center back into the maze, and he moved to stand right in front of me.

Blocking me.

"I heard about Alisa." The groundskeeper's voice was always gruff, but the visible sorrow in his eyes was new. "The kind of man who would take a woman—he's no man at all." He paused. "Nash came to me," he said haltingly. "He asked me for help, and that boy wouldn't even let you help tie his shoes as a toddler."

"You know where Will Blake's remains are," I said, giving voice to the realization as it dawned on me. "That's why Nash went to you and asked you for help."

Mr. Laughlin forced himself to look at me. "Some things are best left buried."

I wasn't about to accept that. I *couldn't.* Anger snaked through me, burning in my veins. At Vincent Blake and Tobias Hawthorne and this man who was supposed to work for me but would always put the Hawthorne family first.

"I'll raze this entire thing to the ground," I swore. Some situations required a scalpel, but this? *Bring on the chain saws.* "I'll hire men to tear this maze apart. I'll bring out cadaver dogs. I will burn it all down to get Alisa back."

Mr. Laughlin's body trembled. "You have no right."

"Grandpa."

He turned, and Rebecca stepped into view. Thea and Xander followed, but Mr. Laughlin barely noticed them. "This isn't right," he told Rebecca. "I made promises—to myself, to your mother, to Mr. Hawthorne."

If I'd had any doubts that the groundskeeper knew where the body was, that statement erased them. "Vincent Blake has Toby, too," I said. "Not just Alisa. Don't you want your grandson back?"

"Don't you talk to me about my grandson." Mr. Laughlin was breathing heavily now.

Rebecca laid a calming hand on his arm. "It wasn't Mr. Hawthorne who killed Liam," she said quietly. "Was it?"

Mr. Laughlin shuddered. "Go back to the cottage, Rebecca."

"No."

"You used to be such a good girl," Mr. Laughlin grunted.

"I used to make myself small." Rebecca's was a subtle kind of steel. "But here with you—I didn't have to. I used to live for the few weeks we spent here each summer. I'd help you. Do you remember? I liked working with my hands, getting them dirty." She shook her head. "I was never allowed to get dirty at home."

Back when Emily was young and medically vulnerable, Rebecca's home had probably been entirely sterile.

"Please go back to the cottage." Mr. Laughlin's tone and mannerisms were a perfect match for his granddaughter's: quiet, understated steel. Until that moment, I'd never seen the resemblance between the two of them. "Thea, take her back."

"I loved working with you," Rebecca told her grandfather, the sun catching her ruby-red hair. "But there was one part of the maze that you always insisted on doing yourself."

My stomach twisted. *Rebecca knows where to dig.*

"Emily looked like your mother," Mr. Laughlin said roughly. "But you have her mind, Rebecca. She was brilliant. Is still." He choked on the next words. *"My little girl."*

"It wasn't Mr. Hawthorne who killed Vincent Blake's son," Rebecca said softly. "Was it?" There was no answer. "Eve's gone. Mom lost it when she couldn't find her. She said—"

"Whatever your mother said," Mr. Laughlin cut in harshly, "you forget it, Rebecca." He looked from her to the horizon. "That's how this works. We've all done our share of forgetting."

For more than forty years, this secret had festered. It had affected all of them—two families, three generations, one poisonous tree.

"Your daughter was only sixteen." I started with what I knew. "Will Blake was a grown man. He came here with something to prove."

"He used your daughter." Xander took over for me. "To spy on our grandfather."

"Will used and manipulated your sixteen-year-old daughter. He got her pregnant," Jameson continued, cutting straight to the heart of the matter.

"I've given my life to the Hawthorne family. I don't owe any of you this." Mr. Laughlin's voice wasn't just harsh now. It was vibrating with fury.

I felt for him. I did. But this wasn't theoretical. It wasn't a game. This might well be life or death.

"Show us the part of the maze he wouldn't let you work on," I told Rebecca.

She took a step, and Mr. Laughlin grabbed her arm. Hard.

"Let her go," Thea said, raising her voice.

Rebecca caught Thea's gaze, just for a moment, then turned back to her grandfather. "Mom's distraught. She started rambling. She told me that Liam was angry when he found out about the baby. He was going to leave her, so she stole something from the House, from Mr. Hawthorne's office. She told Liam that she had something he could use against Tobias Hawthorne, just so he would meet with her again. But when he came, when she went to give him what she'd taken, it wasn't in her bag."

I pictured them someplace isolated. The Black Wood, maybe.

"Tobias." At first that was all Mr. Laughlin managed—the dead billionaire's name. "He was spying on them. He followed Mal that day. He didn't know why she'd stolen from him, but he was damn set on finding out."

"What he found," Jameson concluded, "was Vincent Blake's adult son taking advantage of a teenage girl under his protection."

I thought about the reason that Tobias Hawthorne had turned on Blake in the first place. *Boys will be boys.*

"That little bastard Liam got angry when Mal couldn't give him what she'd promised. He went cold, told her that she was nothing. When he went to leave, she tried to stop him, and that monster raised a hand to my little girl."

I got the very real sense that if Will Blake rose from the dead right now, Mr. Laughlin would put him six feet under all over again.

"The second Liam got rough, Mr. Hawthorne stepped out from wherever he'd been hiding to issue some very pointed threats. Mal was sixteen. There were laws." Mr. Laughlin let out a breath, and it was a ragged, ugly sound. "The man should have slunk away like the rat he was, but Mal—she didn't want Liam to go. She threatened him, too, said that she would go to his father and tell him about the baby."

"Will needed to keep his father's favor to keep his seal," I said, thinking about Vincent Blake's *short string* for his family. "More than that, if he'd come here to prove something to Blake, to impress him—the idea of doing the opposite?"

I swallowed.

"Liam snapped and lunged for her again. Mal—she fought back." Mr. Laughlin's eyes closed. "I came in just as Mr. Hawthorne was pulling that man off my daughter. He got that bastard under control, had his arms pinned behind his back, and then—" Mr. Laughlin forced his eyes open and looked toward Rebecca. "Then my little girl picked up a brick. She went at him too quick for me to stop her. And not just once.... She hit him over and over again."

"It was self-defense," Jameson said.

Mr. Laughlin looked down, then forced his gaze to mine, like he needed me, of everyone here, to understand. "No. It wasn't."

I wondered how many times Mallory had hit her Liam before they stopped her. I wondered *if* they had stopped her.

"I got a hold of her," Mr. Laughlin said, his voice heavy. "She just kept saying that she thought he loved her. She thought—" There were no tears in his eyes, but a sob racked his chest. "Mr. Hawthorne told me to go. He told me to take Mal and get her out of there."

"Was Liam dead?" I asked, my mouth almost painfully dry.

There wasn't a hint of remorse in the groundskeeper's face. "Not yet."

Will Blake had been breathing when Mr. Laughlin left him alone with Tobias Hawthorne.

"Your daughter had just attacked Vincent Blake's son." Jameson was wired to find hidden truths, to turn everything into a puzzle, then solve it. "Back then, our family wasn't wealthy enough or powerful enough to protect her. Not yet."

"Do you even know what happened after you left?" Rebecca asked after a long and painful silence.

"My understanding is that he needed medical attention." Mr. Laughlin looked at each of us in turn. "Shame he didn't get it."

I pictured Tobias Hawthorne standing there and watching a man die. Letting him die.

"And afterward?" Xander said, uncharacteristically muted.

"I never asked," Mr. Laughlin said stiffly. "And Mr. Hawthorne never told me."

My mind raced—through the years, navigating through everything we knew. "But when Toby moved the body..." I started to say.

Mr. Laughlin locked his gaze back on the horizon. "I knew he'd buried something. Once Toby ran off and Mr. Hawthorne started asking questions, I figured out pretty quick what that something was."

And you never said a word, I thought.

"Show them the spot if you have to, Rebecca." Mr. Laughlin gently pushed his granddaughter's hair away from her face. "But if Vincent Blake asks what happened, you protect your mother. You tell him that it was me."

CHAPTER 74

We found the remains.

I brought out my phone, ready to place the call to Blake, but before I could pull the trigger, it rang. I glanced at caller ID and stopped breathing.

"Alisa?" I forced my lungs to start working again. "Are you—"

"Going to kill Grayson Hawthorne?" Alisa said evenly. "Yes. Yes, I am."

Just hearing her voice—and the absolute normality of her tone—sent a shock wave of relief through me. It was like I'd been carrying extra weight and pressure in every cell in my body, and suddenly, all that tension was gone.

And then I processed *what* Alisa had said.

"Grayson?" I repeated, my heart seizing in my chest.

"He's the reason Blake let me go. A trade."

I should have known when he hadn't come with us to find the body. *Grayson Hawthorne and his grand gestures.* Frustration, fear, and something almost painfully tender threatened to bring tears to my eyes.

"Your brother's playing sacrificial lamb," I told Jameson, trying to let that first emotion mute the rest. Xander heard my terse statement, too, and Nash appeared behind them.

"Alisa?" he said.

"She's fine," I reported. *And this time, we'll take care of her.* "Oren, can you have someone bring her in?"

Oren gave a curt nod, but the expression in his eyes betrayed how glad he was that she was okay. "Give me the phone, and I'll coordinate a pickup."

I passed the phone to him.

"This doesn't change anything," Jameson told me. "Blake still has the upper hand."

He had *Grayson*. There was a terrifying symmetry to that. Tobias Hawthorne had stolen Vincent Blake's grandson—and now he had Tobias Hawthorne's.

He has Toby. He has Grayson. And I have his son's remains. All I had to do was give Vincent Blake what he wanted, and this would be over.

Or at least, that was what Blake wanted me to believe.

But Tobias Hawthorne's final message hadn't just cautioned me that Blake would be coming for the truth, for proof. No, Tobias Hawthorne had told me that Blake would be coming for me, that he would box me in, hold me down, have no mercy. Tobias Hawthorne had been expecting a full-on assault on his empire. Assuming he'd projected correctly, Vincent Blake wasn't just after the truth.

He is coming. For the fortune. For my legacy. For you, Avery Kylie Grambs.

But Tobias Hawthorne—manipulative, Machiavellian man that he was—had also thought that I had a sliver of a chance. I just had to outplay Blake.

Take as your consolation this, my very risky gamble: I have watched you. I have come to know you. The words pumped through my body like blood, my heart beating out a brutal, uncompromising rhythm. Tobias Hawthorne had believed that Blake would underestimate me.

On the phone, he'd called me *little girl*.

What did that mean? *That he expects me to react, not act. That he thinks I'll never look ahead.*

I forced myself to stop, to slow down, to think. All around me, the others were fighting loudly about next moves. But I shut out the sound of Jameson's voice, of Nash's and Xander's, Oren's, everyone's. And eventually, I circled back to the Queen's Gambit. I thought about how it required ceding control of the board. It required a loss.

And it worked best when your opponent thought it was a rookie error, rather than strategy.

A plan took shape in my mind. It ossified. And I made a call.

CHAPTER 75

"What did you just do?" Jameson looked at me the way he had the night he'd told me that I was their grandfather's last puzzle, like after all this time, there were still things about me, about what I was capable of, that could surprise him.

Like he wanted to know them all.

"I called the authorities and reported that human remains had been found at Hawthorne House." That much had probably been obvious if they'd overheard me. What Jameson was really asking me was *why*.

"Far be it from me to state the obvious," Thea cut in, "but wasn't the point of digging *that* up to make a trade?"

I could feel Jameson reading me, feel his brain sorting through the possibilities in mine.

"I have another call to make," I said.

"To Blake?" Rebecca asked.

"No," Jameson answered for me.

"I don't have time to explain," I told all of them.

"You're playing him." Jameson didn't phrase that as a question.

"Blake said to bring him the body, and it will be returned to him. Eventually. And when it is, I won't have broken any laws."

It was easier thinking of this like chess. Trying to see my opponent's moves coming before he made them. Baiting the moves I wanted, blocking attacks before they happened.

Xander's eyes widened. "You think that if you'd taken him the remains, he would have held the illegality of that move over you?"

"I can't afford to hand him any more leverage."

"Because, of course, this is all about you." Thea's voice was dangerously pleasant—never a good sign.

"Thea," Rebecca said quietly. "Let it go."

"No. This is your *family*, Bex. And no matter how hard you try, no matter how angry you manage to get—that's always going to matter to you." Thea lifted a hand to the side of Rebecca's face. "I saw you back there with your mom."

Rebecca looked like she wanted to get lost in Thea's eyes, but she didn't let herself. "I always thought there was something wrong with me," she said, her voice breaking. "Emily was my mom's world, and I was a shadow, and I thought it was *me*."

"But now you know," Thea said softly, "it was never you."

Mallory's trauma was Rebecca's trauma—probably was Emily's, too.

"I am done living in the shadows, Thea," Rebecca said. She turned to me. "Bring on the light. Tell the world the truth. Do it."

That wasn't my plan—not exactly. There was one move that would let me protect the people who needed protecting. One sequence, if I could execute it.

If Blake didn't see it coming.

Reporting the body was just step one. Step two was controlling the narrative.

"Avery." Landon answered my call on the third ring. "Correct me if I'm wrong, but our working relationship came to an end quite some time ago."

I'd had other publicists and media consultants since, but for what I was planning, I needed the best. "I need to talk to you about a dead body and the story of the century."

Silence—enough of it that I wondered if she'd hung up on me. Then Landon offered up two words, her British accent crisp. "I'm listening."

I threw Tobias Hawthorne under the bus. Thoroughly and without mercy. Dead men didn't get to be picky about their reputations, and that went double for dead men who'd used me the way he had.

Tobias Hawthorne had killed a man forty years ago—and covered it up. That was the story I was telling, and it was one hell of a story.

"Where are you going?" Jameson called after me once I'd hung up with Landon.

"The vault," I replied. "There's something I need before I go to confront Vincent Blake."

Jameson ran to catch up with me. He made it past me, then turned back just as I took a step that put his body far too close to mine.

"And what do you need out of the vault?" Jameson asked.

"If I tell you," I said, "are you going to try to lock me up again?"

Jameson lifted a hand to the side of my neck. "Is it risky?"

I didn't look away. "Extremely."

"Good." His green eyes intense, he let his thumb trace the edge of my jaw. "To best Blake, it will have to be."

Some words were just words, and others were like fire. I felt it catching inside of me, spreading, as searing as any kiss. *We're back.*

"And once you've bested him," Jameson continued, "because you *will*..." There was no feeling in the world like being *seen* by Jameson Hawthorne. "I'm going to need an anagram for the word *everything*."

CHAPTER 76

After the vault, I made it as far as the foyer before chaos descended on me in the form of one very pissed-off Alisa Ortega. "What have you done?"

"Welcome back," Oren told her dryly.

"What I had to do," I answered.

Alisa took what was probably supposed to be a calming breath. "You didn't wait for me to get here because you *knew* I'd tell you that calling the police was a bad idea."

"You would have told me that calling the police on *Blake* was a bad idea," I countered. "So I didn't call them on Blake."

"We have local PD at the gate," Oren informed me. "Given the circumstances, my men can't refuse them entrance. I suspect the DPS Special Agents aren't long behind."

Alisa kneaded her temples. "I can fix this."

"It's not yours to fix," I told her.

"You have no idea what you're doing."

"No," I replied, staring her down. "*You* have no idea what I'm doing. There's a difference." I didn't have the time or inclination to explain everything to her. Landon had promised me a two-hour head start, but that was it. Any delay past that and we might lose our opportunity to control the narrative.

If I waited too long, Vincent Blake would have too much time to regroup.

"I'm glad you're okay," I told Alisa. "You've done a lot for me since the will was read. I know that. But the truth is that Tobias Hawthorne's fortune will be in my hands very soon." I didn't like playing it this way, but I didn't have a choice. "The only question you have to ask yourself is whether you still want to have a job when that happens."

Even I wasn't sure if I was bluffing. There was no way I could do this on my own, and even though I'd doubted her, I trusted Alisa more than I would trust anyone else I could hire next. On the other hand, she was in the habit of treating me like a kid—the same wide-eyed, overwhelmed, never-had-two-nickels-to-rub-together kid I'd been when I'd gotten here.

To take on Vincent Blake, I had to grow up.

"You'd drown without me," Alisa told me. "And take an empire down with you."

"So don't make me do this without you," I responded.

Fixing her gaze on me with almost frightening precision, Alisa gave a slight nod of her head. Oren cleared his throat.

I turned to face him. "Is this the part where you start talking about duct tape?"

He cocked an eyebrow at me. "Is this the part where you threaten my job?"

On the day that Tobias Hawthorne's will had been read, I'd tried to tell Oren I didn't need security. He'd calmly replied that I would need security for the rest of my life. It had never been a question of *whether* he would protect me.

“This isn’t just a job to you,” I told Oren, because I felt like I owed him that much. “It never has been.”

He’d told me months ago that he owed Tobias Hawthorne his life. The old man had given Oren a purpose, dragged him out of a very dark place. His last request to my head of security had been that Oren protect me.

“I thought he’d done something noble,” Oren said quietly, “asking me to take care of you.”

Oren was my constant shadow. He’d heard Tobias Hawthorne’s message. He knew what my purpose was—and that had to have shed new light on his.

“Your boss asked you to run my security. Taking care of me…” My voice hitched. “That was all you.”

Oren gave me the briefest of smiles, then he allowed himself to fall back into bodyguard mode. “What’s the plan, boss?”

I retrieved the Blake family seal from my pocket. “This.” I let it fall into my palm and closed my fingers around it. “We’re going to Blake’s ranch. I’m going to use this to get past the gates. And I’m going in alone.”

“I have a professional obligation to tell you that I don’t like this plan.”

I gave Oren a sympathetic look. “Would you like it more if I told you that I’ll be doing a press conference right outside his gates so that the whole world knows I’m inside?”

Vincent Blake couldn’t touch me with the paparazzi watching.

“You going to put a stop to this, Oren?” Nash ambled toward us, clearly having overheard our exchange. “Because if you don’t, I will.”

As if drawn by the chaos, Xander chose that moment to pop in, too.

“This doesn’t concern you,” I told Nash.

"Nice try, kid." Nash's tone never advertised the fact that he was pulling rank, but no matter how casual the delivery, it was always one hundred percent clear when that was what he was doing. "This ain't happening."

Nash didn't care that I was eighteen, that I owned the House, that I wasn't actually his sister, or that I would put up one hell of a fight if he tried to stop me.

"You can't protect the four of us forever," I told him.

"I can damn well try. You don't want to test me on this one, darlin'."

I glanced at Jameson, who was well-acquainted with the pitfalls of *testing* Nash. Jameson met my gaze, then glanced at Xander.

"Flying leopard?" Jameson murmured.

"Hidden mongoose!" Xander replied, and an instant later, they were crashing into Nash in a truly impressive synchronized flying tackle.

In a one-on-one fight, Nash could take either one of them. But it was hard to get the upper hand when you had one brother on your torso and another pinning your legs and feet.

"We should go," I told Oren. Nash was cursing up a storm behind us. Xander began serenading him with a brotherly limerick.

"Oren!" Nash hollered.

My head of security didn't so much as hint at any amusement he might have felt. "Sorry, Nash. I know better than to get in the middle of a Hawthorne brawl."

"Alisa—" Nash started to say, but I interjected.

"I want you with me," I told my lawyer. "You'll wait with Oren, right outside."

Nash must have smelled defeat because he stopped trying to dislodge Xander from his feet. "Kid?" he called. "You sure as hell better play dirty."

CHAPTER 77

Vincent Blake's ranch was about a two-and-a-half-hour drive north, stretching for miles along the Texas/Oklahoma border. Taking the helicopter cut our travel time down to forty-five minutes, plus transit on the ground. Landon had done her part, so the press arrived shortly after I did.

"Earlier today," I told them in a speech that I had rehearsed, "the remains of a man that we believe to be William Blake were found on the grounds of the Hawthorne estate."

I stuck to my script. Landon had timed the leak about the body perfectly—the story she'd planted was already up, but it was the footage of what I was saying now that would define it. I sold the story: Will Blake had physically assaulted an underage female, and Tobias Hawthorne had intervened to protect her. Law enforcement was investigating, but based on what we'd been able to piece together ourselves, we expected the autopsy to reveal that Blake had died from blunt-force trauma to the head.

Tobias Hawthorne had dealt those blows.

That last bit might not have been true, but it was sensational. It was *a story*. And I was here now to pay my respects to the deceased's family, on behalf of myself and the remaining Hawthornes.

I didn't take questions. Instead, I turned and walked toward the boundary of Vincent Blake's property. I knew from my research that Legacy Ranch was more than a quarter of a million acres—nearly four hundred square miles.

I stopped under an enormous brick arch, part of an equally enormous wall. The archway was big enough for a bus to fit underneath. As I approached, a black truck barreled toward me from inside the compound, down a long dirt road.

Beyond this wall, there were more than eighty thousand acres of active farmland, more than a thousand productive oil wells, the world's largest privately owned collection of quarter horses, and a truly substantial number of cattle.

And somewhere, beyond this wall, on these acres, there was a house.

"You're about to trespass on private property." The men who exited the black truck were dressed like ranch hands, but they moved like soldiers.

Hoping I hadn't miscalculated—because if I had, the entire world was witnessing that miscalculation—I replied to the man who had spoken. "Even if I have one of these?"

I opened my fingers just far enough for them to see the seal.

Less than a minute later, I was in the cab of the truck, barreling toward the unknown.

It was a full ten minutes before the house came into view. The driver, who was definitely armed, hadn't said a word to me.

I looked down at the seal resting in my palm. "You haven't asked where I got it."

He didn't take his eyes off the road. "When someone has one of those, you don't ask."

If Hawthorne House looked like a castle, Vincent Blake's home called to mind a fortress. It was made of dark stone, its square lines interrupted only by two giant round columns rising into turrets. A wrought-iron balcony lined the front perimeter on the second floor. I half expected a drawbridge, but instead there was a wraparound porch.

Eve stood on that porch, her amber hair blowing in the wind.

Blake's security followed me as I walked toward her. When I stepped up onto the porch, Eve turned, a strategic move designed to force me into following.

"This all would have been so much easier," she said, "if you'd just given me what I asked for."

CHAPTER 78

Eve didn't lead me into the house. She led me around back. A man stood there. He had suntanned skin and silver hair shorn to the scalp. I knew he had to be in his eighties, but he looked closer to sixty-five—and like he could run a marathon.

He was holding a shotgun.

As I watched, he took aim at the sky. The sound of the shot was earsplitting and echoed through the countryside as a bird plummeted to the ground. Vincent Blake said something—I couldn't hear what—and the largest bloodhound I'd ever seen took off after the kill.

Blake lowered his weapon. Slowly, he turned to face me. "Around here," he called, in that smooth, borderline-aristocratic voice I recognized all too well from the phone, "we cook what we shoot."

He held out the gun, and someone rushed to take it from him. Then Blake strode toward us. He settled down on a cement wall near a massive firepit, and Eve led me right up to it—and him.

"Where are Grayson and Toby?" That was the only greeting this man was going to get out of me.

"Enjoying my hospitality." Blake eyed the large box I carried in my hands. Wordlessly, I opened it. I'd stopped in the vault to retrieve the royal chess set. Once I'd been granted admission to Blake's lands, I'd had Oren surreptitiously hand it to me.

Now I set it in front of Blake, an offering of sorts.

He picked up one of the pieces, examining the multitude of shining black diamonds, the artistry of the design, then snorted and tossed the piece back down. "Tobias always was the showy type." Blake held out his right hand, and someone placed a bowie knife in it.

My heart leapt into my throat, but all the king of this kingdom did was withdraw a small piece of wood from his pocket.

"A set you carve yourself," he told me, "plays just the same."

That's not a carving knife. I didn't let him intimidate me into saying that out loud. Instead, I leaned forward to place the seal I'd flashed to gain entrance beside him on the wall. "I believe this is yours," I told him. Then I nodded to the chess set I'd brought. "And we'll call that a gift."

"I didn't ask you to bring me a gift, Avery Kylie Grambs."

I met his iron-hard gaze. "You didn't ask for anything. You *told* me to bring you your son, and you'll get him." By now, Blake doubtlessly would have heard the reports that Landon had leaked. There was a good chance that he'd watched my press conference. "Once the investigation is complete," I continued, "the authorities will release his remains to you. For what it's worth, I'm sorry for your loss."

"I don't lose, Avery Kylie Grambs." Blake's knife flashed in the sun as he scraped it along the wood. "My son, on the other hand, appears to have lost quite a bit."

"Your son," I said, "impregnated an underage girl, then got physical with her when she had the audacity to be devastated at the realization that he'd just been using her to get close enough to make a move against Tobias Hawthorne."

"Hmmmm." Blake made a humming sound that felt far more

threatening than it should have. "Will was fifteen when Tobias and I parted ways. The boy was irate that we'd been double-crossed. I had to disabuse him of the notion that *we* had been anything. What happened was between young Tobias and me."

"Tobias bested you." That was my first thrust in this little verbal sword match of ours.

Blake didn't even feel it. "And look how well that turned out for him."

I wasn't sure if that was a reference to the fact that the only person who had ever bested Vincent Blake had turned out to be one of the most formidable minds in a generation—or a self-satisfied prediction that all of Tobias Hawthorne's achievements would be nothing in the end.

The billionaire was dead, his fortune ripe for the taking.

"Your son hated him." I tried again, with a different type of attack. "And he was desperate to prove himself to you."

Blake didn't deny it. Instead, he brought the bowie knife away from the wood and tested its sharpness against the pad of his thumb. "Tobias should have let me handle Will. He knew the kind of hell there would be to pay for bringing harm to *my* son. Choices, young lady, have consequences."

"And how would you have handled what your son did to Mallory Laughlin?"

"That's neither here nor there."

"And boys will be boys," I shot back. "Right?"

Blake studied me for a moment, then laid the knife on his leg. "I understand you have some friends at the gate."

"The entire world knows I'm here," I said. "They know what happened to your son."

"Do they?" Eve said, a challenge in her tone. The story I was telling—she must have heard enough from Mallory to question it.

"That's enough, Eve." Blake's voice was clipped, and Eve swallowed as her great-grandfather looked between the two of us. "I shouldn't have sent a little girl to do a man's job."

Little girl. On the phone earlier, he'd referred to me that way, too. Tobias Hawthorne had been right. I was young. I was female. And this man *would* underestimate me.

"If I'd brought you your son's remains," I said, "you would have blackmailed me for breaking the law."

"Blackmailed you into what, I wonder?" Blake meant that *I* should wonder.

I knew that it was to my advantage for him to think he had the upper hand, so I had to tread carefully now. "If Grayson and Toby don't leave here with me, I'll give another interview on the way out."

It was dangerous to threaten a man like Vincent Blake. I knew that. I also knew that I needed him to believe that *this* was my play. My only play.

"An interview?" That got me another little hum. "Will you tell them about Sheffield Grayson?"

I'd anticipated that he would counter my move, but I hadn't foreseen how, and suddenly, I couldn't hold my pulse steady anymore. I couldn't keep my face completely blank.

"Eve may have failed at her primary task," Blake said, "but she's a Blake—and we play to win. I'm still considering whether she's earned this." He brandished a golden disk identical to the one I'd placed on the wall. "But the information she brought me when she returned was . . . quite impressive."

Information. About what happened to Grayson's father. I thought about the file, the pictures on Eve's phone.

"I read between the lines," Eve said, her lips curving up. "Grayson's father is missing, and based on what I was able to put together, he *went* missing shortly after someone orchestrated an attempt on your life. Sheffield Grayson had motive to be that someone. I didn't have proof, of course, but then..." Eve gave a little shrug. "I called Mellie."

Eve's sister was the one who had shot Sheffield Grayson. She'd killed him to save Toby and me. "The sister who never did a damn thing for you?" I asked, my throat bone-dry.

"Half sister." The correction told me that Eve hadn't lied about her feelings for her siblings. "It was a very touching reunion, especially when I told her that I *forgive* her." Eve's lips twisted. "That I was there for her. Mellie is wracked with guilt, you know. About what she did. About what *you* covered up."

I'd been ushered out of the storage facility when Sheffield Grayson's blood was still fresh on the ground. "I didn't cover up anything."

Blake brought his blade back to the wood and began carving again—slow, smooth motions. "John Oren did."

I'd come here with a plan, but I hadn't planned for this. I'd thought that by calling the police about Will Blake's remains, I would sap his father of much-needed leverage. I hadn't foreseen that Vincent Blake had leverage in reserve.

"It seems," the man commented mildly, "that I have the advantage on you once again."

He'd never doubted it.

"What do you want?" I asked. I let him see my very real distress, but inside, the logical part of my brain took over. The part that liked puzzles. The part that saw the world in layers.

The part that had come here with a plan.

"Anything I want from you," Blake said simply, "I'll take."

"I'll play you for it," I told him, improvising and letting my brain adjust, adding a new layer, one more thing that had to go right. "Chess. If I win, you forget about Sheffield Grayson and see to it that Eve and Mellie do the same."

Blake seemed amused, but I could see something much darker than amusement glinting in his eyes. "And if you lose?"

I had a trump card, but I couldn't play it—not yet. Not if I wanted even a sliver of a chance that I'd walk away today with the kind of win I needed.

"A favor," I said, my heart brutalizing my rib cage. "Very soon, I'll have control of the Hawthorne fortune. Billions. A favor from someone in my position has to be worth something."

Vincent Blake didn't seem overly tempted by my offer. Of course he didn't, because he already had a plan to come for Tobias Hawthorne's fortune on his own.

After a moment, however, amusement won out. "A game seems fitting, but I'm not going to play you, little girl. I will, however, let *her* play you." He jerked his head toward Eve, then tilted his head to the side, considering. "And Toby."

"Toby?" I croaked. I hated the way I sounded—the way I felt. I couldn't let my emotions take control. I had to think. I had to modify my plan—again.

"My grandson has asked about you," Blake told me. "You could say I have a knack for recognizing pressure points."

Vincent Blake had kidnapped Toby to get at me, to win Eve entrance to Hawthorne House. I realized, in that moment, that Blake had also doubtlessly leveraged me against Toby.

"Eve," he said, his voice carrying the weight of an order that no living person would dare disobey, "why don't you fetch your father?"

CHAPTER 79

Toby's bruises were healing, and he needed to shave. Those were my first two thoughts, followed immediately by a dozen others about him and my mom and the last time I'd seen him, each thought accompanied by a wave of emotion that threatened to take me down.

"You shouldn't be here." Toby kept a handle on whatever emotions he was feeling, but the intensity in his eyes told me he was holding on to that composure by a thread.

"I know," I replied, and I hoped my tone made him realize that I wasn't just saying I knew I shouldn't be here. *I know who Blake is. I know what he's capable of. I know what I'm doing.*

For this to work, Toby didn't have to trust me, but I did need him to stay out of my way.

"You're going to play a game," Vincent Blake told Toby. "All three of you—a tournament of sorts, consisting of three matches." Blake lifted a single finger and gestured from Toby to Eve. "My grandson and his daughter." A second finger came up. "My grandson and the girl who is *not* his daughter."

Toby and me. *Ouch.*

"And..." Blake raised a third and final finger. "Avery and Eve against each other." The man gave us a few seconds to process that, then continued. "As for incentive...well, these things must have stakes."

Something about the way he said *stakes* sent a shiver down my spine.

"Win both of your matches and you can go," Blake told Toby. "Disappear however you like. You'll never hear from me again, and I'll allow the world to continue to believe that you are dead. Lose one of your matches and you're still free to go, but not as a dead man. You'll confirm for the world that Toby Hawthorne is alive and never go off the grid again."

Toby didn't blanch. I wasn't sure if Blake had expected him to.

"Lose both of your matches," the older man continued with a tilt to his lips that I did not trust, "and you won't be coming back to life as Toby Hawthorne. You'll agree to stay here of your own free will as Toby Blake."

"No!" I objected. "Toby, you—"

Toby cut me off with the slightest shift in his expression—a warning. "What are their terms?" he asked his grandfather.

Blake drank in Toby's response, pleased, and then turned to Eve. "Win one of your matches," he told her, "and you can have this." He brandished a Blake family seal at Eve. "Lose both, and you'll be at the service of whoever I give it to in your stead." There was something deeply disconcerting about the way he said *service*. "Win both of your matches," Blake finished silkily, "and I'll give you all five."

All five seals. An electric current swept through the premises. Isaiah had said that anyone holding a seal when Vincent Blake died was entitled to one-fifth of his fortune, and that meant Blake had just promised Eve that if she could beat Toby *and* me, he'd give her everything.

All the power. All the money. All of it.

"And as for you, Tobias Hawthorne's *very risky gamble*..." Vincent Blake smiled. "Lose both, and I'll take that favor you offered—a blank check, if you will, to be cashed at a time of my choosing."

Toby caught my gaze. *No.* He didn't make the objection out loud. After a moment, I looked away. There wasn't a warning he could issue that would be news to me. Owing Vincent Blake a favor was a very bad idea.

"Win at least one game," Blake continued, "and I'll release Grayson Hawthorne to you, with a guarantee that I won't make a guest of anyone under your protection again."

Guest was one way of phrasing it—but as far as incentives went, it was enticing. Too enticing. *If he's willing to keep his hands off my loved ones, he must have other buttons to push. Other forms of leverage.*

Another plan to take everything from me.

"Win both games," Blake promised, "and I'll also swear secrecy on the matter of Sheffield Grayson."

Toby flinched. Clearly, he hadn't known about that bit of leverage his biological grandfather had been holding in reserve.

"Are these terms acceptable to you?" Blake asked Toby and only Toby, like Eve and I were foregone conclusions.

Toby gritted his teeth. "Yes."

"*Yes,*" Eve said, alive in a way that made all other versions of her seem faded and incomplete.

And as for me...

Blake will honor his word. If I won both matches, the truth about Grayson's father would stay buried. The people I loved would be safe. Blake would still be coming for me. He'd find a way of destroying me and all I held dear, but he'd be limited in how he could do that.

"I agree to your terms," I said, even though he'd never given me the option to do anything else.

Blake turned to the glittering, five-hundred-thousand-dollar chess set I'd gifted him. "Well then. Shall we begin?"

CHAPTER 80

Toby and Eve went first. I'd played against Toby often enough to know that he could have ended it within the first twelve moves if he'd wanted to.

He let her win.

Blake must have concluded the same thing because once the board had been reset for my match against Toby, the older man picked up his bowie knife. "Throw this game, too," he told Toby contemplatively, "and I'll ask Eve to give me her arm and use this to open a vein."

If Eve was disturbed by the implication that her great-grandfather would slice her open, she didn't show it. Instead, she held tight to the seal she'd been given and kept her eyes on the board.

I took my position and met Toby's eyes. It had been more than a year since we'd played, but the second I moved my first pawn, it was like no time had passed at all. Harry and I were right back in the park.

"Your move, princess." Toby wasn't pulling his punches, but he did his best to put me at ease, to remind me that even if he played his hardest, I'd beaten him before.

"Not a princess." I echoed my line in our script back at him and slid my bishop across the board. "Your move, *old man*."

Toby narrowed his eyes slightly. "Don't get cocky."

"Fine words from a Hawthorne," I retorted.

"I mean it, Avery. Don't get cocky."

He sees something I don't.

"Eve," Vincent Blake said pleasantly. "Your arm?"

Her chin steady, Eve held it out to him. Blake rested the edge of his blade against her skin. "Play," he told Toby. "And no more hints to the girl."

There was a beat—a single second—and then Toby did as he'd been instructed. I scanned the board, then saw why he'd cautioned me against getting cocky. It took three moves, but then: "Check," Toby gritted out.

I took in the board, all of it at once. I had three possible next moves, and I played all of them out. Two led to Toby getting checkmate within the next five moves. That meant I was stuck with the third. I knew how Toby would counter it, and from there I had four or five options. I let my brain race, let the possibilities slowly untangle themselves.

I tried not to think too much about the fact that if Toby beat me, the cover-up of Sheffield Grayson's death would be exposed. Either that, or I'd have to give Blake something much more significant than a favor to keep it quiet.

The man would own me.

No. I could do this. There was a way. *My move. His. My move. His.* Again and again, faster and faster, we played.

Then, finally, a breath whooshed out of my chest. "Check."

I knew the exact moment that Toby saw the trap I had laid. "Horrible girl," he whispered roughly, and the tenderness in his eyes when he said it almost took me down.

His move. Mine. His move. Mine.

And then, finally—*finally*... "Checkmate," I said.

Vincent Blake kept the bowie knife on Eve's arm a moment longer, then slowly lowered it. His grandson had lost, and as the realization of what that meant fell over me, my insides twisted.

Toby had lost both matches. He was Blake's.

CHAPTER 81

I expect better next time," Vincent Blake told Toby. "You're a Blake now, and Blakes don't lose to little girls."

I caught Toby's gaze. "I'm sorry," I said quietly, urgently.

"Don't be." Toby reached out to cup my face. "I see so much of your mother in you."

That felt far too much like good-bye. From the moment Eve had arrived at the gates of Hawthorne House, I had been determined to *get him back*. And now—

"Will I..." The words stopped, like the question was gumming up my throat. "Can I see you?" I asked.

You have a daughter, I could hear myself saying.

I have two.

Blake didn't give Toby the chance to reply. He shifted his attention to Eve. She basked in it, like he was the sun and she had the type of skin that didn't burn. For the first time, instead of looking at her and seeing Emily, I saw something very different.

An intensity that was Toby's. *Blake's.*

"If I win this game...," she said, steel and wonder in her tone.

"It's yours," Blake confirmed. "All of it. But before we begin..."

Blake lifted a finger, and a member of his security team rushed over. "Could you fetch our other guest for Ms. Grambs?"

Grayson. I didn't let myself fully believe that he was okay until I saw him, and then I let myself think about what I'd won—not just his freedom, but a promise that no one I cared about would find themselves a *guest* here again.

"Avery." Grayson's blue-gray eyes—his irises icy and light against the inky black of his pupils—locked on to mine. "I had a plan."

"Reckless self-sacrifice?" I retorted. "Yeah, I got that." I pulled him close and spoke directly into his ear. "I told you, Grayson, we're *family.*"

I let go of him. The board was set up a final time. Eve was white. I was black. With tens of thousands of diamonds glittering between us, we faced off in a game of greatest stakes.

Based on Eve's level of play against Toby, I hadn't anticipated the challenge I soon found myself facing. It was like she'd watched my game against her father, internalized a dozen new strategies, and learned how I saw the board.

She's playing to win. I was desperate to save Oren, and I had no idea how much of a crime *I* had committed by not reporting Sheffield Grayson's death. But Eve? She was playing for the keys to the kingdom—for wealth and power beyond imagining.

For acceptance from someone she was desperate to be accepted by.

The rest of the room faded away until I couldn't hear anything but the sounds of my own body and couldn't see anything but the board. It took longer than I'd anticipated, but finally, I saw my opening.

I could have her in check in three moves, checkmate in five.

Just like that, I could walk away from here with Grayson, knowing that Vincent Blake had that many fewer ways of coming at me.

But he'll still come.

The assaults on my financial interests, the paparazzi, playing games and boxing me in. *He'll just keep coming.* That thought grew louder in my mind, pushing my focus from my match against Eve to the bigger picture.

For me, *this* wasn't the ultimate game.

I could win, and I would still walk out of here no better off than when Tobias Hawthorne had died. It would still be hunting season. A man who Tobias Hawthorne had so feared that he had left a virtual stranger his fortune would still be gunning for me.

Even without violence, even with our physical safety guaranteed, Vincent Blake would still find a way of destroying anyone, everyone, and everything that stood in his way.

This win right now against Eve—it wouldn't be enough.

I had to play the long game. I had to look past the board, play ten moves ahead, not five, think in three dimensions, not two. If I beat Eve, Vincent Blake would send me on my way, and he'd do so knowing that I was more than he'd given me credit for. He'd adjust his expectations in the future.

You're young. Tobias Hawthorne's voice rang in my mind. *You're female. You're nobody—use that.* If I gave Vincent Blake an excuse to continue underestimating me, he would.

I'd come here with a plan in mind. The tournament hadn't been a part of that plan—but I could use it.

Playing chess wasn't just about anticipating your opponent's moves. It was about planting those moves in their mind—baiting them. After listening to the recording the old man had left for us, Xander had marveled at the fact that Tobias Hawthorne had foreseen exactly what we would all do after his death, but Hawthorne hadn't just foreseen it.

He'd manipulated it. Manipulated us.

If I wanted to beat Blake, I had to do the same. So I didn't take the opening Eve had given me. I didn't beat her in five moves.

I let her beat me in ten.

I saw the exact moment when Eve realized that Vincent Blake's empire was in her grasp—and the moment, right afterward, when Toby's eyes flashed. Did he suspect I'd thrown the game?

Did my *real* opponent?

"Well done, Eve." Blake offered her a small, self-satisfied smile, and Eve glowed, the smile on her face luminescent. Blake turned to me—and Grayson. "The two of you may leave."

His men closed in on us, and I didn't have to fake my panic. "Wait!" I said, sounding desperate—and feeling that desperation, because even though this had been a calculated risk, I had no way of knowing that I hadn't miscalculated. "Give me another chance!"

"Have some dignity, child." Blake stood and turned his back on me as his hunting dog returned to his side and dropped a dead duck at his feet. "No one likes a sore loser."

"You could still have a favor," I shouted as Blake's security began to remove me from the premises. "One last game. Me against you."

"I don't need a favor from you, girl."

That's okay, I tried to tell myself. *There's another option.* An option I'd come prepared for. An option I'd planned for. The gift of the chess set, the fact that I had Alisa waiting for me outside—I'd always known what my gambit was going to be.

What it was going to *have* to be.

"Not a favor, then," I said, trying to hold on to the panic and the desperation so he wouldn't see the deep sense of calm rising up inside me. "What about the rest of it?"

Grayson cut a sharp look in my direction. "Avery."

Vincent Blake held up his hand, and his men all took a silent step back. "The rest of what, exactly?"

"The Hawthorne fortune." I let the words come out in a rush. "My lawyer has been after me to sign these papers for weeks. Tobias Hawthorne didn't tie my inheritance up in a trust. The fine people at McNamara, Ortega, and Jones are nervous about a teenager taking the reins, so Alisa drew up paperwork that would put everything in a trust until I turn thirty."

"Avery." Toby's voice was low and full of warning. Part of me wanted to believe he was just helping me sell the in-over-my-head act, but he was probably offering a genuine word of caution.

I was risking too much.

"If you play me," I told Blake, nodding toward the chessboard, "and you win, I'll sign the papers and make *you* the trustee."

Coming here, I'd been counting on Blake's ego to make him think that he could beat me, but there had always been the chance that he would realize I'd suggested chess specifically because I stood a good chance at winning. But now?

He'd seen me play.

He'd seen me lose.

He thought I was making this offer on impulse *because* I had lost.

And still, he looked at me with sharp eyes and the most suspicious of smiles. "Now, why would you do a thing like that?"

"I don't want anyone finding out about Sheffield Grayson," I bit out. "And I've read the paperwork! With a trust, the money would still belong to me. I just wouldn't control it. You would have to promise me that you would okay any purchases I wanted to make, that you'd let me spend as much money as I wanted, whenever I wanted. But everything I can't spend? You'd be the one making the decisions about how it's invested."

Do you know what the real difference is between millions and billions? Skye Hawthorne had asked, what felt like a small eternity ago. *Because at a certain point, it's not about the money.*

It was about the power.

Vincent Blake didn't want or need Tobias Hawthorne's fortune to *spend* it.

"All of this, for double or nothing?" Blake asked pointedly. Like Tobias Hawthorne, the man across from me thought seven steps ahead. He knew I had another card up my sleeve.

But hopefully just one.

"No," I admitted. "If you win, you get control of everything free and clear until I'm thirty or you're six feet under. But if I win, you make sure that any nasty rumors about Sheffield Grayson stay buried, *and* you give me your word that this ends here."

This was the plan. This had always been the plan. *My greatest adversary—and yours now—is an honor-bound man,* Tobias Hawthorne had told me. *Best him, and he'll honor the win.*

"If I win," I continued, "the armistice you had with Tobias Hawthorne—you extend that to me. End of hunting season." I gave him a hard look, which I deeply suspected he found amusing. "You let me go, the way you let a young Tobias Hawthorne go, way back when."

I willed him to see me as impulsive, to see this as me scrambling because I'd lost. *I'm young. I'm female. I'm nobody. And you just saw Eve beat me at chess.*

"How am I to know you'll keep up your end of the deal?" my adversary queried.

It took everything in me not to allow even a shadow of victory to pulse through me. "If you accept the wager," I said, all wide eyes and bravado, "we'll make two calls: one to your lawyer and one to mine."

CHAPTER 82

What the hell are you doing?" Alisa hissed.

The two of us were—purportedly—alone, but even with no one visibly listening, I didn't want to explain anything that could tip my hand to Blake. "What I have to," I said, hoping Alisa would read so much more in my tone.

I have a plan.

I can do this.

You have to trust me.

Alisa stared at me like I'd grown horns. "You absolutely do not have to do this."

I wasn't going to win this argument, so I didn't even try. I just waited for her to realize that I wasn't backing down.

When she did, Alisa swore under her breath and looked away. "Do you know why Nash and I broke off our engagement?" she asked in a tone that was far too calm for both the words she'd spoken and our current situation. "He was so determined that his grandfather wasn't going to pull his strings—or mine. He expected me to walk away from all things Hawthorne, too."

"And you couldn't." I wasn't sure where she was going with this.

"Nash was raised to be extraordinary," Alisa said. "But he wasn't the only one the old man had a hand in raising, so yes, I stayed." Alisa clipped the words, refusing to allow them more importance than she had to. "I did what Nash *should* have done. It cost me everything, but before Mr. Hawthorne passed, he stipulated to my father and the other partners that I would be the one who took the lead with you." She looked down. "I can just hear what the old man would say about the mess I've made of my job. First, I let myself get kidnapped, and now this."

The mess that she thought I was making right now.

"Or maybe," I told her in a tone that somehow captured her attention, "you've done exactly what he raised you to do—exactly what he *chose you* to do."

I willed her to read meaning into my emphasis. *He didn't just choose you. He chose me, too, Alisa—and maybe I'm doing exactly what he chose me for.*

Slowly, the expression in her deep brown eyes shifted. She knew that I was telling her to believe that I'd been chosen for a reason. That *this* was the reason.

This was our play.

"Do you have any idea how risky this is?" Alisa asked me.

"It always has been," I replied, "from the moment Tobias Hawthorne changed his will."

This was his very risky gamble—and mine.

CHAPTER 83

Blake let me play white, which meant that the first move was mine. I went with the Queen's Gambit. It wasn't until a dozen moves later that Vincent Blake realized my instincts went beyond classic maneuvers. Four moves after that, he took my bishop, allowing me to execute a sequence that ended with me taking his queen.

Slowly, move by move and counterattack by counterattack, Vincent Blake realized that we were much more evenly matched than he'd anticipated.

"I see now," he told me, "what you're doing."

He saw what I had *done*. The young woman he was playing against now wasn't the one who'd lost to Eve. I'd hustled him, and he knew it—far too late.

In four moves, I thought, my heartbeat brutal and incessant in my chest, *I'll have him*.

After two, he realized I had him trapped. He stood, tipping his king, conceding the match. White gold clattered as the piece hit the jewel-encrusted board, the black-diamond king glittering in the sun.

Vincent Blake was a dangerous man, a wealthy man, a formidable opponent—and he had underestimated me.

"You can keep the chess set," I told him.

For a moment, I felt Blake fighting with himself. The lawyers had been there to ensure my end of the bargain—not his. *I promise I won't slowly and strategically destroy you* wasn't a legally enforceable term. I'd bet everything on the only real assurance Tobias Hawthorne had given me.

That if I bested Blake, he'd honor the win.

"What just happened here?" Eve demanded.

Vincent Blake offered me one last hard look, and then he rocked back on his heels. "She won."

CHAPTER 84

Vincent Blake would honor our wager, but he never wanted to see me on his property again. "Escort Avery, Grayson, and Ms. Ortega back to the gate," he ordered his men. "See that the press is dispersed before they get there."

A hand locked around my forearm, suggesting exactly what kind of "escort" I could expect. But the next thing I knew, the man who'd grabbed me was on the ground, and Toby was standing over him. "I'll escort them," he said.

Blake's men looked to their boss.

Vincent Blake gave Toby a foreboding smile. "As you wish, Tobias Blake."

The name was a razor-sharp reminder: I might have won my wager, but Toby had lost his. With a hand on my back, he led me away, back around the house.

We'd nearly made it to the driveway when a voice spoke behind us. "Stop."

I wanted to ignore Eve, but I couldn't. Slowly, I turned to face her, aware that Grayson was exercising ironclad control over any impulse he might have felt to do the same.

"You let me win," Eve said. That was an accusation, furious and low. Her gaze slipped to Toby's. "Did you throw our game, too?" she asked him, her voice shaking. When Toby didn't reply, Eve turned back to me. "Did he?" she demanded.

"Does it matter?" I asked. "You got what you wanted."

Eve had won all five seals. She was now the sole heir to Blake's empire.

"I wanted," Eve whispered, her voice quiet but brutally fierce, "for once in my life, to prove to someone that I was good enough." Her eyes betrayed her, going to Grayson, but he didn't turn around. "I wanted Blake to *see* me," Eve continued, her gaze coming back to mine, "but now the only thing he is ever going to see when he looks at me is *you*."

I'd used Eve to best Blake, and she was right—he would never forget that.

"I saw you, Eve." Grayson's voice was emotionless, his body still. "You could have been one of us."

Eve's expression wavered, and for the barest moment, I was reminded of the little girl in the locket. Then the person in front of me straightened, a haughty look settling over her features like a porcelain mask. "The girl you knew," she told Grayson, "was a lie."

If she thought that would get a rise out of Grayson Davenport Hawthorne, she was wrong.

"Get them out of here." Eve whipped her head toward Toby. "*Now.*"

"Eve—" Toby started to say.

"I said *go.*" A spark of victory, hard and cruel, glinted in her emerald eyes. "You'll be back."

That felt like an arrow aimed at my heart. *Toby doesn't have a choice.*

Without flinching, he escorted me away from his daughter and didn't speak until he, Alisa, Grayson, and I had made it to the truck.

"What you did back there with Blake was very risky," Toby told me—half censure, half praise.

I shrugged. "You're the one who chose my name." *Avery Kylie Grambs. A very risky gamble.* Toby had helped bring me into the world. He'd named me. He'd come to me when my mother died. He'd saved me when I needed saving.

And now I was losing him all over again.

"What happens now?" I asked him, my eyes beginning to sting, my throat tight.

"I become Tobias Blake." Toby had known the truth about his lineage for two decades. If he'd wanted this life, he would have been living it already.

I thought of the words he'd written in the chamber under the hedge maze. *I was never a Hawthorne. I will never be a Blake.*

"You don't have to do this," I told him. "You could run. You managed to evade Tobias Hawthorne for years. You could do the same thing with Blake now."

"And give that man justification to renege on his deal with you?" Alisa cut in. "Invalidate one wager in a set and he could easily argue that you've invalidated them all."

"I'm not running this time," Toby said intently. I followed his gaze to Eve, who was standing on the porch again, her amber hair blowing in the wind, looking for all the world like some kind of unearthly, conquering queen.

"You're staying for *her.*" I hadn't meant that to sound like an accusation of betrayal.

"I'm staying for both of you," Toby replied, and for a moment, I could see the two of us, hear the last conversation we'd had.

You have a daughter.

I have two.

"She helped Blake kidnap you," I said roughly. "She used me—used all of us."

"And when I was her age," Toby replied, opening the passenger door of the truck and gesturing for me to get in, "I killed your mother's sister."

I wanted to object, to say that he hadn't lit the fire, even if he'd doused the house in gasoline, but he didn't give me the chance.

"Hannah thought I was redeemable." Even after all these years, Toby couldn't reference my mom without emotion overtaking him. "Do you really think she'd want me to walk away from Eve?"

I felt a sob caught somewhere. "You could have told me," I said, my voice scraping against my throat. "About Blake. About the body. About why you were so damn set on staying in the shadows."

Toby lifted a hand to the side of my face, brushing my hair back from my temple. "There are a lot of things I would do differently if I could live this life all over again."

I thought about what I'd said to Jameson about destiny and fate and *choice*. I knew why Tobias Hawthorne had chosen me. I knew that this had never been about *me*. But unlike Toby, I had no regrets. I would have done it—all of it—all over again.

Tobias Hawthorne's game hadn't made me extraordinary. It had shown me that I already was.

"Will I ever see you again?" I asked Toby, my voice breaking.

"Blake isn't going to keep me under lock and key." Toby waited for Alisa and Grayson to climb in after me, then closed the passenger door and rounded to the other side of the truck. When he spoke again, it was from the driver's seat. "And Texas really isn't that big—especially at the top."

Money. Power. Status. My path and Vincent Blake's would probably cross again—and so would mine and Toby's. Mine and Eve's.

"Here." Toby placed a small wooden cube in my hand as he started up the truck. "I made you something, horrible girl."

The endearment nearly undid me. "What is it?"

"Blake didn't give me much to entertain myself with—just wood and a knife."

"And you didn't use the knife?" Grayson asked beside me. His tone made it very clear the kind of *uses* he would have approved of.

"Would you have," Toby countered, "if you thought your captor could get to Avery?"

Toby had protected me. He'd made something for me.

You have a daughter.

I have two.

I looked down at the wooden cube in my hand, thinking about my mom, about this man, about the decades and tragedies and small moments that had led all of us to right now.

"Watch out for her," Toby told Grayson when the border of Blake's property came into sight. "Take care of each other." The press had been cleared out, but Oren and his men were still there waiting—and so was Jameson Winchester Hawthorne.

Grayson saw his brother standing there, and he answered on behalf of both of them. "We will."

CHAPTER 85

"The knight returns with the damsel in distress," Jameson declared as I made my way toward him. He glanced toward Grayson. "You're the damsel."

"I figured," Grayson deadpanned.

"What are you doing here?" I asked Jameson, but the truth was, I didn't care why he'd come—only that he was here. I'd won—after everything, *I had won*—and Jameson was the only person on the planet capable of fully understanding exactly how it had felt the moment I'd realized that my plan was going to work.

The rush. The thrill. The adrenaline-soaked awe.

The moment victory had been within my grasp had been like standing at the edge of the world's most powerful waterfall, the roar of the moment blocking out everything else.

It was like jumping off a cliff and finding out you could fly.

It was like Jameson and me and Jameson-and-me, and I wanted to live it all over again with him.

"I thought you could use a ride home," Jameson told me. I looked past him, expecting to see the McLaren or one of the Bugattis or the Aston Martin Valkyrie, but instead, my gaze landed on a helicopter—smaller than the one Oren had flown here.

"Pretty sure you aren't allowed to land a helicopter there," Grayson told his brother.

"You know what they say about permission and forgiveness," Jameson replied, then he focused back on me with a familiar look—equal parts *I dare you* and *I'll never let you go*. "Want to learn to fly?"

That night, I turned the cube Toby had given me over in my hands. My finger caught on an edge, and I realized that it was made of interlocking pieces. Working slowly, I solved the puzzle, disassembling the cube and laying the pieces out in front of me.

On each one, he'd carved a word.

I

See

So

Much

Of

Your

Mother

In

You

And that, even more than the moment I'd defeated Blake, was when I knew.

The next morning, before anyone else was awake, I went to the Great Room and lit a fire in the massive fireplace. I could have done this in my own room—or in any of the other dozen fireplaces in Hawthorne House—but it felt right to return to the room where the will had been read. I could almost see ghosts here: all of us, in that moment.

Me, thinking how life-changing inheriting a few thousand dollars would be.

The Hawthornes, learning the old man had left their fortune to me.

The flames flickered higher and higher in the fireplace, and I looked down at the papers in my hand: the trust paperwork Alisa had drawn up.

"What are you doing?" Libby padded toward me, wearing house shoes shaped like coffins and stifling a yawn.

I held up the papers. "If I sign this, it will tie my assets up in a trust—at least for a little while."

All that money. All that power.

Libby looked from me to the fireplace. "Well," she said as chipper as anyone wearing her *other* I EAT MORNING PEOPLE shirt had ever sounded, "what are you waiting for?"

I looked down at the trust paperwork, up at the fireplace—and tossed it all in. As the flames licked at the pages, devouring the legalese and, with it, the option to foist the power and responsibility I'd been given off on anyone else, I felt something in me begin to loosen, like the petals of a tulip opening to the slightest bloom.

I could do this.

I would do this.

If the past year had been any kind of test—I was ready.

I started taking the leather notebook Grayson had given me everywhere. I didn't have a year to make my plans. I had days. And yes, there were financial advisors and a legal team and a status quo that I could lean into if I wanted to buy myself time, but that wasn't what I wanted.

That wasn't the plan.

Deep down, I knew what I wanted to do. What I needed to do. And all of the lawyers and financial advisors and power players in the state of Texas—they weren't going to like it.

CHAPTER 86

On the biggest night of my life, I stood in front of a full-length mirror wearing a deep red ball gown fit for a queen. The color was unbearably rich, darker than a ruby but just as luminescent. Golden thread and delicate jewels combined to form understated vines that twisted and turned their way up the full skirt. The bodice was plain, custom fit to my body, with airy, translucent red sleeves that kissed my wrists.

Around my neck, I wore a single teardrop diamond.

Five hours and twelve minutes to go. Anticipation built inside me. Soon, my year at Hawthorne House would be up.

Nothing would ever be the same again.

"Regretting letting Xander talk you into this party?"

I turned from my mirror to the doorway, where Jameson stood wearing his white tuxedo—with a red vest this time, the same deep color as my dress. His jacket was unbuttoned, the black bow tie around his neck a little crooked and a little loose.

"It's hard to regret Hawthornes in tuxedos," I told him, a smile pulling at my lips as I walked to join him. "And tonight is going to be my kind of affair."

We were calling it the Countdown Party. *Like New Year's Eve,*

Xander had said, making his pitch for the festivities, *but at midnight, you're a billionaire!*

Jameson held out a hand, palm up. I took it, our fingers intertwining, the tip of my index finger grazing a small scar on the inside of his.

"Where to first, Heiress?"

I grinned. Unlike the introvert's ball, tonight was of my design, a rotating party where we would be spending one hour each in five different locations in Hawthorne House, counting our way down to midnight. The guest list was small—the usual suspects minus Max, who was stuck at college and would be joining via video call near the end of the party. "The sculpture garden."

Jameson's green eyes made a study of my face. "And what will we be doing in the sculpture garden?" he asked, an appropriate amount of suspicion in his tone.

I smiled. "Guess."

"The name of the game is Hide and Go Soak." Wearing a brilliant-blue tuxedo that looked like it belonged on the red carpet, and holding what had to be the world's biggest water gun, Xander was truly in his element. "The objective: utter aqua domination."

Five minutes later, I ducked behind a bronze sculpture of Theseus and the Minotaur. Libby was already back there, squatting on the ground, her vintage 1950s dress bunched up around her thighs.

"How are you feeling?" Libby asked me, keeping her voice low. "Big night."

I peeked out around the Minotaur's haunches, then retreated again. "Right now, I'm feeling *hunted*." I grinned. "How are you?"

"Ready." Libby looked down at the water balloons she held in each hand—and at her twin tattoos: *SURVIVOR* on one wrist, and on the other... *TRUST.*

Footsteps. I braced myself just as Nash scaled Theseus and landed between Libby and me, holding what appeared to be a *melted* water gun. "Jamie and Gray have joined forces. Xander has a blowtorch. This is never good." Nash looked to me. "You're still armed. Good. Steady and calm, kid. No mercy."

Libby leaned around Nash to catch my eyes. "Remember," she told me, her eyes dancing, "there's no such thing as fighting dirty if you win."

I turned my water gun on Nash right as she creamed him with a water balloon.

At eight, the party moved indoors to the climbing wall. Jameson sidled up to me. "Soaking wet in a ball gown," he murmured. "This could be a challenge."

I wrung out my hair and flicked water his way. "I'm up for it."

At nine, we made our way to the bowling alley. At ten, we headed for the pottery—as in, a room with potting wheels and a kiln.

By the time eleven o'clock rolled around and we made our way down the labyrinthine halls of Hawthorne House to the arcade, our gowns and tuxes had been soaked, ripped, and spattered with clay. I was exhausted, sore, and filled with an exhilaration that defied description.

This was it.

This was *the* night.

This was everything.

This was *us.*

In the arcade, four private chefs met us, each with a signature dish to present. *Slow-braised beef soup served with pork buns so tender they should be illegal. Lobster risotto.* The first two courses nearly undid me, and that was before I bit into a sushi roll that looked like a work of art just as the final chef set our dessert on fire.

I looked to Oren. He was the one who'd cleared the private chefs to come here tonight. "You have to try this," I told him. "All of it."

I watched as Oren gave in and tasted a pork bun, and then I felt someone else watching me. Grayson was wearing a silver tuxedo with sharp, angular lines, no bow tie, the shirt buttoned all the way up.

I thought he might keep his distance, but he strode over to me, his expression assessing. "You have a plan," he commented, his voice low and smooth and sure.

My heart rate ticked up. I didn't just have a plan. I had *A Plan*. "I wrote it down," I told Grayson. "And then I rewrote it, again and again."

He was the Hawthorne I'd thought of the most as I was doing it, the one whose reaction I could least predict.

"I'm glad," Grayson told me, the words slow and deliberate, "that it was you." He took a step back, clearing the way for Jameson to slide in next to me.

"Have you decided yet," Jameson asked me, "what room you're going to add on to Hawthorne House this year?"

I wondered if he could feel my anticipation, if he had any idea what we were counting down *to*. "I've made a lot of decisions," I said.

Alisa hadn't arrived yet, but she would be here soon.

"If you're planning to build a death-defying obstacle course on the south side of the Black Wood," Xander said, bouncing up, high off a Skee-Ball victory, "count me in! I have a lead on where we can get a reasonably priced two-story-tall teeter-totter."

I grinned. "What would you do," I asked Jameson, "if you were adding on a room?"

Jameson pulled my body back against his. "Indoor skydiving

complex, accessible from a secret passage at the base of the climbing wall. Four stories tall, looks just like another turret from the outside."

"Please." Thea sauntered over holding a pool cue. She was wearing a long silver dress that left wide strips of bronze skin on display and was slit to the thigh. "The correct answer is obviously *ballroom*."

"The foyer is as big as a ballroom," I pointed out. "Pretty sure it's been used that way for decades."

"And yet," Thea countered, "it remains *not a ballroom*." She turned back toward the pool table, where she and Rebecca were facing off against Libby and Nash. Bex leaned over the table, lining up what looked to be an impossible shot, her green velvet tuxedo pulling against her chest, her dark red hair combed to one side and falling into her face

The world had accepted my account of Will Blake's death. The blame was laid squarely at the feet of Tobias Hawthorne. But once Toby had appeared, miraculously alive, and announced that he was changing his name to Tobias Blake, it hadn't taken the press long to piece together that he was Will's son—or to start speculating about who Toby's biological mother was.

Rebecca had made it clear that she still didn't regret stepping into the light.

She sank the shot, and Thea strolled back toward her, shooting Nash a gloating look. "Still feeling cocky, cowboy?"

"Always," Nash drawled.

"That," Libby said, her eyes catching his, "is an understatement."

Nash smirked. "Thirsty?" he asked my sister.

Libby poked him in the chest. "There's a cowboy hat in the refrigerator, isn't there?"

She looked down at her wrists, then stalked over to the

refrigerator and pulled out a pink soda and a black velvet cowboy hat. "I'll wear this hat," she told Nash, "if *you* paint your nails black."

Nash gave her what could only be described as a *cowboy smile.* "Fingers or toes?"

A yip behind me had me turning toward the doorway. Alisa stood there holding a very wiggly puppy. "I found her in the gallery," she informed me dryly. "Barking at a Monet."

Xander took the puppy and held her up, crooning at her. "No eating Monets," he baby-talked. "Bad Tiramisu." He gave her the world's biggest, goofiest smile. "Bad dog. Just for that...you have to cuddle Grayson."

Xander dumped the puppy on his brother.

"Are you ready for this?" Alisa asked beside me as Grayson let the puppy lick his nose and challenged his brothers to a round of hold-the-puppy pinball.

"As ready as I'm ever going to be."

Thirty minutes to go. Twenty. Ten. No amount of winning or losing at pool, air hockey, or foosball, no amount of puppy pinball or trying to beat the high score on a dozen different arcade games could distract me from the way the clock was ticking down.

Three minutes.

"The trick to a good poker face," Jameson murmured, "isn't keeping your face blank. It's thinking about something other than your cards—the same something the whole time." Jameson Winchester Hawthorne offered me a hand, and for the second time that night, I took it. He pulled me in for a slow dance, the kind that required no music. "You've got your poker face on now, Heiress."

I thought about flying around a racetrack, standing on the edge of the roof, riding on the back of his motorcycle, dancing barefoot on the beach. "Gen H verity," I said.

Jameson arched a brow. "As in generational truth for people far older than us?"

"It's your anagram," I told him, "for *everything*."

My phone rang before he could reply, a video call from Max. I answered.

"Am I in time for the countdown?" she asked, yelling over what appeared to be very loud music.

"Do you have your champagne?" I asked.

She brandished a flute. Right on cue, Alisa appeared beside me, holding a tray of the same. I took a glass and met her eyes. *It's almost time.*

"Piotr," Max said darkly, "absolutely refuses to have a glass on duty. He did, however, pick a bodyguard theme song. I threatened him with show tunes."

"That's my girl!" Xander bellowed.

"Woman," Max corrected.

"That's my woman! In a completely not possessive and absolutely unpatriarchal kind of way!"

Max lifted her glass to toast him. "Elf yeah."

"It's time." Jameson said. I leaned into him as the others crowded around. "Ten... nine... eight..."

Jameson, Grayson, Xander, and Nash.

Libby, Thea, and Rebecca.

Me.

Alisa held a glass of champagne but stood back from the group. She was the only one who knew what was about to happen.

"Three..."

"...two..."

"...one."

"Happy New Year!" Xander yelled. The next thing I knew,

confetti was flying everywhere. I had no idea where Xander had gotten confetti, but he continued to produce it, seemingly out of nowhere.

"Happy new life," Jameson corrected. He kissed me like it was New Year's Eve, and I savored it.

I'd survived a year in Hawthorne House. I had fulfilled the conditions of Tobias Hawthorne's will. I was a billionaire. One of the richest, most powerful people on the planet.

And I had *A Plan*.

"Shall I?" Alisa asked me. Nash's eyes narrowed. He knew her—and that meant he knew quite well when she was up to something.

"Do it," I told Alisa.

She turned the flat-screen television on and to a twenty-four-hour financial channel. It took a minute or two, but then the *BREAKING NEWS* beacon flashed across the screen.

"Precisely what kind of breaking news?" Grayson asked me.

I let the reporter answer for me. "We've just received word that Hawthorne heiress Avery Grambs has officially inherited the billions left to her by the late Tobias Hawthorne. After estate taxes and taking into account appreciation over the past year, the current value of the inheritance is estimated to be upward of thirty billion dollars. Ms. Grambs has announced—"

The reporter cut off, the words dying in his throat.

For the second time in my life, I felt every pair of eyes in a room turn to me. There was an eerie symmetry between this moment and the moment right before Mr. Ortega had read the final terms of Tobias Hawthorne's will.

"Ms. Grambs has announced," the reporter tried again, his voice strangled, "that as of midnight, she has signed paperwork transferring ninety-four percent of her inheritance into a charitable trust to be distributed in its entirety in the next five years."

It was done. It was legal. I couldn't have undone it even if I'd wanted to.

Thea was the first one to break the silence. "What the hell?"

Nash turned to his ex-fiancée. "You helped her give away all that money?"

Alisa raised her chin. "The partners at the firm didn't even know."

Nash let out a low chuckle. "You are so getting fired."

Alisa smiled—not the tight, professional smile she normally used, but a real one. "Job security isn't everything." She shrugged. "And as it so happens, I've accepted a new position at a charitable trust."

I couldn't quite bring myself to look at Jameson. Or Grayson. Or even Xander or Nash. I hadn't asked for their permission. I wasn't going to be asking for forgiveness, either. Instead, I thrust my chin out, the way Alisa had. "You'll all be receiving your invitations to join the board of the Hannah the Same Backward as Forward Foundation soon."

Silence.

This time, it was Grayson who broke it. "You want us to help you give it away?"

I met his eyes. "I want you to help me find the best ideas and the best people to determine how to give it all away."

Libby frowned. "What about the Hawthorne Foundation?" In addition to Tobias Hawthorne's fortune, I'd also inherited control of his charitable enterprise.

"Zara's agreed to stay on for a few years while I'm otherwise occupied," I answered. The Hawthorne Foundation had its own charter, which laid out the minimum and maximum percentage of its assets that could be given away each year. I couldn't empty it out—but I could make sure that my foundation had different rules.

That my inheritance wouldn't stay *earmarked* for charity for long.

Grinning, I handed Libby a sheet of paper.

"What's this?" she asked.

"It's account information for about a dozen different websites I signed you up for," I told her. "Mutual aid, mostly, and microloans to women entrepreneurs in the developing world. The new foundation will be handling official charitable giving, but we both know what it's like to need help and have nowhere to go. I've set aside ten million a year for you—for that."

Before she could reply, I tossed something to Nash. He caught it, then examined what I'd tossed him. *Keys.*

"What's this?" he drawled, his accent thick with amusement at this entire turn of events.

"Those," I told him, "are the keys to my sister's new cupcake truck."

Libby stared at me, her eyes round, her lips making an O. "I can't accept this, Ave."

"I know." I smirked. "That's why I gave the keys to Nash."

Before I could say anything else, Jameson stepped in front of me. "You're giving it away," he said, his expression as much of a mystery to me as it had been the day we met. "Almost everything the old man left to you, everything he chose you *for*—"

"I'm keeping Hawthorne House," I told him. "And more than enough money to maintain it. I might even keep a vacation home or two—after I've seen them all."

After *we* had seen them all.

"If Tobias Hawthorne were here," Thea declared, "he would *lose it.*"

All that money. All that power. Dispersed, where no one person would ever control it again.

"I guess that's what happens," Jameson said, his eyes never leaving mine as his lips curled upward, "when you take a very risky gamble."

ONE YEAR LATER...

"I'm here today with Avery Grambs. Heiress. Philanthropist. World changer—and at only nineteen years old. Avery, tell us, what is it like to be in your position at such a young age?"

I'd prepared for this question and for every question the interviewer might ask. She was the only one I'd granted an interview to in the past year, a media maven whose name was synonymous with savvy and success—and, more importantly, a humanitarian herself.

"Fun?" I answered, and she chuckled. "I don't mean to sound cavalier," I said, projecting the sincerity I felt. "I am fully aware that I am pretty much the luckiest person on the planet."

Landon had told me that the art to an interview like this one—intimate, much anticipated, with an interviewer who was almost as much of a draw as I was—was to make it sound like a conversation, to make the audience feel like we were just two women talking. Honest. Open.

"And the thing is," I continued, the awe in my voice echoing through the room in Hawthorne House where the interview was taking place, "it never really becomes normal. You don't just get used to it."

Here in this room, which the staff had taken to calling the

Nook, it was easy to feel awed. The Nook was small by Hawthorne House standards, but every aspect of it, from the repurposed wood floors to the ridiculously comfortable reading chairs, bore my mark.

"You can go anywhere," the interviewer said, quietly matching the awe in my voice. "Do anything."

"And I have," I said. Built-in shelves lined the Nook's walls. Every place I went, I found a keepsake—a reminder of the adventures I'd had there. Art, a book in the local language, a stone from the ground, something that had spoken to me.

"You've gone everywhere, done everything..." The interviewer smiled knowingly. "With Jameson Hawthorne."

Jameson Winchester Hawthorne.

"You're smiling," she told me.

"You would, too," I told her, "if you knew Jameson." He was exactly what he'd always been—a thrill chaser, a sensation seeker, a risk taker—and he was so much more.

"How did he react when he found out that you were giving so much of the family's fortune away?"

"He was shocked at first," I admitted. "But after that, it became a game—to all of them."

"All the Hawthornes?"

I tried *not* to smile too big this time. "All the boys."

"The boys, as in the Hawthorne brothers. Half the world is in love with them—now more than ever."

That wasn't a question, so I didn't answer.

"You said that after the shock of your decision wore off, giving away the money became a game to the Hawthorne brothers?"

Everything's a game, Avery Grambs. The only thing we get to decide in this life is if we play to win. "We're in a race against the clock to find the right causes and the right organizations to give the money to," I explained.

"You set up your foundation with the stipulation that all of the money had to be gone in five years. Why?"

That was more of a softball question than she realized. "Big changes require big actions," I said. "Hoarding the money and doling it out slowly over time never felt like the right call."

"So *you* put out a call—for experts."

"Experts," I confirmed. "Academics, people with boots on the ground—and even just people with big ideas. We had open applications for spots on the board, and there are more than a hundred of us working at the foundation now. Our team includes everyone from Nobel Prize and MacArthur genius award winners to humanitarian leaders, medical professionals, domestic abuse survivors, incarcerated persons, and a full dozen activists under the age of eighteen. Together, we work to generate and evaluate action plans."

"And review proposals." The interviewer kept the same thoughtful tone. "Anyone can submit a proposal to the Hannah the Same Backward as Forward Foundation."

"Anyone," I confirmed. "We want the best ideas and the best people. You can be anyone, from anywhere. You can feel like you're no one. We want to hear from you."

"Where did you get the name for the foundation?"

I thought of Toby, of my mom. "That," I told the whole world watching, "is a mystery."

"And speaking of mysteries..." The shift in tone told me that we were about to get serious. "Why?"

The interviewer let that question hang in the air, then continued. "Why, having been left one of the largest fortunes in the world, would you give almost all of it away? Are you a saint?"

I snorted, which probably wasn't a good look with millions watching, but I couldn't help it. "If I were a saint," I said, "do you really think I would have kept *two billion dollars* for myself?" I shook my head, my hair escaping from behind my shoulders as I did. "Do you understand how much money that is?"

I wasn't being combative, and I hoped my tone made that clear.

"I could spend a hundred million dollars a year," I explained, "every year for the rest of my life, and there's still a good chance that I would have more money when I died than I have right now."

Money made money—and the more of it you had, the higher the rate of return.

"And frankly," I said, "I *can't* spend a hundred million dollars a year. Literally can't! So, no, I'm not a saint. If you really think about it, I'm pretty selfish."

"Selfish," she repeated. "Giving away twenty-eight billion dollars? Ninety-four percent of all your assets, and you think people should be asking why you're not doing more?"

"Why not?" I said. "Someone told me once that fortunes like this one—at a certain point, it's not about the money, because you couldn't spend billions if you tried. It's about the power." I looked down. "And I just don't think anyone should have power like that, certainly not me."

I wondered if Vincent Blake was watching—or Eve, or any of the other high rollers I'd met since inheriting.

"And the Hawthorne family was really okay with that?" The interviewer asked. She wasn't combative, either. Just curious and deeply empathetic. "The boys? Grayson Hawthorne has dropped out of Harvard. Jameson Hawthorne has had brushes with the law on at least three continents in the past six months. It was recently reported that Xander Hawthorne is working as a mechanic."

Xander was working with Isaiah—both at his shop and on several pieces of new technology that they were *very* excited about. Grayson had dropped out of Harvard to turn the full force of his mind to the project of giving the money away. And the only reason Jameson had been arrested—or *almost* arrested—so many times was that he couldn't turn down dares.

Specifically, mine.

The only reason *I* hadn't made similar headlines was that I was better at not getting caught.

"You forgot Nash," I said easily. "He's tending bar and working as a cupcake taster on the weekends."

I was smiling now, emanating the kind of contentedness—not to mention amusement—that a person couldn't fake. The Hawthorne brothers weren't, as she'd suggested, going off the rails. They were—all of them—exactly where they were supposed to be.

They'd been sculpted by Tobias Hawthorne, formed and forged by the billionaire's hands. They were extraordinary, and for the first time in their lives, they weren't living under the weight of his expectations.

The interviewer caught my smile and shifted subjects—slightly. "Do you have any comments on rumors of Nash Hawthorne's engagement to your sister?"

"I don't pay much attention to rumors," I managed to say with a straight face.

"What's next for you, Avery? As you pointed out, you still have an incredibly massive fortune. Any plans?"

"Travel," I answered immediately. On the walls all around us, there were at least thirty souvenirs—but there were still so many places I hadn't been.

Places where Jameson hadn't yet taken an inadvisable dare.

Places we could fly.

"And," I continued, "after a gap year or two, I'll be enrolling as an actuarial science major at UConn."

"Actuarial science?" Her eyebrows skyrocketed. "At UConn."

"Statistical risk assessment," I said. There were people out there who built models and algorithms, whose advice my financial advisors took. I had a lot to learn before I could start managing the risks all on my own.

And besides, the moment I'd said UConn, Jameson had started talking about Yale. *Do you think their secret societies could use a Hawthorne?*

"Okay, travel. College. What else?" The interviewer grinned. She was enjoying herself now. "You must have plans for something fun. This has been the ultimate Cinderella story. Give us just a taste of the kind of extravagance that most people can only dream of."

The people watching were probably expecting me to talk about yachts or jewels or private planes—private islands, even. But I had other plans. "Actually," I said, well aware of my tone changing as excitement bubbled up inside me, "I do have one fun idea."

It was the reason I'd agreed to this interview. Subtly, I dipped my hand down to the side of my chair, where I'd tucked a golden card etched with a very complicated design.

"I already told you that it would be difficult for me to spend all the money that two billion dollars makes in a year," I said, "but what I didn't tell you is that I have no intention of growing my fortune. Each year, after I balance my expense sheet, take stock of any changes in my net worth, and calculate the difference, I'm earmarking the rest to be given away."

"More charity?"

"I'm sure there will be a lot more charity work in my future, but this is for fun." There wasn't much I wanted to buy. I wanted experiences. I wanted to keep adding on to Hawthorne House, to maintain it and make sure the staff stayed employed. I wanted to make sure that no one I loved ever wanted for anything.

And I wanted *this*.

"Tobias Hawthorne wasn't a good man," I said seriously, "but he had a human side. He loved puzzles and riddles and games. Every Saturday morning, he would present his grandsons with a challenge—clues to decipher, connections to make, a complicated multistage puzzle to solve. The game would take the boys all over Hawthorne House."

I could picture them as children as easily as I could picture them now. *Jameson. Grayson. Xander. Nash.* Tobias Hawthorne had been a real piece of work. He'd played to win, crossed lines that should never be crossed, expected perfection.

But the games? The ones the boys had played growing up, the ones *I* had played? Those games hadn't *made* us extraordinary.

They'd showed us that we already were.

"If there's one thing that the Hawthornes have taught me," I said, "it's that I like a challenge. I like to *play*."

As Jameson had said once, there would always be more mysteries to solve, but I knew in my core that we'd played the old man's last game.

So now I was planning one of my own. "Every year, I'll be hosting a contest with substantial, life-changing prize money. Some years, the game will be open to the general public. Others…well, maybe you'll find yourself on the receiving end of the world's most exclusive invitation."

This wasn't the most responsible way to spend money, but once I'd had the idea, I couldn't shake it, and once I'd mentioned it to Jameson, there was no turning back.

"This game." The interviewer's eyes were alight. "These puzzles. They'll be of your making?"

I smiled. "I'll have help." Not just the boys. Alisa had sometimes joined in Tobias Hawthorne's games growing up. Oren was running logistics for me. Rebecca and Thea, in combined force, were downright *diabolical* in their contributions to what I had been calling *The Grandest Game.*

"When will the first game start?" the woman across from me asked.

That was the question I'd been waiting for. I held up the gold card in my hand and brandished it at the camera—design out.

"The game," I said, my voice ripe with promise, "starts right now."

ACKNOWLEDGMENTS

When I wrote *The Inheritance Games* and *The Hawthorne Legacy*, I didn't know for certain whether they would find a big enough audience to justify the publication of a third book. I had hoped and planned—SO MUCH PLANNING—to be able to share the twists and turns that I knew awaited Avery, but *The Final Gambit* only exists because of the incredible support the first two books have received from my publishing team, booksellers, librarians, and readers. I am truly grateful to everyone who made this book possible.

My editor, Lisa Yoskowitz, has been a tireless advocate for these books from the moment she first read *The Inheritance Games*. It's hard to describe how valuable her editorial insights have been. So many of my favorite parts of *The Final Gambit* are the direct result of Lisa's incredible instincts for what a story needs and her ability to inspire me to do everything I can to take the characters, plot, and world to the next level. Further, as grateful as I am for our creative collaboration, I am just as grateful for the grace, understanding, and support Lisa offers at every stage of the publishing process. I wrote this book during the first year of my new baby's life, in the middle of a pandemic, while dealing with spotty childcare. Lisa, I could not have done it without you!

My agent, Elizabeth Harding, has been a champion for my books since I was barely more than a teenager myself. Eighteen years and twenty-three books later, I am so thankful for everything she has done and continues to do for me and for my books. Elizabeth, working with you is a joy.

I owe an enormous debt of gratitude to my amazing team at Little, Brown Books for Young Readers. I am in absolute awe of the creativity, vision, and work that has gone into getting this series into so many hands! Thank you to cover designer Karina Granda and artist Katt Phatt for creating the gorgeous cover for *The Final Gambit*. You have so perfectly captured this book, and the end result is nothing short of stunning! Another big thank-you goes out to production superstar Marisa Finkelstein, who helped work magic with our schedule to give me as much time with the book as I needed. Marisa, I appreciate all the work you did to make sure the book was what it needed to be when it needed to be—and under a tight schedule, no less!

Thank you also to Megan Tingley and Jackie Engel for their incredible support of this series; to Shawn Foster, Danielle Cantarella, Celeste Risko, Anna Herling, Katie Tucker, Claire Gamble, Leah CollinsLipsett, and Karen Torres for putting this book in front of readers *everywhere*; to Victoria Stapleton, Christie Michel, and Amber Mercado for everything they've done to connect libraries and young readers to the series; to Cheryl Lew, Savannah Kennelly, Emilie Polster, and Bill Grace for making and keeping these books so visible for so long; to Virginia Lawther, Olivia Davis, Jody Corbett, Barbara Bakowski, Su Wu, and Erin Slonaker for their help in getting *The Final Gambit* reader-ready; to Caitlyn Averett for her help at every stage of the process; to Lisa Cahn and Christie

Moreau for their work on the audiobooks for the series; and to Janelle DeLuise and Hannah Koerner for finding such a wonderful UK home for the series! Thank you also to my UK publishing team at Penguin Random House, especially Anthea Townsend, Phoebe Williams, Jane Griffiths, and Kat McKenna.

My incredible team at Curtis Brown has done more for the Inheritance Games series than I ever could have imagined possible! Huge thanks to Sarah Perillo for helping to bring the Inheritance Games series to readers all over the world and to Holly Frederick for working her magic on the television front! I am also incredibly grateful for the help of Mahalaleel M. Clinton, Michaela Glover, and Maddie Tavis.

I have wanted to be an author since I was five years old, and one of the most incredible things about living this dream has been becoming a part of an incredible community of young-adult authors. Thank you to Ally Carter, Maureen Johnson, E. Lockhart, and Karen M. McManus for being lovely conversation partners at the virtual events that helped launch this series. Rachel Vincent is always there when I need to talk out a part of the book I can't quite figure out, and I'm incredibly grateful for our weekly writing days! Thank you also to all my other writing friends; it's been a long time since I've seen many of you in person, but you are all the reason that the community I've found in writing feels like home.

Finally, thank you to my family. For years, while I was balancing a demanding day job, writing, and being a mom to three young kids, people would ask, *How do you do it all?* And the answer has always been *I'm not doing it all alone; I have so much help and support.* Thank you to my parents for being the best parents a person could possibly ask for. They are my biggest fans, an incredible source of support, and the ones who will get in a car and drive two hours to watch my kids and bring me food when there just aren't enough hours in the day. My dad, Bill Barnes, also helped proofread this book, and both my parents helped me create the world the Hawthornes inhabit by answering tons of questions on a whole range of topics!

Thank you to my husband, Anthony, who is a partner in every sense of the word. I cannot imagine a better husband or father, and I am so grateful for everything you do. Finally, thank you to my three small children, the oldest of whom was five when I started writing this book, for the cuddles, learning to sometimes entertain yourselves, and bringing so much joy to my life.

TURN THE PAGE TO DISCOVER WHAT'S NEXT FOR THE HAWTHORNE BROTHERS IN THIS SNEAK PEEK OF

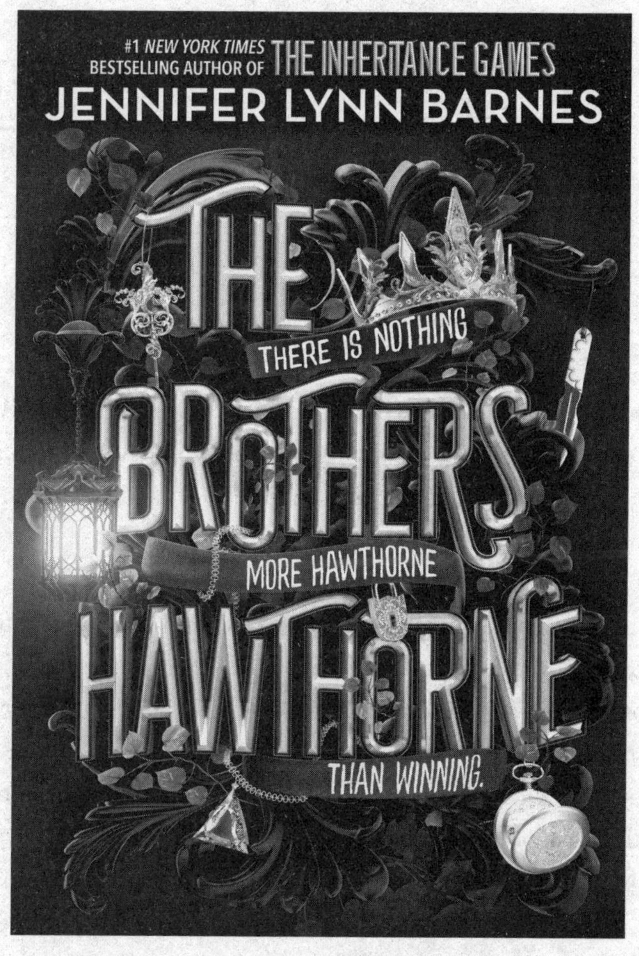

CHAPTER 1

GRAYSON

Faster. Grayson Hawthorne was power and control. His form was flawless. He'd long ago perfected the art of visualizing his opponent, *feeling* each strike, channeling his body's momentum into every block, every attack.

But you could always be faster.

After his tenth time through the sequence, Grayson stopped, sweat dripping down his bare chest. Keeping his breathing even and controlled, he knelt in front of what remained of their childhood tree house, unrolled his pack, and surveyed his choices: three daggers, two with ornate hilts and one understated and smooth. It was this last blade that Grayson picked up.

Knife in hand, Grayson straightened, his arms by his side. Mind, clear. Body, free of tension. *Begin.* There were many styles of knife fighting, and the year he was thirteen, Grayson had studied them all. Of course, billionaire Tobias Hawthorne's grandsons had never merely *studied* anything. Once they'd chosen a focus, they were expected to live it, breathe it, master it.

And this was what Grayson had learned that year: Stance was everything. You didn't move the blade. You moved, and the blade moved. Faster. *Faster.* It had to feel natural. It had to *be* natural. The moment your muscles tensed, the moment you stopped breathing, the moment you broke your stance instead of flowing from one to the next, you lost.

And Hawthornes didn't lose.

"When I told you to get a hobby, this isn't what I meant."

Grayson ignored Xander's presence for as long as it took to finish the sequence—and throw the dagger with exacting precision at a low-hanging branch six feet away. "Hawthornes don't have hobbies," he told his little brother, walking to retrieve the blade. "We have specialties. Expertise."

"*Anything worth doing is worth doing well,*" Xander quoted, wiggling his eyebrows—one of which had only just started to grow back after an experiment gone wrong. "*And anything done well can be done better.*"

Why would a Hawthorne settle for better, a voice whispered in the back of Grayson's mind, *when they could be the best?*

Grayson closed his hand around the dagger's hilt and pulled. "I should be getting back to work."

"You are a man obsessed," Xander declared.

Grayson secured the dagger in its holder, then rolled the pack back up, tying it closed. "I have twenty-eight billion reasons to be obsessed."

Avery had set an impossible task for herself—and for them. Five years to give away more than twenty-eight billion dollars. That was the majority of the Hawthorne fortune. They'd spent the past seven months just assembling the foundation's board and advisory committee.

"We have five more months to nail down the first three billion in donations," Grayson stated crisply, "and I promised Avery I would be there with her every step of the way."

Promises mattered to Grayson Hawthorne—and so did Avery Kylie Grambs. The girl who had inherited their grandfather's fortune. The stranger who had become one of them.

"Speaking as someone with friends, a girlfriend, and a small army of robots, I just think you could do with a little more balance in your life," Xander opined. "An *actual* hobby? Down time?"

Grayson gave him a look. "You've filed at least three patents since school let out for the summer last month, Xan."

Xander shrugged. "They're recreational patents."

Grayson snorted, then assessed his brother. "How *is* Isaiah?" he asked softly.

Growing up, none of the Hawthorne brothers had known their fathers' identities—until Grayson had discovered that his was Sheffield *Grayson*. Nash's was a man named Jake *Nash*. And Xander's was Isaiah *Alexander*. Of the three men, only Isaiah actually deserved to be called a father. He and Xander had filed those "recreational patents" together.

"We're supposed to be talking about you," Xander said stubbornly.

"I should get back to work," Grayson reiterated, adopting a tone that was very effective at putting everyone *except* his brothers in their place. "And despite what Avery and Jameson seem to believe, I don't need a babysitter."

"You don't need a babysitter," Xander agreed cheerfully, "and I am definitely not writing a book entitled *The Care and Feeding of Your Broody Twenty-Year-Old Brother*."

Grayson's eyes narrowed to slits.

"I can assure you," Xander said with great solemnity, "it doesn't have pictures."

Before Grayson could summon an appropriate threat in response, his phone buzzed. Assuming it was the figures he'd requested, Grayson picked the phone up, only to discover a text from Nash. He looked back at Xander and knew instantly that his youngest brother had received the same message.

Grayson was the one who read the fateful missive out loud: "Nine-one-one."

CHAPTER 2

JAMESON

The roar of the falls. The mist in the air. The feel of the back of Avery's body against the front of his. Jameson Winchester Hawthorne was *hungry*—for this, for her, for everything, all of it, *more*.

Iguazú Falls was the world's largest waterfall system. The walkway they were standing on took them right up to the edge of an incredible drop-off. Staring out at the falls, Jameson felt the lure of *more*. He eyed the railing. "Do you dare me?" he murmured into the back of Avery's head.

She reached back to touch his jaw. "Absolutely not."

Jameson's lips curved—a teasing smile, a wicked one. "You're probably right, Heiress."

She turned her head to the side and met his gaze. "Probably?"

Jameson looked back at the falls. *Unstoppable. Off limits. Deadly.* "Probably."

They were staying in a villa built on stilts and surrounded by jungle, no one around for miles but the two of them, Avery's security team, and the jaguars roaring in the distance.

Jameson felt Avery's approach before he heard it.

"Heads or tails?" She leaned against the railing, brandishing a bronze-and-silver coin. Her brown hair was falling out of its ponytail, her long-sleeved shirt still damp from the falls.

Jameson brought his hand to her hair tie, then worked it slowly and gently down—and off. *Heads or tails* was an invitation. A challenge. *You kiss me, or I kiss you.* "Dealer's choice, Heiress."

"If I'm the dealer..." Avery placed a palm flat on his chest, her eyes daring him to do something about that wet shirt of hers. "We're going to need cards."

The things we could do, Jameson thought, *with a deck of cards.* But before he could voice some of the more tantalizing possibilities, the satellite phone buzzed. Only five people had the number: his brothers, her sister, and her lawyer. Jameson groaned.

The text was from Nash. Nine seconds later, when the satellite phone rang, Jameson answered. "Delightful timing, as always, Gray."

"I take it you received Nash's message?"

"We've been summoned," Jameson intoned. "You planning to play hooky again?"

Each Hawthorne brother got a single nine-one-one a year. The code didn't mean *emergency* so much as *I want you all here,* but if one brother texted, the others came, no questions asked. Ignoring a nine-one-one led to...consequences.

"If you say *one word* about leather pants," Grayson bit out. "I will—"

"Did you say *leather pants*?" Jameson was enjoying this way too much. "You're breaking up, Gray. Are you asking me to send you a picture of the incredibly tight leather pants you had to wear the one time you ignored a nine-one-one?"

"Do not send me a picture—"

"A video?" Jameson asked loudly. "You want a video of yourself singing karaoke in the leather pants?"

Avery plucked the phone from his hands. She knew as well as Jameson did that there would be no ignoring Nash's summons, and she had a bad habit of *not* tormenting his brothers.

"It's me, Grayson." Avery examined Nash's text herself. "We'll see you in London."

TURN THE PAGE TO START ANOTHER UNPUTDOWNABLE SERIES FROM JENNIFER LYNN BARNES!

YOU

You've chosen and chosen well. Maybe this one will be the one who stops you. Maybe she'll be different. Maybe she'll be enough.

The only thing that is certain is that she's special.

You think it's her eyes—not the color: an icy, see-through blue. Not the lashes, or the shape, or the way she doesn't need eyeliner to give them the appearance of a cat's.

No, it's what's behind those icy blues that brings the audience out in droves. You feel it, every time you look at her. The certainty. The knowing. That otherworldly glint she uses to convince people that she's the real deal.

Maybe she is.

Maybe she really can see things. Maybe she knows things. Maybe she's everything she claims to be and more. But watching her, counting her breaths, you smile, because deep down, you know that she isn't going to stop you.

You don't really want her to stop you.

She's fragile.

Perfect.

Marked.

And the one thing this so-called psychic won't see coming is you.

CHAPTER 1

The hours were bad. The tips were worse, and the majority of my coworkers definitely left something to be desired, but *c'est la vie, que será será,* insert foreign language cliché of your choice here. It was a summer job, and that kept Nonna off my back. It also prevented my various aunts, uncles, and kitchen-sink cousins from feeling like they had to offer me temporary employment in their restaurant/butcher shop/legal practice/boutique. Given the size of my father's very large, very extended (and very Italian) family, the possibilities were endless, but it was always a variation on the same theme.

My dad lived half a world away. My mother was missing, presumed dead. I was everyone's problem and nobody's.

Teenager, presumed troubled.

"Order up!"

With practiced ease, I grabbed a plate of pancakes (side

of bacon) with my left hand and a two-handed breakfast burrito (jalapeños on the side) with my right. If the SATs didn't go well in the fall, I had a real future ahead of me in the crappy diner industry.

"Pancakes with a side of bacon. Breakfast burrito, jalapeños on the side." I slid the plates onto the table. "Anything else I can get for you gentlemen?"

Before either of them opened their mouths, I knew exactly what these two were going to say. The guy on the left was going to ask for extra butter. And the guy on the right? He was going to need another glass of water before he could even *think* about those jalapeños.

Ten-to-one odds, he didn't even like them.

Guys who actually liked jalapeños didn't order them on the side. Mr. Breakfast Burrito just didn't want people to think he was a wuss—only the word he would have used wasn't *wuss*.

Whoa there, Cassie, I told myself sternly. *Let's keep it PG.*

As a general rule, I didn't curse much, but I had a bad habit of picking up on other people's quirks. Put me in a room with a bunch of English people, and I'd walk out with a British accent. It wasn't intentional—I'd just spent a lot of time over the years getting inside other people's heads.

Occupational hazard. Not mine. My mother's.

"Could I get a few more of these butter packets?" the guy on the left asked.

I nodded—and waited.

"More water," the guy on the right grunted. He puffed out his chest and ogled my boobs.

I forced a smile. "I'll be right back with that water." I managed to keep from adding *pervert* to the end of that sentence, but only just.

I was still holding out hope that a guy in his late twenties who pretended to like spicy food and made a point of staring at his teenage waitress's chest like he was training for the Ogling Olympics might be equally showy when it came to leaving tips.

Then again, I thought as I went for refills, *he might turn out to be the kind of guy who stiffs the little bitty waitress just to prove he can.*

Absentmindedly, I turned the details of the situation over in my mind: the way that Mr. Breakfast Burrito was dressed; his likely occupation; the fact that his friend, who'd ordered the pancakes, was wearing a much more expensive watch.

He'll fight to grab the check, then tip like crap.

I hoped I was wrong—but was fairly certain that I wasn't.

Other kids spent their preschool years singing their way through the ABCs. I grew up learning a different alphabet. Behavior, personality, environment—my mother called them the BPEs, and they were the tricks of her trade. Thinking that way wasn't the kind of thing you could just turn off—not even once you were old enough to understand that when your mother told people she was psychic, she was *lying*, and when she took their money, it was *fraud*.

Even now that she was gone, I couldn't keep from figuring people out, any more than I could give up breathing, blinking, or counting down the days until I turned eighteen.

"Table for one?" A low, amused voice jostled me back into reality. The voice's owner looked like the type of boy who would have been more at home in a country club than a diner. His skin was perfect, his hair artfully mussed. Even though he phrased his words like they were a question, they weren't—not really.

"Sure," I said, grabbing a menu. "Right this way."

A closer observation told me that Country Club was about my age. A smirk played across his perfect features, and he walked with the swagger of high school nobility. Just looking at him made me feel like a serf.

"This okay?" I asked, leading him to a table near the window.

"This is fine," he said, slipping into the chair. Casually, he surveyed the room with bulletproof confidence. "You get a lot of traffic in here on weekends?"

"Sure," I replied. I was starting to wonder if I'd lost the ability to speak in complex sentences. From the look on the boy's face, he probably was, too. "I'll give you a minute to look over the menu."

He didn't respond, and I spent my minute bringing Pancakes and Breakfast Burrito their checks, plural. I figured that if I split it in half, I might end up with half a decent tip.

"I'll be your cashier whenever you're ready," I said, fake smile firmly in place.

I turned back toward the kitchen and caught the boy by the window watching me. It wasn't an *I'm ready to order* stare. I wasn't sure what it was, actually—but every bone in my body told me it was *something*. The niggling sensation that there was a key detail that I was missing about this whole situation—about *him*—wouldn't go away. Boys like that didn't usually eat in places like this.

They didn't stare at girls like me.

Self-conscious and wary, I crossed the room.

"Did you decide what you'd like?" I asked. There was no getting out of taking his order, so I let my hair fall in my face, obscuring his view of it.

"Three eggs," he said, hazel eyes fixed on what he could see of mine. "Side of pancakes. Side of ham."

I didn't need to write the order down, but I suddenly found myself wishing for a pen, just so I'd have something to hold on to. "What kind of eggs?" I asked.

"You tell me." The boy's words caught me off guard.

"Excuse me?"

"Guess," he said.

I stared at him through the wisps of hair still covering my face. "You want me to guess how you want your eggs cooked?"

He smiled. "Why not?"

And just like that, the gauntlet was thrown.

"Not scrambled," I said, thinking out loud. Scrambled eggs were too average, too common, and this was a guy who liked to be a little bit different. Not too different, though, which ruled out poached—at least in a place like this. Sunny-side up would have been too messy for him; over hard wouldn't be messy enough.

"Over easy." I was as sure of the conclusion as I was of the color of his eyes. He smiled and closed his menu.

"Are you going to tell me if I was right?" I asked—not because I needed confirmation, but because I wanted to see how he would respond.

The boy shrugged. "Now, where would the fun be in that?"

I wanted to stay there, staring, until I figured him out, but I didn't. I put his order in. I delivered his food. The lunch rush snuck up on me, and by the time I went back to check on him, the boy by the window was gone. He hadn't even waited for his check—he'd just left twenty dollars on the table. I had just about decided that he could make me play guessing games to his heart's content for a twelve-dollar tip when I noticed the bill wasn't the only thing he'd left.

There was also a business card.

I picked it up. Stark white. Black letters. Evenly spaced. There was a seal in the upper left-hand corner, but relatively little text: a name, a job title, a phone number. Across the top of the card, there were four words, four little words that knocked the wind out of me as effectively as a jab to the chest.

I pocketed the card—and the tip. I went back to the kitchen. I caught my breath. And then I looked at it again.

Tanner Briggs. The name.

Special Agent. Job title.

Federal Bureau of Investigation.

Four words, but I stared at them so hard that my vision blurred and I could only make out three letters.

What in the world had I done to attract the attention of the FBI?

Kim Haynes Photography

JENNIFER LYNN BARNES

is the #1 *New York Times* bestselling author of more than twenty acclaimed young-adult novels, including the Inheritance Games trilogy, *The Brothers Hawthorne, Little White Lies, Deadly Little Scandals, The Lovely and the Lost*, and the Naturals series: *The Naturals, Killer Instinct, All In, Bad Blood,* and the novella *Twelve*. Jen is also a Fulbright Scholar with advanced degrees in psychology, psychiatry, and cognitive science. She received her PhD from Yale University in 2012 and was a professor of psychology and professional writing at the University of Oklahoma for many years. She invites you to find her online at jenniferlynnbarnes.com or follow her on Instagram @authorjenlynnbarnes.

MORE FROM

JENNIFER LYNN BARNES

THE NATURALS

DEBUTANTES

A MYSTERY

THE INHERITANCE GAMES

NOVL  LITTLE, BROWN AND COMPANY theNOVL.com